To my valued reader
Tom

‖‖‖ ‖‖‖‖‖‖‖‖‖‖‖‖‖‖‖‖‖‖‖‖
D1602596

the odds of
HEAVEN

TOM HOUSTON

Thomas Houston
ThomasRHouston@yahoo.com

Print ISBN: 978-1-09839-561-2
eBook ISBN: 978-1-09839-562-9

Printed in the United States of America.
First Edition

CHAPTER I

When Tyler Lacy Whittaker III, or Lace as he was called, left his two-room apartment on MacDougal Street, there was something about the shadows that disturbed his eye. He had just slept off at least a dozen rum drinks from the night before, so he was surprised to find one of those quiet, sunny days, crispy and delightful, for which New York City is justly loved by its residents as they stop to chat with each other: "What good weather we're having! What a string of beautiful days!"

As he came down the three flights of stairs from his tiny apartment, he whistled a little tune to himself. He had been listening to a recording of Maria Callas' 1954 performance of *Norma* at La Scala and a sliver of melody from her aria, *Casta Diva,* was lodged in his mind, but Lace could not hold a tune, and the sound that came from his throat resembled perhaps some sailor's ditty, a pastiche of hit parade melodies or maybe even the warble of a bird

MacDougal Street is a comfortable street, lined with mimosa and small pear trees, and it lends itself to pleasant ruminations during an afternoon stroll or an evening walk or even a short jaunt, such as the one on which Lace was now embarking. It is a narrow street that lies north to south, so that on certain days the sun shines steadily, straight down into the cobbled stones and cracked pavements from an angle toward the horizon. Having tried his hand at photography in his youth, Lace was struck at once by the shadows, or the lack of them, for there were none to be seen at all and, having just listened to *Norma*, the story of that stormy and doomed Druid priestess formed into his consciousness a stage set of stone monoliths and human sacrifice as the sun passed its apogee overhead.

Lace stepped a bit unevenly onto his sidewalk, where he noticed an optical illusion. The walls of those famous Federal and Greek Revival brick buildings bent towards each other, rising mysteriously from their base without seeming to touch the street, an urban Stonehenge measuring time in cycles, with one ray of precious sunlight piercing down an alleyway of stone.

So, lost in a hazy reaction to a street without shadows and in a muddled but sun-struck mood, he ambled unsteadily on sturdy, stout legs out into the world on his way to a late lunch. Lace had put himself together carelessly. He was wearing a tweed pork-pie hat lying just off the center of his head and a camel hair coat of good make and rather old-fashioned design; he was clean-shaven although he had missed a patch just below his chin. The shirt he wore had been plucked from a pile of laundry and there was a small butter stain near the collar. Although people accused Lace of being fat, he was instead big-boned; a large man, standing a little over 6 feet 4 inches, which may be how he got away with a brash, almost bullying personality.

On balmy days, Italian women and young men with tight shirts sat on the uneven stoops of tenements on MacDougal Street, which lies at the heart of a neighborhood that has watched generations of immigrants arrive and pass through. Lace looked one way up and then down the block, looking for neighbors. His rambling, playful mind left behind druidical thoughts and turned instead to Mrs. Finelli whose children, now, were long gone. She was sweeping the sidewalk in front of her building, as she did each mid-day.

"The daughter moved out to New Jersey, what is it now, maybe ten years ago? Has it been that long?" he thought to himself. "Yes, each generation leaves some of its members behind. At least the good ol' neighborhood hasn't deteriorated too much. There's always a sturdy core of people who won't leave for another life just because it's the fashion to think that it's better over there, over the rivers and out into the boroughs and suburbs. Bet they don't even know their neighbors out there, hah!"

Lace nodded and waved foggily to the left at Mrs. Finelli and then stopped for a moment to chat with Anne Rose, who was sifting through refuse left that morning for the garbage men who would come on Monday.

"Look at this," she said, holding a ceramic mouse, in perfect shape except for a broken ear.

She looked vaguely down the street and swung her arm out towards a gnat buzzing around her unkempt hair, at the same time absentmindedly taking in the trashcans and piles of garbage through which she sifted every day.

"How can someone throw away something so beautiful?" she asked Lace.

Pausing to admire the nearly complete rodent Lace then moved on, but he turned briefly to watch Anne Rose's enormous shape make its way down the street. She lived downstairs in Lace's building and they fought often, but he had known her how long? "Known her since she was little…a long, long time. She is a mess, heaven knows, but we watch out for one another here, don't we, old boy? Yes indeed." This old village of a neighborhood forgave him his drunkenness, his leisure, even his awkward poetry and he felt cuddled and coddled, an aging, soft teddy bear.

At last, he headed for a café on the corner called Café Dadilo, a name that described neither a particular place nor was it the name of a person. So far as anyone knew, it was a name wholly invented to sound Italian by an Irishman two generations ago. But whatever its fanciful name, the café was a good spot for lunch. Lace had the unfortunate habit of being thrown out of places where he drank, but lunch at Café Dadilo was safe. Lace wasn't usually terribly drunk until late at night and the places that no longer extended to him their warm hands of welcome were mostly a string of waterfront bars tucked into little squalid stalls along the Hudson River.

At Café Dadilo, Lace was sure to be welcomed, to drink in the elixir of being wanted and expected, and he was meeting Agnes Pranciple who was going to edit a new book of rather risqué poems authored by Tyler Lacy Whittaker III.

Entering, at last, his destination, Lace squeezed the hands of Alberto, the headwaiter, into both of his, giving him a hearty welcome. There were some new paintings along the wall, done in muted colors. They seemed to be nothing but mottled shapes. "Just shapes! Nothingness! What are things coming to?" he thought sharply to himself and then he paused before a gilt-framed mirror to check his teeth. He picked momentarily at his front incisor and then turned for a moment to let his eyes adjust and while they adapted to the darkness he navigated gingerly between tables towards the back until he arrived at a corner table far into the rear of the establishment.

Agnes Pranciple sat facing the door, buried in shadows but still wearing huge sunglasses in thick tortoise shell frames. Despite, or perhaps because her name suggested a schoolmarm, her general demeanor actually cut a swath somewhere between captain of the artillery and bike rider. She looked up as Lace took off his coat and gave it to Alberto, buttered a roll, and said gruffly, "You're late. I've ordered already."

"I'm never late," replied Lace in a stiff, warning voice. He narrowed his eyes and leaned over the table without sitting down. He was, in fact, always prompt and prided himself on it. Agnes Pranciple enjoyed going on the offensive, but she was not going to make any headway with this line of attack and so she sat back, outwardly resigned, and said, "Maybe I wrote it wrong in my diary. Let's get you a martini, you look like you need one."

Lace rocked back and forth for a moment. He had become angry for a split second and it took a second more than that for the blood in his neck to subside, but then, as he settled down, he suddenly realized that Alberto had left him holding his porkpie hat and he looked briefly behind him, vainly, to rectify the omission. Unsuccessful, he turned back upon Agnes and abruptly placed the little round hat on the bench beside him as he scuttled onto the banquette, having forgotten his temper.

"My dear, I do need it. Had a late night out…well, not so late, just…just…."

He sought the right word. "Rambunctious!" he said, with a triumphant spark in his eye. "Yes, my dear, rambunctious! I think I insulted someone, I can't remember for the life of me, but I did insult someone and he insulted me and then someone started something, but then I stood back while someone else got involved and then it started. I think I put money on the fight, but I didn't have any this morning. I suppose I lost the bet."

Grinning, he sat back in the banquette looking, entirely satisfied with himself.

Agnes Pranciple shook her finger at Lace, but she was holding a butter knife and so the tip of her finger flashed a little in the light and looked for a second like a magic wand. She placed the knife with a sharp clink on a plate so that it pointed precisely towards Lace and bit off a piece of roll so small that a particle physicist might have been interested in its structure.

"You will get killed one day and someday soon, so you need to work faster on these poems. My dear, you are a nasty piece of business but if your mind wasn't in some gutter on the waterfront—and those are special gutters to be sure—you wouldn't be able to write these peculiar poems about the damp recesses of fetal memory and all the sexual memories of motherhood and childhood and…and…"

She searched for a word but settled on "…whatever" and at the same time she waved her hand across the table to punctuate an end to her train of thought.

Agnes Pranciple stirred her Rob Roy for a moment with a dinner knife and gazed at her dinner roll, giving it a more devoted, almost motherly stare than could be easily explained by its allure or the circumstances at hand. She seemed to consider the crust during a moment of silence and then continued with a tone of voice that indi-cated she had given some consideration to what she was about to say.

"Your poems are good, you know. *Plaster of Paris Eros* should be out this winter. But they don't pay much. Not much for you to be sure and virtually nothing for me. If I didn't love you, you know. … When are you going to write something that will bring in money? Have you considered pornographic novels or romance? I can get you published at a nickel a word. I know a professor at Columbia who just rakes it in! Writes under a pseudonym, of course."

Lace took this all in with an amused look, ordered a crepe and coffee and skipped the martini for now. "I'm going to the South of Spain," he said as if to answer Agnes Pranciple's prescription for wealth. "I'm going for two months as soon as the money from *Plaster of Paris* is in. You can't stop me so don't try."

He stuck out a little portion of his tongue at her in a merry sort of way, but the tongue looked blue and his face sagged and his eyes look fuzzy and tired. Agnes noticed a little oil blotch on the front of his shirt. She took her sunglasses off, showing eyes that rippled as they reflected the deco lamps in the corners of Café Dadilo. She was a woman now, past the first blush of youth having entered her thirties as quick and striking as a young gazelle. Her hair was black, cut short in a pageboy; her clothes were black; her fingernails were red. She wore only a good watch from Van Cleef & Arpels. It was platinum with a faint gold wash. She didn't wear gold, but colder platinum or a ruby set in a small steely cluster of diamonds was to her taste. Like a cat, she toyed for a moment with a prawn, stabbing first in one direction and then another, poking it into submission, corralling it to make it easier to control and ingest.

Then, in silence, she began slicing one of the prawns into thin slivers as if preparing specimens for biology class and Lace's mind began to wander again, this time to images of his village neighborhood grasping the center of a diaspora of dispersed families, steel trusses and highways spreading out over the land. "Palms grasping humanity," he considered for a second. Perhaps he could write a line of poetry like that. "No, too Carl Sandburg for me," he thought as the silence lengthened between them. "After all, what do I write about? I write about sex and birth and creativity, whatever that is." The word *chthonian* sprang to mind. What a weighted word! "Hmm…. underworld deities of caves and caverns, old gods of caverns, basic forces of birth and death linked to the annual harvest and death of crops…" Remembering a line from T. S. Eliot, "*Driven by daemonic, chthonic powers,*" he was just about to form an image for use in one of his own poems when he was abruptly yanked back to consciousness by three sharp raps of Agnes's fork against the now nearly empty plate. In his reverie, Lace realized that he had somehow inserted an index finger into his nose, so he attempted to recover by bolting upright and scratching the side of one nostril. He stared attentively across at Agnes with his eyes wide open and his finger against his nose, looking a bit like a heavy scarecrow as she peered up at Lace from the table past her eyebrows.

"I have something to tell you."

With that, she fixed a sliver of prawn onto a tine, placed it neatly into her mouth and slowly licked the edge of the utensil.

"Two…no three Sundays ago, when I was leaving that awful opening at Lucille's gallery, you know, the one we call Lucille Lucifer's? Well, I was leaving her gallery in midtown. Were you there? I don't remember. Anyway, there was this man there and he just followed me out. He just followed me straight out onto the street and you know I'm a sucker."

Lace sat up in expectation.

"No, you know what I mean," Agnes sped on, her back straight now without a thought of torturing another prawn.

"Yes, yes, you picked him up," Lace knew the story already.

"Well," Agnes's voice lunged slightly. "I don't think picking up is the right description. We never said a word. I don't remember a word anyway, certainly not an entire sentence. We just went straight to that hotel I know where that Puerto Rican guy Manuel, or Juan or whatever his name was, took me and we rented a room and…and…." She leaned way back on the banquette, now, a lioness in the heat of an African sun, and said, "Momma got schtupped, honey. Momma got squandered sideways. Little Agnes got fucked to a froth. And not only that, Lace, we've been seeing each other and I still don't think we've said a full sentence. Certainly not a paragraph. Momma is a'glowin' in the dark, honey. Momma is doin' it right."

Her outburst done, she found another prawn and without further fanfare gobbled it up whole along with its remaining kin.

"So!"

Lace grinned a big-hearted grin. It was time for a drink now and he called a waiter over for a gin and tonic.

"So…so…so," he rolled the words over his tongue like a brandy, "you worry about my gutters but you've got your own scattered across Manhattan like sewers in the fifth circle of hell. Honey, is he treating you okay? Is he a psycho or anything? If he's a psycho, he doesn't have to be so good-looking, after all."

"He's not so good-looking, actually." Agnes considered for a moment. "You know I like crazy sort of people, but they're usually pretty gorgeous if I do say so myself. He's sort of…." She paused to recall a mental image as she brought the breadbasket over to her. "He's sort of, well, dirty. Dirty red hair, white-boy skin, no sun, sort of skulking in alleyways white, you know. Maybe he's a little crazy, but momma's getting skewered every week now!" She looked like Athena the warrior sitting bolt upright in her chair, or so Lace imagined her, as Athena in the Parthenon all aglitter and eyes ablaze and not just a little radiant.

"I hope you know what you're doing," he said. "I certainly don't."

Agnes Pranciple put down her roll and extended an arm across the table, placing her hand over the large garnet ring that Lace Whittaker had had reset from his mother's estate.

"Lacy."

She looked him straight in the eye.

"You're too old to be starting barroom brawls and you're too old to be writing adolescent tripe about wombs and the wet, gory mysteries of life. That's for college kids. Besides, we're in the 70s for Christ's sake and the Beats are almost ready for bifocals. This stuff is getting passé, honey. You know it, too. What are you going to do, Lace? Good God! You're approaching middle age! Write a romance novel. It pays; for you it will be easy and you might even have something interesting to say with it."

When Lace stepped back out into the day, the shadows had reappeared, long and ominous against the street. He stopped and gazed at them for a very long time. They came and went, stretched and shrank, in endless cycles without end. "No," he thought, "everything ends." Against the unrelenting, ceaseless rising, waning and setting of our sun, underneath things change and wither and die and he felt, after all, unsettled. Perhaps even afraid.

CHAPTER II

This is the journal of one Patrick Harris, me, and I will set out at the beginning my purposes in writing it. It is not a diary, to be sure, because I don't care about documenting that daily clockwork, unceasing, tick-tock unwinding of my affairs. No, I'm writing this journal to look backwards before looking into the present. I intend to exorcise demons.

I am tracking an angst, you see: I'm hunting down a mid-life crisis like a beast in the woods, getting little glimpses of it, seeing little flashes of it like an animal darting through the underbrush. But then again, perhaps I should rephrase the metaphor. After all, I'm no hunter and maybe that's the problem. We might begin with that revelation: that I never pursued any one thing. Never a grand dream, never the supreme goal. So instead, I must start simply by remembering. If my search begins with a tale, the tale requires a beginning that has to be tweezed out of the past. The narrative begins, but to remember its beginning means setting my foot, committing, to one place in time. Which is it, of my disjointed memories, that will lead the narrative and tell the story that arises out of my past to haunt my present and destroy the future?

And what is a story, any story, but a summation of choices and subsequent consequences. Each thing that happens to us arises out of twists and turns of a life that no one understands. A person stands in a doorway looking out or loiters at the crux of a crossroads without a thought of what brought them to that door, how they were caught in the middle of that street or emerged upon that crooked way. It took a thousand steps, each a small decision of no apparent weight or merit, to get a person to some moment when they suddenly stop and say to themselves, "Why am I here, now, in this place? It is dark and I don't know where I am."

First, I'll gather distant relics and try to draw them together to make sense out of today. I will pull together the detritus of my mind.

And, I will begin with this: sometimes I wonder at what makes up my childhood memories. They form me in some way. Not the memories themselves, but which memories, perhaps. Why are some, even the least of them, so much more important than others? That much is inescapable. As much as they belong to the past, somehow you never quite shake some. Then, those are the ones that have trapped me: the un-trappable, uncommitted adult, Patrick Harris. Yes, as I try to resurrect them, they remain elusive. Memories of childhood shimmer like little glimpses of a magic realm. I catch a moment of little Patrick basking in his mother's gaze, but then, with it, comes a flash of a darker moment when Patrick stood, crying in tiny wet pants. These old memories catch the light like tiny, bright Christmas tree ornaments. Without a tree to put them on, to give them coherence, the memories lie around untied to each other like sparkling baubles scattered haphazardly around a gigantic room. The truth is that what remains of my childhood is a sketchy, unreliable, mostly forgotten haze of unconnected recollections. The Christmas tree that I put them on is a reconstruction. It is what I believe the patterns of my childhood must have been to produce those unrelated scenes. But the Christmas tree has changed from time to time and with it the placement and meaning of those ornamental memories. If the Christmas tree can change, it means that it is all made up. My mind makes up a lie so that the haphazard and jagged edges fit into a neat array, prettily laid out across a make-believe holiday shrub.

When I go back to my childhood, I actually fly back through the years like someone hovering and darting over a computerized terrain. I picture things this way, in landscapes and colors, ups and downs. Numbers, for instance, are more or less yellow until you get to the twenties, which are a bluish white. Zero to ten goes in a line directly from left to right with each number the square of a sidewalk. Then, at ten, the numbers to twenty turn abruptly forward to go straight up a hill. The twenties, with their bluish white light, meander slightly left to right again until they meet up with the thirties, which are reddish yellow and climb steps that veer first one way and then another, undulating across an indistinct landscape until the hundreds appear just underfoot. I could trace this walkway of numbers into the trillions if I wanted to, each with a distinctive color and direction, uphill or downhill, stairs or a pathway, winding or straight. Each number is part of a unique sequence in the colors and travels of my head.

When I move back, literally in space and time, I fly over digitized mountains and valleys and steer a trajectory back over recollections from mid-life and through the fractal recesses of early career and relationships gone wild or blown up until I arrive back, through those decades, to a small bungalow in which we once lived. This is where the search begins then. I was perhaps six years old. There, I come to rest with my forehead just a little taller than the surface of a Formica kitchenette barely fitted into the corner of a small kitchen. In the far-back haze of this memory the sun was sepia yellow, filtered through a kitchen window dressed with café curtains. I found the curtains when my mother died. They were covered with red cherries and bright green leaves, just like my memory of them, except that in my memory the colors glow from within like small embers and around the edges, where there is an aura. The curtains, carefully folded away, were cheerful, but faded from sunlight, and I could imagine them across the kitchen window, filtering the sun on that distant late afternoon. So the reds and greens and yellows were flat and real and the cloth was solid to the touch, lengthening the distance between this day and that one even further because the memory is not only separated in time but by the embellishments of imagination.

I come to suspect that this memory is deceptive, maybe even entirely fraudulent, because the Christmas tree upon which I have placed this particular sparkling bauble is itself a fiction. The pieces come together differently as I get older. After all, I am a man who hates the sound of a vacuum cleaner and for many years didn't know why. Then I remembered that if mother was still cleaning when I came home from school, it meant she would be upset and irrational. I was by far an adult when I realized that if she was doing housework so late in the day, she had been drinking. Probably she had been nursing a hangover all day. So there it was, then. A new fact, a new realization that alters everything. The ornaments now hung anew in bright new patterns. Her moods now understand, the silent shadows of our household are snapped into sharper contours.

I will accept that this story out of the past is never a coherent one. How do the good memories of trips to the zoo or to a lake now forgotten coexist with fights and feelings of isolation and loneliness? How do the bright and happy mental fragments of playing with children during recess square with the bitter ones of children who taunted me? Mental fragments indeed! They share with each other no space in the terrain of thought. None of it would make sense if I tried to put everything together into one long story, but in this small house and in this small kitchen at this particular moment on some imagined day in one of the pathways followed out of and back into a vague past. The sun was orange warm and my mother was smiling out of old pictures from the album in my bookcase and in this particular memory as she unpacked groceries she put to the side a long, seductive and mysterious package covered bright with paper and told me it was mine.

What can I do to make the jagged edges fit? Did she ignore me after that? No. I'll bet she told me to wait so we could open it together. She must have continued putting groceries away, but then again, she might have left the room. I can imagine that she needed to go to the bathroom, so reasonable and necessary are other people's actions to the day-by-day unfolding of their own lives. But who thinks like that? This story is my story; it belongs to me. I have to make up the parts that belong to other people, but I also know that there must have been an internal logic to what happened. There is no logical sense to be derived from the impression that stays with me just out of reach like old smells of cut grass or the Shalimar that mother wore, an impression lying just outside of truth or even vague memory that she left me alone, a young boy with a gift that he was not to touch.

No, that could not have been it, even if the feeling that I was being deprived of my gift remains as part of a memory that may be mostly a lie anyway.

But each step must have unraveled slowly, with a steady and sensible idea of what should be done next. What stayed with me ever after is that way that things have, of happening slowly, almost deliberately, necessarily somehow just outside of awareness. Cause and effect, barely perceptible.

Why do I remember this? Was it special somehow? I don't remember that we gave lots of gifts to each other, and yet Christmas was loaded with presents. Didn't we get gifts of new clothes at Easter and little chocolates for Valentine's Day? I think so, but I'm not sure it was quite like that. So I catch the story of my past in yet another lie. Perhaps this package wasn't even exceptional. Yes, I remember that there were happy times. There were promises certainly of trips to the zoo, but probably more promises put off. Promises were not always kept; commitments could be lightly made. I know these things because I'm an adult and I know what life is and it could not have been otherwise.

Whatever analysis I bring to bear now, the fact is that I wanted that gift and would not wait, so in my excitement I tore through the bright paper in pursuit of the gift inside only to find two long, light balsa sticks. Mother had bought me a kite, which, in my rush, I had ruined by tearing apart the paper of the kite itself.

Even in the life of a child, this is a small matter. An adult becomes acquainted with the relative importance of things.

There never was to be another kite. What on earth motivated her to give me this little surprise of a gift? Were kites the topic of some conversation over dinner? Maybe I asked a boyish question from a science class. I don't remember ever having asked for one, but I might have begged my parents for a kite. That's how the fragments get put together in my mind into a terrain, or a Christmas tree. That's how the fragments come together as a story.

But even though the loss of this one gift was a small matter, aside from some disappointment and a feeling of stupidity, I experienced a deep, awful preview of what it means when a small, avoidable moment of action causes irretrievable loss. I met a woman once whose son drowned in the pool while she peeled potatoes. A careless word cost a friend a job. If a careless moment can cost so much, how much more awful is a planned and intentional act that seems sensible and right under the circumstances, but that leads surely and steadily, right before your eyes, into loss or suffering. A small thing. Only an inch different, only a distracted look, only one misunderstood thing and the results are so far beyond what we intend, the punishment so far greater than we could have known.

Of course, time has taught me that life can be forgiving, too. I have gotten away with a great deal. Punishments do not fit the crime, and in the universe of cause and effect people suffer greatly and achieve great things, too, and no one can decipher the exact chain of events from what they did to how things turned out for them. And however true it is that in the way people lead their lives creates the life they live, still, in the limited scope of a boy who is learning from experience what it means to be living, and who draws what lessons he may from each traumatic experience, I drew my lesson from the willful, yet accidental ruination of my kite.

A tree, even a Christmas tree, grows first in one upward sweep out of the ground and then it splits somewhere into branches, first once and then twice. A person learns to look at trees drawn out on textbook pages in school and becomes familiar with the splitting paths that draw a lineage from creatures of the Cretaceous period to Cetaceans and their lordship over the ocean, from great granduncles to second cousins once removed. The branch splits again and again, but when the bifurcations happen as actions played out in time, the path moves only one way. A finger can trace a map backwards and forwards on a page but how do I go backwards along those lines to reconstruct the lesson I took as a little boy so that I can take another direction? Like my numbers, the years into twenty and thirty and beyond have their own colors and move now this way and then that way and no reconsideration of how I came to think as a boy can ever change that.

Perhaps the reason I remember so well such a slight experience is that the tree split in a momentous way. The punishment did not fit the crime, the cause was not related to the effect, not because colorful paper was torn, thereby destroying a kite, but because the lesson I drew grew into the trunk of a tree. I use the word lesson, but it was more than that. It was a way of thinking that grew out of the moment as surely as a forest of mangroves springs from a small root. If my family had been made up of more patient people, if the time or the geographic location had been different, or if my mother had been a different person, she might have spent some time explaining some other lesson to me. Maybe it would have been that not all things come wrapped and hidden from the outside. Most things are what they are entirely. Then again, she might have struck me in anger, had she been some other kind of parent still, and then the growing child would have accommodated heaven only knows what other mix of emotions and methods of handling them. Many children, perhaps most children, would have cared nothing about the kite; would have had no reaction past a transitory and ephemeral moment of disappointment.

But for some reason, this child at that moment was struck by the way we are not given enough information with which to act. It seemed to me at that moment, and for a long time afterwards, that each bold action was a step into darkness and uncertainty and that, if the punishment did not fit the crime, the results were unknowable and possibly awful.

This became for me the great and central unfairness of being alive. Where was the information that Patrick Harris needed to act upon the world; how was I ever to complete the dataset? Some piece of the picture, some fact that would have helped us act differently was always withheld. I had been left with a barely perceptible sense of vulnerability against the unknown and unknowable that seeped into me after mother stepped out of the kitchen and left me with that seductive package. After that, it seemed that stories about the vulnerability of our condition abounded everywhere. Fear of being without information became reflected in the story of Eden and its apple growing out of reach, the inscrutable ways adolescents behave with one another, the administrator at school with his list of secret rules, the bureaucrats at city hall and the lawyers with their intricacies of law.

Then I became a young and then a middle-aged man, and as I became more confident of my place in the world it didn't seem like it was individual people who withheld information from me. It seemed to be the universe itself that would not tell me what effects my actions would have on my friends, my family, my community, and me. And then, the people surrounding me seemed to move within a kaleidoscope, according to ever changing rules and whims that defied understanding. Sometimes my best actions caused uncertainty and unhappiness. Sometimes the least effort brought the best result. I don't know how it happened because when I was younger, I didn't think much about the uncertainty of these effects.

It is later on that you wonder. If I place myself back then, during the time of the kite and probably ten years afterwards, adults lived a secretive life just beyond the borders of what I knew. I remember the moment when I realized that mother and father slept at night and at a sudden the lines between what was plausible and conceivable shifted outwards onto a more distant horizon. Then, as my parents molded my character, sometimes by scolding or punishing, it was rarely because I had meant to do something wrong. The punishment came as a surprise, the result of actions the effect of which seemed unknowable with danger always nearby.

Little Patrick did grow up, of course, and he came to the big city and in that time the uncertainties matured and increased, but the fundamentals did not change, as I begin to see now. The trunk of that tree, planted with the two slim balsa sticks of a kite, had grown and hardened into the base of a tree. And if, in the words of my metaphor, I am caught at the end of a branch with no place left to go, what does one do? I am tempted to scramble to the bottom and cut the entire tree to the ground just to plant anew, but perhaps it's better to sit atop my present perch and survey the landscape from where I sit. There must be more than one way to reshape a life.

Casting my eyes across the horizon, I wonder how I became frozen and when. How did I get so boxed in? The decisions taken at twenty imprisoned me at forty, until I found myself working at the Twenty Eighth Street Flower Emporium each day, day after day unsure of where to go or who to trust. I had traveled first up a broad tree trunk, then onto a smaller branch only to find myself at the end of a twig, fluttering alone in some queer white breeze.

That is the way that a barely remembered moment in childhood caused a thought, which caused a way of thinking, which caused a way of life that never at any moment ever took into consideration that the punishment should fit the crime. But the oddest thing is that ways of thinking can peter out finally. They stop working, while vestiges live on and color everything around them. Perhaps they have grown further and further away from any kind of objective reality until I have been left alone to flutter, abandoned to the wind. And yet I was so sure of myself as a child, I never noticed how the twig was being bent.

My mind gets away from me sometimes. Didn't it seem like the final piece of information is always just out of reach? Isn't this a central theoretical problem for physicists? If that is the way things are, if the universe in fact branched out from a Big Bang, why indeed wouldn't creation itself be nothing but a sudden moment of realization? And why wouldn't a sudden moment of realization be like a child's fixation upon an idea that will only become useless over time?

Even so, the memory or the idea gets placed carefully on a Christmas tree of lies and fictions just so that everything fits together neat, nice and pretty. But if you're not careful, if the memory isn't right and the pieces don't really fit, the whole edifice, the whole Christmas tree, runs dry and dies away as the lights go out. That's what the physicists fear, that everything will just grow cold and die out, even if it's billions of years off and not something I have to worry about on this particular night in pretty damn good shape, if I really thought about it, as I sit writing at the beach, watching the stars and thinking to myself.

CHAPTER III

Anne Rose Morelli hurried home. After her brief chat with Lace Whittaker, she had watched him walk his little, jaunty walk up on the toes after each step with his unsteady whistle as he walked. She was annoyed with him, although why didn't quite come to mind. She was polite, to be sure, but lately being polite made her feel like a little girl among grown-ups and she had known Lace when she was little, even before her mother moved away and left her alone with the apartment. She had been grumpy, generally, of late. Only her hunting kept some kind of sadness at bay, so after Lace turned his back on her and continued down the street for a while with Anne Rose's eyes at his back, she finally turned with a heavy grunt that was nearly a sigh and went on ferreting for the treasures that people put out on the sidewalk. Lately, her excursions had taken her further and further from MacDougal Street. She stopped methodically at each trash can or set of boxes set out on the street for pickup, searching through them for trinkets, jewels, castoffs for her treasure store slowly building at home. Today had not been a great day. Her cart contained only a painted piece of plywood, an old doll and two dresses that smelled of rotted food but would clean up. The old doll needed a home and the plywood would work in between rooms or perhaps as a table. The dresses she would need when she lost weight.

Anne Rose did think a lot about losing weight. She was 334 pounds when she last went to a doctor and she was heavier now. Not that it seemed like it, but her dresses ripped when she put them on and so little pieces of cloth like those she found two streets over would certainly come in handy for that. Then there was the chair that just needed a leg and two old bottles that, being glass a pretty color of green, would catch the light if she put them in her window, the one she liked to leave about six inches open for the breeze against the hot radiators of close New York apartments.

But this morning, people had little to throw away so her wanderings had taken her eight streets over and back. Anne Rose rocked the great bulk of her body back and forth as she placed each foot one only slightly in front of the other to support her weight and hurried against all the laws of anatomy and physics to her home. As she did this, she sang a little song to herself, made up in fragments from a nursery rhyme she had forgotten. She sang in the heavy rhythmic motion of her out swinging legs, "This little piggy went to market, this little piggy went home, this little piggy went to school, la la la la. Ha! Ha! This little piggy…"

She was meeting her aunt, Veronica McGrady, PhD. Anne Rose's mother, in whose apartment she lived, had moved long ago out to Bound Brook, New Jersey, to live with her son in a suburban development, leaving poor (in every sense of the word) Anne Rose to her own devices, with her neuroses and pains and disorders, in the heart and bosom of New York. Anne Rose's mother did not drive. She kept order and home together in the house in Bound Brook for her son's family. Her daughter-in-law worked. They had two young sons and an infant daughter and there was little time to look in on Anne Rose. That was Veronica McGrady's job, both by delegation and inclination.

Veronica McGrady, as the name reminded everyone, was by far the youngest of her siblings and the first to marry outside her heritage. Common as such a marriage might be later, at the time it broke tradition by taking her out and away from the neighborhood called Little Italy. The families made the best of it. After all, the in-laws were Catholic at least. She married an up-and-coming bar owner, Michael McGrady, and they had two sons. Afterwards, she went on to The New School and then to Columbia where she got a PhD in psychology. Then they moved to Port Jefferson and Veronica became head of counseling for the school system. Long as the ride into the city was, she tended to her duties with the regularity of a nurse. Anne Rose knew that Veronica was not to be kept waiting but on this day she felt that her passion for collecting had been cut short by her aunt, which undoubtedly is why she was so annoyed. Nonetheless, she feared Veronica McGrady for reasons she couldn't quite understand, but might have been because Veronica was older, slim and efficient, warm but not suffocating, stern but not mean. In other words, she carried a silent authority and as the family-appointed warden she was not generally questioned by the younger, needy and sad overweight woman who slowly approached her on the street.

As Anne Rose waddled up the sidewalk, Veronica McGrady waited outside her navy blue Buick and smiled at her with a smile that was at once warm because she did in fact love her niece and she understood the abandonment and loneliness that Anne Rose must have felt for these many years after her mother moved away to Bound Brook. On the other hand, if one looked into Veronica's eyes one would find terrible weariness. Her trip into town was two hours long; her work was hard. She no longer enjoyed the mounting hours devoted to administrative routine dictated by the schools and one look at the cart told her that Anne Rose was getting worse. A year ago, she was careless about throwing things out and stacking old newspapers in the apartment. A year ago, Anne Rose was hefty but not morbidly obese. She knew the syndrome, saw its prognosis clear as day and she was resigned to it because Anne Rose would listen to sense no better than anyone in the midst of these disorders listened to sense. And, of course, she was a blood relative. Worse than a stranger, her advice might just as well have been a kazoo playing against the afternoon firehouse sirens. So,she straightened her newly purchased, plaid Claire McCardell Popover dress a little at the hemline and smiled her happy but weary smile and then put her arms around Anne Rose in a truly felt embrace.

"Oh my dear, my dear, my dear, what have you found today?" she asked brightly, trying to mean it.

A careful look crept into Anne Rose's eyes as she paused and glanced up from her cart, feeling patronized. This woman, family though she may be, drove into her life to check up on her and made it clear, behind a façade of concern, what she thought of her treasures. Anne Rose concealed her thoughts and motioned to go into the apartment. Here her possessions, piled against the walls, were layered one atop the other throughout two tiny rooms on the first floor, window looking out onto a back courtyard with a breeze drifting through.

Veronica had to step past a box of magazines and noticed the half-eaten sandwich and partial chicken lying on the sink of a kitchen built along the wall opposite the living area windows. On the stove was a pan encrusted with dried soup. Across the room were two paths allowing access to a bedroom and the bath. Arranged on tables and bureaus that had once been left on the streets were thousands of dolls, ceramics, plates, pieces of jewelry, odd bits of iron and metal and fabric sometimes positioned with care, sometimes carelessly strewn. An enamel dinette table with deco lines painted in red around the edge, pitted and chipped along the sides, supported about a dozen candles and a statue of the Virgin in the center. The Virgin was, in turn, surrounded by three snowmen of various sizes and materials, perhaps twenty angels, partial and broken figures from crèches and three rosaries lying abandoned diagonally across the figurines.

There was no place to sit so they went into the bedroom, where papers and magazines were piled nearly to the ceiling. Finally, they found their way to a single bed and made themselves as comfortable as they could.

Veronica sat straight, hands to her sides, fingers slightly pinching folds in the spattered sheets. She paused a moment to look behind her as she perched tightly on the edge of the mattress before asking, "Did you find anything wonderful today, dear?"

As a sort of riposte, Anne Rose fingered a torn and stained spot near her hem, pulling her dress further up than ordinary modesty would allow. Veronica looked away past the door towards the Virgin shimmering before the rays of a late afternoon sun that filtered through ancient, dust covered windows and added, "Dr. Emerson said you didn't show up last Thursday. Were you okay?"

Anne Rose carefully massaged the soiled spot on her dress, almost without thinking except that she pulled the hemline a little further up, catching with it the bottom of her grayed panties and showing the beginning of her pubic hair. Behind her darkening eyes came the abrupt thought that her aunt and that doctor were in touch behind her back and she wanted to show them a thing or two, to strike back somehow. The feeling wasn't entirely conscious, but it was hard and palpable just the same.

Veronica glanced down and then abruptly, fixedly stared at the Virgin. Anne Rose said, "Fuck Dr. Emerson. Fuck him, Auntie Veronica. What's your idea, anyway? Why are you making these fucking appointments for me?" She didn't raise her voice, she just put a little edge on it, almost like a child teasing a playmate. She took the hem of her dress and the panties firmly between two fingers, rubbing the two materials hard together in a regular, fixed rhythm that matched the cadence of her sentences.

Veronica was surprised but resigned. Anne Rose could be stubborn, but a streak of profanity was new. Talking back this way was new.

"Honey, we all want is for you…well…to live better. And you could live better, couldn't you, sweetheart? I mean…"

She paused, uncertain and careful.

"I mean, your home isn't kept clean. It can't be good to keep food sitting out on the cabinets. We all know you want to live alone, but Dr. Emerson can help you live better. And we all need someone we can talk to."

Veronica reached over and touched Anne Rose's cheek, taking a lock of hair between her fingers.

Anne Rose punched the mattress twice and then used her great, round arm to lift herself up, surprising Veronica who sprang up quickly.

"Fuck Dr. Emerson. Fuck, Fuck, Fuck, Fuck. I found a doll and a mouse, Auntie Veronica and a bottle. There's so much fucking garbage out there; people just leave it on the street. I don't have time to see fucking Dr. Emerson. And the food in the kitchen is still good. Don't say it isn't. I have to straighten out these papers, now, auntie. I have things to do."

Anne Rose and Veronica stood for a moment in the shadows of the bedroom. As the dust motes passed across the Virgin, the statue seemed to turn with the angle of the rays and smile. Veronica did not look at her niece; her attention was resolutely on the statue. "That statue smiles a maliciously sarcastic smile," she thought to herself. The Virgin's red painted lips appeared to snarl upward, an illusion caused, she thought, by a slight break on top of her lip. It reminded her of the Joker's smile on old Batman episodes. A roach, Veronica noticed, had made its way to nap on the rosaries, fitting in with the beads almost exactly. She turned finally to her niece.

"Anne Rose, I have driven two-and-a-half hours to get here. I had a lousy day. It took a lot of time and effort to get that appointment with Dr. Emerson for you. Why won't you go? Don't you think we care about you? You can see how much effort I put in."

Almost immediately, Veronica was sorry. She knew that no one had asked her to do these things. She couldn't obligate her niece.

Anne Rose made her way slowly to the door, picking her way through the growing darkness past the Virgin and her court of snow-men and angels, past the broken umbrellas in an old milk can and steadied herself on a pile of *The New York Times*.

"Jesus, auntie. How do you come here when I have so much to do? I didn't ask you to get me an appointment with that fucking doctor. I didn't ask you to fuck up your fine life to do for me. Don't do me favors. Don't fucking do me any favors, Auntie Veronica."

This last Auntie Veronica," she said with a sneer, her lips curled in sympathy with the Virgin. Veronica following behind found herself jettisoned into the courtyard as Anne Rose opened the door for her to go. She made her way to the blue Buick parked outside as the last rays of sunlight caught a grayish, almost cancerous chip on the right side of the Virgin's rouged cheek.

CHAPTER IV

Agnes Pranciple arched her back. Jonathan moved his haunches slowly around, grinding his crotch hair into her, making her push forward instinctively. He bit tightly into her left tit, leaving it red as he came. Agnes gripped him hard and thrust her pelvis riding him and clenching her teeth hard, sucking him in. Jonathan gave an extra whelp, like a whipped puppy. She liked that.

Agnes didn't know Jonathan's last name. She didn't know where he lived; knew nothing at all about him. She had met him two months ago at that gallery opening and taken him up to a cheap hotel she knew. They met there after that on Sunday's at 6:00. Slowly, their tastes had progressed without discussion.

He lay on top of her, arms outstretched. Her fingers trailed into the nape of his neck, into the long, uncut, wet hair clutching to his shoulder. He pulled out just a bit and slowly, he began to urinate almost into her. It was only a small amount but as he did it, she spread her legs and let the warm liquid overflow her. Pushing it back out, she soiled the sheets, wetness surrounding them like a soft summer's moonlit sea. She trailed her fingers downward stroking his buttocks and inserting a middle finger. With a stroke he reentered and came a second time.

After that, he pulled out. His long, red-haired cock trailed out over the wet sheets and he seemed to drift off asleep. They were careful about not talking. She looked over his white body. She was promiscuous, no doubt about that. But there was something about this Jonathan. They moved slowly in tandem, like assassins in the night. They never talked; sex itself was the conversation between them. Agnes loved being fucked by strangers. She loved the smoky smell of Black men she picked up. She could stroke the smooth skin of Latin teenagers and lick their bodies for hours at a time. But what she loved about Jonathan could turn into absolute filth. The second time they were together, she peeled back his dirty white socks and slowly licked inside his toes. Looking up, she saw no surprise in his eyes. The coolness of his stare excited her. He expected this. He expected more.

Jonathan had not led the way, exactly, but his openness was a kind of leadership, his passivity a sort of command. He seemed to be waiting for something. Nature abhors a vacuum. Agnes filled it, finding things to do. Her eyes became fuzzy in his presence. "Am I out of control?" Agnes wondered. No, she was not so much in his power. Agnes knew she was perfectly in control. Agnes was always in control of herself. She could cut anyone, including Jonathan, dead at a moment. But these times with Jonathan were an inexorable surrendering to some inexpressible need. She bathed in a kind of freedom, like an infant floating in amniotic fluid.

Semen dripped out of the tip of Jonathan's penis and Agnes slipped down to lick it away, bringing him out of his reverie. He raised himself up on his elbow sleepily and looked at her. His eyes were distant, almost vacant. He smiled and showed yellowed teeth under a red moustache. There was a space between the two front teeth from which came the smell of cigarette smoke, making Agnes think of a far-off campfire in the woods. What mystery might surround an unseen campfire in dark woods, smelled only vaguely by a lost stranger? The campfire—stumbling upon or surprising the people around the campfire—could mean deliverance or slavery, succor, redemption or death. A lost stranger in the forest might expect salvation and find despair. Agnes leaned forward again and bit the bottom of his scrotum. Jonathan started, took her hair and brought her face up to his, like an executioner reviewing the face of a newly headless woman. He scrutinized her carefully, looking to see what he had in his hands and then kissed her full in the mouth, discharging spit down her throat, which she thirstily drank and then pushed him away, laughing.

Simultaneously, they rolled away from each other and stood up at opposite sides of the soaked bed. She took a towel, dried herself and began to dress, warmed by the thought that her expensive clothes were to be worn over the dried urine covering her body. Something in her positively glowed from this abandon. Agnes was self-analytical. She was attracted to the thing in her that caused her to behave this way. She was an executive. She was a woman who made her way in the world of business. But somehow this wallowing with Jonathan, if that was really his name, was the essence of control. No one who was not entirely self-possessed could make a way into this world of heedless pleasure. She thought of herself, sometimes, as a priestess in a long history of priestesses who presided over sybaritic rites and these were rites that in ancient times led to the rending apart of lambs and, perhaps, people. Agnes thought of Pierre Louy's *Aphrodite*. In that novel, a slave had been tortured to death by orgiastic pinpricks.

Indeed, it seemed to her that there was a place where abandonment and self-control, ethics and pleasure, love and passion all met and became meaningless. Perhaps it was being relieved of giving these things meaning, not having to pay attention to these things that gave sex with Jonathan its electric appeal. But that wasn't it. Agnes was not excruciatingly polite, tactful or regretful of wrongdoing. She was contained, but not tight-assed. No, in fact sex with Jonathan was not electric. It was riveting, but it was riveting in the way a person being swept out to sea might be riveted. She had read a book about the primitive brain. It seemed to her that perhaps this compulsion for drowning in body fluids, this pig sty of animal activities, hearkened to some dim, reptilian past lived in antediluvian swamps and free of human cares and wants. But then, Freud would put it into the womb, wouldn't he? What would Lace's poems have to say about that? Whatever it was, it drew on something in her as ancient as witchcraft and as subtle and unrelenting as the tides. It felt like it must be the same rhythm that calls the turtle back to its beach or compels a butterfly to fly thousands of miles to reach their mating grounds.

Jonathan took a shower while Agnes got dressed. On the street a loud fight erupted. The street lamp was directly in front of the window and it went on as the sun dipped below the building tops, throwing a shadow across Agnes's bra and giving her just enough light to pull on a maroon cashmere sweater. As she pulled on her snug black jeans, he walked into the room.

"I can't make it next Sunday," he said.

So this was it. He took a joint out of his shirt pocket and lit it, offering a toke to her. Agnes took it and breathed in deeply. She relaxed immediately. They didn't smoke before sex, oddly. He liked to smoke afterwards.

"Do you mean next Sunday or no Sunday?" she asked.

Jonathan was matter of fact.

"A guy is taking me out next Sunday." There was a pause, a sort of arrogance while his sexual ambivalence hung in the air. Then he added, thinking to explain, "I need the money. I never make plans a week away, but I have to go. We're going to the Hamptons."

He paused a moment and then said again, without emotion, "I do need the money," and took another hit off the joint. Then he pulled on his underwear and winked at her, playing with his basket and smiling his yellow, open-toothed smile and sticking out his tongue.

If Jonathan's teeth had not been so cigarette yellow, his breath so fallow, his eyes so narrow, sticking his tongue out in this manner would have been childish and silly. As it was, it was dangerous and dirty, conspiratorial and seductive.

"So, I'll meet you Sunday after next," Agnes said as she adjusted her shoes.

She walked over towards the bureau near the window, through which only the lamppost shown light. She stepped carefully past the sheets that had been thrown across the floor, knocking slightly into the lopsided burnt, brown shade of a floor lamp, which she turned on. Her keys and purse lay on the bureau along with some money. She had gone into the bathroom once. When she returned, all the money was still there. Her keys were still there. The purse lay untouched.

One of the bureau drawers was broken, jutting partially out of the cabinet altogether. There was only one knob on the top drawer. The shower dripped; the toilet ran. The floor lamp buzzed slightly and somewhere down the hall or out on the street a pimp was hitting some whore who screamed into the night.

"Fucking nigger, hit me; don't you go beating up on me, you fucking nigger. Fucking nigger."

She screamed it again and again, as if in a trance. The sound came over the still breeze of the night, a sour perfume drifting in through the open window. Agnes gathered up her things to leave as Jonathan pulled on his pants, turning around slightly. She noticed two long, deep scratches down his back where she had run her nails, blood running freely with his sweat into the crack of his butt. The top of his underwear was already stained red. She liked that too.

CHAPTER V

Dear Journal,

But I'm caught in another memory trap, two memories that can't quite co-exist. Perhaps I was caught early on by the impression that we are terribly vulnerable; that things can go bad in a second. Yet I don't remember myself as a timid adolescent. I think that I was probably overly certain of myself, as young people tend to be, so that as I made my way at the beginning, the sturdy lower branches seemed strong.

Since I was out to take the world by storm, I left home to come to New York by bus. It was a gutsy time and there was little sign that I would ever lose direction. Perhaps it was all bravado, then, when I was eighteen and I was reading Lord of the Rings *as the bus drove through the New Jersey industrial wasteland with the New York skyline floating out of an orange haze further still in the distance, the end of a beckoning quest. As we drove along the New Jersey turnpike, that intrepid Hobbit whose name I forget was climbing into a sulfuric mountain to dispose of a magic ring. Looking out the window at that passing landscape of refineries belching harsh smoke up against desolate flatlands, I found myself in circumstances so similar to that wandering Hobbit that I was struck by how cosmically harmonic it all was.*

 Ah! It was Frodo. The Hobbit's name was Frodo. I remember it again, as the flight over that sepia landscape retrieves another fractal particle of memory and inserts another one of its jagged edges into the picture. It is another edge that doesn't quite fit because this was a time of bravado and I did become fearful in some ways. I was also fearlessly defiant in others. If authority has always bamboozled me, I hate kowtowing to it too.

And in retrospect, however much I felt like I was on a quest, like my Hobbit friend, there was nothing so heroic about it. Really, I was just doing things step by step, heedless and unaware.

I had just escaped the Vietnam draft and I was ready to take on the world. The night before meeting a bus that was to deliver me and about a hundred other new recruits to some army base for the induction physical, I picked up two men who made love to me all night. We drank a lot. The next morning when I looked in the mirror to get ready, I was covered with hickies. That was the damnest thing. It never happened before or since. Just that one night. I was blue and purple with hickies.

So a few thousand of us poured together into a room from about fifty buses and sat along long ivory white tables laid out in long rows where we filled out forms at the bottom of which was the question I was waiting for. The army wanted to know if I had any homosexual tendencies. Well, "yeah," was the appropriate response to that. First of all, they promised to screw you to the wall if you ever, ever, ever lied on one of their forms. Then, too, I had a friend who got a purple heart and also a dishonorable discharge because his gay love letters, which were written from the hospital while he was recuperating from his fucking war wounds, were intercepted by the hospital's commanding officer. And I was an anti-war activist. I had done my share of marching in DC. And Congress never declared this war to begin with, so where did that leave the Constitution and me under it? Hell, yeah, I've got homosexual tendencies, and yeah if you want me to mark the box and own up to it, I will.

After the forms got filled out, we went through our physical. Picture five thousand guys, standing in lines that reached to the horizon, all reading an eye chart. Or there we all were, one after another, bending over and coughing in chorus while doctors peered up our assholes, one hole after another, while they held your balls. What a job. Sticking your finger up about three hundred assholes a day and then going home for a good home-cooked meal with your childhood sweetheart. Thinking back, I have to wonder how it all began for a guy like that. I doubt he began medical school with the express desire to stick thousands of draftees in the butt with the same finger he used to taste cookie batter at home, so you try to picture how it was, maybe, when he first wooed her? You think of him at a soda fountain in a Leave It To Beaver town, proposing:

"Stick with me, kiddo, and we'll have the best life. See this finger? I'm going to stick a million kids up the butt with it so you can have a ranch house, Betsy. I love you, won't you marry me?"

The guys were kidding me about the hickies when a Sergeant, or someone who looked like he was not exactly upper management but had some authority, came striding up to me and showed me the box with my elegantly applied dark pencil mark right through the center.

"Patrick Harris?" He announced, rather than asked, inclining his head in my direction. I nodded to indicate that I was indeed a person who went by that name, standing on tiptoes to see for sure where he was pointing on the form.

"Do you know what this means?" He didn't seem very kind-hearted about it.

"Yeah," I said.

I didn't think I needed to say much more. He marched me, I guess that's what he was used to doing, marching people, so he marched me into a Major's office. I know he was a Major because it said "Major" on the door and I still remember the olive drab furniture, the army drab desk and the wooden chair with slats for a back and rollers on the legs. I forget if I stood or sat, but I guess, thinking back on it, that I had to stand. I certainly doubt that they asked me to make myself comfortable in a wing-backed chair. Maybe I even sort of stood at attention. The Major looked over my papers and gauged me carefully over his glasses.

"How can you prove that you're a homosexual?"

That was a peculiar question that just begged for a peculiar answer, but I was ready for the good Major.

"See where I checked the gonorrhea box? It was up the ass."

It seemed to me the less said the better, but that should clinch it.

Then, continuing his attempts to trap me, "When was the last time you had sex?"

I was still wearing only a pair of underpants and so I turned my shoulder to him, imagining a Geisha in full kimono with the hickies covering me in delicious plum blossom patterns. Very chic when you think about it. Makes you think of art nouveau tattoos all over, and the effect was undeniable.

"Last night," I said, assuming the air of a seductress.

The Major was forced to be business-like, but he was still a little taken aback, I suppose. This was the early seventies, after all, and faggots like me were still expected to lurk out of public sight.

"You are discharged," he said pushing himself back a little in that wooden Pentagon purchase order chair.

The army offered me psychological counseling, which may have shown a benevolent government's thoughtful side, but I was bound for New York and a socialistic bevy of hippies who made their money selling prescription pills and lived in a communal apartment across from a police station in the East Twenties. There were two dykes living there who worked in a supermarket so when the rest of us went in to buy food only about every sixteenth item actually got rung up. We ate pretty well and the rent was, affordably, free and you could do all the hash and acid you wanted and screw everything in sight and so life was looking pretty good. I don't think any of us thought much about the war, though, after that.

But things began to unravel as they do when all your roommates are constantly stoned or strung out. First the dykes began wearing my clothes and then everyone passed out one night and there was no one to let me in so I began to move around a little. I stayed for a while in a flophouse on Bleecker Street called the Bleecker Street Hotel. They've made it into a luxury building and given it a fancy name, but that's what it was then: a flophouse. However, the Bleecker Street flophouse was, so to speak, an upper class flophouse because it was divided into tiny semi-private spaces. I lived in a cubicle with a cot and a chair and walls that went up maybe six-and-a-half feet. The rest of the way to the ceiling had only chicken wire between cubicles. We all shaved at sinks lined up on the stairwell platforms. You paid by the day, of course. We were not people who thought of life in two-year leases.

After I had lived there just a short time, some drunks had an argument over cards and threw a table out of an upper-story window. The table killed an elderly Italian man who had a vending cart on the street. One second he was selling hot dogs from his stand and the next he was flat on the pavement. He was a fixture in the neighborhood, one of the old-timers, an uncle or something of one of the big Mafia Capos. I heard that a long dark car drove up after that happened and one of the Capos got out to talk with the managers. Shortly after that, the building was closed and gutted. It may have become a fancy building, but it never helped make much of the block, if you ask me.

Then I moved into a rooming house on East Fourteenth Street. The roaches used to climb out of the stove as soon as the lights were out. We used to smoke pot and watch them creep out and we'd turn on the lights and try to kill as many as we could before they all disappeared. I lived there with a kid named Ronnie I had picked up who was hustling on the side. That place was the worst place I ever had to live *and then on top of it a mean-looking Puerto Rican guy said he was going to rape me and beat me up. He said, "A cute little bitch like you can't live here without putting out to me," so I moved from there into a little room on the Upper West Side with a bathroom down the hall.*

I was happy there. I started to sketch and bought a set of pastels. The room was near a park and the neighborhood was clean. A maid brought laundered sheets every few days. The hustler kid and I argued and parted ways and I started going down to the Village Bars. After that, it didn't take long. I hadn't been in New York three months before I met a successful doctor and suddenly I found myself driving a gull wing Mercedes and living at the tip end of East 72nd Street. Celebrities lived across the street and the building next door and down the block. People we had only talked or read about when I was growing up were walking their dogs and getting into taxis every day. I was meeting people who took months to look for the best-designed wine glasses, and they used different glasses with different wines. All I had ever known were mother's Fostoria wine glasses, those smallish one-size-fits-all stemmed pieces that she used for all occasions and prized like holy icons. Yes, I had a head on my shoulders and I learned fast at beginning to assemble information. One older guy said I was the most sophisticated eighteen-year-old he had ever met. After just a short time, I knew which wine to order at a meal, who Cole Porter was, what Broadway show people were discussing. Thinking back, I knew how to listen and ask questions that mattered, at least in the company I was keeping. I was good in bed and I was pretty cute, after all.

So you see, Patrick, fragments from the past do begin to come together. Perhaps I was defiant, independent, but to what purpose? I took opportunities as they came, seized them even, but even so and under-neath, I think that I was ascending my tree with no particular aim in mind. Is that how the fear played out? I never had a vision, never looked at a particular branch, high on the tree I was climbing and exclaimed to myself, "I want to go there!"

CHAPTER VI

Jonathan Perry left the Arlington Hotel on Ninth Avenue about 7:30 that Sunday and walked around for a while. He was running out of cigarettes and he needed money and, although he had just finished off two times, he was horny for something. After twenty minutes, he headed down to 42nd Street, picked up a guy from Staten Island, or who said he was from Staten Island, got blown and was paid twenty dollars, which he put towards a pint of whiskey and two packs of cigarettes. After that he got on the downtown Lexington line and headed home to his apartment on Elizabeth Street.

Elizabeth Street, which lies in a neighborhood that is isolated from much of the rest of Manhattan, is the point of an imaginary triangle touching on little Italy, Chinatown and outlying districts of the Bowery. As Jonathan returned home, he paused at the windows of several furniture showrooms that were tucked along the street, the windows sporting bedroom suites that looked like baroque fantasies or settees that looked like the coronation carriage of an English monarch. Plaster Davids sitting on short Bernini columns rounded out the décor of these little groupings, along with wild bouquets of fake flowers. The divans and chairs were covered in plastic. This was the style in

Italian neighborhoods dotting the landscape from Elizabeth Street out to Howard Beach in the far-flung sections of Queens.

Then, right next to the baroque settings of Italianate furniture, were sweatshops for washing and starching the shirts of a white army of uptown office workers. The white collars of the pale-faced garmentos and white-collar Wall Street workers were made presentable here on Elizabeth Street. The Chinese, and the Puerto Ricans somewhat closer to the East River, were only the last wave of immigrants following on the backs of the Italians and Jews. The Jews, the Poles, the you-name-it came through this street as if they were driving covered wagons towards the Cumberland Trail. They set up pushcarts, met, got married, went into business or jobs with the city and moved on out to the boroughs or maybe up to better neighborhoods uptown. Now, the red brick tenements of railroad flat apartments fitted into neat spaces between commercial establishments that served a variety of clienteles. The elderly and left-behind lived here side-by-side with Chinese families squashed into a few rooms. Drag queens spent their nights over sewing machines creating costumes before they went over to the West Side to prostitute themselves with taxi drivers and furtive men on their way home to New Jersey.

Jonathan Perry lived here and liked it. In particular, on nights like this one, he enjoyed gazing into the furniture groupings. They seemed beautiful to him, visions from the fabled lives of very rich people and so far away from the 50s threadbare sofa and TV tray tables of his childhood living room with its yellow brown shag carpet and the blackish coffee stains and the Formica-covered console TV set in the corner with rabbit ears sticking out of it. He would contrast the plain plastic flower arrangement on top of the TV of his childhood with the fantastic rose and peony arrangements behind the shop windows as he stopped momentarily, lost in a dream of wealth and leisure in which he was surrounded by cherubs atop bedsteads, silent servants and satin sheets.

And then, just alongside these images from a fantasy world, the solid reality of his neighborhood asserted itself. Beside the left-behinds from previous generations and the Chinese workers were outsiders who, like himself, had come to live in the cheap apartments of lower Manhattan: druggy poets and sex freaks lived along Elizabeth Street and down the block, just a few buildings away, lived a commune who refused to use electricity and dressed in nineteenth-century clothing.

Jonathan observed these people, nodded, even, to a few of them. The neighborhood did indeed suit him. He was, he had to admit, happy living there.

It was easy to walk up the five flights to his apartment at the rear, the windows boarded across with two-by-fours because he couldn't afford gates against the burglars who prowled across tenement roofs looking for television sets to carry away. There were two locks and a police lock—a rod that stuck into a hole in the floor that was a defiance against forced entry. One by one, he undid them and stood in the middle of his one room looking around, pleased to be home.

Jonathan's place was a tidy home. His mother had taught him that. There was a mattress on the floor and a lamp with a white plastic shade sitting next to it. A small television sat on a stool just in front of the mattress and that was it, except for an army trunk to hold his clothes. The wardroom was simple: four pairs of jeans that flattered his body, six sleeveless tee-shirts, a leather jacket, two flannel shirts, five pairs of white socks, a pair of cowboy boots and a pair of sneakers. That was it. That and the cross with the lord Jesus on it, lying crucified for our sins.

Some cold noodles from the Chinese place next door were sitting in the refrigerator. Jonathan ate them and watched the ten o'clock news. Then he got restless. His mind wandered to sex again so he abruptly gave himself a quick towel wash and changed into a pair of jeans with a revealing tear at the crotch.

When he emerged out into the fall night, the street still was busy with the comings and goings of its residents, the old women talking among themselves on the stoops and out the windows, the hard sound of Chinese gutturals between men playing with tiles at card tables set up in the doorways. A lone transvestite from an apartment down the hall went out at the same time. Her name was Miss Wanda and she smiled at him as they locked their many-locked doors. She smiled, but did not speak. They kept a respectable distance from each other, the habits of people who have grown suspicious over time.

In the Twenties on the Westside waterfront was a bar where young men in faded jeans liked to hang out and shoot pool. Jonathan bought a beer and put a quarter on the edge of the table to wait his turn, watching the other men play and appraising their skill. The pool table was the center of attention, the other customers merely spectators focused on action at the center of the bar. As he waited, Jonathan noticed strangers conversing, sometimes leaving together after some words were spoken. His stomach teemed with the thrill of the chase, the seeking of quarry, and the pool table was the vantage point from which he conducted his hunt.

It took about twenty minutes and two more beers. He was running out of money, but someone bought him a beer and started chatting with him. Jonathan said very little. This was not a man he was going home with so he played it cool, borrowed a cigarette so as not to deplete his own short supply, and played him along hoping for another beer or two. Finally, his quarter was up and he racked the balls, shaking hands with a man named Steve who had won the last three games. Steve wasn't very good but he had been very, very lucky. He had won the last game when his opponent sunk the eight ball on the third shot, but the other two games seemed endless. Jonathan racked the balls with the yellow one-ball smack up front and tight against the others, neat like his room, and stood back for Steve to break.

The break sank the two and the fourteen so Steve chose solids and sank the four. Jonathan sank three stripes, then missed, leaving the cue ball against the side of the table. Steve missed that shot and Jonathan sank two more. Steve sank three, leaving the table open enough for Jonathan to sink his last ball and then the eight ball. He had won easily but not expertly. He was good enough to hold the table in a bar like this, but he was no killer on the pool tables.

Killer or no, though, Jonathan loved spreading himself taut across the worn, soft green velvet, stretching to make shots under the bright light just overhead. Carefully, cat-like he would elongate his torso over the pool cue, legs apart with the small of his back arched, leaving the mounds of his ass open and inviting. Slowly, over several games, he noticed a man in his late thirties with salt-and-pepper hair, just out of the light's circle hovering in semi-shadow. The man's eyes were on him, watching him carefully as Jonathan circled the table, hunter's cue stick in hand. This was the man Jonathan would close in on.

Between shots, Jonathan stood with his stick up, rubbing it against his crotch, standing closer with each turn to the man in the shadows. Finally, the man said, "You're winning a lot, tonight."

Jonathan smiled his yellow smile and blew smoke into the air.

"Yeah. The players suck here." After that, he offered nothing, knowing how to let silence flesh out a response.

"Want a beer?"

Jonathan looked over the man, a small appraising smile broadening under his amber moustache. "Sure." He went over to the table for his next series of shots, winning easily, shaking the hand first of the losing opponent and then, briefly, the next player before returning to the corner and his waiting beer. They stood in silence, surrounded in expectation, while Jonathan played out the game. As he sunk the eight ball and returned to the corner, the man said, "What are you up to tonight?"

"What do you think? I'm not going to make a life out of this, if that's what you mean."

"Let's go back to my place, then."

"Sure."

Jonathan showed the space between his teeth with his easy grin, his eyes vacant and alluring.

Those are almost the last words they spoke that night. They walked six blocks back to the man's place, Jonathan trailing slightly behind, walking the interminable distance to a walkup just below the Lincoln Tunnel entrance in a section known for auto repair garages. Another apartment, sparsely furnished, provided the sense of Manhattan's underbelly that Jonathan knew and had come to expect from its residents. A magazine on a table was addressed to James Garnway.

The man who was apparently James said, "I've got some acid. Want to share a tab?"

"Why not?"

The man, James, dissolved a tab of windowpane in a small glass of ginger ale, offering Jonathan half of the potion along with a glass of pure ginger ale if he wanted it. Jonathan didn't want it. He preferred to wait for the acid to hit. They lay together listening to Donovan sing *Sunshine Superman* as the colors began to dance in the shadows and the melody became warmer and more intense. Slowly, they began to feel around, exploring, snaking their bodies together and stripping away the clothing as each piece found itself in their way. In time, the acid began to surge through Jonathan's veins, the feeling of his erection reminding him of a volcano, although, illogically, the man's pubic hair was becoming a garden with little flowers in it and trees with swings attached to the branches. He mused momentarily, peering down at the swings to see if any children were playing there before the magma of his volcano surged forward again, calling his attention back to the ineluctable demands of desire. He started fucking the man whose magazines were addressed to James Garnway. Fucking him slowly, methodically, the mind racing, collapsing, shadows dancing, little people in the shadows, little people in shadows that drifted away into other worlds where they seemed to huddle in groups, like priests in the vestibule of a great chamber. Still he fucked away, but the idea of priests grouped in a cathedral would not leave his mind. The idea of priests gripped him and toyed with his thoughts.

Time passed. Who knows how much time? The shadows began to glow a reddish brown and the little people wore red. Then the moon rose above the building tops, changing the light and throwing a moving, unsettling kaleidoscope of shapes and colors. As he fucked, the little priests became devilish in the moonlight; their little shadow-caps pointed upwards, their little smiles sharp-toothed. Away in the corners, in the lights and darkness that changed with the clouds over the moonlit sky, the red of passing ambulances and the passing of the night, he was amazed that he could spy into their little world tucked away in the recesses of James' magic apartment. Still he fucked, his eyes vacant, his mind running, his erection volcanic just under the surface, providing the energy that ran the show.

Inside him, the acid mounted in intensity. As he fucked, he looked down at the man with the salt-and-pepper hair. Slowly, at first just the slightest elongation of the man's face was apparent and then after a time, it could have been a year or a second, the man's cheeks flushed red, reminding Jonathan of the red caps and the devilish little priests, linking James with the spirits that inhabited his supernatural realm.

After that, the man under him with his eyes shut became redder and redder still, his face contorting and now his ears elongating until Jonathan was fucking one of the teeming army of Beelzebub. It was all there in this façade of a dark spirit posing as a man, the salt-and-pepper hair turned orange in the light and peeked at the top. The ears pointed outward, the teeth small, knife-like and sharp for attack. Jonathan was not surprised. The kingdom of Satan had pursued him for a long time, until he was weary of it. He could not run; he was a warrior for the Kingdom of God, he knew that. Why he was driven this way, by his volcanic erections and his willingness to degrade and wallow? Why he pursued this odd life he could only guess at this point. But he was sure he was part of God's plan. This was how he did battle, somehow, against the denizens of hell. By going out among them. By playing at their game. God himself had told him so.

Still again, since he was such a warrior, such a great general in the hard conquest over Satan's forces for control of the world, would not Satan himself come someday to make him an offer? One day, he would make an offer to the poor boy of a single mother from the poorest section of Massachusetts, a state everyone thought was rich, except that in his part of it men sat without work for years, remembering their factories and the fishing trade like distant thoughts of childhood. There, the men lurked in poverty, drinking and beating their wives and children. His was the part of Massachusetts where the streets were dead ends and a boy could hear the sound of his mother getting fucked by her boyfriends, not letting them stop when they ran out of steam, demanding in a voice that carried into the small boy's bedroom and out into the street, "Fuck me again, goddamn it. Fuck me again." His mother who littered the house with statues of the Virgin, the cocktail waitress who put body and soul on the table and kept them both alive. His mother who prayed to Jesus in the morning to save their souls and keep food on the table and cried out to Jesus at night so that the men would fuck her again. The woman who taught him everything he knew: that he was the special one and that God would come for him in time. Only later had he thought that it might be Satan who would offer him the world one day and that he must be careful.

There was nothing in Jonathan's world now except for the man called James who slid over the volcano waiting for magma to boil up inside his guts. It occurred to Jonathan that this was the only satisfaction that creatures of the devil could get, the only satisfaction allowed out of hell. But Jonathan's sperm was pure, the armament of his soul. Didn't Paul say, "Wherefore take unto you the whole armor of God, that ye may be able to withstand in the evil day, and having done all, to stand. Stand therefore, having your loins girt about with truth…." Isn't that what the preacher from Cavalry Tabernacle Church used to repeat over and over until Jonathan knew it by heart and knew, like he knew the powers of his own sexual persuasion, that those words were written in ancient times to prophecy his coming? Jonathan knew that his loins were girded with truth, that his semen was the emissary of truth. It was the cleansing agent bursting forth into the hot hellhole of the man he was fucking. It would save the damned.

The insides of his scrotum burst out, like a pimple popping. He thought for a moment…one, two, three, he counted the spasms. The thought of a pimple intruded on him and brought back old memories of blemishes squirting shots of brilliant white liquid. He had been so embarrassed by his bad complexion, but now he knew he attracted people sexually and the thought of it filled him with pride and the acid-induced chain of consciousness melted together white pus and pride and filling so that he knew he had filled the man named James, brought him back to God's righteousness through fucking him and filling him. He had done his battle with Satan's army; he had done it before. The man called James did not come. He groaned with pleasure, feeling the white-hot lava flow into his soul with the redeeming power of God's truth. Jonathan had done his battle and he was tired. They lay there in silence.

Then, through the shadows and in the space of the music that had fallen silent while they fucked, came the dark voice.

"I will give you the world, Jonathan," it called softly to him alone. "I will give you the Northeast. I will give you dominion over Massachusetts and New York, too. Follow me, Jonathan, follow me."

Jonathan did not stir. He had heard this seduction before. The first time was when he was sixteen, after he had fucked little Mary Elizabeth in the confessional after mass. They had smoked a little pot and snuck back into church; all this while his mother talked with the priest and then walked back home. Satan would make him offers and he could resist, but the offers were good and he thought to himself, "God, oh Lord Savior, how long can I serve you if Satan's draw is too powerful for me. Lord Savior, gird me for battle. Keep me from temptation."

And he wanted to *see* Satan. As befitted a great general of the Lord, Satan should come to him personally and make his offer directly. How could he know who whispered these thoughts? Might it be God himself to see if Jonathan were true and worthy? Surely, God might check on him to make sure that he was honorable enough to earn his high estate in heaven, where the singing of God's chosen would drown out the cries and wailing of those condemned for eternity in hell?

They lay together for a time and while the shadows continued dancing, the little men played on with their dark games. Finally, Jonathan got up and dressed without a word and took his leave while the other man slept. With the lights of the hallway glowing wrathfully down upon him, the wrath of the Great Dark Lord whose offer he refused still and whose mission for him he still did not know, Jonathan took stair after stair, turning again and again down from James' apartment towards the street. He was caught, indeed, in hell. Suddenly, his stomach turned sick as he began to understand that the stairs would never end. He would be on the stairs, turning onto another stairway and then another through eternity. He took stair after stair, floor after floor, turning again and again at each stairwell platform, repeating the same action again and again until the fear inside him began to mount. Whatever his hard work for the Lord had cost, wherever it had taken him, still God had forsaken him. Could he be mistaken about his special role?

"Dear God, Jesus, Lord why have you forsaken me? Why am I in hell?" Jonathan almost cried out aloud when he arrived at last on the first-floor landing.

He had found deliverance again, for there before him the tenement door with its glass panes opened onto the street. With relief bordering on euphoria, Jonathan made his way through it at last into the loud and raucous night.

CHAPTER VII

It was late when Veronica got home. Michael McGrady was still out at a poker game with his old buddies over in the back room of the Shamrock Inn, a bar he had once owned. Michael was retired now. He had sold out a few years back and put the money into good investments, soundly watched by a money manager. Veronica warmed some milk and poured hot water into Epsom salts in a tub to sooth her feet. She was bone-tired as she sat down in the small living room of their Long Island house to relax from her difficult day. Soon the *Tonight Show* would be on.

She was sitting in darkness on the sofa turning over the confrontation with Anne Rose again and again in her head, at turns depressed and angry, feeling abused and then resigned, when she heard the door open. Like the mantle clock, the one with the rotating pendulum under a glass dome, Michael kept the rhythm of his hours. He came into the room still in his coat and leaned over to kiss her, smelling of whiskey and cigarettes.

"How did you do?" asked Veronica as he took off his coat and put it away carefully in a small closet.

Michael McGrady chuckled slowly under his breath. It sounded like an old engine getting started.

"That Vinnie. He's a clever bastard; I can say that. I was sitting there with three sevens and he kept raising me, looking me straight in the eye and raising me. So I finally folded and he had one pair. He could stare down the devil himself that guy. And I've known him… what…forty some years? You'd think a guy would know by now."

It was obvious that Michael enjoyed the events of the night. Vinnie was the godfather of their children.

"I only lost about $30, though. Not too bad for being so lousy at poker."

He came around the sofa and sat next to Veronica, perching on the arm and placing his arm around her shoulder.

"And how did things go with Anne Rose?"

Veronica let out a long breath.

"Michael, she's getting worse. She's fatter than last time, if that's possible. The house…what can I say? It's piled high with garbage. There's spoiling food in the kitchen. But she got confrontational. She really…actually she threw me out when I think about it. But I can't stay angry with her. If I drive in there it's my own doing, but I don't think I was there fifteen minutes. And she's acting in a disturbing way. She's getting dirty, somehow…" she paused, remembering what had happened, "…not dirty physically, I mean. She's already that. I mean her thoughts are getting smutty, I suppose. Scatalogical."

"Should we look into having her institutionalized?"

Veronica let silence envelope them as she considered the option.

"No. Of course, I think about that when I'm angry at her, but it isn't right even if it were feasible, which I doubt. Helena would be mortified for one thing, not to mention guilt-stricken for leaving her. But she isn't stark raving mad, after all. She's coherent in her way. And New York is a difficult state to prove insanity. Remember the lawyer telling us about that guy who thought he was the King of France, but his will was probated anyway? And she doesn't deserve to be put away. She does keep her home, after a fashion."

She nestled herself into Michael's arm, pressing her head against his neck.

"But she sure isn't going to see Randall Emerson, you can bet Vinnie on that and make money."

Michael was thoughtful for a while. Then he said, "You're an angel, honey. I always said so. I told my family all the way back: that one's an angel and I'm keeping her. We've made a good life, haven't we, honey?"

There wasn't much to be said to that. They had made a good life together. Raised the children, one a graphic artist in advertising the other one studying law. They kept separate activities, but never took a vacation apart. He bowled twice a week and on Sundays he played poker with the old friends of a lifetime. Regular, like the ticking of that clock in the silence of this house sitting in the woods way out on Long Island. Far out in the yard she could barely hear the crickets calling out to one another.

He hugged her closely, the cigarettes and booze reminding her of a log fire built for an evening in a cabin by the lake. He clutched onto her and then suddenly switched her around, pulling her leg out of the

Epsom salt broth, leaning back so her foot was resting on his lap. He began to massage it and his mind wandered away for a long second.

"I'm not sure I ever told you a story," he began. Then he started again. "Not a made up story, a story about me just after I'd bought my first bar. It was just that corner bar in Elmhurst called the Moose Grill. It was before we were married. You know about this part. People told me that I was going to have to pay out sooner or later and I figured they were right. Vinnie and I knew each other pretty well by that time. Some guys came in and, without coming right out and saying so they laid it all out…you know, what they wanted from me…and I talked it over with Vinnie. I think I knew pretty well that Vinnie knew the right guys. After that, that's when I suggested that Vinnie and I become partners. Anyway, you knew that Vinnie and I became partners about that time, but I don't think I ever told you why."

"I always thought you had to have some sort of deal with the mob. Why didn't you ever discuss it with me?"

"Plausible deniability, I guess," Michael joked. "No, I guess guys didn't discuss business with their wives in those days, especially the tough guys," he said with a teasing wink. "Then it all became the way we did business, 'cause after that Vinnie and I were partners, you know, and the bar business was working okay. And after everything was going alright and I hadn't heard about anymore payoffs, I sort of put the whole thing out of mind. Anyway, after I discussed these guys with Vinnie, he called me up a few days later and said he had a meeting with one of his guys over at the Italian American Club over near Sixth Avenue. Those guys were always experts at saying something but not saying anything, but I could read between the lines. You knew for sure what they were getting at. I took Vinnie on as a partner that day and I never heard another word. And I never had cause to regret it. Vinnie paid his share…God knows where the money came from over the years, but he paid his share and we bought more bars and everything ran smoothly. I never wanted stolen booze, or anything, though. We always did everything over the table and no one ever bothered us."

He paused, pleased with himself, kneading Veronica's foot like Christ before his disciple, squeezing her big toe affectionately. "And then, since we were never bothered again, you know, I just never had a reason to mention it. It's not like I was in business with the mob. It was just Vinnie, and Vinnie, after all, is family now."

Veronica let the story unfold. He was right. This deal was made a long time ago, before they were married. Vinnie was part of the family now, the godfather of her children.

"Then we moved close to each other, the two families. Vinnie and Marie were here all the time or we were there. We joined the same parish, sat at mass together with the boys and John and Emily, all of us together you know, and I never questioned what Vinnie did to keep us out of trouble. You know…what his other connections were. You know a man for forty years. You go to church with him and he's the godfather of your children. He does well by you. He pays his bills. As far as you know, he's an honorable man. You hear him at mass like he means it. And at the same time, you know there's a part of him you don't know about. Like what? Maybe little things, like jewelry in the trunk of a car. But you know he knows about things. Dope. Prostitution. You hear about murders and you think, somewhere there are guys I know who know about this. But these are your guys, you play poker with them for thirty years and you know them the way you know them. If there's another side, somehow it's the part of them that you don't know. And if you did know them that way, I guess they wouldn't be the same people to you."

Michael pondered for a moment and then added, "But he can still make you fold a hand in a pinch."

Veronica laid back, softly stroking his knee and letting him relax her toes.

"Can I get you a drink?" he asked. "You stay right there, I'll be back." He got up to walk into the bar.

"No. I've got my old lady milk."

Coming back and getting resettled, he nestled her foot once again into his masculine hands. Bending, warming, soothing.

"I doubt Marie knows any more about Vinnie's secret life than you do," she said. "But they've been good friends. That's all I know. And good to the children, too. That's another reason why we can't cart off Anne Rose, you know. I've seen the neighbors there. For heaven's sake, she's lived there all her life and she's known some of those people as long as anyone she's known. They keep a watch out for one another. I see people wave at her and they come up and ask about her and she introduces me. Mr. Whitaker I've met and we even had coffee in Anne's apartment when it was clean enough. Oh, that was a few years ago, but we actually visited and I thought 'what nice friends to have.' Yes, I think they watch out for one another in that neighborhood."

"I hope you're right. Things are changing, but I hope you're right."

The clock struck eleven. That clock had sat on the mantle since their twentieth anniversary, a gift from Vinnie and Marie. It had never run down. Not even once. They turned on the *Tonight Show* and watched Johnny Carson's monologue, leaving the crickets outside to their ancient, quiet, calling ritual.

CHAPTER VIII

Dear Journal,

So, it's beginning to come back to me, how I lived and thought those long decades ago, in the years just after I first came to New York. On one hand, I think of myself as defiant in those days, but then another memory creeps in and it seems that the past is up to its old tricks. I was defiant, and yet somehow I wasn't strong. Had I been strong, I might have made my own way instead of drifting about as I did. That's the truth of it, hard a truth as it may be.

Living on the Upper East Side and driving the gull wing Mercedes lasted about two years. That period provided me with the beginnings of a certain kind of education, but I was not a hustler at heart and that was sort of the position I was in. Life with an older society doctor was not for me. I hated sneaking into the theater separately and — what an accident! — being seated right next to my old friend, the aging doctor. "Why Patrick, how nice to see you!" And how did we know each other? Well, we were companions. I showed his dogs. I was this guy who hung around.

Not that I didn't meet great people. And some people knew the scoop. If I had had the heart of a courtesan, I could have been a Madame de Pompadour or something. But then, again, maybe not. I wasn't to the manor born. Those people are trained from birth in a whole series of mannerisms and secret codes. Andy Warhol was starting up the Factory about that time, which makes you think about how a middle-class kid could create a whole artistic persona, but I wasn't prepared to do that. Down at the bottom of my soul I had certain middle-class values and I expected to be treated like some kind of spouse so I seethed and drank too much and started going out on the good uptown society doctor. I could have questioned those values, defiantly turned my back on the middle class. Many people did, but I didn't.

However, to be honest I wasn't going to settle down either. I suppose I wanted to be treated like a spouse, not to act like one. The fact is I wasn't ready for a commitment to anyone. I don't think I would have settled down even if someone had paid me off with great landed estates and herds of prized Holstein cattle. Some people plan out what they want from life, just settle down and get to it, but not me. I was just kind of peddling along, taking things in and learning my stuff.

Anyway, being a kept boy wasn't in the cards so I tried to get a job and found out in short order that I was pretty near unemployable. Not that I couldn't read and write. I just didn't interview well and maybe it showed that I wanted to run the company with little or no experience. Finally, an improbable little family firm that imported hand-made flowers from Asia and South America and sold them wholesale hired me under really horrible working conditions. At first, the offices had no air conditioning and the wife had a bad temper.

She was demanding and arbitrary, but in time she learned to trust me. I think I was a son she'd never had and, without really knowing it, I fell into that role. I've been there for over two decades and I've ended up running the place. In some ways, that job made my fortune, really, but in those days, who knew? Shuffling along turned, in time, to a substitute for a plan.

At any rate I had a little money coming in. Not much, but enough to pay the rent somewhere and buy me enough drinks to get started each evening when I went out. One night I got pretty drunk at a bar in the East Fifties and started drinking everything in sight without thinking that all the glasses on the bar might not be mine. Finally, a man turned to me and asked, "Are you enjoying my drink?"

"Oh yes," I said. "Can I have another one?"

He bought me another one and then a few more after that and we had an affair out of his apartment on Central Park South. Life was easy for me that way. Like I said, I was smart and pretty cute. I forgot to add that I'd sleep with just about anyone.

And then the doctor threw me out, which in retrospect was no great surprise, but at the time seemed like a great injustice. However, I bore my cross with great stoicism and found a little one-bedroom walk-up downtown on MacDougal Street. I've lived there coming on twenty years and I've seen a lot, that's for sure.

Although I can picture the reddish brown of the number five million plus six and can fly over remembrances of things past, I don't remember what year events in my life occurred. There are people who say, "That happened in 1973" or "We went to Cannes the summer of 1985." Not me. I don't even know the year my parents died, but *certain memories are sparkling alive in the mind and ageless. The very crispness of a memory like that is eerie, because anything recalled from the past is a fiction held together by molecules in the brain; the very act of recollection takes place in the present moment and only memory itself suffuses it with brilliance and immediacy. But indeed, sparklingly alive is how I remember the day that I moved into my apartment. It was late summer and hot, hot, hot, like New York in August can be some years. It was one of those days when the children are playing in water spraying out of fire hydrants and the fire department is telling people that if they keep doing that, there's not going to be enough pressure to fight a fire. It was one of those days when the old Italian ladies sat under trees over at Father Demo Square. The men sat outside playing checkers. Lots of people lived without air conditioning back then, but the fans sat in open windows whirling away silently like whirligigs in the hanging gardens of Babylon. I can feel the breeze of those fans against my face, even now, and the tingle of sweat dripping off my eyelids.*

On that day, Lace Whitaker was screaming at the top of his lungs at Anne Rose Morelli. Later, I found out that he was the self-appointed keeper upper of the run-down building I was moving into. He had just gotten back from the South of Spain, which I thought was incredibly chic. He had rented an apartment and stayed there two months, off-season, but for two months nonetheless. He came from an old, Episcopalian New England family that had clearly run out of money and maybe out of time. He was single then. When he took me under his wing, I thought he was gay, but that turned out not to be true. Asexual maybe, but homosexual, no.

Lace made sure the building was kept up. He called the owners when the super didn't sweep and kept at the neighbors who were a noisy, messy lot. None of us exactly had room to spare and it was the custom in these tiny places to let one's belongings flow out of the apartments into the hallways. In Anne Rose's case, her belongings, which were many, I can tell you, flowed out of her apartment's back door into the central court yard where people threw away their trash. Not that much of anyone's trash made it to the city dump. Most of it ended up in Anne Rose's apartment, on a windowsill or on a table or tucked away into a corner.

One of my first boyfriends always said his mother told him, "When you see trash on the street, pick it up." That's always been the motto of my life and it sure was Anne Rose's motto, too. That woman assuredly had an eye for trash.

As I was moving in, these two were having words, which meant that they were screaming at the top of their lungs and using words that people really shouldn't use in public. He called her a filthy old cunt and told her to keep her papers inside where they belonged. He had only been gone two months and the place had gone all to hell. Where did she think she lived, anyway, old fat whore that she was. Her people, he knew her people, were better than that. She dishonored them, him, the neighborhood, the city, the country and the heavenly hosts who were caused mortal pain by her awful behavior, thorn that it was that pricked the lord's forehead ever deeper, the natural effect on cosmic harmony of her thoughtless, even sinful, deeds. He was missing a tooth in front and so these words sort of sputtered out like Daffy Duck mimicking water hitting a hot frying pan.

She told him that he was an old fart of a fruit and that he was tight-assed in the bargain and that he could fuck himself since no one would do it for him. She was wrong on all counts, but that hardly matters when one is loading the ammunition and firing without looking. A person might be surprised to learn that they really cared about each other, as I learned later on. They'd known each other for sixteen years. He knew her when she was a teenager, slim and pretty, so he told me once. And these verbal Armageddons had the regularity of an army drill, or maybe the dependability of tides makes a better metaphor. Anne Rose's stuff would rise out of her apartment like the tides and Lace would rush in to push the tsunami of papers and boxes back into the ocean from which they all came.

Of course, he also got into screaming matches with the super, who was after all pretty worthless, and with the owner and any other tenant who tried to keep a vacuum cleaner or a wardrobe box out on the stairwell. He even called the fire department in once to give everyone a summons. Lace kept us all in shape, I guess.

In time, Lace took me under his wing. Of course, at first I thought he was an older homosexual and I was suspicious of his intentions. Soon enough, though, I saw that that wasn't true. He wasn't at all that way: gay, I mean. He liked having a younger friend, I suppose, and he needed someone to have lunch with, which was his major daily activity—that and reading. Lace had traveled a lot and was raised around some old money that had dried up. He took some more of the sharp corners off my upbringing; rounded off my education and taught me manners and mannerisms that the newly arrived socialite doctor never could have. And unlike the doctor, who had learned everything he wanted to learn from Yale Medical School, Lace read everything he could get his hands on from the classics to science, and his conversation was always infused with an idea or a theory of something or a way of looking at things that I'd never encountered. Even if Lace's always changing and forming thoughts were not always worked out completely in his own mind—were somewhat idiosyncratic to say the least—they were his own creations. And now that I am looking back on it, perhaps they have had a hand in creating me.

I could make it away from the Twenty-Eighth Street Flower Emporium sometimes and we always had lunch on Saturday at Café Dadilo before it closed and after that in a succession of other places. There were very few people he could lecture to. I was young. I listened out of respect if not always out of interest. That didn't matter. The main requirement was that everyone knew Lace by name and made a big fuss when he came in. When that happened, I'd feel like a real swell.

But then, as a friend of mine said, "The best restaurant in town is the one where they know you by name."

CHAPTER IX

"I'm glad you're back, but next time come back with all your body parts. Did the Spanish insist that you leave a tooth behind as a relic? You know how they are with pieces of old saints. Did they want some of your jewelry, too, to make up the reliquary?"

Agnes and Lace were back at Café Dadilo for another late lunch. She was eating prawns again. They were her favorite menu item, served on spinach, but this time she was shaving slices off and pretending they were white truffles. Only last week, some expensive, pungent white truffles had been flown into a four-star restaurant uptown where she had eaten several thin slices on crabmeat. Someone else was picking up the check. She was still savoring the memory, turning the pretend truffle prawn slice over on her tongue and finding it decidedly deficient in texture and taste.

Lace began to sputter through his missing tooth, a piece of lettuce flying across the table at Agnes.

"It was an abscess. Not likely I'd let the dentists there get a hold of me, so I just had it pulled. Wouldn't have the bridgework done there, and there wasn't time of course. But I've been thinking, too. You know what you said last time I saw you about being too old to do this poetry stuff and waste my time all night…you know, what you said about writing and getting on with something worthwhile?"

Agnes was a little embarrassed. "Now Lace, I'm sorry if that was patronizing. You write wonderful things."

"I'm not so sure about that." Lace was serious. "Anyway, you didn't quite put it that baldly, but you got me thinking. I never wanted to become obsolete. Who thinks they're going to be old hat, my dear. Over the hill. Times change, of course, but I always thought I'd stay relevant somehow…stay on top of things as they changed." Another piece of lettuce somersaulted across the space between them and Agnes quietly slipped a protective hand over the top of her wine glass. Lace noticed, from corner of his eye, a new sapphire ring on her finger, but he continued on without remarking on it. "Well, the reason I could get away with writing that poetry is because people were so upset by it. Just the mention of anything sexual, overtly sexual, was enough to get people's attention. I've never been a major Beat poet, God knows, but I could read around town in coffee houses and get a hearing. And I could have a certain notoriety here because America got so stuffy out there…way out there in the great American heartland where everyone wears suits and ties and hats and everyone works nine to five or whatever hours they work. My God, anything out of the ordinary got a hearing. But Allen Ginsburg I'm not. And times are a changing. These days, people are nearly screwing on the streets and my stuff is well, sort of stuffy. Never thought it could be, but there you have it. That's what it is. Stuffy. Silly almost."

Agnes watched him from across the table.

"What about something in prose? Journalism. Porn, for Christ's sake…don't look at me that way. I'm serious. And it will sell. There's a whole line of books about Biker Men or you could just do romances for the lonely…"

"No," he interrupted her. "The thing that got me thinking… no, it was two things, actually. First, I had this silly affair while I was in Malaga. I thought my Willy was wanked out. I thought little Willy was buried and gone in some furrow at the bottom of my belly. But I met this widow; she was traveling through. Had a little money and was enjoying herself and she sort of lead me on and Willy sort of popped up…unexpectedly, actually. Hadn't seen him, really, in years. She moved on but it left me unsettled, somehow, and then the abscess. The thing is that I can't afford to have the work done. It's awful to admit, but I just can't afford it and here I am middle-aged with a hole in my mouth and no way to get it fixed."

He thought a moment and then added, "That was the second thing. The abscess and having no money."

"So, what about writing?"

"Agnes, I'm no writer really. You get to know yourself in four decades—four and then a few years. You ought to get to know yourself. I might be able to write, but I don't have the attention span. I'm a lazy slob. I know that. And I need to start making some money right now. It doesn't have to be a lot, but I need a bit more than what comes in from the little bit mother left me. There's a man in the neighborhood, old Mr. Myers. He's bought up some buildings. Ran an antique shop here for years and took the money and bought some apartment buildings and now he's getting old and he doesn't want to sit at the antique shop all day. He's hiring me to sit there and run it. I do know furniture. I'm going to be an old fart sitting in a dusty shop like something out of Dickens. And I'll get started on the bridgework.

And then, who knows, maybe I'll start writing again while I wait for customers to come in."

At this last suggestion, Lace strengthened a little; he had heartened his own spirits.

Agnes smiled at him. She had been listening closely, like old friends do when one unburdens oneself. She hadn't eaten even one prawn while he talked.

"Lace, I like the plan. I think you'll write again, but that's none of my business, really. If you do, I'll help. If you don't, we'll have lunch. What can I say?"

"Well, I've been running on about my Willy, willy nilly." He enjoyed the joke and then rushed on, "How about your affair? That Sunday affair with Mr. Mysterioso?" He stressed Mysterioso to stress the secret hidden between them, as if they were children trading stories with imaginary friends.

Agnes paused. This was a serious day for both of them.

"Lace, he stood me up. One Sunday he just didn't show up. I waited twenty minutes and went on. I might have been angry, but I'm glad, really…"

A strange look of pain came over her face, a small grimace as if her stomach had just turned and she was trying to hide it. Still, a shadow crept across Agnes's white face nonetheless, red lips curled across her upper lip, tracking a hidden thought that washed through her eyes and then was gone. But Lace saw it. No Athena the warrior goddess, now, her eyes were soft and inward.

"Lace, some time I'll tell you more. The things we did…I just don't know. I didn't know I could. I was so free with him. Because we were strangers, I think. But I don't know where we could have gone with it all. It frightens me now when I think about it. It frightens me because I never even knew his last name. I put myself completely at the disposal of a stranger…put myself totally in his hands in ways I really can't go into. I got driven, sort of. You shouldn't put that kind of trust in people until you know them."

"He didn't hurt you, did he?"

"No. Always honorable after a fashion, actually. I won't explain it all to you just now. And it wouldn't have worked if I had known him, either, so none of this really makes sense."

"Maybe I should keep writing my poetry. Sounds like a theme."

"No…not 'no' to your poetry, of course, but no it didn't make sense. I loved the time doing it with him. It brought out a side of me…" She thought better of proceeding. "I'm glad I went through that, but I guess it's like you. I've reassessed some things. I'm going to work harder at my career. I could go further with the company. Or I could go out on my own and start my own agency. I'm like you, Lace. I'm in my mid-thirties and screwing around, and I guess I just started to wonder what it was about another piece of skin that was so alluring? I'm getting a cat, waiting for a boyfriend. Who knows? But momma's lying low for a while."

"Whatever went on between those two," Lace thought, "it knocked her sideways. Poor thing."

Then he said out loud, "I think one has to know what to nourish in life and what to let die off…or cut out entirely, for that matter."

They sat in silence for a long while. Agnes finished her prawns. Lace ordered a brandy. It was a little early in the day, but what the hell. You didn't talk like this with someone, not even an old friend, all the time. Your insides didn't go on show very often. It wasn't time to call it an afternoon yet.

"How did you find things on your return?"

"I felt like Odysseus home from the wars and, what was *that*, ten years of wandering? The building was in an uproar, of course. Had to light into that Anne Rose…you know, the mad maid on the first floor. Penelope and her tons of knitting flowing out into the courtyard and up into the hallways if I'd let her. It makes me furious. And it was on that awful, broiling day so my temper was none too good, I can tell you! She's got things piled to her roof in that place like the Collyer Brothers, which is unsafe for all of us. Think of the fire hazard. And then she starts putting things out in the courtyard. What a fight. I think we had neighbors looking out of windows a block away to see what we alley cats were doing to each other. And then there's a new kid by the name of Patrick just moving in and he stops and watches the two of us like we're two loonies. And speaking of loonies, he's a little far gone himself. A flake actually and a bit on the other side, swinging a little loose at the hips, if you know what I mean."

"My dear." Agnes was happy the conversation was getting cute again. "Do I ever know what you mean! I've got eyes in my head and you're talking about things changing on us… Well, Queer is the next big wave. It's going to be bigger than hula-hoops, mark my word. Maybe it's the love that dare not speak its name, but it is the coming thing, I can tell you. I can spot a fad and this one's a comin' fast. Momma says, 'Get ready, cause the queer folk are gathering out there somewhere over the horizon and they're takin' over.'" She spoke in her best Harlem accent. "I don't know whether to circle the wagons or bake a cake…and decorate it."

"Perhaps. Maybe he's one of the advance guard, sent to check us all out and report back. Anyway, he's moved in and he's a lost soul, poor thing. He's got a white boy afro, skin-tight bell bottoms and a peculiar turquoise belt buckle with love beads around his neck. Dressed all the rage, I suppose, but no class and no direction. He's going to end up in no good if he's not careful. I think I'll sort of adopt him. Not that I'm one of the great immortal wise men, by any means, but old Lace might steer him out of trouble if he'll let me." After a quizzical glance upwards, he added, "Maybe I'll start him on Montaigne. I always think a young man should read Montaigne's *Essays*. Teaches a person how to think. Sixteenth-century, but a modern mind and thinking for yourself in the sixteenth century was a triumph."

Agnes thought to herself for a moment and almost whispered "Montaigne" to herself with a sense of amusement as if remembering a fine old lover and good times next to a fireplace. Then she snapped back to attention.

"That sounds good, too, honey." Agnes looked at her watch. "Let's get the check. It's on me."

CHAPTER X

Rennie Rodriguez was pastor of the God's Covenant in Righteousness Church, which operated out of a storefront on East Houston Street. His was an uncertain flock. Drunks from the Bowery came here, sometimes for coffee or to get out of the bitter winter cold and sometimes for spiritual sustenance. Pastor Rodriguez was in the business of saving souls, a hell and fire-breathing dragon who preached like a southern preacher from the Kentucky hills. God's Covenant in Righteousness Church was not too far from Elizabeth Street. Jonathan Perry had begun to stop in there.

Lately, things had been getting out of hand. He'd been picking up tricks on 42nd Street and along the Westside Highway. His prices had been going up; he'd gotten some telephone numbers that turned into regular tricks. He'd been picking up women, too, and his number had gotten around with them, so men and women were calling him at home and little by little he'd gotten into a business at it. He had even made it out to the Hamptons once with a guy who had given his number to some friends and gotten him into some S&M stuff. Then a couple of months later he went out to the Hamptons again and ended up staying for two weeks. Never got back to that woman he was screwing on Sundays. They were getting ripe with each other, but it was no loss. He moved on without regret and Jonathan didn't linger over regrets anyway.

Then the guy from the Hamptons gave out his number and one thing led to another, the recommendations got to a dominatrix on the Upper East Side and she brought him into her business to do a few gigs. They whipped one guy bloody, then got together with a guy and his wife and things got pretty rough. The couple liked it, but boy, things got awfully rough.

The dominatrix introduced him to some fetish clubs. The people were into cutting, role-playing like mamma and baby, some man dressed in diapers and playing baby coming on mother's breasts. Sometimes, the guys shit in the diapers and then they came on mamma's breasts and that's when things really began to get out of hand for Jonathan. Some of the scenes were a little too foul. As things were getting intense, Jonathan sought refuge in Rennie Rodriguez's Church of the God's Covenant in Righteousness. It was easy walking distance from Elizabeth Street.

There were a few ladies from the neighborhood in Rennie's church and they kept it running for him. They gathered around, these women left over from the sweeping migrations of previous generations, a flock of adoring, exotic and elderly birds hovering around the great man who wore sharp suits and sported a bristle of brindled gray/black hair. These were ladies from the tenements who had not moved on out to the suburbs, or they were Puerto Rican woman from the projects. They were Catholic Ladies, for the most part, who had converted to Charismatic Christianity. Maybe it was the mystic qualities of old-time religion, but then it hadn't been a big switch for them because sometimes they were already not too far from Santoria or Voodoo. They went into trance states and talked in tongues anyway. If it was the saint spirit that possessed them or the ancient African saint-goddess or the Holy Spirit, it was all the same to them and pretty much all the same to Rennie Rodriguez. At home, they turned the saints to the wall to punish them when things got rough or they kept photographs of their enemies in the freezer, knowing that to do so kept people from doing them harm, just as scissors hanging over the doorway to their apartments cut apart evil as it attempted to enter. They all knew judgment day was coming and coming soon. They were ready and the old men with their pints of whiskey knew judgment day was coming, too. Only they weren't ready. Those men were scared. Scared to the tips of their boots, if they owned any when they came in.

And then one day in came this young guy, fresh as a day in spring. A little pasty and teeth scarred yellow from smoke, but he spoke the Jesus charismatic lingo and he knew his Bible verses and he began to help out. First he helped set up and take down the chairs. Then he helped make coffee. He did that for a few months and became a fixture, very quietly and helpfully, always polite. He gave a testimony one Sunday night at prayer meeting. He talked slowly and quietly in a way that riveted them all, bolted them right down to the very seats in which they sat:

"My name is Jonathan Perry and I came here from Massachusetts. I hope God loves me because my sins are going to catch up with me one day. I don't know why I do what I do. I came from a poor family in Massachusetts. I don't remember my father. He died when I was young and my mother raised me. She was—is—a whore. She brought her boyfriends into our house and screwed them in front of me when I was a little boy."

This was not entirely true. She had never had sex in front of the boy. But he could hear them late into the night. That part was true enough.

"I guess that I tried to run away from all that when I was still real little. I played outside in the yard alone. She wouldn't let me play with the other kids, so I played alone outside and downstairs in the basement. Always alone. So I started with a lot of bad habits. I started...I started...playing with myself, you know, a lot. Then in high school I had sex with some of the women and got them into trouble and ran away. I smoked a lot of dope then too and...and..." He waited a moment for effect. "And I sold myself to some older men to get to New York and get away from all that. But before I left, I knew something was wrong. I knew it in my soul, because the Lord Jesus was speaking to my heart."

Yes, Jonathan knew the lingo, for sure. "Jesus was speaking to my heart and so I went to a little church there...up there in Massachusetts, I mean...and I spoke to Pastor Jimmy and we decided to call upon the Lord to cast out the devils that were in me. I know the Bible says that every devil creates seven other devils. We called upon Jesus to rid me of my devils and I gave my life to Jesus right then and there. Then, when I was saved and all and ever after that, I've been doing God's work in the world. After I was washed in the blood of Jesus, I have been carrying a sword for God. And I want to help Pastor Rennie with his work for God."

Jonathan got the effect he wanted. Heaven rejoices in each sinner saved. The old ladies in the church opened their arms and bosoms wide to receive him and hold him close in the Savior's redeeming love. And maybe, too, their sons had not always turned out the way they had dreamed. Maybe Jamie had crude tattoos and left Rikers jail only to return again and again, or maybe Angel wore dresses and came home late, or Victor didn't spend much time at home anymore since leaving New York University grad school, but this new kid promised the resurrection of those old motherly fantasies and it seemed to them that their lives had become fresh again, redeemed and filled with promises that might even be kept this time around. Pastor Rodriguez gave him more responsibility. Jonathan had the family he was looking for.

His testimony was not quite true. Did he know that? He hadn't sold himself to men in Massachusetts. He did that after he got to New York. None of the girls in Massachusetts bore any of his children. He hadn't had that much sex in Massachusetts. He was too much a loner for that. He hadn't been accepted in high school. It would have been a bitter pill to remember that their favors went to the popular boys, the basketball stars and the quarterbacks. They avoided the pimply kid who hung back in the shadows, getting poor grades, destined to move on one day, always keeping one step ahead of the hurt that long ago wore a hold in the pit of his belly. Perhaps he put these memories out of mind because they were painful. Perhaps they brought him back to the holes inside him that gave the devils their hiding places; the holes they used to creep into his soul to begin with. The demons crawled into those holes and waited for a chance and perhaps they held onto the hope that Jonathan's mother had instilled into him that he was a special one, a lone special child in the wilderness waiting for his special moment.

But Pastor Jimmy of Cavalry Tabernacle Church had prayed with him for God to remove his devils. And Pastor Jimmy had given him bus fare. Not for New York, of course, that evil witchery of a town, but for Boston where Jonathan might find work. But Jonathan had come to New York instead to give his testimony one Sunday night and to find himself embraced by the improbable ministry of Pastor Rennie Rodriguez, his elderly church ladies, and the whiskey-smelling, wheezy old men who crawled in on their bellies to receive coffee and forgiveness.

And things went okay for a while. For about a year—probably even a year and a half—Rennie Rodriguez paid Jonathan a small salary and Jonathan cleaned up, made coffee, sat up chairs, bought toilet paper and typing paper when they ran out. Ran errands. Sometimes he made telephone calls and helped out in the office. But spare time runs hard on a boy. Every once in a while the dominatrix would call. The money was good and the small voice in his head wanted him to go. And he couldn't quite squeeze from his mind the nagging force of that realization that he was somehow anointed. The idea was in his mind that he was God's chosen worker as sure as if a telegram had been delivered right into his hand, the cold hard fact coming to him right after he came inside Mary Elizabeth. And the way the message came to him that night with the man and his acid tab in the walkup. God was trying to reach him to do his business, and God moved in mysterious ways.

The work with the dominatrix, the control he exerted with her over her minions, was real somehow. His allure was real enough and it was easy for him to cast his spell. It must be that it was all in God's work. And the dominatrix didn't call too often; just enough to keep in touch, set off some guilt and let Jonathan work it all out in his head late at night. He would sit up at night until all hours working it out in his head whether he was really backsliding into a life of sin or whether God really moved in his own ways to work his will in the world and was not beholden to man's morality when he chose to strike. That much was clear. God did not behave according to men's morals. Why would his messenger on earth?

What interested him, really fascinated him, was that on the outskirts of the dominatrix's practice there were these Hail Satan types. As they wallowed and cringed and begged and cried out for their just degradation, they prayed to mighty Satan. Some of them did, anyway. The Hail Satan types were a people unto themselves, involved in their own cosmology and system of logic, perhaps, but to Jonathan they were part of something sweeping. They provided evidence that his story was unfolding sensibly, inexorably. The path was opening before his very eyes. To follow this path was to follow the Lord's way into the thick of battle. This is what he realized with a childlike quality in the very, very dark hours of the late night after he returned home from his gigs. Jesus said to enter the kingdom of heaven as a little child. That meant not to question, but to have a simple faith. And as he realized this, he realized that he was being led to study the occult so that he could know his enemy. He was to fight Satan on his own turf. That is how he came to frequent a small store dealing in magic items and metaphysical books that was positioned exactly adjacent to a wholesale furniture warehouse near Sixth Avenue where MacDougal Street joins Houston Street.

CHAPTER XI

Veronica and Michael drove into New York on a Sunday afternoon about three years after Anne Rose refused to see Dr. Randall Emerson. For a while, Anne Rose had become so hostile that Veronica's visits became infrequent. Veronica had asked a woman from the neighborhood, a girlhood friend who was now with the Ladies Auxiliary Chapter of Our Lady of Pompeii on Sixth Avenue, to call on Anne Rose and ask for her help at church. Florence Finelli was her name and she had done it gladly because, as it turned out, she lived across the street and it was easy to do. And as it also turned out, Florence Finelli was concerned anyway because she watched from her window and, as she saw everything that happened on MacDougal Street, she saw Anne Rose bent over the garbage cans, elbow deep in trash, wearing her soiled and torn dresses tight against her growing body.

And the old friendship was still there, too, between the two women, the suburban career woman and the village church lady. Despite their different lives and the great difference in their educations, the childhood relationship had held fast over the years. They kept their pact a secret from Anne Rose, talking every week or so on the phone. Sometimes Florence Finelli was able to get little donations of items from Anne Rose's household warehouse towards church bazaars. Sometimes Anne Rose came to a church dinner or to Saturday bingo. Between them, they kept an eye out.

And nothing much changed. Anne Rose stayed at about 334 pounds. She kept wandering further and further away from MacDougal Street to search out her treasures. Three years ago, there was no room in her apartment for more wonders, but the Virgin must have provided. Just like fishes and loaves, the space within that apartment miraculously increased to accommodate thousands of other items.

On this Sunday afternoon, three years after Anne Rose jettisoned her aunt into the courtyard of her building, the Virgin was surrounded by a heavenly host of creatures. Her retinue still included just three snowmen, but the crèche figures had grown with the addition of porcelain camels and jade elephants, fake Han horses and little doll babies that lay in bits of shredded ornamental papers and pieces of drinking straws picked up from off the street. More rosaries, perhaps thirty of them now, were placed with beads and bits of rhinestone so that the Virgin and her court seemed to live in a sparkling palace that came alive, especially in the sunlit late afternoons of fall and winter.

Anne Rose was anxious. Time had passed and she was no longer angry. Uncle Michael was coming too. She had straightened up her home a little. There was no food lying around on the counter along the kitchen wall.

"The Holy Mother has such beautiful things around her," Veronica began as they inched into Anne Rose's apartment. "Did you find them all? You are so clever, Anne Rose. Do people really just throw these lovely, nice things out onto the street?"

She hugged her close and Michael added, "What wonderful taste in things you have. I can't believe you find all this lying around."

For Veronica and Michael, this Sunday outing was long in the planning and they had discussed carefully the attitude they would take. A month or so earlier, Veronica broached the subject one early evening as they barbecued hamburgers outside in the yard.

"Michael, we can't just leave things as they are with Anne Rose," she began. "I've been thinking about it a great deal, and matters just won't do as they are. Families need to talk and see each other. We can't have it, this cloud over Anne Rose and us."

Michael worked at kneading the hamburger patties into neat, round circles as he listened to his wife.

"God knows I wish Helena would do more and that boy of hers could do more for his sister, but I guess we have to realize that they've got their life and they're not going to change it. Janet works. They've got the kids and Helena can't or won't learn to drive. She always was the old-fashioned one. And I don't think she ever liked Anne Rose very much. It may be just as well that they're not in touch more. Anne Rose doesn't need more rejection from her family, after all."

Michael looked up from his work. Veronica was setting out the old checked tablecloth and putting ketchup and mustard, plates and flatware out for their evening meal. She had clearly been thinking about Anne Rose for a time.

She continued. "Then, I was talking last week with Flo Finelli. I don't think anyone in that neighborhood really thinks anything's wrong with Anne Rose. Sure, she's simple; we all know that. But she talks with other people. She goes to church suppers. She eats too much, but if we started jailing people for that the jails would be fuller than they are and we wouldn't have construction workers to build the prisons! So maybe she was right to be angry with us...me...I might have been patronizing to her, after all."

"Honey," Michael wanted to allay her self-recriminations. "Remember how it was, though. It looked like she was going crazy on us. She blew up all of a sudden, got way over-fat, which was a health concern at the very least. She started hoarding things. Then it seemed like for a while she got abusive. We didn't know where it was going to go."

"Yes, yes, I know." She straightened her apron abruptly and turned slightly away from Michael, waving him away. Veronica was not engaging in self-recrimination. She was in pursuit of a solution to what seemed to her to be a family problem. And she had finally hit on what that solution might be.

"Maybe it looked like she was going crazy, as you say, or maybe we just wanted her to live according to our standards. In any case, and maybe more power to her, she wouldn't stand for it. Honey...Helena and John aren't going to do it. They never have and they never will and that's that. We need to get back in there and get back into contact with Anne Rose."

They talked about it until late at night and they decided that they couldn't fake any part of it. They came to the idea that accepting Anne Rose and her eccentricities — indeed they would consider them eccentricities rather than pathologies — was the way to be genuine in their affection and true in their emotions. And it worked. Anne Rose did not hear anything uppity in their voices. On this day, they were not being patronizing.

Veronica continued her plan for a Sunday visit first by calling Anne Rose and feeling her out and keeping in touch, as always, with Florence to take the pulse of Anne Rose's mood. She found out that Anne Rose lived among her neighbors on MacDougal Street easily, one of the fixtures of the little neighborhood with her going-outs and coming-ins each day monitored like everyone else's, with the waving to and receiving from her neighbors those waves of greeting that people give to each other from across the street, from their doorways, as they pass to and fro between the errands of their everyday lives. She engaged like any normal person in passing phrases — "How Are You; I'm Fine; How are You" — that keep people connected, if only tentatively, no matter what paradise or hell or sewer they might hide behind their eyes. How crazy could she be as long as she got along with her neighbors, especially if getting along with one's neighbors was almost the definition of sanity?

It seemed to them now that Anne Rose, the dear girl, had not gone stark raving mad after all.

So today on this perfect Sunday, the couple drove into Manhattan the two-hour, long drive, taking the Southern State Parkway because of its park-like terrain. They drove along the Meadowbrook into the Grand Central through the Midtown Tunnel and down to MacDougal Street. It was as fine a drive through views as close to gardens as they were likely to get. It had been a beautiful sun-filled drive into the city.

And as they entered her apartment, Anne Rose reached over the same stack of *New York Times* that still sat near the doorway next to a milk can stuffed with broken umbrellas. The stack had grown taller, but contained only copies of the *Sunday Times*, a testament, Veronica noted with approval, of some degree of organizational attention.

Veronica thought to herself, "It is odd how stable this home is. Nothing changes here, really. Everything that was here last time is here now."

She stood at the door to let her eyes accustom themselves to the new light. "And there's order, too, to this chaos. The pile of *Sunday Times*, the broken umbrellas all together in a can, the little creatures all around the statue! Now, I see the whole picture: the Virgin, the magazines, and snowmen. It's just that there's more to it; more to see."

Anne Rose reached over the papers with her strong round arm and brought up a small doll with ratty hair and a plaid dress. One leg was bent backwards and one eye would not stay open.

"I found this yesterday. Isn't she pretty? You'd think someone would fix her and try to keep her. Wouldn't you, auntie? What do you think Uncle Mike?"

Uncle Mike allowed as how had never seen such a pretty doll. All that was needed was a little washing. That would be all that needed to be done, and it would be easy to do, and then the doll would be good as new. That plaid dress was a nice dress, too. It was funny, when you thought about it, that anyone would cast off such an adorable little figure.

And so the conversation went along because the day was pretty and none of them, not Anne Rose nor Veronica nor Michael, wanted even one thing from any of the others.

First, they washed the little doll and somehow Michael got the eye to work and together they pushed and prodded the leg back into place. Then, they went out for a walk and Veronica and Michael consented to look into trash with Anne Rose. Together they found an old side-table, which Michael carried, and a stack of books that Veronica was able to fit in the tote she carried over her shoulder. Anne Rose walked behind pushing her cart, gathering up a new batch of treasures and placing them into its well. She was sharing these glittering treasurers, perhaps for the first time, with people she loved, and she was happy.

Then they bought calzone from a corner store with a counter looking out onto the street and they bought sodas and then some ice cream while they sat in an ice cream parlor on Bleecker Street. Finally, just as they turned a corner on the final approach to MacDougal Street, Veronica saw the tip of a little statuette sitting on the cement just behind a metal trashcan. She bent down to pick it up and pulled out of the shadow an owl. About eight inches tall and made out of some metal, it was heavier than it looked and it glowed with a greenish patina. Actually, it was a good piece, nobly made and simply designed, although there was a significant dent into the base. It was true. People threw out the strangest things.

Veronica turned to Anne Rose, giving her the statue as if she were making an obviously special gift. And the younger women cradled it, placing it carefully in her carriage and carting it with the other items off on the last leg of their day's journey.

What a wonderful day it was for Anne Rose. Not since her girlhood had she lived so happily through a day. They arrived back in the late afternoon. They called Helena and John and Janet and talked maybe for half an hour. Anne Rose was on the phone for at least half that time. John promised to drive Helena in some time soon. Anne Rose got silent with that. She looked pleased and she held tightly to her dress as they sat and pulled the sides down so that the folds stayed especially neat.

Then, they placed each beautiful found object carefully together around the apartment in places that seemed to open up to absorb them, containing each and every one as if the space had been ordained for just that little creature or cloth fragment or picture or stick of furniture. That is how each item, a frog, was kissed and turned into a prince. And the owl, that happiest of creatures, found a place nearest the nurturing blue skirt of Anne Rose's holy mother, on the deco table within the bosom of the Blessed Virgin's retinue.

They had found two little stoneware dogs, sleeping and curled up, each only about an inch long. These they added to the sparkling court of the Virgin, along with the camels and the frogs, elephants, horses and angels, the saints and black-a-moors that abounded around the goddess's figurine and did unto her their silent homage. At last, once again, Veronica noticed the Virgin's smile. It was marred only slightly by a small chip on the cheek. But now it was no longer malicious. Not on this happy day, this special day, this perfect, spectacular fine Sunday that had come as a gift and seemed, like a kiss from the angels, as if it might bring unfortunate, poor Anne Rose out of her long and desperate exile.

CHAPTER XII

Dear Journal,

It was a bit hard to handle, that untamable mixture of defiance and aimlessness, so what I ended up doing was settling into MacDougal Street and keeping my little job at the Twenty-Eighth Street Flower Emporium. Now, as I write it all down, the memories still have jagged edges that don't fit. I don't remember having any sense of purpose, and yet the job at the Emporium grew into something worthwhile. I went out most nights, drinking hard and playing hard. I got to be a club kid, I suppose. Out at midnight, in at dawn, but not a complete club kid—the ones with spiked hair and black kohl-lined eyes; the ones who give their entire lives to a certain style of living. I dabbled in the club life and dragged my ass into work. I was young and I had stamina and things happened to me that made life glamorous. I met people who stayed around and became friends. I'm still in touch with people from that era, so I can say that there are strands in my life that worked out, became substantial in their way. I've watched them grow older with me. We run into each other on the street and trade stories, bring one another up to date. They fade in and out of my life, becoming closer at times, even friends for a while, and sometimes

TOM HOUSTON

they fade back out and become passers-by again, acquaintances. That's the process, I guess, as things sort themselves out day by day. Patterns emerge and collide; they are strong and then they are weak, they are mean and kind, raunchy and delicate, substantial, but they can ebb away, too.

This all come to mind because there was, at last, one particular substantial thing that broke apart, a strand that came undone, the tattered and frayed thread, a branch that broke and withered. The bright paper with nothing inside but sticks. It began when, one night at the bar of a restaurant that catered to older gay men on the Upper East Side, I met a man with the daunting name of Constantine Spirotikos.

"Call me Connie," he said as he slipped a flashy arm covered with several heavy and clanking gold chain bracelets around my waist and so I did call him that whenever we saw each other, which turned out to be nearly every Tuesday and many weekends for nearly two decades. It was a situation that was perfect for both of us.

Connie had been born in Astoria, Queens, into a raging Greek family. He had a brother who owned a machinery and die cutting company in Long Island City and lived a boozing, brawling rich suburban life with a wife, three children and a mistress. There was also a sister who was quite a beauty and had made it through Bryn Mawr to marry an industrialist. They lived in a country club community near Detroit where she sat on the board of a museum, played the role of society matron and mothered a heroin-addicted son. She had a wild kind of good looks, and was hard and intelligent. It took a lot of work to be in her company. They were quite a family and they demanded a lot out of life and people, but what Connie wanted they wanted for him and they took me in for what I was: Connie's sometime unconstant companion, but certainly not as a full and completely equal spouse.

Growing up, the pervading philosophy in my family was to get a good job and lie low so, from where I stood, Connie led a fabled life. He started out buying antiques for one of the big department stores, but he was hardly shy and before long, to hear him tell the story, he had become quite a man around town. By the end of World War II, he knew just about everybody and began to veer towards show business. He wasn't shy about telling stories and dropping names. He'd spent time in Hollywood and knew all the stars from the Forties and Fifties. I never met any of the big names through him, but other people corroborated the stories. He was a sometime songwriter and Broadway backer and did some producing off Broadway as well, and a couple of times he helped produce plays on Broadway, too. He wasn't one of the well-known public names, but people around town knew him. Growing up in New York, he'd been part of the glamorous Harlem days, frequented clubs like El Morocco and the Stork; he was bigger than life in a lot of ways, a big drinker and gambler. He wore brocade dinner jackets and more than a few rings. His favorite set of tuxedo studs and cuff links were emeralds set against white enamel. He insisted on having all his formal wear made at Brioni decades before Brioni was available in the United States. He became used to buying his clothing in Italy during the Fifties and never got over that habit, even after it was no longer necessary to visit Europe in order to get good things, and no longer even particularly glamorous.

Then he was also twenty-five years older than me, graying and balding and paunchy. I'm nearly as old as he was when I met him, so I understand that he was beginning to live in a world he didn't quite understand. In general, people were becoming less formal; the Age of Aquarius had dawned and the allure of drawing room society was fading away and being replaced by the New Wave artists and Andy Warhol's factory. When he'd describe an outing in New York society, the description reminded me of an old black and white movie with fake English accents, but it was exactly the aggressively chic clothing and the jewelry and his airs that made him eccentric and gave him a sort of power over me. Power over me was the magic, the success and the curse of those years with Connie. Oddly, I have never been attracted to older men. Connie was a complete anomaly and in the end I have to admit that the relationship would never have worked if he hadn't sort of raped me when we had sex. Week after week, year after year, there was this almost physical struggle to get me into bed and then this rough, unrelenting screw with me pretty well held down. That's just the way we did it. He asserted his power over me. I understood perfectly when Jackie married Aristotle Onassis. There was something about Connie's large, brutal body, the snarl to his face, the hardness of his conceits that attracted and repelled me and made the sex with him hard and satisfying. They say that power is an aphrodisiac, but my experience suggests that it leaves subterranean traces of anger whenever it is exerted.

At the same time, in a peculiar way, Connie was also a dandy, showbiz all the way, and had worked years to get into that society that so interested him. He was the guy those ladies on Fifth and Park Avenues would call when they needed a man to even things out for dinner. There were some great rich women who liked to go out with him because their reputations were safe. If their husbands were out of town, going to a play and being seen at restaurants with Connie caused no suspicion. The friendships were real, no doubt about that, but I remember once he confided to me that a Palm Beach invitation hadn't come through because he wasn't, "born to those people," as he put it. I don't know if things are still that way or if they were really that way then. Maybe he just thought that was the reason, whereas in truth he was a little difficult to take, sometimes. Or maybe he wore too much jewelry for the Palm Beach crowd. Still, he considered them friends and when they snubbed him he was hurt.

The decades passed and we never did make a final commitment to one another. With only Tuesdays and some weekends spent with Connie, I had plenty of time to play the field. We weren't possessive and we didn't ask about Monday, Wednesday, Thursday, Friday or the many stray Saturdays and Sundays. For a long time, I saw every play on Broadway with him, most cabaret and any movie worth seeing. I met lesser lights from Broadway and Hollywood. And I came away from those years with nothing, absolutely nothing, to show for the contacts I might have made. I met people who made stars out of themselves later on; people with wills of iron and wits as sharp as the fangs of hungry cheetahs, but all the while I was circulating with Connie's crowd, I was merely his silent sidekick. Where another person might have made friendships that stuck, I remained his little silent adjunct, his hang-around kid, never sensing that I ever had a distinct person-ality in myself. When I was around him, I was just an appendage, I felt like a kind of possession and so I can't complain if in the end I was forgotten by the people in his circle.

Why am I writing down all of this? It seems that I begin to cap-ture some of the essence of that angst I've been searching out. That growing sense of failure that was so vague when I began my journal.

Still, I wonder sometimes how it really was; not what my memories mean in retrospect, but what the quotidian mechanics were that drove me from one moment to the next and led bit by bit to always narrowing pathways out from my past, step by step as I traversed first one branch of the tree and then leapt blindly onto another smaller branch to reach at last this twig, this cul-de-sac, this small spot. That trajectory is made up of thousands of little points, like the points of a line connecting two spots on a map, and each point is literally a point along a succession of decisions that take a person from one moment to the next. I look back to the years with Connie and in those past moments I find a stranger instead of myself. I didn't stand up to him. I couldn't stand alongside him. Why was that? What drove me to choose again and again the smaller path, the littler branch, the direction that led to the safest spot, until I have come to a point from which I can travel no further?

Ah, then. Can I see what boxes me in? A glimmer of it, I think. Ultimately and despite a certain wildness of character, it was the safe life I pursued. I do what I know to do and I do what I know how to do. I repeat the patterns that take me home, again, to the green tip of the same leaf, blowing as it does in a warm, white, comforting breeze. This kind of life would be paradise for so many—fluttering in a soft breeze sounds like an ad for a Caribbean vacation after all. But if it is the truth that sets us free, which truth is it? Is it safety or risk that I've wanted all along?

So, from Connie I might have learned to be free from past preconceptions, free to act and to develop, but instead he exerted his power over me and I remember feeling from it an awful sense of confining security. Perhaps it felt best to rest, inert in his embrace, but being in a person's power, I have learned, will bring anger at last. There is no doubt that I still am angry at Connie. There is a deep regret, too, because I might have been more assertive with him. I don't believe that he would have stopped me. Avoiding confrontation, letting him make the decisions was a pathway in itself from the main trunk to the smaller confines of one of those branches and now it seems apparent that the choices to act and the choices not to act, all of them create regret when the choice costs more than it brings back in happiness or wisdom or strength. A person tries to draw something good out of what they've done or who they've become. One tries to create an image of happiness and if that isn't possible, a person makes wisdom or strength—anything positive—out of their experiences so that the books are balanced in the end, so that you can still make something out of nothing, salvage your life when all is said and done. But the internal life remains untouched by that. At final last, I sense that I can only be satisfied or not, content or not, happy or not. No matter how many justifications or balancing acts one perpetrates on the psyche, the only way to live a larger life is to grow into it.

Regrets. One night I asked Connie what his greatest regret was. I don't know what I thought he'd say. I probably figured he'd regret not having worked harder or going through more school—he had quit before graduating high school. Whatever I thought he was going to say, his reply in retrospect was more profound than anything I antic-ipated. It was more profound because he was older, perhaps, but I think more because he lived in a larger world than I did and he saw things from a wider perspective. And it was also profound because it wasn't pop-psychological or philosophical; it had to do with the day-to-day technology of living. Still, at the time, I didn't think his answer had much to teach me, which is odd because it lies at the center of what I'm facing now.

There I was, still a hellion of a kid who had escaped from the suburbs, rebellious against little concentric circles of petty family quarrels and church feuds and small-town gossip that a child of my background might be excused from thinking made up the social world. Rebellious yes, but not against things that had any weight. Connie moved in a world of larger concerns. Raised by a fierce and raging father in the world's largest metropolis, he made his way into it at the age of sixteen by running away and living with an older man who was a mentor to him. Even when he had his first regular day job, designing windows at Lord and Taylor's, he was writing songs and making his own money and then he pushed his way forward through business acumen and a sharp insight into what made the theater work. Many of his backers were the kind of society women who had known many lovers and held salons for the greatest people of our times. Others headed corporations and held in their hands thousands of lives. They were men and women who made or influenced decisions at the top levels of government and business. His idea of work was to move within this sea of people. He frequented every party, sat through thousands of dinners and met thousands of people, keeping their names in a vast Rolodex. When someone's interest might be served, when an introduction might be made or a project could use a push or expertise or plain money, Connie would dip into his vast Rolodex and make things happen.

Looking back on it, of course, I think people often didn't like Connie very much. He worked hard at his game. He risked looking silly, pushy, glad-handed. He wore makeup and he made up more as he got older. He never accepted the baldness and paunch and his fading glamour in a gay world that was more and more youthful and bright and open, experimental and odd. But I realized, later, that he ran in a club that accepted certain oddities in its members. One night we watched a TV host interview a former British Prime Minister, who was asked what it was like to have known all the great people of his time. The Great Man reflected for a second and then replied that men and women who operate at the extreme top positions of government and literature, philosophy, art, the dance and diplomacy are all artists and accepted one another as such. Life at its fullest potential, he seemed to say, was in itself art. So in retrospect, I think people accepted Connie's brocade jackets and rings and face blush, because he, like them, was an artist at what he did.

With Connie, I suppose that I was, a child, really, at the knee learning. I asked a question about something as profound and personal as regret and I expected an answer that conformed to my small suburban expectations. I expected that he would regret a mistake, perhaps: a sin of commission, but his one regret was a sin of omission. "Follow through," he said. "The people I've met, and I didn't follow through." He sat there a moment, silent and sad in disbelief at the wasted possibilities that he had let slip through his fingers, the smaller branches taken, the cul-de-sac to which inaction leads.

Yet for the most part, I have always remembered what he said because underneath it the comment described something astonishing about the context of Connie's relationships with people. I think at the time I placed his remark in a simplistic context of social climbing and name-dropping. I don't think, though, that Connie looked at it that way at all. No, he thought of people as a vast web of interests and concerns, capable of great kindnesses and cruelties. He had said once, "You can't imagine the things people have told me," and then he shook his head from side to side in sadness and silent horror. There's no doubt in my mind that he had the inside dope on everything from mob executions and kidnappings to the peculiarities of love, the private turmoil and kindness, the petty meanness, the tyrannical madness of hundreds of people. He thought of himself as a central part of the fabric, the weave, the thread and the coloration of this great cloak of humankind.

I, on the other hand, was a suspicious lad and had a thousand considerations about people. I thought myself too good, too moral and unsullied to look at what my interests were, but actually I was too careless and too selfish to see what might interest other people. I didn't believe that friendships should serve an agenda and certainly love should be about romance. It never occurred to me that caring for people might mean actual actions taken for their benefit. I fell in love with idiots time and time again. Lace would tell me, "My boy, we all have to make our home under a tree. It might as well be a good tree as a bad one. And it might as well be a rich tree that provides good fruit as a poor one that doesn't." After all, if you do love someone, don't you want to provide the best possible? That's one regret. What kind of friend was I, after all? Was I, who claimed to be disinterested in selfish intent, capable of knowing and serving the interests, the wants, needs and desires of my fellow humans?

The project of remembering as best I can those years with Connie and searching for the truth behind what transpired has caused an image, a phantasm of the imagination, conjured out of the stuff of memories, but not a sepia landscape of awakened memory like the *backwards flight that returns me to my mother's table in that far-off kitchen. No, there are times that memories evoke primary colors that explore underlying recesses of the brain and these memories are described in symbols: dreams, spirits of the mind, evocations of lost senses. Last night I dreamed that I was swimming in cyan blue water surrounded by swirling, orange fish. They were fish, but somehow some of them morphed into people too, people from the past, so that I found myself traveling back to my life back then. I swam first in one direction and then another, but always alone. At the same time, these people I knew became schools of fish, together, bunches of fish darting together one direction and then another, but I just watched them and never engaged with, never became a part of, those gleaming schools of comrades swimming together first one way and then that way and always together.*

That was the image that stayed with me when I woke up, fixed in my mind as I stumbled out of bed to make a cup of coffee. Then I tried to get a fix on my emotions. Watching from the sidelines didn't make me feel lonely, I'm sure of that. I think I felt bewildered by those schools of fish, watching them dart hither and thither together, an ensemble, in each other's thrall.

If dreams express the subconscious, don't they still have roots in our conscious world of experiences and viewpoints? It is not lonely, necessarily, to be an outsider; to be alone is not to be lonely. There has to be a place for the fish that doesn't chose to swim in a school. But surely last night's dream unearths my feelings about that time in such vivid hues because being a spectator was not a choice. For me, it was a mystery how people always seemed to go to clubs together, how they rose through the corporate ranks together, lifted weights and went to school together, phoned each other for dinner each afternoon and met together in groups at night for a last drink before going to bed. But if I wasn't a member of a group that went out drinking together, that part was okay. I enjoy solitude. The part of that blue watery dream that triggers a shock of regret is that, just as in the dream, I sat on the sidelines and watched aloof, all too ignorant of how those schools of interlocking creatures cooperated with one another to make a way through the world. Together, they opened up possibilities for one another, learned from each other, built with each other, combined and created.

So those are the emotions of the matter, coming as they do through symbols out of a dreamscape painted in the brilliant, primary hues that I know to be the colors of dreams. But emotions are just as they are and even a dream arising deep out of the subconscious must be interpreted with one's conscious philosophy of how things work. I believe it was Samuel Johnson who wrote an essay on how people have to discard old acquaintances as they rise through the ranks. Of course, he was writing in the eighteenth century when rank was stark and hierarchical, but when I think about those fish swimming together, I realize how the dream breaks down at the conscious level because even if people swim together as they start out, their lives begin to differ. We undergo a winnowing. People begin together at a corporation, or as freshmen at university, but after a while, some are promoted above others and then Samuel Johnson's comments begin to apply because the new Executive Vice President is no longer just one of his old school chums. Unlike the fish in my dream, his situation has changed and he stands apart and makes decisions about others, decisions that influence the course of other people's lives, so that in a way he's become something distinct, a larger and more commanding part of the fauna. To be cut away from the pack is not unusual, then, but rather a part of the act of living and, I suppose, of growing. There are those like me who tend to be alone by choice and others who are forced to it, but in the best case a person separates from the crowd because their lives grew into something larger whereas I have become alone because life has grown small.

I can't shake the images of that dream because it leads me to the uncomfortable conclusion that I've had only a few friends. I never did swim with schools, have always been an outsider at group activities. The feelings that remained with me are also true. This is what I know. It is not lonely, it just something I don't understand, a bewilderment. Alone, I went to clubs and picked up men. I had a job and an apartment. Lace and I are friends, to be sure. There have been others, too, but Connie's friends I thought at one time were mine as well, though that turns out to be a delusion. I saw Connie once a week and many weekends. He had a place in the country. We traveled some. If it wasn't precisely the suburban life of my parents, if it sometimes had the trappings of glamour or wit, it was still a familiar life, always the familiar, never too risky, always tried and true. In my mind, and as far as I knew, it might as well have been a life recreated from the small, circumscribed stockade of the life I knew as a child.

At the same time—and to be fair to myself—despite my relationship with Connie, I also went my own way, going out at night, dancing at clubs, watching plays, going to cabaret, seeing, watching but I can't escape the fact that I also was dependent on him like a button sewn onto his wide, luxurious fabric of people and experience.

Connie's crowd risked large, failed big, reaped huge. They were haves whose names you might know, but sometimes they were has-beens breathless to make a comeback. There was a baroness who wore a rhinestone red-baron helmet to parties and sometimes appeared in public supported at the arm by two young men-for-hire. There was the beautiful, kept lesbian who fronted bars for the mob and an ancient chanteuse with her prostitute boyfriends. There was the wife of the former President of a small republic and the wife of the president of a foreign national bank. There were playwrights, cabaret performers, oil tycoons and ship owners and one or two British lords. They were sometimes broken down and sometimes building up, but they had one thing in common. They didn't appear to be afraid and, to me, they seemed to know instinctively what they wanted, and while I stood still, alone, watching, they acted. Standing still, like an audience member in standing room only, I was dumbstruck and awed and watched them like actors on a great stage.

That is what I regret; that I was merely an adjunct to Connie's life and, although I learned a lot, the great and mighty, the gifted and the grand were never able to help me much. Since I conceived of myself as a pure and disinterested soul, I neither gave nor took. I hate looking back at things through a lens of regret. We are told that we can do nothing about the past, that optimism and hope are the key to the future. But how can one grow if one does not confront the past without flinching. Yes, to be sure I learned a great deal by watching. That is true. Doubtless I got an education, but towards what end? Had I been more available to the experience, more willing to learn how to swim first one way and then another with my fellow fishes, Connie's wide ocean of fortune, less defiant and aimless, many of those great people would have been happy to help me. I needed only to join in. Perhaps I was afraid of being eaten alive.

As it is, I have very little to show for it. I had a friend who when he was asked what he did replied, "I don't do, I am." That always sounded wise, and perhaps it is, but just now it seems nomadic, untethered and even lost. It is too detached and just now, I believe it sounds a little bewildered too.

None of those people stayed in contact when Connie died.

CHAPTER XIII

Connie lay in Cabrini Medical Center near Manhattan's Gramercy Park with IV drips inserted into his arms. Ashen white, small, circled into a ball like a larva, he was dying. Earlier, people died swiftly from AIDS, but no longer. This caused some consternation to his soul. It was an amazement after all: nothing worked in his body anymore. His bowels emptied themselves on their own schedule and at their own whim and fancy. Same with his bladder. His stomach wanted nothing to do with food, or his body for that matter. His fingers no longer clasped, his legs could not withstand the few pounds left on his body. Yet his mind was active. So far as he knew, he was unaffected by dementia. Tired he was, yes, he slept a lot, but his mind was alive and, indeed, he was in a consternation.

True, people died swiftly from AIDS, but because there had been medical advances —so-called—since the outset of the plague, one could live maybe one or two years after the sicknesses began as the doctors treated each of the afflictions and disorders as they cropped up, one by one and then in a cascade, as the body, overwhelmed, ran down and fell apart into the dust from which it had been made.

Bit by bit Connie, who had never depended on anyone, came to depend on Patrick. This was never supposed to be. They lived apart in largely separate and parallel lives, but it was Patrick, now, who slept over or checked in. It was he who called the doctor each time a collapse occurred. They began by hailing a cab and getting him to the hospital and later Patrick rode with him in the ambulance since the collapses were now real emergencies.

It began with exhaustion and fever, days in the hospital ending in a release that was really an expulsion into a hostile environment that attacked him as soon as he returned to it. They let him go home for a short period of rocky health and rising hopes before the abrupt bad times came again. Thrush on the tongue, high, high fevers for no apparent reason but possibly, they said, Micobacterium Avian Complex. Every time Patrick was there, Connie found it impossible to turn to his family. His sisters were sympathetic, even kind, but there was a gulf between them. He became a stranger in this awful sickness, a kind of leper. Understandably, they were afraid for themselves at the beginning. No one knew for sure how the terrible plague was being spread. They had the maids scour their apartments with Clorox after Connie visited. In time they became less paranoid as more information became available, but it was how the disease was contracted that built a wall between them. He had always been a homosexual of the old school: mixing socially, but not necessarily closely with others of his kind. It had seemed tawdry to him somehow and when the gay world exploded and gay men began to build networks and families among themselves, he had looked on as an outsider. Now, lying in a small vulnerable ball he realized how it was that he'd always kept Patrick at bay. He never thought of him as an equal, certainly. More than a toy. A sexual necessity, perhaps. Somehow not full grown.

How much had that changed now? Connie's mind wandered over his past, his sisters, his father's suicide, the body swinging from a rope discovered by the little boy when he was six. Now, dimly, he sensed that he possessed the mind of a dying man.

Patrick drifted back into it. Always there helping, solicitous, he had been a stalwart lad, okay, but it didn't seem to matter much. The nagging feeling that had been bothering him, a sense that he'd forgotten something was there again. He realized what it was. Never got around to mentioning Patrick in his will, but what did it matter now? Did the kid expect anything? Why would Connie do that? Leave his money to an outsider. Blood was thicker than water. He'd fobbed fake, low-grade jewelry off on the kid, second-rate watches. The kid never noticed or complained. Somewhat on purpose, Connie thought, he had invested the least possible and achieved the maximum returns: sex for less money than a hooker, conversation for less money than a psychiatrist, company when he wanted it and no more.

And so, Connie's conscience was absolved at last as he lay there. He thought of more immediate matters. Somewhere nearby he heard a drip, drip, drip. Maybe it was a click. A sink? Perhaps one of the machines that monitored him or kept him alive. It repeated and repeated, droning, dull and methodic. Would there be a light? At the very last? He wondered at that, but all he saw now was a ball of darkness against a background dimmed and gray.

CHAPTER XIV

Business was good for Marjorie Carbonoy. She had always been the best in town, but changing times and looser sexual mores had brought more people to her thriving atelier, a richer clientele who were willing to pay more. Her customers called Marjorie Carbonoy "ma'am," a fact that sometimes amused her. Once as she had watched a BBC broadcast about the Queen of England, she learned that after one has referred to the Queen as "Your Majesty" one time, it is proper to address her as "Ma'am " thereafter. Thinking of the similarity in title amused her because the titles did not proceed from the same cause. Indeed, most objective observers would admit that Marjorie Carbonoy's position in life was somewhat different from Her Majesty's. It was somewhat different from most women whose position in life would elicit a "ma'am". Yet "Madame" would not have been quite proper for her all the same. It was Marjorie Carbonoy's business to dominate people and to feed into their deepest desires. Not their pleasures, mind you, she fed their desires and the people who came to her bent their knee to her indeed and, crouching on the floor in front of her, gladly called her "ma'am."

So when middle-aged men, or anyone else who had been intro-duced into her select circle of customers, would call and she prepared the whips or slings or shackles and restraints, she was a little amused at those who groveled at her feet and called her "ma'am".

Marjorie would do anything except kill people. There were those looking for that kind of thing, but she wouldn't do it. If somewhere there lives a stereotypic whore with a golden heart, maybe Marjorie would be that whore. If the good and honest laws of a country were to be based on crimes with victims only, if indeed all the consensual acts of adults were to stand unfettered by the magistrates, Marjorie's life would be as exemplary as a saint's. No one came to her unwilling or unbidden; each person came from their own motives. It was her specialty to dig deeply into someone's innermost psyche—some might say psychosis—and fulfill it, no matter what it might be.

Of course, good-hearted people do not often do unto others what Marjorie was capable of doing. In the fast and voguish society that she inhabited by necessity, she might seem like the well-known New York society dermatologist, whose mild manner and vaguely effeminate way belied his ability to pierce a cyst or perform a quick operation oblivious to the pain of his patients. After all, if the pro-cedure had to be done, did you want the doctor to be delicate about it? Did you want your mistress to be squeamish?

Marjorie could place razor blades into a balsa strip with just the tiniest sharp edge showing through and draw the strip lovingly, searchingly along the back of a customer. She could pierce a man's testicles slowly, urgently with the needle of a syringe, holding the sack of his balls firmly in her manicured hands like a seamstress darning a sock. She had taken anatomy courses so that she could pierce a woman's body with long needles. She knew how to place clips along a path from a spot on someone's genitalia, along their stomach and tits, onto their neck and then yank the clips off without tearing the skin. And she knew how to tear the skin too, just a bit.

But she would not kill.

There were those who wanted her to kill them. They nosed about, contacted her outright or slowly let their desire be known. She had taken medical courses and knew how to string a person up. She also knew how to bring a person out of a drug overdose and how to give adrenaline shots. She had saved lives, but she also knew how to choke them until they almost passed out and then release them. She knew how to bind a person tightly in duct tape so that only the mouth showed, or only the nose. People came to her for these things and more, and she knew to watch closely because if the nose plugged up and the mouth was taped shut, a person could die and she would not kill people. But she had heard about things. In her position, people had told her terrible things. They had asked her to do terrible things.

Marjorie Carbonoy had always been the best of her field and the people who came to her paid top price. Anyone in America would be astonished at her list. Those from the everyday walks of life couldn't afford her. The people who came to Marjorie were people you read about. People in government and business and from society visited Marjorie or, very often, asked Marjorie to put together little scenes for them, like tableau vivant or little dinners for six. They used Marjorie more or less as they would use a party planner, although Mistress was a bit more specialized and, of course, she got through on the private line.

And the things people asked her to do, this big-bosomed, almost kind woman with her tall, lanky frame and long, red hair. A man asked her to pour Amyl Nitrate on his chest, dripping the liquid in the shape of a pentangle, and then to light it. She branded the shape onto his chest and over his nipples, the scar shining garishly ever after. People like him were motivated by drives of religious ferocity, drives she could not even pretend to understand completely. She didn't have to understand things completely. She had never exactly analyzed what came naturally, even if she was always a bit removed, somewhat detached and perhaps the tiniest bit entertained to sit goddess-like over her clients as she bound up the disjointed parts of their psyches and brought out inner parts of their nature that they needed to express in order to feel whole.

She understood what her clients needed without thinking much about it and a piece of her remained detached as she watched the burning mix of chemicals char a satanic symbol onto that man's chest, as he pumped himself faster and faster until he ejaculated into his hand, exhausted and wounded. She didn't understand why a person would brand a satanic symbol onto his chest, but she serviced those drives, nonetheless.

Marjorie was not a religious person. She might have turned out that way, of course. Raised by decent people in Minneapolis, she went to good schools and took away a major in political science from the state university, but her people were never church-going people. No, she was secular and a businessperson of this world; a healer of souls perhaps in this world, but not a slick seller of hope for the next. She served the interests of her clients and knew better than they did what they wanted out of their lives. The man with the pentangle was what she called a Bogus Satanist. She coined the term. What did these people believe anyway? If you bought the Satan bit, didn't you have to buy the God bit too? And who was going to win that battle? Weren't you sort of playing the losing side? She pretty much marked it up to some kind of twisted logic that sharpened sex for some people, people who had gotten sex all mixed up with religion in their youth. They came when they thought of screwing around with their God. Well, for her it was all smoke and mirrors. Even sex. It was all smoke and mirrors and the more smoke and mirrors she provided, the better the fees.

She had even been wondering lately if she even liked sex very much. She was so disassociated from it, really. People had all these deep agendas that seemed hardly to do with sex at all. Maybe she even hated sex and as she thought back over her life, she could understand why. Being in the business of providing subterranean urges was not the same thing, exactly. Being in the business of sex was not exactly the same thing as sex itself.

She had gotten out of Minnesota once and for all and never looked back at those people and that small town and the boring, clapboard houses rotting like teeth along a slimy mouth and the stinking brown rot yards with rusty swing sets, strewn with plastic tot-toys that never were picked up as they accumulated layer after layer of soot and lay forgotten and blackened in the rain and muck and gray of her memory. Still, she did escape once and for all from the promiscuous girl reputation that hung over her all the way into college. How her decent and doting parents never found out, if indeed they never did find out, she could never explain to herself. Perhaps they had begun looking the other way when her old granduncle started playing with her just before adolescence. Even then, as soon as he told her it was to be just "their little secret" she knew that she had her grip on him. Later on, of course, she heard that she had been a victim, but somehow, right from the start, she knew instinctively that other people's secrets gave her power. "Their little secret" really meant *his* awful secret and she knew without being told that he would pay a high price to keep it that way, so she started extorting money from him. Not that she came right out and said, "I'm blackmailing you, you bastard." No, even at thirteen, as the subterranean rage grew up inside her, she knew how to trade on that early sexual blossoming, her swelling breasts and that lanky, honeydew voluptuousness. She curtly requested $5 at first, and then demanded some clothes. After that, she never looked back. And an intense hatred for her granduncle helped her along.

Indeed, Marjorie never felt sorry for herself; from the moment she discovered how to manipulate people, she felt powerful, so when she began to hear reports from the feminists that she had been the victim of male-dominated transactional sex her reaction was to become angry at them. Still, she wondered if the anger wasn't a reaction to something true. "What of it," she thought to herself during brief periods of self-analysis. If she was victimized, it was also the way to freedom after all. Perhaps there were incipient feelings of trust, aspiration, hope that were cut off to her forever, but, she thought, her childhood rape led ultimately to a path taken, not a way denied.

Now business was doing just fine, thank you very much, and it was ingenuity that kept her on the top, so to speak.

One day, she cut down a young, submissive fellow who was hanging from a rafter suspended across her ceiling. Marjorie was wrapping up after a scene. He had been brought in by one of her better customers, who said of him, "He'll do anything with anything on two or four legs." He was young, possibly early to mid-twenties and he had a great tattoo of the devil covering his entire back and a cross upside down covering his stomach. Before they started, he took out a vial of crystal meth and snorted a heaping, long line of it. With that he became excited, an erection almost bursting out of him as they hung him up with shackles and rope. He had wept out, "Hail Satan" quietly a few times as he hung from her ceiling, wrapped tightly. That's what the customer liked: total control. The boy had never been touched. He was wrapped tight as a mummy and hung from the ceiling and never touched, although his eyes had been left open to watch the other people.

After everyone else left, he produced the vial again and, nodding with a questioning glance that silently asked if his mistress gave permission or wanted some of the drug, he took another enormous snort. Marjorie hadn't really noticed the boy. Her lack of response was not so much permission granted as boy ignored, but as the speed began to hit, he began to chatter and, for some reason, she let him. He loitered, hanging his head in a shy sort of way, as he dressed slowly, obviously looking to unburden himself to her. That happened sometimes. Marjorie was nothing if not an authority figure and it was not hard to understand how it was that people who had shared with her their most hidden secret life would share the added secrets of their souls: problems with spouses, business reversals, feelings of powerless and failure that a public person cannot tell ordinary people about. Sometimes, people would start talking about something small and end up stumbling onto what mattered to them most, but Marjorie never talked back, except perhaps to pose a short question every now and then. Give and take in this game was dangerous. Silence was the golden rule. Silence kept her authority intact and fed the fantasy. If she stayed silent, they might return, even after spilling their guts, but a conversation would be deadly. To be a cipher and to listen. Marjorie was good-hearted, after all, and she had some time and her sadism was oddly interlaced with a small portion of affection, too, which made her clients open up to her.

"People think Satan doesn't exist," he said quietly, tying a shoe. Marjorie did not reply.

"People think Satan doesn't exist," the young man said again, softly. "But he does."

"Why do you follow him, boy?" asked Marjorie as she wrapped a whip around her hand and put it into a studded storage chest.

"He is Prince of this World, ma'am. God doesn't run the world, Satan does. What choice do we have? But also, Satan is a better master. Satan allows us pleasure. What pleasure does God give us? Satan gives us freedom to be what we are; to explore what we really are. It always seemed to me that it was Satan who loved humans for who they are. When I was a boy, we read the Bible all the time. No one could live up to God's demands. There was God one moment wiping people out for nothing, absolutely nothing, and then smiling and saying all was forgiven. One verse would be about love, the next about hate, the next about love and tolerance, the next about killing your enemies. There are verses telling you to kill people for nothing and followed up by versus telling you to forgive everything. Jesus begins by talking about love and ends up talking about coming back with a sword to kill."

"The boy's either a fucking two-penny philosopher or he's stoned," Marjorie thought to herself. She knew enough about drugs to know how the crystal was making its way through the boy's brain so that the thoughts came flying faster and faster, making connections that were sensible to him but not always to other people.

"Either way, stoner or thinker, he's deluded, an idiot, off on one of those religious, sexual tangents." She saw it so often and it was always so stupid. She was only partly listening. There was another gig later in the evening, but she turned to look at him at last, assessing him. Although she hadn't really noticed him before, now he started to come into focus.

"How does a creature like this come to be who he is?" she wondered to herself. By all appearances, he was a waif, really small, willowy and physically weak. It didn't matter to him which sex degraded him. He had no work, no career. His living came entirely from being available for sex and he seemed entirely bound up by a willingness, even a compulsion to submit. For most people, the scenes at Mistress Carbonoy's were a part of life generally unrelated to their business, social and married lives. For this boy, masochism was a way of life. Perhaps it was the drugs. Crystal was highly sexual. She conjured up for him a childhood littered with abuse, running away from home as an adolescent and hustling city streets. Everywhere on the streets were highs to be had. Maybe she was wrong, though. Pop psychology didn't always explain things that run deep in people. For all she knew he came from a good family, had some kind of education and was actually holding down some kind of job. But that didn't seem likely. And it was so ordinary for her men to collapse after their sexual release and jabber on and on, opening themselves up to her. Her mind wandered to individuals, the disjoint between what they did with her and then the hopes and dreams they conveyed to her afterwards. A gangster would talk about a house with a lawn and kids, still black and blue from the beating she'd just given him. Which piece of an individual was the true piece, she wondered? And what about her dreams? Where, indeed, had her dreams lead her?

Vaguely, she heard the waif incessantly prattle on. "Well, what about him?" she mused almost angrily. "Where will it all lead for him? Is there a part of him that's real and a part of him that isn't? A true soul, free, clear and ordinary and a false part, created by drugs and sexual fantasy fueled by strange beliefs?" She pondered his fate with kind of detached amusement. But finally she snapped to. "Child-like though he is, he's still an adult and he's not my responsibility once he's out of here," she decided. That was enough reflection for Marjorie's taste.

Meanwhile, the submissive young man sat and tore duct tape from his arms, which took away patches of hair as he ripped, and he continued to develop his philosophies. Perhaps he had little opportunity to actually expound them, at least to another human being. Perhaps somewhere in that submissive behavior of his was a guiding desire to be understood by his mistress, snuggle into her breast, gain her acceptance, regain his mother's love.

Swept up by the methamphetamine, he rattled on with increasing intensity. "Then I began to think," he continued, the volume and speed of his voice increasing, "what is God hiding? First we get one face and then we get the other…you know, an opposite face. It doesn't depend on anything you do. It doesn't depend on what your last action was, what face you get. It's random. That's if you really read the Bible and don't just listen to what the ministers make up out of the Bible. They take what they want to make their stupid little points on Sunday. You get love or you get a sword. It just depends on the day. That's when I began to think, 'Satan is just God on a bad day.' God on the rag."

At that moment, he became animated and gesticulated abruptly, throwing his hands over his head and tossing a cute little head of long and unruly brunette hair. He struck her like a little ragamuffin doll suddenly sprung to life in her corner. Marjorie began to laugh, breaking her rule of silence for a quick second, but she caught herself. Instead of reacting more, she took a moment to glance in the mirrors that surrounded her playroom. She paused for a moment to notice that her breasts were becoming pendulous and that her ass was robust. Her upper thighs were almost muscular. She enjoyed the sight of it. Marjorie was not thin. Her men wouldn't have liked that. The planes of her body were rounded and voluptuous, her bright pubic hair shaved away except for a small tuft left behind. Still, the boy saw her muffle a momentary chuckle and he laughed, too.

The kid misunderstood the twitch upwards in the corners of Marjorie's lips as a reaction to what he was saying and assumed he had engaged her at last. "No, I mean it. And it is funny. I thought there's something weird here. Either Satan and God are the same thing, or if God is so screwy…I mean if God is first judgmental and angry and then kind and loving and then turns right back around mean again. Maybe Satan is the one getting a bad rap. Maybe we're not getting his side of the story. Maybe he's less screwy than God. Even Jesus says first one thing. He says stuff about loving one another. Then the woman comes to him in Matthew and he tells her to get lost, she's not one of the people he came for and the disciples talk him into listening to her. Jesus is going to come back in anger and kill his enemies. This is the same guy who tells us to forgive everything. Maybe the God who wrote the Bible is the bad seed and Satan is, well, the even-tempered one. How do we know for sure?"

Marjorie looked at him for a short time and, weighing whether or not to tease him, decided that she had already laughed once, so she countered by poking at him gently, "You know, some people say Satan's best trick is making people think he doesn't exist."

"I've heard that, too, I don't think I agree with it." He looked up out of the corner of his soft eyes and his look silently added, "Ma'am."

Then he went on. "What would that matter to something as powerful as Satan? They both want our eyes on them; him and God. They both want us to think about them all the time. That's the old saying, 'You are what you think about, or a man is what he thinks.' Something like that."

Focusing now on preparing for her next gig, Marjorie pulled out a drawer and began to extract long rolls of wide, medical bandage and several mats of the kind intended for yoga exercise. But what he had said to her triggered a thought. As she unfurled the gauze, she began to think to herself, perhaps half-aloud, "I always did think that the real Satanists were those religious people, the fundamentalist Southern Baptist types who think and talk about the Devil all the time. It has to be that way: you are what you think about most of that time, sure enough and finding evil everywhere is the surest road to damnation. They—that whole damned religion—get so completely focused on Satan and what's bad about the world and their neighbors and the rest of us that they don't think about anything else. If that's where their minds are, those church people, they'll end up in hell all right. If they're not there already…those little church groups…must be hell on earth to live among people like that!"

Inside her forehead, blood began to roil against her temples. Church people annoyed Marjorie, mightily. She had had more than one brush with them. They did make the meanest customers and were bothersome opponents. There had been a needless court case recently and the thought of it made her chest seize slightly with anger, but she shouldn't have let her guard down with this little strumpet of a boy. She stopped herself, freezing up and looking away to focus attention on her preparations.

The boy did not notice her preoccupation or perhaps it was in his needy nature to divert her attention back onto himself. What a fine feeling to have a big-bosomed, lanky woman pay attention to him, tie him up and then listen to his theories. The air expanded inside him.

"But I think people have it just the opposite. A lot of times, what people think of as Satan is really God and what people think about God is really Satan. They might be the same thing, but if they're two separate things, then that's what I think. For instance, you know those pictures of hell where people are on fire and they're screaming and yelling? But, you know, lots of people experience pleasure where most people would have pain. I think those are masochists and Satan, or God, understands that pain is pleasure to them and so what they are really getting is endless pleasure. It's backwards; kind of topsy-turvy, but maybe Satan is the God of people who are turned inside out. My Satan is as good, maybe better, than some people's God and he's as good to me as people say God is good to them. And I have pleasure in my life. A lot of them don't."

"So, you gonna get fucked over if God and Satan battle it out in the future?" Marjorie was still not sure how seriously to take this conversation, but the boy was young, she was passing time and she might never see him again.

"Maybe, maybe not. But you can't go by anything as unreliable as the voice in the Bible. Who knows if there's gonna be a battle, even? If you can't count on God to be kind or angry, to be there or not for humans, you can't count on what he has to say for the future. Even his plan for humanity kind of sucks. It's not what we would ask for ourselves, that's for sure. He's just sort of sticking us with it. And for what, to sit around and praise him; tell him what a pretty tie he has on and how nice he looks or how witty and fine he is into eternity. Isn't that what he's looking for, people sucking up to him for his eternal glory? But we don't get anything out of it. Satan understands the insides of your soul and gives you what you want. Like you, ma'am. You know, just like you. At least he understands the insides of my soul. And if the Bible is nothing but propaganda, why believe it any more than you would believe that Russia is really going to bury us just because they say it. Or if we don't win Vietnam, the Russians will invade California? Would you? Believe it, I mean."

"I don't give a shit, boy, if you want to know. Do you always think this fucking much?" She wanted to lower the book on him and get back in control.

He paused a second. "Do you ever smoke cocaine?"

Marjorie might have been suspicious. She never did drugs. The mistress had to be in control to be the best in town. She never did drugs, but her clients did. Ordinarily, she was careful about who used them and she never let anyone she didn't know well see anyone else doing them. She had to be careful. The last thing she needed was a drug bust. The next gig coming up that night, though, was going to be a special drug scene. "No," she said truthfully, but in a tone that immediately reasserted her authority over him.

"Sometimes when I smoke cocaine...you know, free-base...I begin to get a high buzz in my head. It's a particular buzz, real high and squeaky. It's a special sound that I know. When that happens, all of a sudden something appears as real as can be right in front of me, or in the apartment. Sometimes it's a person, sometimes it's a devil. I see them as real as I see you and one time I even reached out and grabbed hold of it. It was a man in a silk jacket. He had blue eyes and gray hair and I grabbed him by the ankle because I was sitting on the floor. His leg was like a bone. I remember that really well. And then he just disappeared." The boy looked at his fingers. "He disappeared right out of my hand." He considered for a minute as he tied his last shoelace and finished the thought. "I think they travel on sounds from another dimension."

"Spooky as hell," thought Marjorie. "This boy's a loon, but it sort of explains why some of my folks go in for the hokey Satan stuff. At least the people who seem to think about it." She still thought that most of them probably didn't think about it much, just got some sort of deep but oddly cheap thrill. But why the thrill seemed to run so deep was a mystery to her.

"Look here, boy." Marjorie had a sudden thought. The news that the boy free-based gave her a sudden inspiration. "I know what we're going to do with you just now, you little fucking slave, so you just stay here with your mistress. I've got some people coming up and you're just the ticket for them." She turned sharp with him. "You're staying here. Take off your clothes, scum, and get me that duct tape and the bandages from over there."

Then the boy went silent, smiled as much as he dared, and followed to the letter.

When, an hour later, Jonathan arrived, Marjorie's young trick was wrapped back up with two holes, one in the rear and one around his mouth and nose showing a gaping hole and a waiting tongue. He was not suspended from the ceiling. He was lying on the floor, on his back, waiting for anything to happen, his body and soul safe in the open, benevolent, if not loving, hands of his temporary version of Lord Satan and more to the point Mistress Marjorie, dominatrix.

Jonathan had been specially requested for tonight. The guest of honor, whose tastes were peculiar and who did not want to be seen, was the much-photographed girlfriend of a Rock star. She was fearful of the Rock star's anger if word got around that she loved to satiate herself upon the bodies of strange men who caught her fancy. Jonathan caught her fancy from a picture Marjorie had of him and Jonathan, that night, had his eyes bound so that he could see nothing at all, not even by peeking out the sides. He was lying on his back, right next to the young boy.

The Rock star's woman liked to get her men stoned and have her way with them. She cooked her free-base cocaine herself, carefully measuring a dollop of bicarbonate of soda against a heap of pure white Colombian powder, bringing it to a quick boil in her little bottle and stirring it quickly and efficiently with a metal piece to bring together the oily congealing substance that swam to the top and cooled into white rocks. These she sprinkled carefully into a pipe, placing the stem into first Jonathan's mouth and then the boy's and lighting the iridescent pebbles with a small torch until they boiled. As the white, pearly granules seethed, they gurgled lightly, sizzling as they created a lustrous smoke. One by one, the boys breathed in deeply, letting out silken white clouds. The Rock star's woman followed them, breathing in and holding long and then she began to work Jonathan with her tongue. She inserted him into her. She rode him. She licked him and smelled him. She rolled him over and licked him, she rolled him back and played with him all the more.

The boy she used for a toilet, peeing down his throat and forced his tongue far into her. She never turned him over. Never used him any other way, but he gurgled with joy as the liquid rushed down his throat and her pleasure was evident as he used his tongue back at her in ever-widening and urgent swirls. It was obvious to Marjorie that the kid was an adept.

Again and again, she made the two young men draw the white, hot cloud into themselves until their minds buzzed with a shrill, high sound. But who knows what they saw or thought behind the walls of their bindings, inside the closed cubicles of their minds? Neither Marjorie nor the woman ever asked them. Neither boy ever spoke a word, but Jonathan did experience a vision under the smoke's heavy influence. There was a high, shrill buzz and then he saw in a scene projected as if it were actually in his field of view a boy walk out of a door and stop in the center of an empty room. He looked blankly in Jonathan's direction and then walked back through the opening into a dark void, but as his body disappeared he turned around and his head stayed, brilliantly lit, floating in the black doorway. Then, suddenly, there was another man too, well-dressed and perhaps middle-aged, who seemed to have stepped out of another door. Then the older man turned, left the imaginary room through a hole, something like a door but more like a floating hole in a white, glowing white wall and as suddenly as he had appeared, he was gone. Methodically, then, the phantasm stopped moving and turned into a still frame, except that the still frame was just one of a series of still movie frames that stood simultaneously next to one another and extended out as far as the dreamscape could take him. Then the celluloid-like frames began to splinter and fragment into fractal shapes, first yellow and then orange and finally faded into brown and then into black, as if they were being burnt and melted by the hot light of a projector. But the face of the young man stayed alive in Jonathan's imagination, burnt against the back of his retina and seared into his memory.

Meanwhile, the Rock Star's woman never spoke; she was engrossed entirely in her scene. The smoke made her oblivious to anything but the use of these mindless exotic animals. To her, these speechless toys were there for her pleasure or perhaps they gave her some solace against the Rock star's bad temper or they filled some empty hole in the middle of her very being that could only be filled by white smoke and young men.

There was much more cocaine as anyone needed and even as much as they wanted. They kept up their Dionysian fury until the next day when the woman had to go and start her long, painful reentry into the real world. She had bags under her eyes. She was puffy and tired and still not sated by the two men whose ears rang and whose minds boiled and who had been prohibited from seeing anything. She rode Jonathan all night and still the cocaine forced her to work harder, grinding herself into him, moaning and crying as Marjorie kissed and caressed her, assaulting her anally, forcing her tongue into her harder and harder as the woman's needs grew into an insatiable fury. For the Rock Star's woman, the time could never come when she was finished. Night passed, the morning grew late and the hour came when she had to pull herself away from this obsession that had become fiercer now than when she began fifteen hours earlier. It was hard to get her to stop, to quiet down and understand that she could never go away satisfied and that her intense pleasure would not give her any place to rest. It was painful, sometimes, how bitter the withdrawal from this intensity could be. How painful it was to rip one's self away. The Rock star's woman could not do it without being forced.

"The bitch is doomed," Marjorie thought with a tinge of disgust, "but she is not my responsibility once she leaves here." The emotion of disgust surprised her. Being judgmental was not a usual part of her business plan and the sudden rush of self-righteousness disconcerted her, but that usual aura of detached amusement had worn thin. It happened seldom, but it happened now, that she felt disdain for one of her clients. Perhaps it was because this woman wasn't acting out any deep-seated emotional need, she was merely playing with urges made greedy by drugs. "And that," she thought wearily, "is as boring as it gets."

The Rock star's woman left about noon the next day and Marjorie undid Jonathan's blindfold, let him wash up and let him go. Then, she unwrapped the boy and let him take a long shower.

What Marjorie never did know, however, was that Jonathan had seen the boy's clothing in a pile outside the bathroom when he put his clothes back on. It is possible that Jonathan forgot that he had seen the clothing, too, because forever after he remembered that he knew the boy from having seen his face in that floating vision. Perhaps that part is true as well, but the fact is that he waited outside the apartment building until he recognized the boy who emerged out onto the street in the jeans and black jacket that had been left in that pile. Jonathan approached him and introduced himself and they went home together. For two weeks, or thereabouts, they had an electric affair until they split and went their separate ways.

During that time, they smoked a ton of cocaine together and Jonathan learned how to score it and how to cook it. And the boy, to be sure, told Jonathan about his theories of the devil and the cosmos and how God and Satan were maybe reversed, with God being the evil one. Or maybe they were just one thing anyway, where identity and good and evil, abandonment and self-control, ethics and pleasure, love and passion all met into some kind of a moral singularity at the center of the universe and became nothing recognizable as human at all. Jonathan had picked up metaphysical flotsam in his occult reading, bits and pieces that tried to bridge the gap between science and eastern philosophies. Perhaps, he reasoned, God was the moral equivalent of the hot, hot white soup of particles and energy that existed in the first billion trillionth of a second, when the universe was created out of the Big Bang and the laws of physics had yet to apply and the characteristics of yin and yang, good and evil, order and chaos, light and darkness, even matter and energy had not emerged. Yet in all their sharing of sex and cocaine, Jonathan never told the boy that he was sure he'd seen him in some sort of otherworldly divination, even though his eyes were wrapped in bandages at the time. "Who are you to understand the ways of God," Rennie had said. So, like the Virgin Mary when she learned that she was pregnant with God's child, he stored these things away silently in his heart.

CHAPTER XV

"Brunch, my darling?" Agnes was on the telephone to Lace and it was a Sunday morning.

"After church, my dear." Lace waited for the reaction.

"What? You old reprobate. Are you drunk still? Were you out last night?"

"Yes, as a matter of fact. And I got quite drunk, but that is no matter. I've started going to St. John's. Looking into my Church of England roots, my dear. Why, I don't know, but I've been going now for three weeks. I sit in the back and I don't follow along much but there I am. And I'm reading Thomas Merton. God help me. I've begun the slippery ascent towards the mountains of God. Heaven only knows what I'll find there."

"Be careful. I hear it's a cheap motel. Those mountains have slippery slopes, you know. Can't you find the wider path? Isn't there a freeway or carpeted stairs or an elevator or moving sidewalk or something? How about Eric Butterworth or Isaac Denison or someone you can follow and understand? I always figured that they were the real Sherpa guides to the mountaintops of God."

"Church is over by around 12:30 and it's a half hour walk back over. The Stove and Grill at 1:00?"

Sadly, Café Dadilo had closed its doors several months previously. Alberto had opened a restaurant uptown where Agnes sometimes ate, but Lace did not leave the Village except under circumstances as rare as the sighting of a Yeti. Still, he was not dismayed. Already Lace knew the waiters and owners and barkeeps of The Stove and Grill and because it was a place to have lunch, they never had the opportunity to see Lace become loud and obnoxious and never had to ask him to leave and never come back.

The Stove and Grill did not have banquettes. Agnes was waiting at a table in the back when Lace arrived in coat and tie. His face was still flushed red from the night before. The day outside was bright and it took a moment before his eyes adjusted and he made his way to the rear of the area near the bar. Scattered about were tables, mostly empty at this time of day as the waiters waited for the Sunday brunch patrons to arrive. He used the twilight created by low overhead lights and a myriad of tiny table candles to pick his way through the white and red check tablecloths. Finally Agnes appeared to him, nestled in shadows, waiting with a drink in hand. He smiled wide as he sat down. Even in semi-darkness, his teeth gleamed to perfection.

"The dentist did a nice job," said Agnes, as she curled her lip in a catty grin. "Good enough for a toothpaste commercial. May I offer you some Listerine to drink?"

"I love going to church hazy," replied Lace, ignoring the swipe. "It's sort of in keeping with the liturgy. Don't look too closely, or faith disappears. Everything in amber light, vague, you know. That sort of thing."

He called over the waiter. "Can I get a drink yet? Well, then, I want a gin martini, dry. Almost no vermouth. Just vapors of vermouth." He glanced at Agnes. "I've been to church, now I can relax."

"Now, what is this all about, my dear? There are other ways to explore one's roots."

"You know perfectly well, Agnes. You started it all. What am I going to do? I don't think people who, well, work for a living and put all that time in day–to-day let their minds wander so, but then how do I know? I'm no judge. I wrote that poetry for years. I'm not writing it now. I ended up no Ferlinghetti. I can tell you that. I've ended up the creek instead of On The Road. I haven't had a crisis like this since I read Hermann Hesse, for Christ's sake. When I was ten." He stressed the word "ten." "I sit in that antique store and I wonder where have I gotten to. I read, of course. I read a good deal, and I think. I need to go away for a while."

He looked at her forlornly and tossed his head.

"Good Heavens! I'm burbling like an infant." He took a napkin and dabbed at his nose.

A waiter brought his dry martini and Lace gobbled down the olive, ordered Fettuccini Alfredo and drank the martini in two swallows before the waiter had a chance to leave. He asked the waiter for another and turned back to Agnes.

"There, I needed that. Might as well be drinking straight out of the bottle. This is all catching up with me Agnes. Catching up with me. Not that I'm an alcoholic. I don't think so, anyway. In Spain I only drank a little wine at lunch and at dinner. I had things to do and then that affair…"

"That affair?"

"I didn't let on, but an affair does do a man good. A woman, too, for that matter, but I'm talking from my perspective. It was good to see my old, shriveled Willy again. It was like running into a schoolboy chum. Made me feel virile and alive."

"Do you encounter Willy in the hymnal? They've changed the service since I was a girl."

"Don't scoff at God, my dear."

"I wasn't scoffing at God. What does an Episcopal service have to do with God?"

"You have a point there. You have a point there, indeed. It's all theater, I suppose, but I go into that church and sit in the back and they go through this routine, this regular routine that they've been going through for centuries. Some people call it cant. I've called it cant. But just now, it seems like ritual. Ancient ritual. And it gives me roots. I hate saying, 'It centers me.' Sounds like those New-Age imbeciles who clutter up the Village these days. But it grounds me."

The second martini was delivered and Lace toyed with the stem of the glass, taking just a sip this time.

Agnes looked across the table at him and a little sneer crept across her lips as she folded a piece of lettuce into a neat origami and placed it near her mouth. "I don't see why you have to find solace in that retrograde church, Lace."

"Are you starting something with me?" Lace sat his drink down sharply and pointed his fork downward straight at her, glaring fixedly over its arch. "Look here, I don't go poking at you for sleeping with any two-bit bum and looking for god knows what from every piece of prick in the city, so don't pull any shit with me."

"Sorry, Lace, sorry." Agnes knew to back off, even if she thought that Lace's reaction was outsized. "You're right, we don't judge one another and I'm sorry to be flip. Really, I didn't know this meant so much to you. What's going on?"

Lace played with his food for a moment to let the blood settle and looked over Agnes' head while he regained control. He wasn't sure himself why he had snapped at her, but he didn't dwell on it. Finally, he said, "That's a good question. Did you know that the church is starving for priests, but there are waiting lines to get into the strict contemplative orders? Maybe I was just born that way, you know, to ruminate over things, and I know that I've got a lot of time on my hands. I doubt many people have the luxury to think themselves into a stew, but then there are two or three things that…"

"Yes?"

"Well, when I was a child, I used to get this awful feeling. It would creep over me sometimes and I'd have to think of something else fast to keep it from flooding over me…no not over, so much as through me. It's hard to describe, but I'd feel like I was a huge something, a spirit or an intelligence, something, but that I was too big to fit into the body they'd given me. I very much felt that someone had given me this body and it wasn't a good fit, somehow. Too small for the sensation I was feeling and it would give me a panicky feeling of claustrophobia, like I was holed up in a tiny space. That feeling basically went away…in time it went away, with adolescence, I suppose. I guess I have it sometimes even now, but basically it's gone away. I do still remember how awful it felt."

"And other things too?"

"I don't know if people have these sensations, you know. It would make sense that people wouldn't share them if they did happen. And it's hard to describe things that are out of the ordinary. People dismiss things like that. 'Oh, you were just light headed,' or 'are you sure you weren't dreaming?' And of course you can't convince people that what you felt, or saw, was extraordinary. You know your own dreams and what lightheadedness feels like, and you know that those sensations are different from the extraordinary ones. But do people believe what you tell them?"

"Lace, you know I've wondered if sex-craving people like me just aren't more physically sensitive in those gonadal nether-regions, or if we don't somehow get more of an experience out of sex than ordinary people. Is it simply a matter of how many nerve endings you've got? It's similar, if you think about it. I will never know how other people experience it, the sensations of sex. I remember a guy saying that he blacks out at the moment of climax, which means that he has no sensation of it at all. That's got to change how he feels about the act itself. Come to think of it, he was more interested in the process, foreplay in other words, than the climax itself. Differences of sensation that we can't verbalize with one another could explain lots of attitudes. For instance, it would be easy for a guy like that to be a puritan. Sex might not mean that much to him simply because the firing squad down there doesn't fire very well. In other words, in a way I guess I know what you're talking about because I can't ever know how other people experience something compared to how I experience it. I'm transported. But even if it all boils down to being physically more sensitive, the end is result is that, for me, sex with a stranger is a mystical experience, but I can't explain it. I just know that some people see it as I do, but we never discuss it. I have to say, though, that most people don't seem to experience sex the way I do. I think the psychologists have it all playing out in our heads, the product of our upbringing, so we're acting out old dramas in bed, but somehow with me it feels more physical than that. But just try to explain that to your therapist. He'll have you searching for reality in your past experiences and to hell with your actual orgasm."

"Maybe you've got company in the sexual revolution, honey. But, of course, it boils down to personal experience and that's hard to share. There's another experience, too. I've been sitting in a room and suddenly the air comes alive somehow. One moment I'm sitting in my world, my universe, and then suddenly the atmosphere itself begins to change and somehow the atoms themselves, the air itself, begins to sparkle. And the colors. The colors around me become electric and I have a sensation, not that I'm dreaming, but that I've been transported into a world that is somehow the real one. Every speck of matter is alive and bright. I don't mean some goofy space ball sense of everything being infused with a higher consciousness. I mean, maybe that's what it's all about, but I'm talking about an actual experience and not some hare-brained philosophy. On the other hand, you get to understand what Plato was talking about, because at the same time I know, no, I sense that what I'm experiencing first-hand is the ideal, the true world; that I've somehow emerged into another dimension that's made out of the real stuff and that everything is just like it's supposed to be. Maybe Plato had the same experience and that is why he thought about things as he did. After you've spent a second or two—that's probably all it is—in the ideal universe, this one seems like those shadows on a cave wall. Of course, as you say, any modern psychoanalyst would probably trace all this back to some childhood trauma."

"Well, possibly Jung wouldn't discount those, what are they, experiences or feelings. Sensations, maybe. I think that sex is like that, sometimes. I mean, transporting, like that. Do you ever feel transported?"

"No. Not often. Every now and then…or maybe often. I suppose I don't have anything to compare it with.

"So anyway, all those sensations lead you to church?"

"Church is one place to start looking for answers. I don't think that the church has the corner on these matters. What I suspect is that there's something deep down in me that creates a longing to explore these things. And I'm not alone. One need only read Varieties of Religious Experience, after all. But whether or not others have similar experiences, I can't shake myself out of the feeling that everything around me, well, lacks reality and until I find out what that ideal dimension is about, I'm going to feel sort of like a starving man. I'm lucky. I have some money and time. I don't buy Christian theology. I don't think there's a god who sent his only son for sacrifice. But sacrifice and the mysteries of creation are the essence of the sacred. We know a lot, scientifically, but the search for what is sacred goes back to the beginnings of human consciousness."

"And was all that poetry part of this?"

"In some way. Not on purpose though. I was just trying to be avant-garde, most of the time. But now that I'm not writing that silly stuff, I find I need to toy with something more substantial in my mind."

The tempo of Lace's voice began to quicken. He looked directly at Agnes.

"Of course, you've got to figure that it's sexual at its core. Sex is the creative urge. Sex and territory may be at the root of everything we do. And I guess even the territorial instinct is just about increasing access to sex. Anyway, defining the sacred is not a quest for the faint-hearted. I've been reading about how the Greeks looked at it all."

"You are serious, my dear. But why aren't you reading Freud instead of Thomas Merton. And why St. John's? Aren't you looking to Christianity to define what's sacred for you even though you don't see it as a true description of reality?"

"I said something back there about ritual as theater. The church as theater." He tried for a moment to remember. "Anyway, you know, of course, that originally the theater grew out of Dionysian rites. The comedies were started out of the rites in Sicily of all places and they wore a huge, fake penis on stage as a matter of ritual until the fourth century AD. Willy's been on stage since the beginning of time. A goddamn child star! He just hadn't been making an appearance for me. So much for the sanctity of ritual, I say. And tragedy came from acting out the fate of Dionysus. He was a semi-God—son of God, actually—who gave himself to save humankind. In fact, the worship of Dionysus included eating bread that was said to be the body of the god. So much for the sanctity or the originality of Christ. Christ is just a remake of an earlier model…and everyone had a god that had been resurrected. The Egyptians had Osiris. Baal was one, so Jesus is a retread they drummed up to capture the Roman Empire. And it helped, I suppose, that Jesus and his Dionysian story was in the recent, historical past, yesterday really, and accessible compared to some god of myth who belonged in the distant, unreal and unreachable past.

"Of course, God the Father and Christ the Son, the Emperor Constantine liked them because they mirrored his authority on Earth and the whole thing had happened right there, underfoot so to say, in one of his own provinces. So, he used them to help unite the Empire and give his regime divine authority.

"You see, before that the emperors became gods because they were greater than other humans and did things that were so superhuman that they seemed divine and so, as happened with the greatest of humans, they were accepted into the ranks of gods. I mean, just think of the escapades of a Julius Caesar or an Augustus or a Mark Anthony and Cleopatra. Or Alexander the Great; now there's a guy who did well! Or at least until he didn't!" With that, Lace giggled lightly. "They seem superhuman to us even now. What Constantine needed was to have his authority reinforced here on Earth to give him authority in a failing empire. Christianity, at least as he created it, taught that Constantine's government was the earthly extension of heavenly government. So much for the sanctity of Christianity as a religion. It was a ploy to tame the masses from the start. Not the opiate, as Marx says, so much as fluoride in the water."

Lace took another drink of his martini and wiped his mouth off with a napkin. He swirled his tongue over the new bridgework. He wasn't used to it yet.

"I do get started, you know. It's just that sitting around that store gives me plenty of time to read and precious few people to discuss it all with."

"But I certainly don't understand how a ploy to tame the masses is currently soothing your torn and shattered soul because it has turned from cant into ancient ritual. Isn't that transubstantiation?"

"You're toying with me again, but I forgive you." Lace winked at his old friend. "What I'm coming to is something like this: Dionysus is a deeper model of an elemental human drive, deeper somehow than the Christ that replaces him, more attached to the real human soul. These are truly ancient psychological themes, honey. Ancient. Ancient. More ancient than Christianity, that's for sure. It's just that Christianity touches on something ancient, and sacred. I'm not sure exactly what makes up the sacred, whatever those things are they have something to do with what makes us human. I suspect that…probably there's no objective definition of it…for you, a sort of Dionysian frenzied sex has elements of what we experience as sacred. I'm not sure what the sacred elements are, to be sure, but I do suppose they touch on the most hidden parts of our psyche. Certainly, for the Greeks, Dionysus was something like Freud's Id, whereas Apollo, god of sculpture and order, for instance, would be analogous to the Ego. And think of something else. Dionysus was torn apart and scattered, I think. Mutilated, but he rose again. The rites were always frenzied. Resulted in animals, maybe humans too, being torn apart. That's in prehistoric Greece, Minoan times maybe, but anyway he went to Hades and rose again and saved us all through regeneration. I think he makes vegetables grow, too. Think of compost! But anyway, it all has to do with those innermost drives that have to be controlled by learning, society, civilization…The Id is mutilated, scattered and goes underground, but that is the creative force when all is said and done. Perhaps the sacred deals with things like that. These are still concepts that fascinate the therapists, but that doesn't mean that the ancients didn't understand them, perhaps better than we do. And deal with them better, too."

Lace shot a quizzical look, afraid he'd gone on too long. The fettuccini arrived along with Agnes' lamb shank.

Lace speared a pea and said, "If Dionysus is a harvest deity, he's responsible for these too." He tasted it and looked upwards for a second. "Thanks be to you, Dionysus." Then he glanced down at the floor. "Or maybe you're down there, old fellow. Where the growing takes place. Anyway, the celebration of the mass goes further back and deeper than Christ and the Nicene Council. It celebrates something primeval in humans. Of course, the mass on the level of what takes place goes back to Roman court ritual, but on some level the mystery extends back to the Dionysian rites. I don't know exactly what that is, but I feel it, just these days lately, but I feel it."

"Well, with all you say, the thing that the ancients got right was the feminine side of nature: Isis, Astarte, the mothering goddess of creation. Where is that in Christianity? And if you're seeking something primal, something like your poetry used to talk about when it was at its best, then don't you need the other side of the mystical coin? Where is the Yin to your Yang?"

"At least the Episcopalians haven't forgotten the Virgin Mary!"

"Oh, Lace, don't talk to me about the blessed mother! I do have something to say about how Christian theology treats women! I know, I know! Mary is supposed to be the mother goddess, sort of anyway, and the perfect woman by some kind of standard, but by my stars, she's a sort of bimbo; why she's nothing more than a man's ideal of a loving, willing slave. Where is the lusty, sexual woman in the idea of Mary Magdalene, or in any of the Saints for that matter? Can you find me a real woman portrayed positively anywhere in Christianity? Mary is impregnated by God, without her consent, and deems it a favor?! Gimme a break. Some female fertility goddess! She comes across sounding more like a simpering rape victim. All well and good to beg the almighty father on behalf of humans, but she doesn't have any real power in and of herself. All very convenient for the men, to be sure."

"I can't disagree with all of that. Still, if one is searching for something out there it's better than those Protestants or Muslims who only have a father figure, and a stern one at that, as if women count for nothing at all in this world. At any rate, while I see your point, the church services address only a part of what I'm looking for. A continuum, I suppose, and a long history of intellectual and moral teaching. But those old mysteries of birth and rebirth, regeneration… you know, the endless cycle of creation, maybe it's created a subconscious sense of itself that our DNA has replicated millions of times reaching billions of years into the past. And it's that thing, it feels like it's in the DNA after all that almost compels me to look at how the ancient pagans looked at things, to explore the Mass, to ponder my navel, dearest one." He tapped his knife twice on the edge of his plate and then pointed it at Agnes with a clever grin.

"I think you're still writing poetry about wombs and gore. Tell me true, darling. You're still writing poetry in your closet, aren't you? Or are you doing it on a Louis Seize bureau plat in that fancy store of yours?"

"I'm not writing about it, my dear. I suppose I'm trying to live it. In fact, there's an eighteenth-century bureau plat with ormolu heads of Dionysus as mountings, so just try to get away from the ancient gods, sweetheart. But really, I'm old enough to feel bound together by tight wire and I can't get loose. Barbed wire, sometimes. And, you know, I've watched people grow old and they go back to their old religions and they become fearful. You watch and you just know that they don't want to make the final mistake. They've been told ever since they were children that they'd go to hell and here they see the end approaching and, well, there's that hell thing. So they take the safest road."

"That's not what you're doing, though."

"Hell, no! I'm looking for religious ecstasy. St. Teresa of Avila, getting pierced by Christ, white-hot sort of ecstasy. And I sure as hell don't see that I need salvation. From what?" Lace cocked his head and looked for a moment like he was going to throw a hat into the sky. "I don't know, Agnes. I just want to break out of a mold and I don't know how. I'm not even sure what the mold is."

After that, there was a long silence and when one, or perhaps the other, said something it was unremarkable so that the subject changed to light topics. They talked for a time about nothing much, split the check and went out into the bright Sunday mid-afternoon and walked towards Washington Square where New York University students played bongos and danced in groups and acrobats danced in the sun and beggars asked for small change from anyone passing by. Couples young and middle-aged made out on the grass. Soft and under their breath, young men asked if Agnes or Lace wanted "smoke? Smoke? I've got great smoke." The two of them walked arm in arm, exulting in the mere crush of humans, lying akimbo, scattered helter-skelter across the park landscape of tall summer sycamores, oaks and silky grass.

Finally Agnes said, "You know, Lace, I do know something of what you mean. A woman feels justified by someone wanting her too, you know."

"You mean about Willy being in demand?"

"Yeah, sort of. We'll call her Wendy. Wendy needs to be in demand too. Sleeping around makes me feel wanted, it's true, and I'm not sure I want to be locked in like those people." She waved her arm in a motion that included the student lovers intertwined on the grass. "No, I'm sure I don't want that, but I'd like someone to stay around for a while, after all. Then, I suppose, I'd feel validated because they'd like me as well as my being a great piece of ass, or whatever. Do you think I'm getting ready for the lover thing?"

Lace didn't answer right away. He just squeezed Agnes' arm and smiled at her. After they had walked away in silence, he said, "You'd be robbing the town of an easy lay."

"Well, that's one reason not to get tied down. Got to think of the public weal, after all."

As the day passed into early evening, Lace and Agnes saw Anne Rose and her aunt and uncle passing across the street about a block up.

"What were their names?" Lace thought to himself.

Anne Rose was dancing a little step and seemed to be singing. He could see that her cart was partially loaded. Uncle what's-his-name was carrying a few items and as they walked together, they all laughed. Then the aunt bent down to scoop something up off the street, which she gave to Anne Rose. Anne clutched it to her heart like a little girl and placed it neatly into her carriage. Auntie, the one he'd had coffee with those years back, took her husband's hand as they walked. Lace held Agnes close and hugged her tight, shoulder to shoulder.

"What was that sudden affection all about, Lacy dear?"

"I don't know, Agnes, but all of a sudden, I felt very happy. Very happy indeed."

CHAPTER XVI

Who on earth could possibly gather together the strands of what made Jonathan do what he did? Rennie Rodriguez was an honorable man, even a good one. And yet with no malice of purpose, believing only in his principles and doing what he must have been driven to do, he helped spin a thread that led as surely and steadily to that awful night as a straight highway leads out of rolling hills down to the central metropolis.

His church and its little band of exotic brown ladies reached out into their community of lost people, men mostly, who were hopelessly enslaved to drink or sometimes drugs. They came into the warm from living in boxes and in from the sleet and rain, smelling of shit and urine. In the doorways, they mated like dogs, oblivious to who or what they were screwing. To know them was to discover that they weren't gay or closeted homosexuals. They were simply blind with intoxication and they acted out their carnal impulses blindly, without eyes to see. But passers-by could see them sometimes. Naked and masturbating, not knowing where they were, they stared out at you with eyes that were blank and dark. What inner world did they inhabit? People stopped and stared and then moved on, but these tortured men returned the stare and saw nothing as they stooped to shit, or pissed on themselves and trickled onto the street or sucked each other off in the dark shadows and the vacant lots south of Houston Street and east of Elizabeth.

But Pastor Rennie worked among these men, giving them coffee and, in time as his ministry grew, he was able to give them a little food besides donuts. He trained his women to refer these men to social agencies and public services.

And so Rennie's church grew in stature and in good works; he hoped to make a difference in this awful place. Indeed, Rennie was a good man and fulfilled, he hoped, the confidence his Christ placed in him. When the vagrants awoke from their slumbers, the long drunken slumbers from which they remembered only vaguely what private things they had done in public and they began to wonder what had become of them and how they could possibly atone for their shame, they came to Pastor Rennie and, in God's name, he forgave them. That was something, at least. They left the little Church of God's Righteousness forgiven to live into another day.

Jonathan worked with the pastor for over a year and a half. He became a part of the congregation. He was helpful. The women loved him. They would do anything for him, brought him rice and beans and chicken and rice and lasagna. He was grateful. Took it all home and told them how good it all was next time he saw them.

At the same time, Jonathan did his gigs with Mistress Carbonoy and after that year and a half, he began to collect some of the fetish magazines that were beginning to come out in those days. He wrote to some post office box addresses listed among the ads and found out about various clubs—whipping clubs, incest clubs, clubs that swapped wives, stories, satanic ritual clubs—all extreme sex clubs. He was becoming fascinated and he frequented the West Side Highway and 42nd Street and he picked up easy money. The demons went away for a while. He didn't ask questions. Pastor Rennie didn't go on about sex. What for, on the Bowery? Drink, not sex, was the problem here. Everything else stemmed from that.

Then one night he did a gig for the redheaded dominatrix uptown and met this guy who introduced him to free-basing. There they had been that night, both blindfolded. The other guy bound, gagged, blindfolded, you name it. The memory of that strange scene stayed with him, like the light taste of the cocaine smoke itself, filling his lungs with its buzzing aroma. Whoever was making it with them kept shoving the free-base pipe at them; made them smoke the cocaine. It surprised him. It had almost no taste; just a tinge of a fishy odor. A little oily. Again and again they made him take a hit. He began to black out, fade in and out, and little by little he began to see through the blindfolds into another world. It was odd. He couldn't explain it and never tried. Not to anyone. But there he lay as someone was fondling him and suddenly he saw out of and away from the darkness of his blindfold into another world with another boy standing naked, without a blindfold, beside him. As he remembered it now, the boy looked at him knowingly and nodded. The memory of that evening came back to him often, a sort of constant companion, and when he toyed with those images in his head, he remembered that it was that boy, whom he had never met before their session together, who had appeared in his vision as clear as day. He knew that because although he'd never seen the boy before, he knew exactly who he was when he appeared on the street afterwards and after that they had lived together for a while. It was that boy, all right. Sure as shoot'n.

It hadn't impressed him at the time, but one part of that memory now seemed remarkably mysterious. In that phantasmic vision, just before the boy entered imaginary space, just before they inhabited that floating room, together, for a period of time that he couldn't measure, a high-pitched buzz began to sound in his ear. It was metallic in tone. Then it died away, but it came back when a man walked in from an empty door behind the boy and smiled at them both. The man was nondescript. Jonathan couldn't describe him now, but it must have happened just before that kid had become just a floating head, before the scene stopped and shredded into those skittering still frames. The man stepped out of that door into a room in his mind, smiled with his teeth bared into a wicked smile, his cold eyes leering at him and the boy naked beside him, and then he stepped back into the door. In an instant he was gone, Jonathan found himself back in darkness with a woman licking him. Hovering just out of touch was the red-haired prostitute who put it all together along with the cocoon-like boy.

Those were the separated actions that he remembered now, seared against the back of his mind. Jonathan was hooked, obsessed with finding answers to unanswered questions. Where did that door go? Who was that man? And the high-pitched buzzing sound. Did that have anything to do with the messengers who slipped into and out of his visions? The episode, with its strange and intangible experiences, became mixed with those assembled and hard memories of real things that he trusted in his mind to be absolute and solid, like dinner and hailing a taxicab the night before last. It had been too real to fade back into memory and it seemed too solid to have been a mere hallucination.

From the boy he learned how to buy, cook and smoke the precious cocaine. They smoked and screwed obsessively, but Jonathan made it into Rennie's church still and did what he had always done. It seemed to him that he continued doing the church chores just as he had always done and he basked, as always, in the love of his church family. At home, though, he began a collection of sex videos. Some of them he purchased homemade from private sources through his specialty clubs and these showed exotic scenes that were not for the faint of heart. He and his boy watched them all night, inhaling the white magic smoke and waiting for the high, white metallic sound, the herald of beings from the other side of what they came to experience as some kind of dimensional divide.

The boy told Jonathan about his theories, which made sense under these new circumstances. Who can ever know whether Jonathan, having heard about creatures out of the beyond from books and this half-mad creature of a boy, had really begun to make them up in his own mind? He had been reading about the occult, after all, on his own and he had become acquainted with texts that described how to conjure up spirits. Before, he had regarded those things as Satanism, the lore of an enemy whose ways he needed to learn. Then, from the time that nondescript man stepped out of a doorway just as someone was licking the back of his body, he sought an explanation for these new experiences, for the visions continued. That he was sure he'd seen the boy before meeting him on the street was a kind of proof that special information was being fed to him, but as time passed what he thought about most was the knowing smile that that man had given him and the high-pitched tone that seemed to announce his coming.

But because he also knew that he was the special one, first to his mother, then to god, he also began to suspect that the spirits of these phantasma came from that divine being who was neither good nor evil but all things in one.

As he became more and more fascinated, Jonathan's life began to revolve around the metallic sound, which did seem to repeat itself whenever the various creatures that he met stepped into his consciousness out of some void. And they were a varied lot. The first was that perfectly normal man, but later as he continued smoking the white vapor there were great demons, giants who were hairy and hoary with great white teeth and long nails. There was a beautiful woman with great gray eyes, like Athena, he thought, although only her head appeared, huge in his living room like a great stone Toltec head. And there were radiant creatures bathed in light and covered with feathers that shimmered and looked like the rainbows that light reflects when it shines, refracted into oily water.

How much of their separate hallucinations the two young men shared is anyone's guess. Some of them Jonathan only remembered later on. They didn't talk much when they smoked; they writhed in a sort of limp sexual epiphany that never quite reached climax. They argued a lot, after a while, over jealousies and drugs. The boy moved on and Jonathan spent more time again at Rennie's Church.

At the same time, Jonathan made trip after trip over to the occult and magic bookstore near Sixth Avenue. He wanted to see whether any of the creatures that rode across space and time on the high pitch of his white smoky dreams were listed in the occult materials that he found there. Then one day, looking through a book on Mayan magic and ritual, he came across a frieze from a temple and there he found the God of Death. The God surrounded by skulls. The God that drank blood, sometimes referred to simply as "God L" by the archaeologists. But whatever scientists may make of this deity in their scholarly papers today, centuries ago someone had painted a wall fresco of a creature. Perhaps the one that had appeared to him in the night.

So, Jonathan had found a name, finally, for a creature from the beyond, but who knows what he really found? One would say, rather, that his mind made it all up and he found something similar to one of his hallucinations in that reference book on Mayan magic. Perhaps the Mayans, too, smoked cocaine and because the drug did similar things to the axons and synaptic nerves of the Mayan priests, the peculiar mix of drugs, serotonin and electronic impulses fired by a particular pharmacopoeia created the same dreams for them as well. Perhaps there are deep human memories from the reptilian past buried in our brain that come out of all of us as hallucinations when they are released by these exotic, subtle and treacherous substances. Perhaps, as Jonathan thought, he had at last been approached by divine beings from the other side. Perhaps they were all from one, supreme power that was trying to reach out to him. Is it possible that this is the way that they communicated? Was this the secret of the sages? Perhaps even Christ Jesus himself understood this, receiving his divine transmissions in an altered state from the almighty father who was greater than good and evil, from he who combined happiness and despair and whose ways are ever unknowable and who, could he not, communicate through this divine white smoke, the white wind of the Holy Ghost himself, and make a conduit through the high pitched buzz so that his emissaries could enter into this lower world.

But how was Pastor Rennie to know anything of all this? Even so, one cold Sunday morning late in the winter he began to preach in his usual way. Pastor Rennie's way was to begin in a quiet voice and build, like a black Baptist preacher. He would walk out into his flock, turning first to one person and then another. As the morning went on, he would rise in measured cadences, rolling like waves across his flock, first soft, then hard and angry, then withdrawn and then again forceful and strong.

Cajoling one, he might say, "Now, Manuel, you have sinned again. Haven't you Manuel? Your wife loves you, but you've left her and your family again. Run away from this demon, Manuel. You have fallen again, but God loves you still. Pray to Jesus, with us, William. Pray to him with us." Rennie would place his hand against Manuel's head and pray to have his devils removed. Sometimes the man would faint, having been struck dumb by the hand of God.

Then again, Rennie could be more severe, spittle growing on the side of his mouth. He would take a man by his shoulder and shake him and say, "This man is taking the wide way to hell. Beware of the wide way. The Lord demands harder things. You have been seen fornicating. You will not give up drink. My man, you are lost without Jesus. My man, you are lost without Jesus and you are prideful, filled with the demons of hell."

Then Rennie would look upwards and cry out to the devils inside these bewitched men. "I command you in the name of Jesus to come out of this man. You must leave this man alone, now. Now!" And again at a feverish pitch, "Now!"

Rennie would shake a man by the shoulders, shaking the booze breath straight out of his lungs and banging him on the head until his eyes shown bright and fearful of the Lord's minister and maybe even the gates of hell itself. He would cast his face close to the man's, bearing his gaze down into the eyes of this lost soul and piercing down into the recesses of a man's madness to retrieve what was left of who he had once been and bring him back in "Jesus' name, Amen." White spit spun off Rennie's face like the tops of waves in a high wind, flaking away to splatter these vagrant faces and wake them to God's mercy.

This Sunday, Pastor Rennie waded through his congregation, the women watching as usual, prayerful. He laid hands on a young man who had been out on a binge, but was still wearing the good clothing he had gone to work with a week earlier before he disappeared into an uncontrollable mist of booze. He bent down over an older man and shook the demons out of him, crying out to God and Jesus to drive the devils out. Again and again, he shouted out to the demons, in the name of beloved Jesus, to leave this poor body and return no more. He commanded them in Christ's name. They were chained and gagged by the precious blood of dear Jesus. They were prohibited from returning.

Then surprisingly, unaccountably, Pastor Rennie turned upon Jonathan. The pastor's eyes had rolled back in his head, as if they saw something that was not in the room with them at all. The white spittle had grown against his cheek, it gathered from whirling, combustible clouds into a growing storm. It swirled like rain puddles under the feet of charging horses. The spit shot out of him in jets as the rising and falling jetties of his speech called upon God to wreak vengeance upon His enemies of good in the world, called upon God and his warrior Son to decimate the forces of Satan and the denizens of hell. He turned upon Jonathan and called upon God's powers to eviscerate the forces of hell that lay like a poison in the very midst of this precious flock. He called upon the savior not to save poor Jonathan, but to rid his vulnerable church of the demon that had made its way into their very heart.

Jonathan's stomach turned and he felt sick as his face turned white and then red with horror. Sweat gathered on his palms. What was going on? Was Rennie Rodriguez possessed?

"The Lord has told me that you have stored the instruments of Satan away in your home," the minister thundered. "He has whispered in my ear that you have turned against him…and against me! Turned away from his grace. The Lord's word says that the only sin that cannot be redeemed, even by the savior's blood, is blaspheming against the Holy Spirit. You have blasphemed. There is no saving you, Jonathan Perry. You are beyond our help here. You are beyond God's grace. You are beyond redemption, cast away from communication with God. Get you gone, instrument of evil. Get you gone."

The pastor seemed to be acting according to some unseen force, for with that, Rennie shook an astonished Jonathan by the shoulder, picked him up and pushed him towards the door. The elderly women of his flock gasped. They held each other's hands and looked at one another, imploringly. What were they to do? What could they do? Pastor Rennie had been talking to God and he knew best. What sadness. What a look of sadness and mortification came over that poor boy's face. What a lost look, a hopeless look as he was ejected into a light snow onto Houston Street.

How did Pastor Rennie know what might have been in Jonathan's apartment? Is it possible that a voice told him about the implements for smoking and cooking cocaine, the fetish magazines and videos and the books on the occult? He used the skills of an investigator to stay informed about his flock, it is true, but it is equally possible that Jonathan was acting strangely and Rennie knew by instinct what the glazed look in his eyes meant. After all, Rennie did not act by reason, but by faith and feeling. He sensed like a cat hunting in the dark, sensed what Jonathan was doing late at night because he had spent so many years among drugs and alcohol, seeing them abused on the streets, watching them stalk the people of his flock like fetid monsters, destroying the life of the community and the men who fucked in doorways and pissed against the walls of stairways as the dear women from his small congregation went up and down those stairs to their tenement homes and tried to avoid the yellow steaming streams of urine and the wickedly unpleasant smells. Perhaps he was trying to protect his little community from the rotting erosion of broken bottles and used syringes that littered the streets just off East Houston on the way to Elizabeth Street.

Whatever the pastor's good intent, Jonathan was ejected that early Sunday out of the only family he knew for reasons that mystified him. He feared that God had really told Pastor Rennie about his secret life. There could be only a couple of reasons for this. It could be that, as he had come to suspect, God and Satan were indeed one entity and he was being faced at the moment by the random consequences of God's meaner side. It was also possible that he was being moved on to do God's work. He was being moved out of Rennie's family because God required actions that went beyond good and evil and

Rennie did not understand this. The pastor's work for the Lord did not require great understanding, the understanding of great things that was required of a lone warrior for God who was an advocate for humankind and a general against Satan's hordes. But then again, if Satan and God were the same being, perhaps he was a general advocate on behalf of humans in God's court. Wasn't this the explanation for Jesus' death? Why did God demand a human sacrifice, the sacrifice of his son made human? It was because humankind required an appointed advocate before the thunderous and mighty, the irrational ever-changing and terrible face of a God who was sometimes a God of love and sometimes a God of wrath, who turned first one face and then another towards humankind, endless into eternity, without reason and without rhyme. Jonathan was the next in a line of such advocates, those appointed to intercede for mankind before the great blue and sparkling throne of the Almighty.

And if he was to be forced into solitude, cut off from the very humankind he was to save in order to meet his terrible fate, so be it.

These were the terrible ideas that formed in his head as he remembered how he been special since boyhood, alone, special and pampered by his mother as he lay alone in his bed and she cried out to her men to fuck her, moaning without ceasing far into the morning hours. As Jonathan muddled over these possibilities in his mind, he knew this with increasing certainty: creatures from beyond space and time were prodding him. They had combined to move him in a certain direction and towards uncertain goals, which only they knew. However the great wheels of fate worked, the path through them had now closed down to one narrow way, as narrow as the eye of a needle. Jonathan had no way to go but to follow the creatures that were clearing a path before him. He was utterly alone among unsuspecting and unaware humans in his journey towards greatness.

CHAPTER XVII

A nne Rose began to work with the other ladies at Our Lady of Pompeii. They folded her into their activities. Flo Finelli got her a little job, helping make phone calls and arranging bazaars. More and more, Anne Rose would give small items to the church for rummage sales and sometimes she would buy cookies baked at the Italian bakeries that lined Bleecker Street and donate them when the ladies set up tables along Sixth Avenue. Her duties were light, but the work gave her structure and she had less time to wander the streets. Her weight did not change, but she didn't get heavier.

Nonetheless, around the virgin on the chipped art deco enamel dinette, the small court of retainers continued to grow into a crowd of devout worshippers. There she added frogs and a knight and bishop carved from Mexican agate from a tourist's chess set. In the corner beside the milk can containing broken umbrellas, the *New York Times* magazines had been doubled at the base so that they could continue their tall ascent towards the ceiling. Sitting nearer her long kitchen, the refrigerator, stove and sink in a row along the wall, was a new card table with a slightly dented top where someone had pushed downward too hard. On that table sat a multicolored ashtray about eighteen inches wide filled with marbles, potpourri and shiny bulbs that Anne Rose had found on a Christmas tree thrown out last February.

One Sunday, after early Mass, Anne Rose took an elongated path down Sixth Avenue onto King Street and there on the brownstone banister of the stairs up into the entryway of a building, stacked one atop the other, were six books. There were two books of no particular interest to her, a paperback of Christopher Isherwood and one of *Justine,* and two books that were cheap romances. But of the other two, one was entitled *A General Survey of Psychical Phenomena* and the other was *Mythology of Mezzo America.* These two books she placed under her massive arm and took back to MacDougal Street where she placed them on the table next to the sparkling, multicolored glass ashtray filled with the colorful objects that so delighted her.

Then, Anne Rose readied herself to step in and spell a few of the ladies at church who were running a bazaar, pausing to gaze at the moving shadows that played across her possessions. The sun had reached its zenith for the day and the brushwork of sunlight through her windows was just about right. Her days had rhythms and she always knew from the shadows and the light when it was time, as if her life were played out on the surface of a sundial. Anne Rose had decided to take the two books as a gift to Our Lady of Pompeii's rummage table. Meanwhile, she washed herself out of a chipped, enamel basin in a leisurely way. Long ago, the plumbing in her apartment had ceased to work well. It sometimes scalded her when she took a shower, so she sponged herself out of a bed pan that appeared one day, thrown out with the belongings of the man with a nice smile who had lived just one block over and who had died last year. Sponging herself gave her freedom to walk about her home and inspect her massive heap of belongings. They gave her a kind of pride of ownership, like a pirate reviewing jewels and doubloons that would never be spent. She could imagine running her hands through a buccaneer's chest of treasure, just like the movies, and her mind wandered, briefly to films she had seen. How long it had been since she'd gone to one! "I'd like to go sometime," she thought vaguely, but then the thought of treasure returned and with it the tactile sense of sifting through mounds of precious stones, red and blue and green, and the golden touch of old coins and necklace chains entranced her. As she massaged herself with the dimpled, round loofah, she became entranced by the voluptuousness of it. Her other hand sifted through the tepid water in the bowl, like an oar, stroking. In her imagination, her hands dipped into a liquid treasure chest with a slow, clockwork, circular motion, and as she daydreamed, she stroked her breasts and the furry interior of her legs with the same motion, the sponge pressed hard against her body's surfaces as she slowly and deliberately cleansed those erotic and tender tissues that hummed under the gnarled surface of her large round body with its soft, deep pits and crevices.

Anne Rose's mind seemed to leave her as she became transfixed by the rhythmic motion of her hand and a pulsating sensation built up inside the deep folds hidden within her legs. She drifted away into some kind of dream, down red ladders and velvet ramps where her multi-colored emeralds and rubies lay spread all about until she ventured onto a hidden subterranean lake, where she dreamt herself to be a Victorian lady dressed in Lincoln green velvet, adrift alone in a wooden boat, her fingers plunging into syrupy, silent waters. She stroked the roiling waters in her enamel bowl silently, hearing the drops of water slide from her fingertips and feeling the ripples of excitement extend out along her legs, building intensity as the tiny waves sparkled with growing frequency.

Behind the boat, water swirled as it drifted, first slowly and then faster. The water whirled more violently as her fingers propelled the bark towards an inlet hidden behind a spike of land, where she could not see. From just out of sight, behind the hills that sloped down to water's edge and hid the inlet, came a noise, at first the noise of a waterfall, but then it became a hammering noise that she couldn't distinguish. Was it out of place? The notes came at her insistently, not like the rush of water at all but some sound that didn't belong at the bottom of red ladders and velvet ramps at all. The thundering was not water; her eyes opened slowly.

Suddenly, there was a knock at the door and she jolted upward out of her reverie. The sun had shifted along its orbit, sending streams of the old, ochre luminescence brushing against the virgin's cowl, marking her blue warmth and touching softly against the chips and scrapes that did not show in every light. Anne Rose awoke from her distant cavern of thought and emerged from the deep lake to realize that Veronica was supposed to meet her today and accompany her to a bazaar. They were to help sell from behind one of the tables. Veronica was now banging insistently against the metal apartment door.

Anne Rose quickly threw aside the sponge and grabbed a robe that her mother had given her last Christmas, a cotton flower pattern against gray from one of the 14th Street stores. She had tried to keep it clean, but it did not wear well. It was cheap and took on the gray tint of cheap clothes. But it was from her mother, who had sent it through Veronica and Michael. Her mother had not come last Christmas, claiming ill-health. Her brother and his family kept her mother away and she let them. Anne Rose knew that her mother would have come had she been allowed and so the robe took on a precious quality, the tangible evidence of her mother's love.

Veronica was at the door as Anne Rose opened it. "That landlord of yours has to do something about locking the outer door. Can you speak to him about it? Hello, honey," she said in breathless haste.

"Lacy Whitaker has told them a thousand times," Anne Rose retorted, brushing off Veronica's demand with an impatient flick of her hand. She raised her eyebrow as if to say, "What can I do about it?

"Look." She touched the two books.

Veronica picked up each one, shifting and turning the volumes in her hands, studying them. She leafed briefly through *A General Survey of Psychical Phenomena* and put it aside. *Mythology of Mezzo America* she looked at carefully examining several color plates carefully. "This is nice. Where did you find it?"

"Around. I took a walk around after mass this morning. People leave such things behind, auntie. Can you ever believe it?"

"Did you look through it? The pictures are very good."

"No, auntie. No time. I wanted to be ready for you," Anne Rose lied to please.

Anne Rose stepped into the bedroom and put on a loose blue dress with lace trim. At the hem, the lace had come loose and dragged a bit. Here and there, the dress was discolored, but even with the spots it was clear to Veronica that Anne Rose was making an attempt to keep her clothes cleaner.

"You are a trooper, Anne Rose. I don't know how I'd keep my clothes clean without a washing machine in the house. How you get them to the Laundromat and get them back I'll never know."

It had taken a long while, but Veronica and Michael had come to understand the comings and goings of Anne Rose's life. "How different," it occurred to her, "my suburban life is from a city dweller's…and what a long road it's been to understand the differences."

For Veronica, whose life had been spent raising children, the mechanics of errands were tied to car pools and station wagons and wound in between football and basketball games and then darting into the city for her classes. After that, for a decade now she had driven each morning to work in the school system. At first she did not understand the rhythms of city life, taking dirty clothes to the laundry to be done and folded, picking it up in the afternoon, buying just enough food for each day and carrying food home long blocks from a grocery store rather than loading bags into a car. These alien habits, the methodology of day-to-day living for an urbanite, took time for Veronica to uncover and decode. Getting to know her niece, after she and Michael finally thought to pay attention, had been like an anthropologist studying a tribe of people indigenous to a remote region. There were patterns imposed upon Anne Rose by her surroundings. Unlike Veronica who was cloistered alone in a car as she did her daily errands, Anne Rose chatted with perhaps a dozen people every day as she made her rounds around the neighborhood, tracing and retracing the same pathways to gather up people's castaways. She made a myriad of acquaintances from walking about, buying groceries, taking out the laundry, going to her rummage sales and these patterns repeated themselves again and again until they became a kind of tribal ritual.

"I'm ready now." Anne Rose had touched up her face with a little blush and some eyeliner; a new and hopeful sign, Veronica thought. And indeed, the sun was drifting a little lower and showed now the rose blush of the virgin's cheek, casting long shadows among the tributary court of knights and bishops, frogs and angels. She took up the two books.

"I'll take these for the sale." The plates of friezes found in Central American temples were very good indeed. She was becoming proud of her ability to draw odd and interesting items into her realm and, if she chose, to pass them back out into the world, value added by her peculiar tastes.

They walked in silence the short distance to join Flo Finelli at one of the tables where the women from Our Lady sat together. Some tables were laid out with pieces of cut glass, bowls, cups and ceramics. Others contained knit wears from various places in South America, hats, sweaters and scarves that looked to be from somewhere in the Andes. At the spot, where the three women sat together, were many pieces found over the past months by Anne Rose and the three had even talked amongst themselves of setting up a flea market table at one of the local weekend fairs. Was it possible? Little by little Anne Rose had begun to develop an eye for the castoff. Bit by bit, the colors and qualities of these old items had an adopted allure that might even be saleable. The women discussed these and other matters and had begun to joke a little about the tiny, new priest recently assigned to Our Lady, when their animated talk was interrupted by the slow interruption of a man with sandy blond hair and a moustache that barely covered a gap between his teeth.

Jonathan was walking past the tables when his eye landed on the books' titles. Veronica noticed him first. His jeans were not skin-tight, but they were worn tight enough to show the contours of his body and ripped with the air of a man who is used to attracting others for sex. To Veronica, he was a city creature, lithe, urban and dangerous. She was instantly aware of him as Anne Rose and Flo continued their conversation unhindered.

Jonathan looked slowly through Anne Rose's two books. He read intently from a few pages of *A General Survey of Psychical Phenomena* and put under it under his arm. As he opened *Mythology of Mezzo America,* a subtle, startled expression came over his face. His eye narrowed and he took in a short breath and then he asked, "How much for these?"

Oddly, although it was Veronica who noticed him, he fixed his long look at Anne Rose, ignoring Veronica and Flo as if he only expected Anne Rose to reply even though she was caught up in her conversation. Yet it was Veronica, who was silently alert and aware of his presence and so there was every reason to address the question to her, but Jonathan's eye darted directly from the two books to Anne Rose as if the other two women were not present.

Even so, Veronica replied, "Five dollars each." Her voice ran colder than she expected.

Jonathan looked abruptly at her as if he had been pulled away from a deep sleep, interrupted from a private reverie of his own. His eyes were vacant, but Veronica felt that she had intruded upon him. Oddly, her hands felt cold. She shifted her folding chair, planting it firmly in place, staking a spot on the ground and rubbing her palms together. Then she leaned forward and squared herself directly against Jonathan.

"Do you want them or not?" she asked.

Jonathan stooped over, hunching his shoulders as he rummaged around in his pockets, extracted ten dollars and handed the crumpled bill over to Veronica. He took the two books and turned away to walk down the street, but not after his eyes had deliberated once again and too long on Anne Rose.

CHAPTER XVIII

Cizin, great god of earthquake and death, ancient king of Mitnal and Xibalba, that terrible subterranean land of death and the most horrible of nine hells for the peoples of Central America, lay sleeping and forgotten in the dry dust of his majestic caverns. He had other names too, depending on the expanded tribes who prayed to his various names. The Toltecs, Mayans and Aztecs variously called him Ahpunc or Ahpuch or Yum Cimil. As he slumbered, put away in some place hidden from our notions of space and time, he dreamt of that faraway epoch when he had once been a mighty deity to generations. They, out of respect for his bloodthirsty appetite, slaughtered a million human beings, ripping their hearts from living bodies with black obsidian blades.

To a god such as Cizin, life stretches in cycles measured over millions of years. His other self, his mirror self was Chac-Tlaloc, god of rain, god of sustenance, that kindly enemy and lover, brother, mate and nemesis. Chac the creator and opposite, bringer forth of life, whom he had not seen in a thousand years, was the missing piece, the hole ripped from his very essence. Buried deep underneath the inchoate consciousness of humans, he lay unwanted and unknown, driven out by those marauding Spaniards and invading priests who had superimposed their own god and cosmology over his noble race of warriors. Cizin stirred from his sleep, lonely and alone.

He remembered the old days. It was Chac who had given life and sustenance each season and, with each cycle, balanced the chaos let loose by the great underworld lord, Cizin. Without Chac to dance rain upon the land, without Chac who made human life itself possible, Cizin, lord of the ninth-most center of hell itself, he who had demanded the devotion and debased fear of three civilizations and ten million men, this molder of molten souls, ravenous devourer of living hearts, whose hymns were sung in the name of Cizin, Yum Cimil, and Alpunc, was nothing but dust, asleep on the floor of his dark red kingdom somewhere beneath but still, outside, the green contours of this earth. Without his divine brother and lord Chac to create life, Cizin's world had died, leaving him alone and only half alive. How, he wondered, could the world survive without someone to stir the pot and bring disorder to the world? From chaos were all things made new. This is how the very core of creative energy came to be. He remembered his power to destroy and smiled to himself. Was there no one now to unloose the chords that bind up creation into a solipsistic ball so that life can create itself anew?

Images of his history came to him as he awoke. Something insistent called at him and brought him to consciousness. He dreamt of the old times: at his greatest, he would appear as a bloated corpse, adorned with bells. Sometimes he was represented with the head of an owl on a human body. Even today, Indians of Central America and Mexico believe that someone will die when an owl screeches.

But for the transcendent gods, ages pass as long cycles grind them between proud wheels that travel a relentless trajectory through time. Even as the lives of humans are marked with a shorter cycle of three score and ten years, this once powerful and great God lay forgotten in his cavern, his life measured by the eons of his own cycle, waiting for his own merciful death. But that would not come yet for a long time. Instead, so long as humans exist, he would remain half- asleep, half-awake, now dreaming of his superb past, now descending even further into unreachable dimensions that inhabit recesses of imagination, like someone continually drowning but never dying just below the sea's surface. But to Jonathan, as he struggled for some vague interpretation of what he saw and believed about his extraordinary world, it became clear that there was from this world a silver chord of sound that ties us to distant, dimly experienced and otherworldly dimensions. To him those far worlds were real places lying further from our senses than theoretical physicists can suspect and closer to touch than our own skin.

And so it was that one night around three o'clock in the morning Eastern Standard Time, Cizin Ahpunc Ahpuch, great god of earthquake and death, ruler of the dead, lay sleeping and forgotten in the dry dust of Mitnal, land of death and the most horrible of nine hells. It was at 3:00 in the morning Eastern Standard Time that he was awakened by a high, pitched buzzing in the air around him. He had called out to men, commanding them to adore the name Cizil, Yum Cimil, called to them for devotion and sacrifice, but now he was himself being called. For a mighty God, even this lord of the hidden reptilian remnants of our mind, when a human cries out from the innermost, chthonian chambers of his heart, it is an elixir not to be despised.

When humankind seeks such a god, the call takes a form that cannot be ignored. Around such a divine being, who lives just beyond the reach of ordinary perception, the air literally breathes and comes alive with small flecks of earthly desire and longing. What might be, to mortals, the atoms of oxygen and nitrogen, the helixes and wavelengths of electrons or gluons, perhaps the sharp and veering pathway of charmed quarks or the stretched vortexes of Calabi-Yau shapes, these moments of what we call matter become fixed in time and space and begin to buzz. They begin to sing a siren's song. To human ears the buzz sounds like a high-pitched squeak, but an ancient deity knows the call of human imaginings. Such a deity was made to answer the call of human hearts.

Cizin Ahpunc Ahpuch awoke steadily as a singularity developed towards the edges of his realm. The walls of the ninth-most pit of hell began to open up and through it grew, at first merely a recess as if it were a cloak closet dimly lit, but at last through the thin, fine points that maintain a necessary distance between physical dimensions, a winding hallway, like a silken silver thread, opened.

Taking his favorite form as a dancing skeleton, he held to his empty, dark mouth a smoking cigarette and wore around his neck a collar made of disembodied eyes dangling by ribbons of nerve cords. The great god Cizil had not been called for over a thousand years and he would adopt the shape for which he was most feared and venerated. Arising from an ancient and lonely sleep, he made his way into what had grown into a glowing hallway with walls that hummed like the sound of bees in the millions. He followed its shining, bluish corridors, coming finally to the other end where he found himself, at 3:04 in the morning on Elizabeth Street in New York City. As Ahpunc stepped out of the passageway through time and space into a sparse and neat apartment with only a mattress, a trunk and a lamp on the floor and a television set on which played a pornographic video showing three, hairless young men squirming together on a black mat, the great god looked into the eyes of Jonathan Perry. Jonathan Perry stared back for a moment with a longing that struggled to emerge through his narrow blue and vacant eyes. Ahpunc could see in this young man generations of the kind who bowed down low to him and sent to him their very hearts as blood offerings. It was remarkable. Such was the willingness of human beings to appease the very things that torture their souls.

Such a moment of sustained human supplication cannot be held suspended in imagination for long. Indeed, a god dare not suspend the fundamental realities of physics for so long a time. A human cannot suspend them. Ahpunc looked for a moment with longing in his old and ugly heart. He remembered the obsidian sharp rituals of his ancient peoples. They had created and sustained him and his good, kindly brother Chac. How lonely he had become. Lonely and tired. Jonathan gazed back as if to salute an old friend who had suddenly appeared on a receding shore. Then the tunnel between them collapsed and the connection between them was severed.

Jonathan leaned across his mattress to pick another white pebble of cooked cocaine out of a chipped green saucer. Carefully, he placed it into the stem of his glass pipe, lit it with a small propane torch and heard a sizzling sound as the hard substance was transmuted into pure white smoke and made its hungry way into his lungs. But that was all, only the sizzling sound of the burning white coal. He could not bring back the high-pitched sound. The creature that had appeared to him would not return tonight.

The next morning, Jonathan slept late. Around noon he climbed slowly up from the mattress on the floor and pulled on his old jeans. Then he finished off the small kernels of cocaine that were left scattered in the green saucer, so that the jagged edges of his life rounded into smooth curves. He left his apartment and stepped quietly around and around the turns of the stairways from his apartment down onto Elizabeth Street and he floated contentedly past the elderly women of the neighborhood and the bums lying in old newspapers as he made his way to the bookstore near Sixth Avenue.

In such a state, the things that happen to a person seem to achieve a supernatural flow, connecting them to each other so that they no longer seem like mere happenstance. As one event comes upon the next, they seem to merge together into the stream of a pre-ordained story. Perhaps, at these times, imagination punctures some sturdy barrier placed between dimensions and ruptures a natural wall between cause and effect. Perhaps in our saner, more solid world, a cause dissipates before its full effect can be felt. Like subatomic quantum particles, the uncountable possibilities of a particular event may cancel out one another before they bring an effect into being, so that their trajectories through time and space are irretrievably lost. However these things may be, the lines of cause and effect, that ran from his mother's passionate screams in the dark, through Jonathan's life in New York, his rejection by Pastor Rennie, his affair with the young masochist and the appearances of beckoning demons, now converged into a most extraordinary occurrence.

Jonathan made his way, as he often did, to the bookstore near Sixth Avenue and spent no more than thirty minutes there. He enjoyed leafing through the books on magic and the occult and today, at the top of a stack near the front door, was a new compendium on magic and on the glossy cover was a photograph of the Venus of Willendorf.

The picture fascinated Jonathan. Inside the flyleaf there was a general description about the Venus, a Paleolithic statue, one of the earliest ever found made by human hands. The round, armless, almost formless rotund anatomy of this ancient fertility symbol seemed to speak directly to him from across unbroken threads of time. She was fat, earthy and fecund. He read about the magic, female and fertile qualities of this earth-bound Venus, who had been carved of bone by some person sitting beside a campfire, perhaps in a cave, some distant ancestor whose mind must have searched the twinkling bowl of heaven and considered the magical mysteries of how life recreates itself again and again from out of the dark and mysterious folds of women's anatomy and drew a comparison with the endless rebirth of nature from out of the womb of the earth itself. There, in that ancient figurine, lies the earliest expression of any attempt to explain why we are conscious beings and how it is that we perpetuate our kind through the endless cycles of generations.

The book went on. Her powerful hidden and eternal mother-hood was the central worship of these stone-age people who, perhaps, understood better than us the web of life. She incarnated the magic through which human life and spirit were created and, by extension, from her great thighs came the bountiful produce of earth itself. She was the earth. Again and again, in the lore of primitive tribes, it was the Venus or someone like her who was inseminated each year by gods whose powers lie in the sky, lying over the ready and receptive land.

Jonathan was no scholar, but each piece of the knowledge that he was gleaning seemed to fit together into a story. He leaned against the side of the store's back bookcase, reading on, learning about the rotund thighs of this Earth Goddess and how annual rites of harvest have been reenacted by humans since before memory to celebrate and cajole these goddesses so that the magic would not cease, so that human souls and nourishing grains would continue to flourish out of the female deities: inaccessible, dark recesses of the female interior, the humid caverns, the warm earth where the soil was hot, fertile and magical.

These were the mighty and good, the creative forces that a magician sought to harness. He had learned already of the damp fermenting gods like kindly Chac, brother and lover of Cizin, whose glistening rain and powerful, opalescent semen were like white currents of creative energy pitted against those of erosion and chaos. But these forces achieved their power within the folds of women. They required her powers, unseen in the dark like waters that change into wine, mystically hidden away from the sight of man in sealed amphorae. He read that any great magician, any mage whose magic is based on unfolding powers of the cosmos itself, sought to balance these two irreducible forces.

Jonathan thought for a moment of the dominatrix and lingered for a moment over her power over her men. Where was the balance before the throne of God almighty? Where was he, that specially chosen person, who was to redress the balance between creation and chaos? Had an emissary not visited him this very morning around

3:00 am? He knew that the white, powdery substance that anyone could purchase secretly from under the counter of the Borinquen Bodega at the corner of Elizabeth Street, that very same and illegal substance which was, when cooked over a flame with bicarbonate and distilled into hard substance and smoked, what brought to him emissaries from the other side. Bit by bit, they told him a story and step by step seemed to teach him what his special role in the salvation of humankind would be.

And the young man had rounded out the story. God and Satan, Good and Evil, were finally indistinguishable. God was all things and made no distinction. He required sacrifice, for reasons that he need not explain. He had sacrificed the Lamb of God, he caused humans to sacrifice to him. He took the lamb to slaughter himself and required blood from the very universe of his creation. The messengers came to him from the same God and they led the way.

As Jonathan left the store, he sailed in a state of steady bliss around the corner and onto Sixth Avenue towards Our Lady of Pompeii, along that part of town where tables are laid out on Sundays and second-hand items are displayed for sale. As he came to Father Demo Square, he approached a table behind which sat a group of ladies engaged in animated conversation and laughing among themselves. Lying before them, with the other bric-a-brac, he spied two books. Jonathan was past amazement. He had come to expect amazing coincidences. By now, the line between coincidence and cause and effect had become entirely blurred. It seemed as though random events no longer existed, as if every occurrence led one to another down a straight path of revelation. Whatever Jonathan did, wherever his path led, in some vague way everything that happened to him converged so that the rules of randomness no longer applied. So it was that at the end of a string of what otherwise would have seemed to be coincidences that happened throughout Jonathan's walk to the bookstore and then beyond to Sixth Avenue, Jonathan's unfolding story culminated in what, to him, could only have been a miracle. There before him, rising out of the pavement behind a little card table covered with second-hand merchandise, the great Earth Goddess appeared to him in the flesh. Sitting behind the table, was the Venus of Willendorf herself, come somehow to life and talking, just as anyone might talk, with another woman.

Then, as Jonathan kept one eye fastened upon his enormous goddess, he opened up *Mythology of Mezzo America* and turned first one page, then a second. The third page opened to a plate of Cizin, mighty god of earthquake and death, ruler of the subterranean land of the dead, also known as Ahpunc or Ahpuch, great king of Mitnal. There in this book he was pictured as a dancing skeleton, holding a smoking cigarette, wearing around his neck a collar made up of disembodied eyes dangling by ribbons of nerve cords.

Of course, there are those who will say that Jonathan's hallucination of the night before had merely taken a form vaguely similar to the plate that spread out before him. For such people, the only admissible possibility is that Jonathan's imagination was the result of some hallucination which itself was the product of his pineal gland in a fevered state. How can such a reasonable argument be refuted? Might one simply suppose a spark of memory from the night before triggered Jonathan's unreliable imagination so that it seemed that a pathway of revelation laid itself open to him? It is easy for the humans who create Lord Cizin to believe that the random events in their lives actually spell out a divine plan so that the strange instant at which a high-pitched buzz rises to a squeal and the edges of a room melt away to admit an apparition and opens in its turn onto a succession of moments that are all the related, the preordained, the personal plan of a divinity.

No. No scientific analysis can conjure away the fact that this pathway led, no matter how, to a certain table on Sixth Avenue and that, for Jonathan, the goblin who had come to him last night with his esoteric message was now made real before his very eyes, described and pictured in detail by the book that he held to scrutiny in his hand. And moreover, standing immediately before him in the flesh, after just reading about her, was the very Earth Goddess incarnate. Ahpunc, lord of Mitnal, devourer of souls and bringer of chaos, was now linked in his mind to the earthly and very real incarnation of the Venus of Willendorf in the person of Anne Rose who sat behind the table upon her great and fecund thighs, unaware even of Jonathan's presence before her.

CHAPTER XIX

Dear Journal,

So, as I look around me and place these memories into some context, perhaps I am beginning to decipher what it is, this peculiar angst. For one thing, I notice that very few people ever actually question themselves to begin with. That may not be all bad. Many of these are simply people of action, I suppose. Their lives are a series of actions taken, although usually in a small way, made up of small choices, but they don't seem to look deeply into why they do what they do or where these things might lead in the end. Are they the lucky ones? Surely, though, mine is not the only life hedged in by an accumulation of countless thoughts and choices. Most people seem to accept that this is inescapable. They move through routines that take them back again to the same homes, the same families and jobs, cooking a meal each night, watching their favorite television programs, rereading books that they've come to love, shaving again and again. The same razor, the same brand. The most fortunate among us make the best of it and create rituals and beauty out of their routines: a silver handled razor, a special teapot, The Times *crossword on Sunday. Couldn't*

I just settle in for the long run? Am I asking more of myself than I am capable of giving?

Connie and I were more or less together for quite a number of years and our life, too, settled pretty much into a routine. Some would call it exciting and some would call it frivolous, depends, I guess, on your point of view. I don't think I missed anything of interest in town during those years. I went out every night and hit every club, saw every play. But even then, the constant cycle of plans the opera season, cabaret, dance clubs seemed sometimes less like activity than passive voyeurism. We would let entertainment wash over us as if we were daydreamers on a beach, lying at the edge, inert in the undulating waves.

But always something kept me from being seduced by routine. Although I kept company with Connie, I had plenty of affairs, too. We never did see each other more than a couple of days a week and weekends sometimes. Should I have made more of a commitment to him; ventured more? There seemed to be no reason to do that. I don't think I was in love with him, ever nor, probably, was he in love with me. Perhaps by the end I had grown to care for him, and perhaps that's something akin to love. But wouldn't love have motivated me more? What was missing was passion. Wouldn't I have been driven to make more of a life with him if I'd really been in love? People say it is the companionship that makes things last, but don't half of all marriages end in divorce? People may not know what made their marriage fail any more than they know how it is they've ended up aflutter and utterly alone lying beside the very person they look to for company. All I know is I was never passionate for Connie. Not even lustful for him. He was just the person I happened to be with and so my life took one step to the next, up the trunk, out onto a branch, onto the next smaller bifurcation of the soul.

My cousin found our great grandmother's diary a few years back. There was an entry for every day during World War II yet she never wrote anything about the war or even anything a person might have heard over the news. Nothing from the newspapers or the radio ever intruded upon her life. She wrote about canning tomatoes or how the people at the church supper enjoyed her rhubarb pie. The family lore has it that she would lurk under people's windows spying on them from outside if they were listening to music and dancing or she thought they were playing cards. Then she'd jump up and rap on the pane and accuse them of sinning. She lived in a small town in Kansas. I suppose they thought of her as the local crazy woman. She belonged to some little offshoot church and she was a fanatic, so the family said, and indeed that's how I learned the word "fanatic" so that it meant to me only a wrinkled-up old woman and the cramped handwriting of her letters admonishing me to believe in Jesus and stay far away from Satan and his snares. That diary is what remained of my great grandmother, but if you try to flesh out the memory of her, fit the sprinkled baubles of her life onto a Christmas tree, her story, too, must have had its own structure, its own system of trunks and branches.

But the quotidian details of her life hide the fact that she raised ten girls all by herself. A falling tree killed her husband one day and so she raised an entire family and the girls, who all married pretty well, creating a clan as they went through their lives. They all turned out okay. Still, even with bringing up those girls and the tribulations of being a single, poor woman making ends meet, there was nothing in that diary except for canning tomatoes and attending church suppers and making dinner and thanking her god for his presence. Nothing more.

I suppose that someone reading this journal would think that my life amounted to the same thing. An entire generation was born and people died and started businesses and blew up buildings on the Gaza strip and machine-gunned each other in Belfast. Pol Pot killed millions of people out there in Cambodia and AIDS killed a couple hundred thousand and it seems today that I knew most of them, but my diary would read like an endless string of theater events and dinners or cabaret and business meetings at the Flower Emporium. Even the benefits for AIDS organizations and memorials begin to merge into the flow of functions, day in and day out. I went to work, out to the country, back to the city, out to the clubs. I saw Connie according to the rules of our relationship, which allowed me plenty of time to pick up men whose names I no longer remember and so I had quite a few bounces in the hay. Some of those guys stayed close and became friends—the best of friends, really, if not always the closest, since we have so little to hide from one another, and no axes to grind.

I suppose, too, that this was my way of making ends meet, my sub-stitute for canning tomatoes and going to church dinners. But there are moments that stand out from the routine and those stay with you, embedded in the past like particularly bright ornaments on the Christmas tree. Indeed, there are some chance encounters you remember out of all proportion to their place in the continuum of your life. There are moments that in your recollection of them did not lead to anything—were neither effect nor cause. They seem to stand outside the ordinary markers that memory tells us led to one branch and then another. You cannot ascertain any logical meaning to these anomalous moments, and yet they contain an unbidden power over memory. It is in this evanescent way that strangers intertwine themselves for an hour and communicate something to each another through some unspoken, tactile, non-symbolic system of language that we could never express through something as awkward as words. I don't know exactly what hunger two people, unknown to one another, fulfill. I have spent an hour with a stranger and explored him in a way that Connie and I never did in twenty years of talking and steady lovemaking. And if lovemaking brings intimacy with the person you love, it's been my experience that there are intimacies that cannot be shared with people you know well. Once two people know one another, isn't intimacy not just sharing who I am, but who I know you expect me to be? If I love you, won't I want to fulfill that role and yet as I do so, don't I guard myself, pretend a little, and so fail to achieve the very co-joining that we both claim to seek? There are interests to safeguard after all, a status quo to keep, a person to protect.

Does the promise of revealing yourself on the most elemental level explain the urgency strangers feel for each other and the way the physical and emotional barriers fall all at once to an outpouring of lust, while social and mental barriers are irrelevant. Only with strangers does this happen; who they are and what they mean to us is of no consequence. Only with strangers have I been able to express my craving to fold myself into another body.

But, of course, what takes place between people as they glide between giving and taking pleasure with one another, silently speaking through touch and emotion and, perhaps, even smell, is naturally heightened with a stranger. People say that sex creates intimacy within a relationship and I don't doubt that that can be true. Connie and I knew each other's ways in bed and we had a shared repertoire, if it comes to that. That is a shared intimacy on the level, perhaps, of vacations together, the secret language of special words and phrases, songs from long ago, that people string into a sense of togetherness. But it is one thing to build a system of intimacies with someone over time and to share a piece of one's own, most intimate nature with anyone. Indeed, if I had not explored parts of my psyche with strangers, I doubt I would have any idea that they were parts of my personality at all. So, in that way, I opened up to express deeply submerged elements of myself through giving and taking pleasure with those I'd never met.

The question, it seems to me, is whether we should or can really ever release those ancient, animal urges with people we know well. I, for one, cannot give over that much power to another person. It is a different kind of power from what I gave to Connie. Could I lose myself utterly in another person without giving away my sense of self-worth? I was acquainted long ago with someone who had a nervous breakdown and as he spiraled into madness he sought out strangers to unburden his soul of its most private secrets. People do confess their private turmoils to one another, but that is an attempt to cure the loneliness of a person's mind. But while friends over the years talk of the intimacy they achieve over time with a lover, I know from secrets they have shared with me that parts of them are withheld from their partner. And I know that that they withhold something physical from one another, too.

Lace refers to the Dionysian aspects of what it is to be human. Somewhere in my physical being is a need not so much to lose control, but to meld control entirely with another person. The need is so elemental that I would not be surprised that it has at its core the desire of the DNA itself to unravel and join itself to another strip of the genome that has been split and laid bare to receive its complementary set of instructions. Only at that level, of course, is it possible to meld entirely. Otherwise, we cannot do it, although the impossibility of it doesn't keep us from trying. But that need, built as it is, from the very ground up of ourselves, results in a kind of sex that is Dionysian and to lose oneself for an hour in the rites of that daemonic god is to confront the daemonic part of yourself without any artifice whatsoever to hold you back. All ages have acknowledged this kind of passion, of course. The Greeks embraced it under specific circumstances, the Victorians feared it above all else, but it is nothing new, although lots of people think they invented it.

I came across something by Thomas Hobbes, writing in the seventeenth century, in which he calls lust a "pleasure or joy of the mind, consisting of two appetites taken together, to please and to be pleased." I would add "spontaneously, when the people involved are strangers. And when two people communicate in this way, combining their appetites for the giving and taking of pleasure, you can become completely accurate about who they are underneath, even though you would begin to form some kind of mirage out of them if you were to know them socially for even five minutes. You will never know them as well again as when they were a stranger to you and your only agenda was out in the open and straightforward: to give them pleasure and to receive pleasure back again as its own reward. As is, the very people who should know each other well lead relationships full of denial and self-deception with hidden agendas, role-playing and expectations. People call that intimacy, but perhaps we should coin another word for it.

In those years, living as I did as a perpetual adolescent in the heat of desire, with plenty of time on my hands and the city at my feet, I met my men and made love to them without asking anything from anyone, without commitment or conversation. Yet of those magnificent men, some, with a wink of goodwill and an hour of their time, could reach so far into your heart and soul that they left you gasping for more. Sometimes I'd run into them at the theater that night, these men whose names I never knew. We'd nod and smile at each other, but you knew when not to approach. You knew that because you had learned to know them. You had said everything to them you needed to say and you needed to say no more than that.

Then there are other people you remember because there was something about them. Sometimes someone will come to mind because he got drunk and slept over and tossed and turned all night. I remember very few of the men who started calling and tried to get romantic or start dating, the affairs that sputtered and died before they even started, but I remember some who caught me up in some kind of wet and lusty magic. And then, there was one man I especially remember because he was the only one out of the entire bunch who frightened me. After that experience with him, I never took anyone else up to my apartment on MacDougal Street. After that, I became very careful.

Connie and I had come back early on a Sunday from the country and I was walking back from the Fourth Street subway stop at dusk when I caught the eye of a sexy, sort of handsome guy who was hanging out at the corner of MacDougal and Bleecker. Normally, I wouldn't remember any of this, but some memories are etched into your mind along with the setting for them and the retrieval of those memories is recalled in slow motion.

Anyway, he looked at me and I looked at him, he followed me and I led him up to the outer door of my apartment building, waiting a second for him to catch up. No one in the big city needs a long conversation. He just came up after me into the apartment, I got him a beer and we sat for a second on the couch until I put my hand on his leg.

Then he said, very quietly, "Do you let many strangers come up here like this?"

"Sometimes." I remember feeling instantly on guard, coming awake with the awareness of danger.

Then he added, "Have you ever made a mistake?"

I'll never know if my response to him kept me safe. I always have been pretty good in dangerous situations and I've been in a few of them. I didn't tense up. I stayed relaxed. Confident, I countered, in return, "Have I made a mistake with you?"

He was handsome in his way, but rather sexy than good-looking. He had reddish hair and a moustache. And he had that gap between the front teeth. I happen to love that gap between a man's front teeth; I always think of the Lady of Bath in Chaucer. I think that's one of the sexiest things a guy can have, that and a cleft chin. And I remember how he smelled of cigarettes. I never did smoke, but even today, with tobacco companies on the run and smoking considered kind of tacky, the smell of cigarettes on a man's breath is erotic to me. It must go back to some early but unremembered sexual experience. The taste of cigarettes in spit, the smell from deep down a man's throat as we sit side by side, these awake a sensual desire that I cannot wholly explain. An awakening comes from the pit of my bowels as if smoke itself is forming in the center of my chest and finds its way to the tense muscles of my stomach. It is an entirely instinctual reaction, its cause unremembered but formed somewhere at my roots. Funny. Some other experiences can be conjured out of memory like genies out of a bottle, exact and seemingly intact; they come when you call them. But others leave their residue in feelings, desire, old reactions and vague fears, ghosts lurking just around corners, witches under the bed.

Heady stuff. First the hint of smoke on his breath, then that remark which added to the tension in my stomach with an alerting shot of adrenalin. He took an easy look at me. It wasn't a malevolent look. He certainly wasn't a kind person, I could tell that from his eyes. They were empty, somehow. He could have been creepy, but there wasn't anything creepy about him and I don't know why he asked that creepy question because all he said in reply was, "No, you haven't made a mistake."

I sometimes think that if I had gotten nervous or scared, he might have scented fear and become excited. Perhaps he was looking for prey and didn't find it in me. He stayed for a while and we had sex. It's funny, but I don't remember that part at all. I don't think it was good or bad, but it must have been indifferent. When we were done, he simply held out his hand to touch my forearm and said, "My name is Jonathan. Maybe we'll run into each other again."

So indeed: no strangers in my apartment after that! And for a while I even took a different street home from the Fourth Street station. I didn't know what he meant about "running into each other again" and I didn't want to find out. I think that he was genuinely interested in having sex again as far as that goes. But as I said, the product of unhinged lust is confluence with another human being. Then to follow it to its conclusion is to know that person utterly. No, I don't remember the sex itself, but the connection between us as strangers was still electric, still Dionysian, but somehow disquieting exactly because it had given me the opportunity to look into his soul. There are indeed decisions that make up individual points in the arc of a person's life and at the same time, taken together, the points come together to form a person's essence. As we sat together and maybe as we had sex, I knew without a doubt what those points had combined to form. No logic can express what I felt to be true, but I knew to respect the darkness of his being and to stay far away.

After that afternoon, I always told people, "No one gets into my apartment unless I'm so familiar with them that I know where their mother went to school."

CHAPTER XX

The Myers Store sat on 11th Street, a cross-town side street only a few blocks uptown from MacDougal. There were other antique stores along with town houses from the 1890s arranged in a row along the street and the black iron, lace-like banisters along door stoops gave the appearance of so many Victorian widows in black mourning dress. Situated near the corner of 11th and University Place, Myer's Antiques was at street level and sported a delicate bay window for displaying the goods that attracted a brisk carriage trade.

Lace worked at the antique store for seven years, coming in each day around noon and leaving at six. When he first took over the store, the inventory relied heavily on old bits of china and bric-a-brac along with furniture that was rather old than antique. But Lace gained a good deal of knowledge about the antique trade and began to take some Saturdays and Sundays off to go upstate or out to the New Jersey countryside. There were plenty of auctions and estate sales. The store became more his than not and he slowly rotated the items and replaced them with pieces of better quality and known provenance. As the antiques became more expensive, the profits grew and as the store reflected its change of taste, word of it spread among shoppers, decorators and other people in the trade. The deal worked out well for Old Mr. Myers and for Lace.

His proudest coup was the purchase of a Herter Brothers knockoff that he bought from a young man in Brooklyn. It started as an innocent transaction. An ad in *The Sunday Times* announced the sale of some second-hand furniture and Lace went out on a Sunday morning after services at St. Johns. The fellow couldn't have been more than twenty-two and he was selling off his mother's estate. The dark, Brooklyn apartment was filled with the rambling, archaeological detritus of lives going back to the start of the century. None of it was any good, except for one piece, a bureau, that was crowded into the long wall of the dining room. Over it hung a bad print of a Dutch landscape, vaguely reminiscent of Van Ruisdael. The room was badly lit by a cheap brass plate chandelier recently purchased from the Bowery discount lighting places.

But Lace noticed the bureau, which looked something like a Herter Brothers piece and he figured that with some cleaning up it would do all right in the shop. The store at this point didn't often get furniture of the highest quality with aristocratic provenances. A lot of what Lace tended to find were old reproductions of still older styles. It didn't surprise him to find this slightly later knock-off of the distinctive Herter gilded age style and so he wrote a check for $2,500 on the spot and arranged to have it transported to the store.

Lace was not averse to stripping some paint on a cool afternoon, or repainting or refinishing a piece that was old but not particularly valuable. In fact, he had found that including some faux finished side tables or bureau from time to time seemed to spike interest in everything. Still, the Herter Brothers knock-off, he judged, shouldn't be refinished altogether. The old black surface was soft and smooth in better light and the gilded insets of carving glowed softly. He pulled out a drawer, the bottom of which had been covered in aging and dirty felt and so, as a first step, he pulled the cloth back to expose burnt-in carved lettering which read, "Herter Bros., New York 1880."

He had accidentally bought the real thing. He sold the piece two weeks later for $25,000 and sent an extra check for $5,000 to the young but unknowing lad. Why not, after all?

The store hours were not onerous. He scouted for furniture on some Saturdays while the young fellow from downstairs, Patrick, sat in for him. Lace was fond of the boy and thought perhaps their friendship had done him some good. Settled he wasn't, but he had been seeing an older man now for some time and had learned some manners. It was a pity that he didn't save anything. He went to clubs, drank too much and was careless, but he held down a job and had taken on some responsibility as he approached the lower cusp of middle age with the careless abandon of someone who saw only a future of eternal youth. They had lunch often and their lunches kept Lace feeling young. Patrick was a window onto an exotic night world of bars and after-hours joins and dinners with celebrities whom he met through his producer friend. He and his not exactly full-time partner, Connie, went to everything, so associating with young Patrick helped Lace keep up. But Lace knew, too, that he filled a gap for Patrick that Connie, older though he was, did not. Lace had education and background and these he tried to pass on to Patrick. He thought he could count on being a mentor for decades more, the fatherly instinct surprising him. If he didn't really care how mature the kid became, at least he could add a bit of wisdom and broaden his horizons by suggesting the readings required by classical humanism, sprinkled with a bit of philosophizing here and there, which to Lace was the only kind of education that mattered. And, yes, Lace had to admit that he did care about the man that might finally emerge from the spirited and wayward foal that had landed in his charge.

Sunday mornings Lace went to church and immersed himself in its music and rites. For him, the celebration of Eucharist brought a sense of closeness to something overwhelming and eternal. When he took into himself the wafer and wine out of the chalice, his emotions rose. Lace felt transported backwards in time through an ancient line of rites and ritual that predated Christianity and spanned generations dating back even to the rising of consciousness itself. To his mind, he was immersed in a great river that swept humankind out of that unrecorded past towards some distant place, another firmament somewhere in the future. Afterwards, he often drove out to the country where he would stay until Monday night. The store was closed Sundays and Mondays.

Shortly after his fifth anniversary running the store, on a Tuesday morning, the phone rang.

"You'll never guess what happened to momma," Agnes said without having to announce herself.

"If momma got schtupped last night, I think I don't have to guess. Or have you found the writer on whose back Madame's millions will be built?" Still the poet, Lace was happy with his alliteration.

"Lace Lace Lace. Be serious. I am. Two Sundays ago, I met someone. About my age. Met him at an AIDS benefit. But he's straight. He's perfectly hetero. I'm sure of that." She was defiant. "Not that we've slept with each other, so maybe I do wonder about him. But

I think I can tell that he's really interested in me because we've had three dates and we're talking about things and taking some time. And he's a writer, did I mention that? A journalist really, but maybe I can help him get published. But then, maybe I shouldn't, you know?"

"Careful, honey."

"I will be careful, but the dates have gone awfully well. He kisses me…I mean really kisses me…so it's romantic, but, like I say, he's taking time and going slow. New experience for momma, honey. What do you think?"

"What do I think? Well, first of all I'm glad you've given me so much information about him. Why don't you marry him right away and find out about him later? Does he have a name, for Christ's Sake? Honest? Is he well known? Does he have another agent who's doing something for him?"

"Yes, yes. William Morris and all that…and his name is Robert. Robert Silbers…and he doesn't need me to make him rich and famous, unless he's lying, of course, and if he's doing that I'll find him out soon enough. No, he's moderately successful. He's just had a piece syndicated in a dozen newspapers and a piece for *Popular Mechanics* and William Morris is handling a novel, which I haven't read."

"All that sounds awfully close to what you do for a living to be comfortable, my dear, but you'll know best. Best wishes to the bride and write when he proves he's not gay."

"Very funny. I'm giving him two more dates and I want to see his apartment. Then I'll know whether I think it might go somewhere. Sound fair enough? Anyway, there's hope, don't you think? I don't usually go for gay men; not like Lucy Lucifer, anyway. If that one falls in love, you know the guy's gay for sure, but do you think maybe I've found someone who's just not indefensibly sleazy? I'm not sure what the difference is between a guy who's nice to be with and a raging homosexual, but I figure the drapes will lend a clue, so two dates and an apartment viewing. Then I should know how to proceed. What do you think? "

"Fair, my dear. Maybe even sensible, but perfectly fair in any event. You are nothing if not fair, although come to think of it you're really a shrew in your natural state. What am I thinking of? You've gotten the better of one or two deals, have you not? Left a few people bloodied and senseless, as if you needed me to remind you."

"Just closed a hell of a deal on Friday. Had to work my ass off, but it's done now. And if I do say so myself, I do think my clients are better off for what I do for them. Are you suggesting otherwise? Speaking of deals, what's doing at the store? Passing off fake faux finished tables for Boule? Any more word on working a deal with Myers?"

As it happened, Old Mr. Myers, as they referred to him, was now old in fact, proving, Lace and Agnes joked, that if you insist on something long enough it will actually happen. He had been divesting himself of worldly attachments and as he turned his thoughts to matters of more eternal weight, he offered Lace a buyout for the store on very good terms.

"We actually have some very good things in at the moment. Just picked up some wonderful furniture at an estate sale up on the Hudson River, but that aside I suppose the news is that I talked to little Patrick from downstairs about helping me out. I know he's a bit flaky, but he's up to doing this and they've been giving him a fair amount of responsibility at the job. He's doing okay at that. He can use the dough, which he's always short of, and he can watch the store when I'm out. It'll work out okay, I'm sure of that. I'm working on a new name for the store by the way. What do you think of Eternal Items?"

"Take two aspirin and call me about it in the morning. Really, Lace, if you sleep on it, you'll think of something better. What's wrong with Tyler Lace Whittaker III Antiques? You want people to think you have something of value, don't you? What's the use of that pedigree name if it doesn't add some class to your storefront?"

There are easy periods for people and it happened that during this time, for both Agnes and Lace, things continued to work out well. The smooth and easy season lasted a couple of years. Agnes saw Robert Silber's apartment on the next date, for dinner, and she stayed well into the night. Whether it was because the draperies were simple linen on hooks hung carelessly across the living room and bedroom windows, or because he was sexually deprived, he took her to bed and performed satisfactorily. They got on with each other well enough, she thought. Sex wasn't electric, though. But he seemed to care about her: what she thought and how she felt and he asked questions about her. He liked to kiss and he liked to cuddle.

"Intimacy," she told Lace. "I've taken Basic College Psychology. Intimacy is the hump. I'll wait for us to grow together sexually. Everyone says that sex gets better with intimacy. He's very nice, you know."

Indeed, everything was as Robert presented it. Publishing gave them conversation in common and yet he had the sense not to talk real business with her. He had been at the AIDS benefit because he donated some time in order to be helpful and was invited to the affair as a perk. They did ordinary things together and developed a secret language in common—talking about art openings they'd gone to, the plays or movies they'd seen. They walked in the park. Robert began to spend lots of time in California on a screenplay he'd been asked to do.

As the two years passed, Robert did more and more work in Los Angeles, developing a miniseries on the worsening AIDS epidemic and getting himself known as the author of articles for women's magazines. He wrote from a woman's point of view under a pseudonym. Everyone marveled at the way Robert could see the world through female eyes. They rented a house in New York State near Monticello and got in with a crowd of couples. Agnes worked more on her own and stayed more and more out in the country house until her trips into town became intermittent and brief. But she and Lace stayed close.

Meanwhile, Lace built up the store, bringing in gift items to mix with the antiques. It was Patrick's idea. It developed out of his work at the Flower Emporium. They did the store up like a living room, with flower arrangements that they sold at a hefty markup and knickknacks sitting around on Queen Anne or Mission tables. They invited people to lounge on an Empire sofa, getting a feel for the velvet upholstery and lying snug against its contours. With a steadier income, Patrick reupholstered chairs and settees so that they were ready to take home and use. They no longer handled anything that looked beat up and needed repair. They pushed an eclectic look and did mailings to the trade for a series of teas. They mounted exhibitions for young artists. Little by little, the name of the store, which was Lacy Whittaker Antiques, got around and a clientele developed. In time they could afford advertising and they were written up a few times in trade magazines. Yes, Lace, Agnes and even young Patrick, who was not very young anymore, were doing just fine.

CHAPTER XXI

After Jonathan left Anne Rose's table late that Sunday afternoon, he crossed Sixth Avenue and took a table in front of a café with a direct view of his Venus of Willendorf. Having achieved a clear vantage point, he ordered a cup of black coffee and watched them, thumbing through *Mythology of Mezzo America* and reviewing an entry on the Mayan God of the Underworld. He was sure that the vision that had emerged from the blank wall on Elizabeth Street was just as he saw it before him now: a skeletal man with sunken eye sockets—almost hollow eye sockets—with skulls dangling around his body. And yes, almost surely there was a cigar or something sinister hanging from the otherworldly god's lips. And yet at the same time, Jonathan remembered piercing eyes, despite the fact that he was sure the eye sockets were indeed hollow like a skeleton. Yes, he thought about how that didn't make sense, reflecting back on the night's phantasm, and somehow, even though he remembered how empty and black the eye sockets were, he was still struck by his memory of fierce and murdering blackish brown eyes.

The immediate, euphoric effects of smoked cocaine had left him some time ago and he felt jumpy, but he was too fascinated with the books to move on. The pigment began to drain from the color plates, giving them the sallow hue of old Kodachromes left over from his childhood. But the temple friezes portrayed in the book jumped out into his roiling mind nonetheless. Old gods peered out, daring him, communicating their thoughts to create a direct link between them. Like a cloud just starting to form, an incoherent thought began to dawn in the center of his brain, just below the crown of his head. Indeed, a narrow way, some indistinct pathway which he could not yet quite make out was opening up clear before his very eyes. The ivory gray mists were parting and he began to sense and then see before him in ever-brighter colors the awful act that he would be required to do. It was not for nothing that a god of death, easily identifiable as such, had appeared to him, immediately followed by the goddess of creation in the flesh. As he read into the mythology of those ancient Americans, for whom darkness and light, creation and death, up and down for that matter, were different sides of the same coin, he began to understand something. Everything had its opposite quality, dualities expressed in revolving orbits of time that crushed everything between them and in so doing, expressed the full and inner essence of all things. He saw that creative forces must be fed by bloody sacrifice because destruction and creation are forces that must remain in balance, one giving way to the other in ceaseless cycles. This was the eternal secret in which he was being instructed. Creation must be accompanied by destruction. It was required that someone become the destroyer and the awful idea that finally came to dawn on him was that he was the chosen one, just as his mother had foretold. So now, at last, the task itself had become clear to him.

In time, the women packed up their belongings and the Venus left with one of the other women. Quickly, Jonathan left some bills on the table and got up to follow them. He did not have far to go. The women took a quick route across town on Bleecker Street and turned directly onto MacDougal, entering an old tenement building a couple of blocks down.

Jonathan lingered on the block wondering where the next step would lead. He wanted to mellow his mood and he thought that if he cooked some free-base he might find the next answer, but he didn't want to leave the spot. Then, in time, a man left the building and turned to appraise Jonathan, the long look of a gay man on the prowl. The guy wasn't bad looking. The fading high turned sexual and Jonathan felt a stirring in his pants. He marked the fellow's face hard and weighed him in his judging mind, noting the smallish upturned nose, dark, thinning hair and rounded cheekbones. He wasn't a bad looking man, all in all, but Jonathan stood motionless, watching the small, lithe body walk away from him along the street. Then he turned away and returned back to Elizabeth Street to renew his high.

After that, Jonathan loitered time and time again in front of the building on MacDougal Street, watching the Venus come and go, but never seeing the gay man again until one Sunday afternoon as he had nearly begun the walk back across town to go home. Suddenly, the two ran into each other and Jonathan purposefully cruised him, instinctively slowing down and gazing into the man's eyes. It was easy for Jonathan. It was always easy.

And indeed, the man reacted as Jonathan expected, catching his eye in return and slowing down. They caught up with each other in silent courtship in front of the building and went through a front entrance down an outer corridor and through a courtyard. It did not surprise Jonathan to see the Venus in the courtyard. He was past surprise by now, everything was a message, a sign. She was sorting through refuse sitting in front of her door and she hummed to herself, unaware of anyone's presence. The words of her song were nonsense and they especially caught his notice: "Two men in a dinghy/ Two little men/Two tots went singing/To catch a little hen." She chuckled to herself in amusement, leveling all her concentration on a pile of objects that looked to Jonathan like pure flotsam. The song and the litter lodged themselves into his mind and he searched there for some hidden meaning, but there didn't seem to be any message in the words of her made-up rhyme. She swayed to the tune of her melody and began to sweep a small leaf strewn patch in a corner of the courtyard as Jonathan turned to catch up with the young man who was holding the door open for him as he said, without leaving room for a reply, "I'm Patrick."

Entering a back building, the two men entered a dark vestibule and climbed a stairway to the second floor. Once inside a pleasant if small apartment, they sat for a moment in silence on a daybed with a tie-died throw covering it, until the man began to make his move by placing his hand on Jonathan's thigh.

But Jonathan's mind was elsewhere. How easy it was to gain entrance to this building with its glass front door and no one near enough to the entrance to hear the sound of breaking glass. And he now knew where the Venus lived. Again, he wondered at the way creatures appeared to show the way. How easy the pathway was. How fascinating and strange. And out of nowhere this man had come to show him how the final steps of his awful assignment were to be accomplished.

Could this stranger possibly have any inkling of his precise place in the great master plan to which he, Jonathan, alone among humans, was privy? Did he know that he had been sent to show him where the Venus lived and how easy it was to reach her? Jonathan asked, very quietly, very steadily as he gazed directly into the man's eyes "Do you let many strangers come up here like this?" Suddenly, he was aware of an antique clock somewhere in the room, ticking, and then a sliver of darkness, like a shadow, descended between them. The sun had gone behind a cloud. As the light shifted, the clock ticked, back and forth for what seemed like an immeasurable period. In the silence between them, he felt its hands measure the passing of time, which was nothing more than revolutions of those grinding, great wheels of force and destruction that had called him to be their servant.

"Sometimes," said the man. He tightened just a little. You almost might have missed it, but he was hesitant. Suspicious. He might have leaned back in fear, but he did the opposite. He leaned forward and hardened his eyes, looking directly at Jonathan. He looked for a second like a small, wiry warrior and his knees looked tense, as if they were set to spring.

"Have you ever made a mistake?" Suddenly, Jonathan felt slightly malicious, countering the man's quiet alarm. Upping the ante. He was becoming aroused.

Oddly, the man smiled.

"Have I made a mistake with you?"

The directness of the question surprised Jonathan. The man's eyes narrowed, serious. Was the question slightly threatening? Jonathan liked this unknown man who confronted danger directly, acknowledging his uncertainty and putting fear on the line. The combativeness of the response brought him up sharp. The atmosphere charged with fear and sex; two people entirely unknown to one another in the most vulnerable of circumstances. They were wary adversaries; they were hunters like mountain lions on the prowl and they were ready to mate. Jonathan became erect.

"No." The man was in no danger, of course, he thought to himself. "I wouldn't hurt a fly," he thought, and then he caught the thought and he knew that he was a meek soul who was compelled to judge the quick and the dead so that the meek ones like him might inherit the earth, as Reverend Jimmy had said. Pride swept him up and turned him languid as he heard himself say out loud, "No danger at all. Hey man. Blow me, why don't you?" Jonathan unzipped his trousers and leaned back to enjoy the sexual release. The two men had circled around one another, hard to know who was the hunter and who was the prey. That excited Jonathan. It was a good climax, particularly intense, and he left in a good mood, emerging into the courtyard where he lounged for a moment to examine the terrain.

"Too bad," he thought. "I'd like to get together with him again." But Jonathan knew better. His future would not include the young, brave and stern man. He was set on another task and he cast about for the huge woman singing her tune. There was no one. The door to her apartment was shut. There were trashcans and a table and chairs and a high heap of what appeared to be garbage astride the door, opening directly onto the central courtyard that led to the dark cave of the Venus' lair. Two windows also opened to the courtyard, one slightly raised. There were no security bars. In the corner was a small pile of newly swept leaves, partly brown and partly orange, that caught the lengthening shadows of late afternoon.

And as he left the building Jonathan learned something else. The front lock did not work properly. With a little manipulation, it would suddenly jar open. Now, the way opened entirely before him, wide and well-marked. He went back to Elizabeth Street to get high and curl his mind with the pure, white smoke that tightened around his plans and his narrowing destiny.

Once back at his apartment on Elizabeth Street, Jonathan lit his glass stem and listened to the sizzle of the white rocks, breathing in the cloud and waiting for the high buzz and the emissaries to lead him. He had been feeling edgy; too much time had elapsed between hits on the pipe and the drug felt good in his body, loosening the tight ends, massaging his anguished mind. But there were no apparitions to come that night. He smoked again and again, but never seemed to get really high. Finally, Jonathan decided that this was the night to act. He knew what he had to do.

He had laid in a store of goods in anticipation: some rope, duct tape, a box knife, a hunting knife, a small hammer. These items he fed into a knapsack and threw it over his shoulder. As he began to leave the room, he suddenly had to piss, the urge running chilly down his spine. The extra wait reminded him to take his stem and he took extra time to cook more free-base, expertly adding just the right amount of bicarbonate and watching the oily substance gel into precious hard little rocks that made the smoke of his dreams. He added a small blowtorch to the cache and set out, locking the many locks and turning to slide down the many stairs onto his journey across town.

He met Miss Wanda coming up the stairs. "Mmmm, honey, ain't seen you in a while. You okay?" She peered at him, upward past her red painted eyebrows. The last two words dripped like syrup in her fake, Southern drawl.

Jonathan smiled at her, "Been okay. Sure." He winked at her confidently, feeling maybe a little higher than he thought.

Miss Wanda looked at him for a moment, appraisingly. She raised one finely drawn eyebrow and leaned against the banister, whistling under her breath. "Mmm, honey. You sure you okay? You need anything, you come over to Wanda, you hear now? You look a little under the weather to Wanda, now, honey. I'll take care of you." She smiled big at him, a smudge of lipstick flicked at the bottom of her prominent upper teeth.

Jonathan smiled, but he felt apprehensive. He was used to being cocksure, living in a protective thicket of certainties. He grinned his yellow grin and his eyes unfocussed enough to give him a silly, stoned look. Wanda laughed and turned to go up into her room.

"That's a promise, honey. You come over anytime and Wanda'll take good care of you, sweetheart." She let out the last word, stressing it as if she were blowing out smoke and Jonathan thought he saw a cloud of vapor rise past her painted lips towards the high tin ceiling.

Jonathan wanted to follow her, that black chick with firm, nice breasts and long dick. He wanted to follow the intriguing curves of her body. The smoked cocaine brought sexual urges to him in strong waves, but he turned against them and rushed away onto the street.

On the uneven and littered stoops, the same old men cackled at conversation and their bent-over women stooped over the tiles of their card table game as he slid away from them all and continued down the street. Tonight the noises they made were crisp against the sky and sharp in his ear, cascading up and then down the tenement walls like the ping of an old-time arcade game's metal balls. As the sounds faded behind him, their staccato consonants evoked images from his books and he almost sensed the presence of ancient crones summoning spirits from the dark. The small of Jonathan's back was tight and in his raging mind he felt his tight thighs swinging forward like a jaguar hunting through the Yucatan jungles or even an owl spreading its wings to search out prey.

It was late, but Jonathan took plenty of time to get across town to MacDougal Street. Time had stopped for him. As he walked slowly to his destination, the city's nighttime rhythm subsided. The night lights receded to hazy purple star-like clouds. Pedestrians dwindled away until they seemed to walk within their own shadows. Then, almost suddenly, he arrived.

The old apartment house was dark. He jiggled the lock, which fell away with a simple, sideways click, and he walked briskly back into the courtyard. There, a window leading into the Venus' apartment was slightly open and, as Jonathan pushed it upwards, it slid easily, without noise. Effortlessly, Jonathan made his way across the windowsill. Light from the courtyard was enough to see once his eyes adjusted. He remembered his earlier sensations. It seemed to him, indeed, that he had extra-sensitive perceptions this night, but now instead of feeling taut like a jaguar about to leap, he had the night sight and the quiet stride of a cat on the hunt. He thought of a cougar. Then, he noticed a glowing ball of red light emanating from somewhere near the back of the strange and crowded room. Like a burnished river of blood, it ran out of the dark corner and cast an eerie halo across a statue of the Holy Virgin.

Pausing to take in his surroundings, mostly black shapes tumbling here and there with a shadowy light splashed across everything like a rose blush, Jonathan slowly made out a clearing in the forest of objects. In it, the Holy Mother stared at him from across the room, surrounded by a silent dark retinue and looking at him straight in the eye with a sad, patient gaze that said to him almost audibly in a whispering lament, "If you must come, I am helpless, but know that I am sad. I am lament itself, incarnate." He thought back to the church of his boyhood and sex in the confessional and he knew that that lady of his childhood and the church of those far-off priests were powerless to protect against chaos. "Perhaps the cardinals know how order in the cosmos is maintained," he thought to himself. Jonathan basked in the glory of his special revelation. "I am the bringer of death and the creator of order." Had he read that somewhere? The man who invented the atomic bomb had said it, he remembered now. "I am become Death, the destroyer of worlds." Vishnu.

Finally, he had his bearings and crept unnoticed into Anne Rose's bedroom where she slept on her side. Jonathan tiptoed behind her. Because of her weight, she took long, labored breaths that buzzed as she exhaled. Beneath a flowered nightgown, he could barely see the rise and fall of her diaphragm. Jonathan stood quiet for a long moment. He had already taken out the hunting knife. It was effortless. The blade drew across her throat. The violence forced her to rise upward, flinging her right hand across her body before falling back onto the pillow. At last, Anne Rose's dying breath sputtered blood across the bed and into her tiny room.

Then like ravenous harpies, a thousand voices descended upon him from which one stood out over the others. He thought he heard his mother's voice calling, but it came as a sharp jolt lasting only a second as it cried out his name. With the shrill sound came the memory of his mother screaming aloud during those long ago nights, demanding her men to fuck her again, stay with her, make her crazy, keep aloneness at bay. She would bang the walls and berate her lovers to fuck her again and the little boy would lie awake at night and try to get some sleep and take his silent breakfast with strange men the morning after.

He fought away the insistent voices and concentrated on the business that he had been called forth to complete. And how was he, Jonathan, alone among men to continue this awful deed? When he stood before the throne of god almighty in supplication for the human race, he alone would be responsible for the symbolic act to which he was now committed. The mother goddess in whose womb the mysteries of creation were worked out had been sacrificed. Now her womb must be fertilized, just as Chac fertilized his brother Cizin, great god of the underworld and death. Now he was to finish the sacrifice. The symbolic rite must be complete.

He had not come with an exact outline of what he was to do. Ideas flowed through him like electricity. Outside in the packed living area, a red glow still seemed to light the darkness. It illuminated the doorway into the dead Venus' bedroom, reaching out to him, providing a flow of inspiration.

Jonathan pulled the weight of Anne Rose against the bed so that her head lay down against the floor and facing upward with her arms outstretched beyond her. The blood still trickled across the room darkening into filthy carpeting. Then, without thinking, but because he suddenly had the urge to do it, he pulled against her nightie, ripping it open and pushing his hand directly into her vagina, feeling the still warm force deep inside Anne Rose's cold legs. After that, almost methodically, he turned and masturbated, spraying semen from his body into the dark, dying cavern that was made to receive and revive the creative force from his body, for his was a body designed for sex and for the work of an anointed one. Just as Chac had done, he left his own powerful but unpotentiated elements inside the nourishing, hidden, magical womb of his Venus of Willendorf. There her sacrifice could work its magical transformation. The effort left Jonathan breathless; the sensation of climax nearly tore him apart.

Once again, he was impressed by the super-sensations of the night. He had been gifted with a heightened sense of awareness, of feeling. He found that he could creep silently and see in the dark. The ease with which the door and window opened to admit him on his supernatural errand was further proof that he had been guided. The sensation of this breathless climax was an additional gift and now, the Earth Goddess had been fertilized, impregnated and offered up to heaven. What more could Jonathan do?

He paused to check the flow of ideas that seemed to crackle in the air around him and spotted a long-leafed plant, sitting askew just outside the bedroom, near the kitchen. The leaves stood upward like spikes and suggested themselves to him. The Venus did not just bring forth human life. The life force contained in the Venus created all living things; it permeated flora and fauna, brought forth animals and the abundance of harvest too. "Harvest," it hit him. He should leave a plant offering. Jonathan plucked it from its terra cotta holder and planted it, dirt and roots and all, inside Anne Rose's vagina as a final offering to the gods in whose service he enacted these terrible deeds. It was done now. A living offering from the earth had been planted within his offering on behalf of humanity to a voracious and demanding god. Now, he knew, the act mandated of him was complete.

Stepping around Anne Rose's torso and into the gory, red light, he washed his hands in Anne Rose's sink and then buttoned his tight, torn jeans. Pausing for a moment, he took out a couple of tiny pebbles, placed them in his pipe and lit them with the torch. The smoke entered his lungs, glazing over his nervous energy and tightening his mind.

As Jonathan's world became smooth, the red light turned gold like honey dripping from the side of a beehive. With it, a sliver of moonlight cast a delicate wash of brushed silver across the virgin's retinue, highlighting an owl. Like the insistent buzz of a gnat, a small memory darted to the front of his thoughts. He stood up from a small red plastic chair. Where had he read that when an owl cries, a person will die? There again, the signs were plentiful if one cared to look. Jonathan took up the owl in his hand and clasped it carefully. One by one, he placed the statue, his glass pipe and the other items back into his knapsack. As he turned to go back out the window through which he had come, he noticed that the red glow was gone from the corner behind the virgin and her silent court stood vigil around her in a darkness that was black and cold as the center of ninth-most hell.

CHAPTER XXII

Immediately, Agnes knew something was wrong. In Lace's voice, she detected a deep, dry rasp, the strangled sound of a throat shut tight with anger, fright and grief.

"Someone killed Annie Rose last night. Some fucking bastard, Agnes." He quavered for a moment. "I knew I should have written that asshole landlord about the front lock, but she…she was sleeping with her window open. No bars or anything. Why the hell would she do that? God knows she wasn't bright. Who the hell would do it? And why Anne Rose, Agnes?"

Agnes didn't say anything, unsure how to proceed. Robert was good at this sort of thing. Good old measurable, sensitive Robert, off in California at a Save a Redwood convention or something. Writing something for the Sierra Club, was it? Robert was always reassuring, but then she didn't need reassurances, she needed someone who talked straight and damn the torpedoes. Her mind darted far away to her own dissatisfactions for a moment before returning to what Lace was saying to her. The impact of what he was saying didn't quite hit her at first, but Lace had gone on without her. "Anyway, the police were here this morning. I think she'd been there for a day or so from what I hear. Her aunt found her. We're all under suspicion, I suppose. There's been a detective talking to everyone in the building, of course. And everyone's got a rumor. Anne Rose had money tucked away, or she picked up a street person to give him a night's sleep or you name it, someone's got a take. You know how she was. You know, Agnes, we used to scream at each other. She was filthy, goddamit, but she was a simple creature." He thought a second and added, "And she sure helped keep the streets clean."

Lace let out a small little skittish chuckle that resembled a rapid burp. The torrent had run its course, ending in the shallows of his dark humor.

"Oh, Lace, I'm sorry. Do you need me? I can drive in." Agnes was in the country, Lace surmised. His phone call had been forwarded from the city number.

"No. No. It's not like we were brother and sister, just neighbors. But I knew her for a long time, Agnes. I'm angry about her. I mean, how could anyone murder a poor defenseless and not-altogether-*there* woman? And then it's such an awful waste. We could have...I should have written Sneider Management about that lock. This used to be such a safe neighborhood and now who knows what goes on anymore. And why did she have to leave that window open? And then we all feel vulnerable. Do we have to look over our shoulders all the time? Was it really a robbery? I mean, someone could just have easily followed me in the door or put a knife to my throat and forced me to take them in. And then the detective what's his name...Koklensky, I think...he talks to you for half-hour and he's polite and all that, but you feel under suspicion so my mind's been running away with me for a while, like the *Fugitive* or something. No, don't come into town, but just let me go on like this a few more times, okay?"

"Sure, kiddo. And sorry, honey. Life's a bitch. You can't live with it and you can't live without it."

Lace chuckled again, low. The constraints against his throat were gone. "By the way, there's going to be a funeral, obviously. I think I should go. Would you go with me? I won't know anybody, except the aunt, of course. It'll feel awful to be alone, but I think I have to go."

"Sure, just let me know when."

"Thanks," he said and then he rang off.

Lace was right. There was a Detective Koklensky, Walter Koklensy, who was investigating the murder. It was lucky for Veronica that she was a strong woman. She had come into the city and dropped by to see Anne Rose, using her key when the doorbell wasn't answered. She had had to face her niece lying draped from the bed, blood hardened against the floor and flies buzzing around the corpse. She called the police immediately. She touched nothing. She waited there, hands folded, fingers white with her polished nails biting into the opposite hand, until the police came. Then she went to the station to make her statements. She met Walter Koklensky a day later.

For his part, Koklensky went about the investigation with a gnarled grimness, but below the surface the detective was a maelstrom of emotion. He assessed Veronica and thought he understood what lay beneath the remote stillness he encountered. He didn't want to tell this quietly bereaved woman that this murder was the worst he had ever seen in seven years serving on the force. There were things people did to one another that defied imagination: little girls raped by their fathers, children whipped and killed. He had seen these things and they were awful, but this perpetrator, this criminal, this asshole had gone out of his way to defile his victim. Like a filthy Jack the Ripper, he had left his peculiar mark. Maybe he was like a skunk spraying his territory. The apartment had not been ransacked and, from statements made by Veronica McGrady and a careful assessment of the crime scene, there seemed to have been no robbery. Satanic perhaps, but he didn't quite believe in ritual murders. Anyway, this one was just too plain loopy. A goddamn plant, for Christ's sake? But as a detective, he had to remember. There was always something else to look for. Always something under the surface…but a messy, dirt-laden, ice-cold, fuck-you of a scene like this one puzzled him. He sought a motive and found none. The lab had found semen ground into fucking miracle grow house plant soil, which had been smeared over the woman's private parts. It had to be someone crazy, a guy who would do that. Koklensky was grim and angry and sad for the strong, straight-backed woman. It was a blessing that she had immediately called the police, sitting in the kitchen until they arrived. She had never inspected the scene. She never understood the extent of what happened to her niece. They kept in touch, but he tried not to push himself onto the McGradys.

The neighbors didn't seem like good leads and none of them had seen anything. People had known the victim for a long time, some of them. Some of the building residents sort of knew that the lock was easy to jimmy. No one had really realized that the victim slept with her window open. No one had noticed, perhaps, or the victim opened it late at night after her neighbors were in bed. People on the block expressed surprise when they heard about the window and then they shrugged. Anne Rose Morelli was regarded as a good-natured simpleton. Perhaps she slept with the window open all the time or again maybe she just left it open that night. No one knew for sure. They gathered in small groups, forming and dispersing like groups of dancers who had been choreographed to assemble into small huddles and look together towards the building on MacDougal Street, and then to talk, point in unison and shake their worried heads before emerging from the groups they had formed to move forward with their separate lives.

Within a few days, a funeral was arranged at Gannon Funeral Home with the internment at St. Paul's cemetery on Long Island. Lace called Veronica McGrady. Her number was in his book from a day many years ago when he and Mrs. McGrady had run into each other on the front stoop and shared their worries about Anne Rose. That was the day they ended up having coffee in Anne Rose's apartment. They had traded numbers, just in case. Now the case had happened and some sense of appropriateness said that he should go to the funeral of this woman whom he'd known since she was a young maiden, slim and full of energy for life. It surprised him to remember her that way, so long ago now, in her youthful promise.

Agnes met him and they took the subway up to Pennsylvania Station in silence. Together, they took the train out stop after stop past Babylon and caught a cab directly to the cemetery just as the service was beginning. Not many people had come out. Lace recognized some local ladies from Our Lady of Pompeii. The detective on the case was there. Lace and Agnes stood next to Koklensky during the ceremony, exchanging a few slight comments about the weather and how nice the people who had shown up were, but neither said anything of substance and it didn't seem appropriate to ask about the case. Perhaps detectives always came to check out who came to the funeral, like a murder mystery, Lace thought. The McGradys were there with another couple. Afterwards, Veronica McGrady came up to Lace and extended her hand. She wobbled as she reached forward. Lace was surprised to see that she was a little drunk.

"Thank you for coming, Mr. Whitaker. It was very kind of you. Very kind." She trailed off, looking behind her for her husband who approached with another man.

"Mr. Whitaker, this is my husband, Michael McGrady."

"Lace. Please call me Lace."

"Thank you," said Veronica. "Yes, call me Veronica, of course." She looked at Agnes.

"This is Agnes Pranciple. Agnes, Veronica McGrady…."

Lace halted not knowing the two men, one of whom extended his own hand in a firm handshake and offered his name.

"Michael McGrady."

Lace liked him immediately. He noticed pools of sadness in the man's face, underscored by dark circles under his eyes.

The introductions almost finished, Lace noticed that Veronica slurred her words somewhat, but her manners remained correct. There was a momentary lapse and then she added, "And this is Vincent Morelli, one of our oldest friends." Lace looked into Vincent Morelli's eyes as they shook hands. In contrast to Michael McGrady, his eyes were black like small fragments of glinting onyx and, as the two men shook hands, a spark of dark emotion combining wariness with suspicion sped across their interlocked hands. Was it malevolence? Lace wondered if one could capture the spark of a menacing look like that in slow motion, tracing its pathway back into those stark sockets and discovering the inner thoughts of a hard man like this one. Yes, you could capture it, he concluded as people talked around him. You captured it in your chest and measured it with a contraction of fear.

"One of our oldest friends," Veronica continued as Michael and Vincent walked away talking in hushed voices. Her voice turned sour against the wet afternoon, hard like a woman who has turned bitter with her burden and plenty of alcohol. "You can't imagine how she was, Mr. Whitaker…Lace…Agnes. You can't imagine. If we ever find out who it was I can tell you…" she looked down at the open hole and the casket lying at the bottom of it. "I can tell you, Vinnie is suspicious of everyone right now, but if we ever find out who killed Anne Rose, I'll see to it…Vinnie will…" then she thought better of what she was saying and waved her hand violently at her side as if to push everyone and everything away. "And what will it matter then… what will it matter?" She began to cry as she turned away to rejoin her husband and his cold, black-eyed friend. As she walked away, her arm kept waving behind her, quick and disjointed.

CHAPTER XXIII

Dear Journal,

I don't know who could have done it. I went out for breakfast and to pick up the Times. *When I got back, there was a police barricade around the doorway made out of those yellow tapes they use to cordon off a crime scene and they were taking Anne Rose out of the apartment covered on a stretcher. I never found out all of the details, didn't actually see Anne Rose, for that matter; just saw a big mound in a black body bag. I remember thinking, oddly, that she looked like a huge chocolate bar. Fitting, if you think about it, but an odd thought under the circumstances. I heard her throat had been cut, but not much more unless you count in the rumors, which were many. I think Lace knew more, but he didn't share information with me. He went to the funeral. They had known each other for thirty years.*

Within a day or two, the neighbors made a little altar, a kind of potpourri of memories outside the apartment on the sidewalk. There were Polaroids of Anne Rose taken with the women from Our Lady of Pompeii and there were flowers and candles. A few people left poems or little notes and about a dozen Mass cards were poked into the sides of her front windows. The little altar stayed there for weeks, the snapshots and Mass cards getting soaked and dirty and the candles lit from time to time. Someone kept replacing the flowers, too.

And now there's a detective named Koklensky who's came around several times. He asked me questions. Pretty obvious questions; more like questions that he has to ask like where we all were that night. Easy for me. I was with Connie at a small off-broadway production. We were planning to go to a quiet bistro afterwards, an easy night out in view of his deteriorating condition. That's also the night Connie collapsed and then went into his final descent, so I was at Cabrini Hospital, waiting for news that didn't come until one in the morning and then the news was that he had died. Connie's illness from AIDS had reached its natural end, but against the odds we planned somehow to take in a play in an astonishing denial of what was actually happening that took great effort to attempt. So, by the end of the night he was gone, and that was an end to it, all the last years of feeling ambivalent towards him. Finally finished, and then I came home and went out for breakfast to begin thinking things over and maybe read the Times *and talk matters over with Connie's family and the next thing I know there's yellow tape around the apartment building and a few days later detective Koklensky arrives to ask me where I was the night in question. He asked everyone questions. I pretty much always assumed that someone thought Anne Rose had money stashed away or I figured it was a random burglary. Soon after, the landlord put in a good lock. I don't know if the family ever brought a lawsuit, but I don't think so. I think the landlord has to have been notified by certified mail before the fact and I don't think anyone ever thought to do it.*

But death is all around these days.

It's true that I haven't absorbed Connie's death. His sister arrived that night around midnight and after she arrived, she was the only one that mattered to the doctors. She was next of kin and the family just moved in. They've taken care of all the arrangements. Nothing left to do but come home. Come home and put together the fragments of our decades together only to discover how little physical evidence is left behind: some jewelry, a few photos, odds and ends—these scraps and odds and ends, tatters that make up the jagged edges of memory. They don't fit into a coherent story at all. Even my childhood can be assembled into something coherent, but these years tell me nothing. So if the three decades with Connie are only shards lying about with dull edges that fit no pattern, it's easier for the moment to focus on poor Anne Rose. The startling and gruesome death of poor Anne Rose.

So anyway, the detective asked lots of questions and I began to feel paranoid like they'd discover something that would appear to lead to me and with Connie dead and unable to back me up, they'd say something like I'd slipped away long enough to do the terrible deed, maybe after the second act or before going to Sardi's or maybe we'd never gone to Sardi's at all and it was just my word for it and I'd be charged and the circumstantial evidence would incriminate me. I'm sure I've been watching too many thrillers or TV dramas, but I've heard about convicts who spent twenty years in prison and then they'd discover someone else did it. When I heard those stories, my heart would close tight and I'd get a worried feeling in the pit of my stomach. Of course, you know all those fears are just a floating sense of vulnerability, but it does happen, after all. There were those childcare workers in Massachusetts and Florida who were charged with molesting children and putting them through satanic rites and they lost everything and spent time in jail. Then it was pretty well proved that the children were swayed by the interrogators and pushed into agreeing with the psychologists who were actually religious zealots obsessed with Satan. It turned out that the prosecution essentially made everything up. Perfectly innocent people trapped in a mess not of their own making and sold down the river. I saw an interview recently with the prosecuting attorneys who still maintained the guilt of those people, despite all evidence to the contrary. They had that wild-eyed look of people who project evil out from themselves and onto their view of the world. There's a look in the eyes of those people and it scares me. I fear becoming prey to true believers, but that fear brings back lost feelings, that old fear of being left alone, unprotected, adrift and astray.

It seems that Anne Rose's sudden death and losing Connie, literally, in a heartbeat has made it seem that a person can be swept out to sea in a moment with no warning. I think you might call that feeling "vulnerability," but writing it makes it seem weepier than the feelings I have, which feel less like a baby cuddled up in a fetal position than, well, that old sense of sitting alone at the end of a twig aflutter in that old white breeze.

I think of Anne Rose sometimes. I think of her often. She was a child in an adult's world and she had found a place among us. Her dresses were dirty and she roamed the streets in search of who knows what. She searched the way drug addicts and alcoholics search for something, with a sense of compulsive desperation. Anything to fill some kind of hole in her soul. I suppose everyone is looking for something, but some people are driven mad by the search. I don't know if Anne Rose was mad—crazy mad—but she played around the edges of madness, and yet she had her place in our little world where we held her close. When I think of Anne Rose, I think of the crazy people in some Indian tribe before the white settlers came. Before the true believers got to them, the white settlers and their missionaries who knew how people are supposed to be instead of who they are. I imagine that the crazy people had their place then. Perhaps they were the shamans or the ecstatic dancers or the woman who bathed all day in the stream and cried out to unseen spirits. If you were to read magazines and newspapers or listen to the evening news, it would seem that there is no place for people like Anne Rose anymore, but here on MacDougal Street there was a place made for her. She did nothing that I can see to make the world better. She didn't work and she didn't create, but still I think of her often.

However much they fought and for all her girlishness immaturity, Lace, I think, has been badly hurt by Anne Rose's death. He's became silent and moody. He sits at the store lost in his thoughts. He spends less time in the country and I step in for him more, driving up to Westchester or out to New Jersey to review the auctions and estate sales. And when I do that, driving alone in the car, my mind wanders back to her because maybe I'm compelled to search for something the way Anne Rose was. Of course, I don't see myself spending days and nights sorting through trash bins just because I need to fill gaps in both time and the space in my home. But I still saw in her the human desire to search and so I wonder how different she was from the rest of us. I understand looking and looking. It could be curiosity; always looking towards the next horizon or under the next rock. Maybe it's the hunting instinct, part of the genetic makeup of the human species, and it might even be a good thing and not something even to wonder about. But if that's the case, then a person has to accept that they'll never be satisfied and it almost seems to me that a person would start dying if they find what they're looking for, end the search and be satisfied with things as they are. I suppose that would be like a leaf at the end of a small branch waiting for that warm breeze to take it away.

* * *

It's been months, now, since Connie died and it's time to turn to it at last. His family took care of everything. They treated me as dearest friend of their family member, which I suppose I was by then. God knows, I had not been happy with Connie for a long time. Maybe years, even. Age had made him arrogant and difficult and I had begun to feel trapped. He dropped names, told everyone how much he'd spent on everything, wore more and more makeup and he put on weight. I didn't feel it was up to me to judge how a person handles getting older. He talked incessantly about aches and pains and he seemed terrified that his vital juices were draining out of him. That much I could sense, but it wasn't attractive and over those last years he had been unattractive to me physically and mentally, too. I thought I should stay loyal, but then to whom was I staying loyal? My old friend Connie? This man who died was someone different from the person I'd been involved with originally. He had become someone unpleasant. In time, I think now, I would have had to back off, resolve it somehow, and even break it off if I had to.

Our relationship changed around us in the final years. It wasn't anything like what we had begun with. And yet one stays on. I felt a sense of duty and I watched as he grew frail and thought, "You can't leave now, Patrick." But he became almost abusive and it was difficult to hang on. Guilt and duty and memories of how things were once. These things kept me going. And then Connie died and his relatives closed in on his death. As for me, any sense of our relationship has faded away and after all those years with him there's so little left that even memories won't nourish me because, in the end, there's no story to tell.

He never mentioned me in his will, which surprised and hurt me. We never discussed property, never having lived together. In the end, even after all those years, neither of us had ever been willing to really commit, preferring our independence. It seemed better to stay free and, looking back, I don't regret that decision. Still, he hadn't mentioned me at all. Had I completely misinterpreted his feelings? Did we stand for nothing? Looking back, even after all this time, it seems that I spent those years with a stranger.

CHAPTER XXIV

"So what the hell am I supposed to do while you're away?" Agnes was half joking perhaps, but she was serious. Matters with sensitive Robert were not good. "I'm mouldering out here in the country like some fungus on a fucking tree, you're taking off to play castanets, Robert's in Arizona sitting under a crystal pyramid or something. Fuck the both of you."

Having called to say that he was going to Acapulco for a long stay, now Lace pictured her pacing the living room of the cabin, looking out to the annoying, babbling brook that she said made more noise than ambulance sirens on the way to a hospital. She had been talking this way for months. "There isn't a noisier place on earth," she would say. "First there are the damn crickets and then someone's dog over in the next holler starts up and that starts a vulture screeching somewhere. There are tree frogs and gnats in your ear. On a still night—well, there is no such thing as a *still night*, but on a night with no wind—the insects and dogs and cats and tree frogs and crickets can drive you hysterical. It's a wonder farmers die with any of their hearing left intact and it just leaves you praying for a breeze in the trees to drown it all out. Then the sun comes up and the birds start in, which is enough to drive you straight to the vodka bottle. Actually, this morning it *did* drive me straight to the vodka bottle."

Robert, of course, was up at dawn running. He knew a finch from an albatross, which to Agnes made him Audubon. She complained about the drives back and forth to New York, and the cost of gassing up the car. While he tended a small vegetable garden and ran several miles, she paced back and forth behind the glass windows looking out over the property like some caged gerbil and called her writers, culled manuscripts, set up book tours and personal appearances and wrangled with publishers.

Then Robert would fly off to some airhead convention. Just now he was in Sedona working with a New-Age group. They were laying out large patterns in the desert with stones and scratches in the earth. According to Robert, they were using spiritual vortexes that magnified their peace-loving effects upon the world as they carved great, spirit designs upon the rocky red earth. But, because they were cutting and scratching delicate desert topsoil, environmentalists were accusing them of doing damage that could not be undone in a millennium. Where was all that fucking peace he was creating? Not here by any damned shot. "Not here," was the thought that underlay her mood these days. "Not here in the pit of my stomach or in the conversations that fail to satisfy and the lovemaking that isn't what I need any more. Not in the life we're supposed to be making together. Some fake, pretend peace out there beyond the horizon where it doesn't play out and doesn't signify shit. That's for fucking sure." So that's how she pretty much thought and that was what infuriated Agnes. Robert had a fey quality by which he divorced what he thought he was doing from what he was actually doing. In her view, while he tried to make the world a better place, some fatal misunderstanding of how the world actually worked caused situations that were worse than those he found. He wouldn't turn around and confront what was actually there in front of him. He had a knack for muddying the waters, worsening the misunderstandings that make the world a lousy enough place to begin with and a worse place even than that if you don't fix things when they need it. Pretty words to oil rusted hinges.

Still, all that might have been well and good for Agnes if his clumsiness was played out only on the world stage, but on a personal level she wasn't getting what she needed out of Robert. His domesticity and his willingness to listen bode well at the beginning. He was up in the morning to make an apple pie. He cuddled in after dinner and listened to her talk about business and he said "yes, yes" and "Oh, yes, we all feel that way sometimes" in a way that made her feel better at first. Early on, she always left Robert feeling comforted. But as time went on, she began to sense that she wasn't being listened to at all; at least she wasn't being heard at the level she wanted. Out of their conversations came no new ideas and never an outright criticism or even a mere suggestion. He just provided comfort, which tasted to her like a constant diet of oatmeal cookies.

Robert's softness when he interacted with Agnes became a metaphor: the softness of his body, the spongy quality of his ass—which never got firmer no matter how much he ran—and finally his softness in speech and action were all mixed up in her mind so that now, when he came to her soft in bed, she even had to work to get him ready to fuck. He seemed vacuous to her, empty and flaccid and floating. In bed, he was too concerned about what pleased her, worrying about her reactions to him and whether he had done everything to her satisfaction. "God, what I'd do for someone who just *fucks*! Just take his own satisfaction and ride me with that!" she complained to herself, annoyed and vaguely disgusted. It took time, but she began to think back to the hours with Jonathan. He took what he wanted or waited, forcing her to fill a void. But he hadn't been vacuous. The void he left for her to fill was an empty place demanding to be entered; a mysterious cavern that cried out to be inhabited. Robert left her empty. Yes, he would have done far better to have satisfied himself and carried her to climax with selfish gestures.

Bit by bit, the country house filled with little vessels of home-making: sponge wear, mixing bowls, crockery pitchers, a Hudson River landscape. Agnes had tried to get him interested in sponge wear, but then Robert found a silly sponge wear duck and began collecting ducks instead. Any kind of duck, cheap or not so cheap, would do. They began to inhabit corners and gather dust. Bookcases cluttered slowly with small found objects that cloistered Agnes in their grasp and gripped her closer and closer as she spent less and less time in the city, growling against her confinement with mounting rage.

The two of them danced around each other like mating insects caught in a dull summer breeze. As their embrace tightened, the relationship became ever more carnivorous. She became demanding as he tried to listen, holding her into the night until she became smothered by his embrace and broke loose. Then she walked around the living room in circles behind the sofa, making her points by attacking with a voice that rose up harsh against the soft, country evening. Exasperated as Robert cooed at her, she hated the way he talked and didn't act and didn't even talk about action and then she became rough and mean. Outside, all the while, crickets kept up their monotonous drawn-out creaking chatter. Like dark spirits, they, too, remained hidden away in their unlit, removed hiding places. They, too, hovered outside the windows of this lonely house in the woods, just out of reach, talking, interminably talking but untouchable and unthinking.

No, Robert and Agnes were not working out and Lace had listened to all this before. He took her tantrums in stride, continuing with his news.

"Wanderlust, my dear." Lace countered her jab, voicing enthusiasm over his travel plans and pulling Agnes back to the original conversation. "I have to fly away sometimes. You know I'm a brittle thing and I don't want to stay in New York just now. Can't, really, if it came to that. Little Patrick can handle the store; he's done a bang-up job so far. But for you, Agnes, what can I say? I am sorry you're feeling so all alone."

"I'm *not* all alone." Agnes knew as she said it that it was a lie. "No…Yes, well, I am alone just now, you know." She paused. "Rats."

"Agnes, you're stronger than iron, honey. I guess I hate leaving you, really I do, but don't you think you'll work things out with Robert? Three's a party, or a crowd or too much ballast, isn't it? What can I do if I stay?"

"Screw working things out, Lace. With what? Talking to Robert is like playing with silly putty. He'll seem completely in sync with what I say, eyes all teary and curled up on the sofa like some damned puppy and then he bounces off in some weird direction that has to do with his conception of a loving universe and both of us unique creations of some goddamn thing so we end up talking about his meaningless vision of pure love and compatibility while what I just said gets thrown out the fucking screen door. If I never see another screen door and a fucking back yard and, god almighty, another screaming neurotic babbling brook, it'll be too soon."

"Well, princess, the way is clear. Why don't you just drown him in that annoying brook and be done with it?"

"The fucking brook is even shallower than he is! But it's fear, I guess. Fear…not stark raving fear. Well, maybe not fear at all exactly. I don't know, Lace, I just can't screw up the courage to plain out leave him. What's wrong with me anyway? I've got like six ovulations left in my entire female life and what of it anyway. I don't want a kid. I don't want to get old. I've got two months before my tits hit my knees when I run. I don't think I'm afraid of loneliness. I was happier single, I think but I'm not sure. Am I afraid of getting old alone without a man? God help me if that's what it is. Why did I want him in the first place?"

"Well, in the first place did you want him? I thought he just grew like Topsy in your cabbage patch." Lace thought that over for a moment. "No, the cabbage patch and the back yard came later. He just grew like Topsy, plain and simple. Now here he is, the immovable force."

"The immovable non-force is more like it. I'm giving it some more time, I guess, Lace, but really, what am I looking to you for? I'm a grown girl. If I'm stuck in a mountain holler it's my fault and I'll have to haul myself out. First step is to come in from the farm. I'm driving in next Sunday. Lunch, honey?"

"Sure. Same place at 2:00?"

"Done." And she rang off. The outburst saved her for the next round with Robert. She wasn't so worn out and angry. Strength in confession, she guessed. Agnes took out some notes and called Random House. She was ready to get back to work.

CHAPTER XXV

After the sacrifice, Jonathan's sense of destiny seemed to pass. He smoked some cocaine, but far less and after a time his desire for it disappeared altogether. The apparitions no longer appeared to him and he felt vaguely forsaken. Now that the sacred mission was finished, he imagined that the magical, evanescent creatures had moved on to other tasks. He was not hurt or annoyed, really, even if he had been abandoned. He was a man, after all, who needed a rest after a long and arduous project. He floated insensibly from one day to the next, keeping his tiny apartment tidy. He scored fewer tricks. There was less money. Somehow his sexual drive left him; Marjorie Carbonoy called once and he went over, but the electricity was gone. He performed well enough, but for some reason what had been riveting was now simply tedium. He was not asked back. Perhaps Jonathan's diffidence had ceased to be alluring and Marjorie's clientele was ready for new diversions. He did not dare to go back to Rennie Rodriguez.

For a while the few tricks that he did score around Times Square, the handouts of his mother and neighbors or a trickle of dollars from public programs seemed to tide him through. Six months after the murder, his mother died. He did not go up for the funeral. There was nothing to go up to; there were no family and later there had been no real friends outside her charismatic Catholic church. Members of the church tried to contact him, but his phone had now been cut off. The letter came too late and he didn't recognize the name of the woman whose signature appeared at the bottom. He didn't respond at all.

Oddly, as if the spirit of Anne Rose had returned to inhabit him, he began to pick up items off the street and on Sundays he spread them out on a blanket over off Sixth Avenue near where he remembered seeing the churchwomen and where he had bought the books that had so fascinated him. Now they seemed dirty and they held no interest for him. He noticed that they smelled of acrid smoke and sensed that they had been saved from a fire. He was able to eat and pay the rent, not always on time, and from time to time he scored some cocaine to cook. But now that the apparitions were gone, nights alone with the glass stem and the fine, white pebbles of cocaine lost their interest, too. Slowly he stopped the drugs and began to observe the solid world around him. He did not pick up men and women the way he had. He would fix his sexual stare at people, but somehow they stared forward and passed, leaving him and his hollow, yellow stare behind.

It was, indeed, very strange that he continued to pick items up from off the street and he began to catalog them and order them in his meticulous, neat way. Sometimes, he would go to the library and research them and in time he bought a card table and sat up at a regular spot right along Sixth Avenue, among the other second-hand dealers and the ladies from the church and South Americans plying shawls and the Koreans with turquoise and pewter jewelry. From time to time, his research would bear fruit and he would discover that some discarded piece or another had some real value. Then he would leave the apartment on Elizabeth Street early in the morning on Sunday and go first to the Twenty-Sixth Street market or to the dealers in the stalls around 25th Street and trade it to the better dealers. They began to acknowledge him with silent nods and sometimes a cheerful greeting. One day, he knew, he would be one of them with his own shop, in from the bitter cold and the wind-swept drizzle that descended in winter and away from the hot sun of summer.

The awful moment when he killed Anne Rose sank back under a serene, submerged swamp of memory. All of the rich tapestry of his apparitions and the quest to complete his divine mission belonged to another time, but when he did reflect on those past events he felt that he had been adrift in a story not of his making. It was not for him to wonder why or how he had been singled out like Moses who floated on the Nile straight into the arms of Pharaoh's princess. In some way that he could not describe, he had done great things for God. The language of small, charismatic sects had in some ways created him. It was their cosmology that explained to him that there were intercessors for humans with god; that he might come before the great throne of God almighty to plead the case for man; these ways of thinking provided a platform for defining what he had done, for clearly this God required sacrifice. After all, had not God sacrificed his own son and who else besides? Not just the fat, fertile woman whom he had killed, but himself as well. God had given and worked through his sexual magnetism. That much had been clear to him always. God had taken the euphoria of sex and the languidly powerful magic of those apparitions to work his majestic and inscrutable design. Jonathan was left now with a day-to-day life of small objects traded up for greater objects. Just as his god had used a lesser object, enhancing his value, Jonathan sought to add value to these small, found items. He bent over his new craft with the concentration of a counting house clerk, knowing that he had done great things for mighty beings; that he had to go on with life. Jonathan gave it no further thought than that as he moved on easily, without regret.

A year went by and it is possible that Jonathan forgot where he had gotten the greenish owl that he secreted away with his pipe and took with him from Anne Rose's apartment or perhaps he no longer cared where he got it. He took it one Sunday morning and placed it with the other items that he was gathering for sale. It sat all day on the table on Sixth Avenue and no one bought it. After three weeks, Jonathan noticed a chip showing white on the base against the vert-de-gris finish. He touched it up, but still it did not sell. The statue became one of his display's fixtures, sitting usually near the back, looming over the smaller objects in front.

It was on one of those muggy hot days in summer that Jonathan looked up from an *Antiques* magazine to see a woman stopped along the sidewalk, two or three steps back behind someone who was fingering a watch. She looked familiar somehow. She looked at him hard, her face so contorted that Jonathan's heart seized. For a moment, he feared that a terrible blow had befallen her and that she might require emergency medical assistance. She stared at him intensely for a long moment so that Jonathan averted his eyes, pretending to see something to the side of her.

Veronica stepped forward and reached to the back of the table picking up the owl and grasping it in her hand. She remembered even the chip at the base and saw it there, dressed over with some coloring, but still evident. This was Anne Rose's owl. The one they had found on their outing together that fine, sunny day so long ago. She became calm; steely calm. She held the owl firmly and gathered her resolve, thinking furiously. She couldn't just buy the owl because it had to be traceable to this person. Yet it must be here when the police came. She couldn't let it get out of her hands; she couldn't let the trail evaporate. She was a little unsteady, a little light-headed.

"How much for this owl?" she asked. Was that really her voice, so level and even that she could hardly believe that the sounds she heard were her own? Blood pumped audibly through her ears. "No suspicion," she forced herself to think. "He mustn't get suspicious of me."

"$20.00."

"I'm out of cash. Can you hold it for $5.00 and I'll come back with the rest?" She congratulated herself on her good thinking. That should buy some time.

"Sure. I'm here until five. Be sure to get back before then, okay?" He barely noticed her as he spoke.

That was that; so simple; so simple and direct.

"Oh God, don't let someone else offer more," she thought as she hurried to the nearest payphone to call Detective Koklensky.

CHAPTER XXVI

Dear Journal,

A couple of days ago, Lace took me to lunch. He was jauntier than I've seen him in some time, in fact happier than he's been in the half a year or so since Anne Rose's death: more cheerful and a bit flushed. I guessed he had had a couple of drinks earlier. He announced that he wanted to leave for a while and go to Mexico. He has a right to sublet his apartment for a year and that was what he is going to do. And he's found the right person, a young female college student to tend shop; the perfect person he hopes. He is off to Acapulco—he had a place lined up already—and he's going to live there for a year.

The general idea is to hire someone to sit in the store. "But it needs someone to run it, which is something you could do part-time," he said to me. "I just want to get away." Beyond that, there was nothing in detail worked out in his mind.

That sounded fine to me. We're closed on Mondays anyway. We could just close on Tuesdays as well and hire someone from noon to five or six on Wednesday through Friday. I wouldn't even have to leave the Twenty-Eighth Street Flower Emporium.

All that sounds simple enough, yet there's still this nagging Connie thing hanging like a dark mist around me and I'm only beginning to separate out feelings. I sort of know the mix of emotions at this point: There's something like guilt, because I had ceased to love him, really, and felt trapped, stuck for a long time. And then, because I didn't have the nerve to say no, I continually felt raped by him, not just sexually but generally. Connie was some kind of authority figure to me by the sheer force of his gargantuan will. I lost my nerve around him and hated myself for it, so I became guilty and angry with myself for wasting those years. Still, I must admit, I think I was fond of him, although if you keep company with someone for years and years that turn into decades, what's supposed to happen? Is what I felt fondness or resigned comfort? Wasn't it like that, a lot of times? Year turned into year and you got used to things. You got used to being together and as for the excitement: wasn't it supposed to die out anyway?

Now that he is dead, all that anger at myself has burst out. Am I such a wimp that I can't stand up to people, assert myself, stand on my own?

I criticize myself for not being assertive, but I never allowed things to get too close, either. No need to push back, I suppose, as long as we stuck to seeing one another on Tuesdays and some weekends. I think he would have agreed to a clear definition of our relationship, a real marriage. It's not that he hadn't proposed. All that's in the past, but still. At the end, what really existed? More than a roll in the hay, less than what exactly. He didn't even include me when he thought to write his will and his daunting battery of friends haven't kept in touch and generally it feels like I wasn't much up to making anything very substantial out of any of it.

Well, Lace knows me too well not to notice a dark cloud hanging over my head these days. He hadn't said much, and I didn't want to intrude on him. Anne Rose was a blow to him. But over our lunch he suggested something concrete: a partnership, a step up from just pitching in when the need arose.

After he put his proposition to me, I paused for a long time.

"Well, I don't know," was the first thing out of my mouth.

"What do you mean, you don't know, my boy?" Lace sounded really concerned. It was almost amusing the way he fussed with his napkin and looked away, but I know he was thinking as he folded the cloth and placed it carefully in front of him on the table. He wanted his arguments to be persuasive, I think. He added, "This is what you've been doing anyway and doing a good job too, if I might say so. You don't have to give up anything and you have plenty to gain."

I know I sat in silence for maybe half a minute, because I actually didn't know how to answer him.

"Something about Connie, isn't it?" Lace ventured, half question, half statement.

"No, not Connie directly... I'm sure not. It's just that you commit to something and then nothing comes of it in the end. At least that's how I'm feeling these days."

"First of all, you never did commit to Connie." I remember Lace pausing to adjust himself for a fleeting second and I got a feeling he was about to unburden himself of something he'd been thinking *about for some time. I know him pretty well, after all, and when he fidgets it means he's giving something some thought, so after folding and unfolding his hands in front of him like a pianist about to start a concerto, he continued, "Well, that's unfair, I suppose. Not for the world to judge the strength of your commitment, I suppose, and you were together for twenty years. I do think he could have remembered you, my boy. I know you weren't after the family jewels, but something would have been nice. But I'm not Connie, this is just a business set-up and we can have the agreements written out."*

I was silent. It wasn't just Connie. Nothing from all those years seems to be surviving his death. If Connie's friends weren't staying in touch and the family kept polite and distant, what were they saying about me? Did I have what it takes to pull this off?

"Do you think I'd pull out on you? I'm sorry, Patrick. He was an arrogant asshole sometimes. He just was. You know it and though there's no point speaking ill of the dead, there's no reason mincing words either. Maybe it was your good judgment that made you think twice before moving in with him. Maybe you kept your distance for good reason. There's no helping all that now, but do you think I wouldn't live up to our agreement?"

Lace knitted his brow and gauged me for a long, appraising minute and then continued his train of thought.

"No, not just Connie, I imagine. I can't advise you on relationships, dear boy. Don't have any myself. But I'll tell you about something I've been considering…thinking about, you know."

I had known Lace then for well over twenty years and yet it was only then that I learned something new about him. He read a good deal at the store and if I was a little late meeting up with him, I would find him busy reading something. Over the years he introduced me to the classics: from Julius Caesar's Commentaries and Montaigne to Proust and Sartre. I ran into him once or twice reading under a tree in Washington Square Park. So I was well aware that Lace read a good deal, but I always assumed he read literature. I never noticed that he read science or technological stuff. It surprised me when he reached into a tote and took out a book on particle physics since he seemed to me to be a literary sort of guy. Carlisle or Lamb, maybe.

He sat back for a moment, took a sip of his brandy, which he nearly always ordered after lunch, absentmindedly played with his napkin which he unfolded and folded once again, finally leaving it in a heap on his plate. Fidgeting on that scale means he was really taking time to construct what he was about to say, something either complicated or delicate. Then he launched into his new topic, "New interests, young man…Got to keep the old mind in working order. Never read science much before, you know. Well, maybe the social sciences, history, philosophy, that kind of stuff, but there's something to finding out how the world works you see. The hard facts, if anything is a hard fact, which has something to do with where I'm going with this."

As I write all this down, it astonishes me how imprinted on my mind it still is. Maybe that's because I felt that it promised to be an important conversation. It was only a few days ago, so memory still serves, but I think there's something more at work. Maybe…especially…because it happened so recently, the memory of it is being moved from near-term to long-term memory, so you catch those old stories in the process of formation, like layers of sandstone laid down into the formations of geologic time. And I sense, now, that memories from the distant past *are themselves changed as recent ones overlay the perception of events from long ago. But isn't long-term memory just another trick, just another bunch of Christmas tree ornaments fitted together so that the fragments fit together into a story? The pieces made up of Lace's cloth bag, his napkin, the brandy and flecks of food on his side of the table fit together into a narrative just as my mother's kitchen table and the cherry covered café curtains under sepia light fit into my memory to make sense out of a story. Over time, and this has happened over just the last two days, the past takes on a particular sense only because of what you've come to understand later on. Instead of being a fixed thing, it is warped by its own future. New ways of thinking throw light not just on the present but they also change perception of the past. The story that grows from a kernel planted earlier in time is actually a story told backwards, the cause and effect are reversed. Perhaps lunch with Lace is so clearly etched in my mind because it has been a first step to understanding something new. I think I have begun to see something differently and my mind tries to reorder the past in order to substantiate the present.*

Whatever the case, on that day, whether during a routine lunch or a construct of memory, another junction, another bifurcation, has begun to open before me. There is a sense of something that at last will answer this awful sense of failure, that will draw me away from the leaf at the end of a twig, back past the forks along the branches that led me here, back to some larger way of seeing things. Lace had discovered physics and he liked to expound, too, and so he proceeded to do just that.

"There's something about what's bothering you and the way the world works, somehow. It's a malaise people have and you're not alone in

it. Anyway, that's what I think, or I sense it about you. No, I can't tell you about people. But it seems to me that the world works in a certain way, from the very bottom up. The basic stuff of matter itself is fascinating. Of course, it makes for fascinating reading for me, but, more to the point, it's fascinated some of the greatest minds in history. The weird fact is that we know nothing about the very heart of things. We can't trust what we see of the world and we can't measure it at its most fundamental level. We can't even be certain exactly where a simple particle is and how fast it's going at the same time. We can't get a fix on it. Whether that's the actual truth of things is anyone's guess, but it is our experience of it. And then there's the question, is it really a particle at all, because if we look for a wave moving through space, we get a wave. But if we look for a particle, voila! We get a particle!" He sat back and softly clapped his hands like a magician saying 'voila' and producing a white rabbit. "We get what we're looking forward to getting and the underlying objective reality of things is as slippery as holding onto Jell-O. And it's not that I don't understand it. No one understands it!"

He shrugged his shoulders and threw his arms out with a quizzable expression as if to accentuate the weirdness of it all.

"The closer we look, the fuzzier the picture becomes so that the more precise we are the less we know. Part of it is, of course, that when we look at such small things, the pressure of the light we use—the photons themselves—distorts any measurements we try to take. But, as I said, matter is either a wave or a particle. It can't be both things, yet it is, depending on how we try to measure it. So what are we dealing with, this thing we experience as solid? That may be the question for a theoretical physicist, but it's not what interests me at

the moment. The question for me isn't how it is that we never know precisely what we're looking at, the real quandary is how we can end up knowing anything at all. The very center of the world we inhabit is made of uncertainty."

I sat back in my chair, listening carefully. Obviously, Lace was using some kind of metaphor, but just how it applied to me was a mystery.

"The surprise is that, just as soon as we realize we can't know the exact whereabouts and speed of a particle or even understand on a fundamental level what state it exists in, we can very quickly be certain of the particular probabilities. And it's these probabilities that make up the world we trust, not anything we know about the thing itself. Actually, the equations that describe these uncertain things are the most precise ones in science, which means that their relationships are quite dependable and we can trust how they're going to act under certain circumstances. At the heart of matter and energy is nothing particularly definable and yet almost immediately, as we step away from that uncertainty, we know to a very precise degree how these uncertain things interact."

I guess I was getting impatient. "What the hell does this have to do with Connie and the business and that I'm not sure about any of it"

"Now, now my boy. I'm really just saying that everything is unknowable from the ground up. It's designed that way, Patrick, at the base of it all. If, that is, there's a designer at all, but whether or not there's a supreme designer, it seems at any rate that that's the way things are: just a mist of stuff at the bottom of everything. Still, we build things that aren't solid at their very center. We can erect buildings, because, taken together, elementary particles become dependable. Statistically, *the particle will exist in a definable way. It's all we need to build an entire city out of uncertainty."*

The afternoon was getting on and it was time to get back to the Twenty-Eighth Street Flower Emporium, so I looked vaguely at my watch and then Lace checked the time on his and we agreed silently that it was time to wind things up. We called for the check.

As we got up to go, Lace went on. He began to stand, but seemed to think better of it as he considered for a moment. He sat down and he fit the book back into the tote. It seemed that he was confused about something and then his eyes widened into a look of genuine amazement.

"This new reading of mine has gotten me thinking about something we experience in normal life. Every day every one of us places absolute trust in something we don't truly know. Think of this: at a red light, cars come to a halt and pedestrians pass in front of them and no one thinks for a moment that one of the drivers, on a whim, might step on the accelerator. We know nothing about these people. We know that people sense the world, interpret things, in entirely different ways so that sometimes it appears that people hardly see things the same and yet we put our lives into their hands, trusting that all people will, first of all, see the color red in similar enough ways to interpret the color red in the same way—as stop rather than go—and that for whatever reason they will not run us over. Can we be certain that people who stop for us at a red light for us see that light in the same way we do? In fact, we probably don't see colors the same way as others do. There's been research. They've shown people the same simple stripe of red on a white background. You know what? Different people's brains light up in different areas, which means that we don't process the same

information in the same way, so maybe what we see is not exactly the same as what other people see. Perhaps it's not the physical fact of red that we all agree on as much as the difference, the relationship of red to green or violet or Siena Sunshine at the paint store.

"I've come to the conclusion that we know nothing of people's intentions or values in anything approaching an absolute way. How they think can be a complete mystery to me, anyway, and yet we place enough trust in them that we expose our very lives. Sometimes our trust isn't warranted and a car will continue through the light and maybe even a lunatic will start up and mow down someone, so once again things can get fuzzy if we look at individual events, but overall things like that happen so seldom that it lands in the newspapers and we know that those people are robbed of something, that they're a statistical anomaly. We even know that those exceptions prove the general rules of behavior, and it doesn't keep us from trusting that essentially all drivers see red light in some way equivalent to the way we see it and that they see us, too, and will let us pass in front of them without harming us.

"It's an idea that permeates the universe, Patrick. Like a basic particle, we have no way of judging how people will behave if we only focus on one point in time, even people we know quite well, and they behave quite surprisingly sometimes, but we do know how people act in general and we build our lives and create cities and civilizations. Still, it is possible to build something solid, even from a heart of uncertainty. It is possible to learn how the world works to a fair degree of accuracy. We learn what individuals can and can't do, or perhaps more importantly what they can provide within our relationships with them. But considering how crazy people are, it's a wonder we

can trust relationships at all. It seems to be at the heart of how the world works that the closer you look, the less certain you can become and yet…and yet it all works out and we can build a life with a fair amount of trust."

Then, as he got up, he finished with a parting shot. "Wasn't it La Rochefoucauld who said something like 'it's easier to know mankind in general than any one person in particular'?"

At the mention of La Rochefoucauld, I realized with a certain satisfaction how many years Lace had been schooling me. I had come to New York with a middling education. How was it that I knew about people like La Rochefoucauld, or Montaigne or about Elizabeth I's speech to her troops? I had learned from the society doctor what was chic and what glass was right for a Bordeaux and from Connie I had learned how people might make their way in the world, but Lace had been a mentor to me for years, teaching me, discussing things with me, and arguing with me. Have I learned, somewhere along the way, how to think? In essence, he had shared with me his thoughts: what people give one another and what we can rightfully expect, not in moral terms but in the objectified language of science that describes how things work rather than why they ought to be. I was immediately grateful to him for it because it seemed to me then as I stood up to leave our luncheon, as it seems to me now as I write this, that the humanist education he provided is coming into play to make the world more understandable, even if the understanding of it takes time, the accumulation of knowledge, and a journey across branches of a tree that is always growing into the future despite the uncertainties of space and time.

CHAPTER XXVII

Veronica was driving back from an appointment with her hairdresser. Time had healed much of her hurt and the ladies at the salon, back behind the strip mall on Commack Road, no longer took pained and circumscribed measures to protect themselves from her grief. Time was, just after Anne Rose was killed, that the other women avoided her gaze. Of course, they offered their condolences. Then they stayed away from her after that.

The exception was Flo Finelli. Together, they weathered the storm, speaking regularly and lunching together often. Flo Finelli was a part of Veronica's grief, a part of the wound, a part of the healing and a part of the scar that remained.

But the ladies from her suburban life were different. Each in her way had followed the same emotional route that started with expressions of sympathy and ended as the women protected themselves and then detached altogether. Veronica's first appointment after Anne Rose's murder had been just before the funeral. The clients who were there that afternoon, she remembered who they were, Marie Gladler, Jane O'Reilly, Wilma Reider especially, circled around her, clutching at her and squawking awkward phrases like ducks at the city pond. Veronica had carpooled their children after Little League and entertained them in her home. The women at the salon gathered around her that day, touching her, hugging and speaking at her. They sent condolences by the fist-full. There was a heap of Mass Cards still lying in Veronica's desk drawer, the drawer in the kitchen near the refrigerator where she always stood to write checks for household bills.

But by the next appointment, things had changed. She began to realize that the words they spoke to her in condolence were formula phrases that people use. "I'm so sorry, Veronica." "If there's anything I can do."

"What can you do for me?" she thought. "Can you ease this grief? Can you explain to me who would do this thing? Can you give me a why? Can you tell me what this pain is that won't go away, the one that runs scarlet through my dreams and stains each waking day. My morning coffee is sour with pain. The orange juice is rancid in my throat and each day aches. Can you help with that?"

No, she knew, of course, that they couldn't help with these things and she would not be needy; wouldn't look to them for things they couldn't give her. The women from her life out in the suburbs were now bystanders, blurred faces in a crowd that you saw from a speeding car, mannequins with lacquered hair and perfect nails sheathed in shiny, new SUVs with glossy tires. Oh, each one, she knew perfectly well, had a private sorrow, but not one of them had ever come across a rotting body infested with flies. They had their private injuries, but all they suffered seemed insubstantial to Veronica, small petty quarrels and hurts of suburban life, it seemed to her these days, and she gripped with steering wheel with anger as she thought about it.

No, Flo understood and they could talk, but she wouldn't ever go to those women. Never.

That is how Veronica thought about it, but, of course, the fact is that the women from the beauty parlor and the blocks around her house didn't want to intrude on Veronica's private sorrows. Bereavement must have shown in her aura; it was an electric kind of mourning that glowed around her like a dark soul-force halo. The ladies were afraid of her, steering clear of her vulnerability and hurt, which deep down they felt might be contagious and made them feel vulnerable in turn. And they didn't know how to approach her from the closeted safety of their daily lives where death had been banished forever by good food and happy thoughts and all the future shone bright in the careers and families of their children and the happy lawns and barbecues of their own hazy, fortunate summertime days. To them, Veronica had ventured away, into the dark, unknown crucible of the city and had come back burnt to her very soul.

As a result, Veronica's visits to the grocery store or the salon or the five-and-dime were met with odd silences and eerie politeness. People avoided her somehow, embarrassed by their ineptitude and frightened away by goblins of uncertainty. But that exile from the community of woman passed and slowly Veronica reintegrated back into their world and the talk at the salon returned to light chatter about family and friends, patter about town talk and television. There was a comfort to it, the little things that make life go by like clouds passing overhead aimlessly on a calm day and then over time, the days passed more and more quickly like the fast forward in a film vignette.

Then Veronica found the owl and Detective Koklensky proved that the accused really was the killer. There had been no lack of clues at the scene. The trial was short; there was no doubt at all. The awful matter of Anne Rose was getting resolved and Veronica was prepared to move on with her life. Sometimes the scene from the apartment on MacDougal Street came back to haunt her but not often. She was a strong woman. She had moved on from Little Italy out to the suburbs, raised two children and been a good wife. She had gotten her degrees, built a career. She had done the right things, the expected things except for marrying an Irishman. She could move on, now, beyond the bloodied tinges of this one tragedy.

Her hair newly done up, bobbed and sheared in a new style, she drove quietly down the neat streets, past her ficus hedge, turning at the postbox. She parked the Buick in the driveway. The garage door was open so she went that way, in through the kitchen where Michael was on the telephone.

At first she heard only "Yeah, yeah, that's it. Okay." But she also knew the tone of voice and because she had been married to Michael McGrady for over four decades, she knew that he was talking to Vincent Morelli.

"Sentencing is next week," Michael said. Then he said "Okay. Okay," and then he hung up.

He turned to Veronica as he placed the receiver onto the wall unit next to the refrigerator where the magnets held reminders and recipes and the notes to each other that let each of them know where they would be, when they would be home, what dinner would or might be. That refrigerator, or the one before it, was a constant glue of communication that over forty years bound them together more tightly as a couple than even one person alone can be with their own psyche. Sometimes you didn't know yourself how you felt, but thousands of little notes about every conceivable matter had built a web of little events, a web linking them together from every corner of themselves. Over each of those years, every one of the decades, there had stood a refrigerator, the Maytag and the GE and this new one with the double doors and the slick, black finish, each one of them the solid center holding them fast together. So, Veronica knew without being told what Michael had arranged with Vincent Morelli. Vincent had been a good business partner and a fine godfather to their children. They never asked questions; never asked any favors. On his own, Vincent would have had his revenge, but he needed to sense that he had Michael's permission somehow.

Michael turned to Veronica and his face was grave, ashen and sad.

"God, he looks tired," she thought.

He did look awfully tired. He had not actually had to ask a favor of Vincent because Vincent himself was outraged at Anne Rose's death and the manner of it. All Michael had to do was let Vincent know that the matter was in his hands. "Handle it, Vincent. Let me wash my hands of it because I'm a good man, an unprepossessing man, an unprepared man for the hate I feel." Veronica saw the tumult of those vague thoughts in Michael's eyes and she knew that he hadn't thought any of it out in a conscious way, even if she knew all of it instinctively and consciously. But Michael, sweet Michael was a good man. He had been a good husband because those were the qualities that had made him a good bar owner. How many people had he steered into Alcoholics Anonymous from his bar? And he kept in touch with those guys, too. Made sure they made it. Drove a couple to meetings at the start and always kept a list of meetings at the bar and the number of AA, too, so he could suggest it.

Sweet Michael had been hard hit by Anne Rose's death. This was not the world he knew, an evil world where people did things like that. Vincent Morelli had protected Michael from that kind of world and Michael protected himself so that the bars had been a place for male camaraderie, a place where people—mostly men—came together and unraveled their souls and slowly, as men do, reveal how they felt and what they thought and what their simplest dreams were underneath the complex outer layers they needed to show. That is what Michael brought to the people who surrounded him and protected him from cruelty.

Yes, Michael looked awfully tired and sad at a new unforeseen world in which he had just conspired with his partner to kill another human being in terrible revenge for his terrible acts. All Vincent wanted was his permission. They hadn't really said it straight out, but that is what the conversation meant, even if they flew around the subject like a butterfly trying to land on a poisonous branch willowing in the wind. Once again, Michael was saved from having to confront cruelty dead on, as if the butterfly had been saved from landing too hard, able at last to move on, saved by its own timidity. He always relied on Vincent for these things, if you looked back into the past. "It's true," thought Veronica, "You're partners with a man for your entire adult life. You don't have to come straight out and say the thing." Yes, Michael had given his consent and Veronica knew this even though she had only heard 'Yeah…yeah...okay…"

She had watched and listened and taken note as this moment approached and she knew it for what it was and somehow she cared less than she ought.

He was tired and ashen and sweet, too. He looked at her as she stood there by the door and he walked over to her directly with three long hungry steps and he took her by the shoulders and clutched her close to him and held her tight. His face lay down next to her neck and he pressed his eyes into her shoulder. He didn't hold her like a husband. He held her like a wounded child grasps at its mother for solace and comfort against what can happen to you. He wrapped his strong arms around her shoulders and held on and he quietly began to sob.

"It is an awful thing to murder another human," she thought. "It is an awful thing to be sweet and kind and careful of others and then to exact your revenge on another human being. It is the kind ones who remember that the murderer is a human being and to feel sorrow in the first place. He is that kind of man," Veronica thought to herself in a reverie as she held her husband to her breast. He had begun to heave in his sobbing, like a child who can find no solace, like a child who cannot climb into his mother's lap. She understood that he was terrified. He was not afraid of being caught. That wasn't it.

"He is terrified that he could do this. One can think about an awful act. You think 'I could kill this person or that person.' You fantasize in your rages about what you could do and even what you might do, but you think you wouldn't really do it. But you can," she thought. "You can and then you meet something in yourself that terrifies you and the world isn't safe anymore because you're caught unprotected and you realize, abruptly and at last, that there's no safety anymore at all, ever, and you grieve at that when you cry and then you want your mother."

For what seemed to be an age, Veronica held Michael as he sobbed like a baby whose finger has just touched boiling water for the first and only time. Yes, she knew that cry. She had raised two children. A baby knows nothing about the world: only a mother's milk and the warmth of her breast and then he finds in an instant that something in the world is dangerous and mean and strikes like an arrow from nowhere to put fear in your soul and a blister on your finger. Michael had found that the world can form a lesion on your soul, too.

"He is a sweet man," she thought again as she held him and he sobbed still, the crying unabated. But Veronica knew that he—they— had done what they had to do by conspiring with Vinnie to assassinate a killer who deserved the death penalty. She had already thought about it enough, steeling her courage against the day they would do it. Her fist was already closed, her knuckles white with resolve. They would wreak their vengeance on that evil, little man for what he had done to Anne Rose. She did not cry. She had done that and now the women at the beauty salon chatted to her about small things that did not matter and she would not let that feeling of safety be stolen away from her again. She was a strong woman who had raised two children and was a good wife to her husband and she would go on.

"He will be killed in his turn and what of it?"

She thought about it without flinching, but now that it had been arranged, her thoughts were suddenly no longer on revenging Anne Rose's murder. Her mind turned to other things. They were low on breakfast cereal. She would make Swiss steak for dinner. And then, too, she needed to call the children. They hadn't spoken in several days. That is how her mind began to wander away from grief and back into the routines of her daily life, even as Michael held on to her still, the heaviness of his breaths softening, the despair of his sobs quieting as tears pooled against the pit over Veronica's shoulder blades and the salty liquid ran from his eyes shut tight down her right breast and trickled in a cold pool against the top of her mothering and ready nipple.

CHAPTER XXVIII

Sedona's giant, red boulders are thought by some to anchor vortexes into other worlds. Whether this is true or not, there are people who are caught up in an emotional eddy, swirling in towards the gorgeous scenery as if they were caught in the tightening circles of a whirlpool. When he was with Agnes, Robert without knowing it was hovering near the outermost circle of an eddy. He was doing the laudable thing, the proper and sensitive thing. The thing to be praised. He was putting in time alleviating the pain of those suffering from a new and devastating illness called AIDS.

However much the emergence of AIDS formed a new community of gay people in the public mind, Robert was not affected by that. He did not think of himself as gay in a cultural sense, at least, and being an outsider caring for afflicted people suited him. Detached by nature, passive at heart, he could feel part of something without putting anything crucial about himself at stake.

He met Agnes at an AIDS benefit. She was with that awful gallery owner friend of hers. There were photographs of lower East Side drug kids. Heroin addicts, mostly. They chronicled the underside of a flood of young people pouring into the cities. Kids prostituting themselves, smoking dope, shooting up. The pictures were hard to look at, spoons lit underneath by lighters, needles stuck unattended in the arms of passed our addicts. He winced to see the needles. Some people were saying that AIDS was from shooting drugs, but that didn't square with what he saw. People with decent jobs, people like the suburbanites he knew were getting it. Even so, he wasn't close to them. Maybe they did things he didn't know about, yet somehow equating the new disease with drug use didn't quite square.

Agnes swept him up. He'd been wondering if he was bisexual, perhaps, surrounded as he was by gay activists, AIDS activists, it amounted to the same thing. He was used to laudatory compliments from people. He was doing the right thing, on the side of the angels. He imagined people saying, "You know that Robert? What a good person, a nice fellow." That's how he thought people thought of him, but Agnes would have none of that. She took him by the scruff of his neck like a puppy and more or less pulled him up into her apartment. Robert never had had much sex, so the first weeks with Agnes were a party with no thought given to his moral and ethical bona fides. They fucked, she saw what she wanted in him—he knew that somehow—and he stayed with her out of inertia, because that's how he knew to live and because to break off wouldn't have been nice. Robert was a nice fellow.

Somehow, they found themselves in Connecticut and Robert became involved with environmental causes. The New York watershed was important and there were the migratory patterns of ducks to think about. He got involved and became the office manager for a preservation society. He started collecting ducks. Cartoon-like ducks, pottery ducks, silly ducks, kitsch wood decoys used in the slaughter of real ducks, all would do. He didn't connect the decoys with hunting, strangely, although when a country soul mentioned duck hunting he would wince inwardly at the sad thought of wounded fowl. He would never have said anything, since he was far too nice to do that, and he deflected any notion that decoys played a role in killing ducks. The collection gave him something to do and the AIDS problems were forgotten, left behind in the city. He didn't bring up his experiences there. In Connecticut, it wasn't considered a nice topic.

He survived with Agnes because of the country. She had these friends. A stuck-up ass named Lace who, in turn, gave emotional shelter to a little guy, a sort of ragamuffin named Patrick who kept company with a crazy godforsaken Greek named Constantine. Then there was Lucille whom they called Lucille Lucifer, the woman who was with her when he met Agnes at the gallery. Lucille was too glad-handed for his taste. Too pushy. Not nice. Connecticut was better because the people were nice there. He liked that about them.

They pulled at one another from odd directions. She never would have moved to the country—even part-time as she did—except for Robert. It was one thing to socialize within the confines of a community in crises that seemed to need him. He could bury his head in that, but Agnes' life in New York of theater, parties, lunches and work turned him off. He thought of it as shallow, whereas his work was meaningful, but what he didn't see was Agnes' deep interest in people and how they interacted. Hers was a life of action, a day-to-day doing of things with and for people that involved an interconnectedness that eluded him. This he did not see and he also failed to understand that his own activities were born from an inner passivity: he looked to these needy causes to solve his own inner desires, but the people and the causes themselves meant little to him.

Of course, it was the sex. Robert was generally asexual. He didn't seek it out. If approached by a guy he became flushed, embarrassed, a little insulted to be seen as just a sexual being. Agnes more or less manipulated him to bed and, assuming the top position, rode him home to the best climax he'd ever had. Mind you, he had never known climaxes of great intensity, so the bar was set low. But then he'd never been with anyone as experienced as Agnes and, given his natural passivity, she could pretty well have her way with him. That's how it worked at the beginning.

But Robert was not a person to make things work. He let things work and if they didn't, well, then he didn't think it out too much. As Agnes became exasperated with his softness, he spent all his time in the country and she spent more time in the city.

Under the circumstances, it is not surprising that Robert found himself gradually absorbed into the orbit of a Wiccan matriarch named Naomi Kaplan, who had taken the name of Mother Wanderstar. In her younger days, she had studied Edna St. Vincent Millay at Bard and spent some time seducing, sometimes physically, but more often intellectually, pretty nubile women from Vassar. Naomi—Mother Wanderstar—became a zaftig and general-purpose earth mother upon whose great belly lay many passive, furrowed brows. Robert found his place among the various wandering souls who suckled, metaphorically and metaphysically at her great tits. When Mother Wanderstar decided that advanced beings were soon to visit Earth through the Sedona vortexes, and that it was imperative that she be first in line to greet them, her brood was bound to follow. It was all ethereal and spiritually conceived, of course, but being first to receive the bounties to be derived from newly arriving multidimensional strangers didn't sound too bad either.

That is how Robert found himself in the beautiful, red deserts of Arizona scratching long, straight lines into the delicate topsoil. There was the possibility, too, of paying for the trip by writing an article on environmental issues faced by a desert inundated by tourists, the irony of which was entirely lost on Robert. The thoughtless trauma etched into red sand, begun to give the aliens direction to a landing strip somewhere between Coffee Pot rock and Walnut Creek, came very quickly to the attention of locals who found reason to disagree with some of Mother Wanderstar's premises. Far from being helpful directions to superior beings, there were those, and they were powerful enough to get their ideas across, who thought that these lines were scars inflicted upon the earth. They pointed out that the Naxca lines show that scratches, just like the ones Robert's people were etching into arid desert topsoil, last indefinitely. And those people who didn't see eye to eye with Mother Wanderstar thought that this scarification was a sort of sacrilege. They put a stop to it, time went by and no aliens or six-dimensional superior beings appeared, or if they did, they didn't inform Mother Wanderstar and her folk. As a result, the group began to disintegrate slowly.

But all kinds of people stray though Sedona and one, a guy named Jasper, who hailed from San Francisco and liked to wear a little bit of leather, took a liking to Robert. Their relationship was not sexual at first. One might think it never did become sexual in the way that people ordinarily define sex. Jasper started a conversation with Robert at a local breakfast joint and soon realized that Robert tended to do what he was told. Jasper was good at picking up on this—his entire sexual persona depended on it—and he was good at moving slowly and methodically so that Robert was performing certain, simple sexual services on Jasper soon enough without much fuss or bother. It was control that Jasper was looking for. A blow-job or ironed shirts added up to about the same thing, but adding these things together actually did add up to something serious.

For Jasper, Robert's commitment to being a good boy meant doing the best he could for Jasper, which, in turn, caused Jasper to fall in love with Robert. When Robert saw that look of love in Jasper's eye, he wanted to serve Jasper's needs even more fully. And so it went, with Jasper more in love with Robert as time went by and with Robert more nestled into Jasper's protective chest, more alive in the basking warmth of Jasper's approving gaze.

Ultimately, they settled in that happy embrace in a small adobe house somewhere between Sedona and Cottonwood, Arizona, and they may still live there unless death has parted them.

CHAPTER XXIX

Agnes came into the city, disgusted and tired, decidedly and at last ready to leave Robert behind once and for all. She arrived at her flat Saturday night and surveyed the deteriorating surroundings, taking stock. The enameled aubergine walls, colored the brightness of fingernail polish, caught Agnes' attention. They were in need of touching up. Several vases were full of brown flowers. She hadn't thought to throw out the blossoms and clean them the last time they left for the country. That annoyed her. Just how much had her life fallen apart during their deadly sojourn up in the hills? She started to dust, but stopped in the middle. It didn't seem worth dusting when the fucking walls were chipped. There were some old magazines and newspapers that needed to be thrown out, too, and she needed to clear up her office space. She could start on all that tomorrow. She went out to buy a *New York Times* and then curled up to read, falling asleep around 1:00 a.m.

Sunday was bright and cold, light streaming in hazily through the sheer draperies. She had forgotten to draw the blinds, used to the small country windows with their tiny panes. Agnes took her time making coffee and dressing and then decided to have brunch at Le

Goloue on Madison Avenue. She took along the *Sunday Times Magazine* and sat by the window on a banquette, enjoying the tender warmth of late morning sunlight, ordering an omelet and sipping on an extra strong Bloody Mary while she waited.

It wasn't until the omelet arrived that she looked up to notice a new arrival sitting at the table next to her along the long banquette. A sideway glance caught her eye. He looked away briefly, then back again. He was watching her, Agnes realized, maybe, the start of a flirtation. It caught her off balance, early in the day as it was, and because he caught her unawares she found it sexually unnerving. He was older than she liked, perhaps in his mid-sixties. At any rate, he was well past middle age, whereas forty-five was usually old enough for her. "Well," she thought, "I've got fifty years well in hand myself and I still look pretty damned good and maybe I'm developing a taste for mature men; wouldn't that be the charm? Agnes! Enough romping with children. It's time for a man."

Still, the stranger did unnerve her somehow, a clinched feeling seizing her throat and a chilling nervousness catching her stomach for just a moment. "Butterflies after the life I've led!"

He said, "I could call the waiter for salt, but it seems more charming to ask you. I think they've neglected my table."

"Of course…" she paused and then said, "I'm Mother Theresa, you know. Raised by nuns, the Sisters of Mercy in fact. Far be it for me to see your table left neglected. How about pepper, did they forget that too?"

"Kindness is one of my virtues too. Especially to strangers. But I didn't learn it from nuns. Probably picked it up from the Talmud in Hebrew school. It certainly wasn't my parents."

He could have been in his very late fifties, she thought, but that was parsing ages, splitting hairs. He was at that age when maturity and success make a man virile. He was a big man, too; probably had hair on his back. A man with a big waist and a swagger. No, this wouldn't do. She thought of her younger men, that man who pissed in her, the youthful Manuels and Jorges from East Third and Avenue A. Those men. Awful Robert seemed juvenile all of a sudden. The thought of Awful Robert gave her pause and made her think, "Why not? Let's go romping with the stallions at stud."

Agnes turned partially towards him and eyed him up and down, obviously appraising.

"Careful what you ask for. Ask for salt and you might get the whole salt lick. You might just get the whole fucking Nevada Salt flats. The nuns told us to give a little extra."

"I knew we were missing something at Synagogue." He smiled and extended his hand, moving towards her along the cushions. "Alan. Alan Gold. I have a flat on Lexington Avenue because I stay in town during the week. This is rare to be in the city for a weekend. We live in Hewlett, my wife and I. The kids are grown and moved out, now. Just Hannah and me."

"Direct," thought Agnes. No jerking around and pretending. Wife right out in the open, or else she had misread him. Just a lonely guy out prowling? But why mention his wife if he was trying to pick her up? That was it, she thought. He hadn't said anything to her at all that could be interpreted as sexually leading and she had responded to the most innocuous request with an innuendo. How clumsy! That was her jaded way of looking at things and she was annoyed with herself. Annoyed and embarrassed. Anxious, too, which felt worst of all.

Alan looked down for a moment and smiled to himself, looking up to her with brown sly eyes. She liked the light in them. They were sharp but mild and they had a twinkle in them. He looked playful.

"Most men aren't usually very up front, I guess. Sorry." He had noticed her discomfiture and Agnes realized with a start that he had read her mind and taken it as proof that she had been aroused. "But I like to start off with my cards on the table. I've been in business for forty years and that's always how I deal with people. Cards on the table, out in the open. Look at this *punim*. I'm lousy at poker."

"So it's the old story. Hannah doesn't understand you. You need consolation." She looked down at the table and pointed with her eyes, "From a salt shaker?" It came out more brittle and bitter than she intended.

"Hannah understands me very well. It's been a partnership and a love story, of its kind, since we met and we've been married a pretty long time, raised a family, seen some disasters and grief. Done well together. We have enough money. At some point, we just started to think differently. Or maybe we started to feel differently. I may not know the difference, but we thought, 'Why are we being so traditional?' I had a mistress in town. We'd been together for ten years and it never made a difference to what Hannah and I did together. We were a couple on Long Island, Marcy and I were a couple here. Then I found out that Hannah was having an affair on weekdays just the way I was. They were in love and I loved the life Marcy and I had, even if I didn't necessarily love her. The kids were gone or getting ready to move on. Our lives were made, why unmake them? Hannah and Ben see each other on weekdays. Of course, they have to be more circumspect in a small town, but they manage it and they're really pretty devoted to one another. Hannah and I have *schule* and all those obligations, and all the family duties and our house and the finances and forty years of marriage and a good friendship. If that's not love…"

"What is?" enjoined Agnes. "You certainly make something complicated sound simple."

He reached under the table and took her hand. "I like things simple, it's true. But sometimes there's an asp in Eden. Things get un-simple even with the best of intentions and all your aces in plain sight. Marcy and I broke up a couple of months ago. It's not," he paused to consider something for a second, "at least I don't think it's because of the situation. She wanted marriage, but I still think she accepted things the way they were. But we were getting acrimonious. Why bother, I thought. Really, Hannah is the unbreakable relationship, but not so with Marcy. No reasons for difficulty, so time to move on. I guess the will to work things out wasn't there. That's the danger, of course. You know, the danger when things are simple and the commitments are loose. The ties were easy to break even after ten years, but maybe it was just time to let go"

"There we agree. Same with me. Mine's a wimp called Robert. I know it's rude to speak ill of the ex, but things have just dwindled into nothingness. I've just come into the city to collect my thoughts and start redoing the apartment, which is to say redo my whole friggin' life."

That didn't sound quite right, Agnes thought. Not the right kind of detachment. Alan was going to think she was still with Robert. Oh well. What of it?

"Anyway, my apartment is a shambles," she added. "It's my home and it's gotten out of shape. Time to get back on track."

"I see. Newly broken up. Hope I'm not intruding on your sorrows." He put his hand lightly on top of hers as it lay on the banquette.

Now or never, Agnes thought to herself, and then she picked up her hand, with his palm on top of it, and moved it over his leg, just above the knee. Alan took a long look at her and a slight grin was the only expression on his face. He made no motion for a long second, but his eyes held her hand in place. Then he took just the tip of his pinky and lightly pushed her hand towards his crotch where, to her surprise, she found a thick and ready erection.

"Whoops," he said with a voice that cracked a little like a horny adolescent boy, "Time to call for the check?"

He hailed the waiter and asked for the bill, "One check," he said and paid it. They left two omelets, hash browns and fruit salads on two tables, essentially untouched. Also left behind was a splatter of egg that Alan had flecked from his lip onto the table cloth when Agnes grabbed him.

Alan Golden's apartment on Lexington Avenue was about as far from Le Golou as Agnes' and he took charge as soon as they hit the street, expecting that they would retreat to his place. She let him guide her there and through the rites of lovemaking. He was quiet and experienced, taking a long time rather than going quickly with youthful exuberance. She lay back and flung her arms wide and let nuance overflow her. He had, indeed, a hairy back which should have been repugnant, but wasn't for some reason. She began to stroke his back and the masculinity of it made her arch forward. He had hair on his penis that rubbed rough inside her, the extra friction catching and sparking her on. The finish was severe and noiseless and she grasped him close as they came.

Afterwards, as he buttoned his shirt Alan looked at her sidelong and Agnes noticed the same boyish eyes with the twinkle in them.

"Say, I've got an extra ticket for theater tonight. Want to go?"

"Marcy's hand-me-down?"

"Well, yes, I suppose, except that Marcy's gone for good so it's neutral territory. I'd love your company. I'm serious. I'm in the garment business, plain old Seventh Avenue *schmata* salesman. Own my own company in bargain women's wear. We sell to Wal-Mart, mostly. Not chic, but I have millions. That's not to boast, Agnes, just to let you know who I am. I'd like to take you out and see what happens. I think we could like each other very much."

"Here's who I am, Alan. I just broke up with a loser. I'm independent as hell. I'm an agent, literary agent. Hard as nails, I think. I'll go with you tonight. Yes, I could use a date and I'm ready for a date with a guy who takes charge. Just don't expect anything. That's who I am."

"Fair enough. I'll pick you up at your place, say, Seven thirty? We'll eat afterwards, if it's okay with you."

"Seven thirty, then."

Seven thirty came and with the promptness of a courtier, Alan appeared wearing an elegant and simple suit and Ferragamo shoes of the more classical sort. Outside, waiting, was a car: a plain Town Car driven by his usual driver. "His dresses may not be chic," thought Agnes, "but the man may be."

It was the following Thursday, after a performance of Turandot at the Met, over dinner at a small, good French place in midtown, that he handed her a small package. It was an elegant, simple set of diamond clips in a Tiffany package.

"Please don't think this is rushing things, Agnes." There was a level sincerity in his voice. "I'm not trying to make you beholden. I'd like you to have these and, if you'd like to continue, there'll be more to come. We can have a good life together, be together, do things. If you can live with the constraints, I think I can make you happy."

CHAPTER XXX

Dear Journal,

Now Lace has left us for at least a year and gone off to Mexico. For over two months, I didn't hear a thing from him and I let him be. He may have been jauntier and more cheerful than usual the day he handed over the store to me, but I know he left town with a broken heart.

He left me with Agnes Pranciple as a contact. Agnes Magnus, I've always called her. Sometimes Agnes Dei or Agnes Opus Magnus because she was a lot of work and I never thought she liked me very much, so I end up working doubly hard with her. She made me jump through hoops to please her, which, of course, I was never able to do. She would screw into me with a line of questions if I ventured an opinion and always made me feel as if I'd just expressed the most foolish thought possible under the circumstances, perhaps even pushing the outer limits of what may have been considered foolish up until that particular moment in history. Agnes had always stopped into the store every now and again, but no longer. Lace avoided mixing the two of us. She always made me nervous. She was an imperious woman to be sure, but since Lace adored her, she came with the territory. It was a good month before I felt much like calling her for

Lace's address in Mexico, since Lace had never given it to me and I still hadn't heard from him. I consider that strange, but I sense his self-exile to be a sign of how tired he was of the store and his day-to-day life in New York generally. He didn't have a telephone, so Lace and I have kept in touch by mail. He never did get a telephone, which considering how much he loved to chat or gossip or lecture shows how much solitude he needed.

Early in the summer of this past year, I took over day-to- day operations of the Twenty-Eighth Street Flower Emporium and the owners cut me in as a working partner and began to step out of the enterprise altogether. I've made Lacy Whittaker Antiques a natural part of my little but expanding empire. We use it as a retail outlet for the flowers, it's became a regular stop for decorators and we're doing well. I can hire people to look after it and still use weekends to search for merchandise. After years of doing that, I have plenty of contacts. It's not all that hard and it has been fun.

Meanwhile, gay guys have begun hanging out at the gym as part of our new, ultra-butch, we'll-show-them urban culture. We've graduated from bushy hair, tight jeans and moustaches to biceps and triceps the size of redwood trunks, boasting about chest sizes and sporting abs as hard as sidewalks. It's taken a while, but I've been swept along, too. I couldn't stay up at night going to clubs as much as I was used to doing and I guess the gym gave me some of the same thrill. Then, like a million other men, I met someone at The New York Health and Racquet Club. In Benny's case, the immediate attractions were a cleft chin and a cute butt. He could also lift fifty pounds more than I could and he seemed to like me. He called me and then kept calling me. We added dinners and movies to sex and he still kept in touch, and little by little we sort of got to each other. He is cute, for sure, and I was complimented that he seemed to be so attracted to me.

On the other hand, Benny was a waiter and, as I got to know him, he seemed to change jobs a lot, which made me a bit shy about considering him stable enough to commit to. I was used to Connie, bigger than life and a dealmaker of the first order. Now, here was Benny who drifted along and bounced from restaurant to restaurant, maybe a little too like me if you think about it, which is to say two people just bouncing around in one relationship seemed like an invitation to go nowhere. But we began seeing each other and then things got more serious and we became that sort of primary social unit that people who are seeing each other to the general exclusion of others become. But we didn't live together. We just sort of were together.

One thing I saw immediately about Benny, though, was that he was honest and kind and simple in the sense that he wasn't constantly contorted by complications. He also wasn't very aggressive or combative. He didn't want much out of life, it seemed to me, but yet he was—is—content. After Connie, Benny is easy. He doesn't demand a lot from me, which means that I don't feel I need to change, as I did with Connie who was always teaching me something. We're comfortable together and we wear on each other like a fire on a cold winter's day, not crackling sparkling fire so much as cozy warm embers that you snuggle in front of and sip a good cognac.

So, while I suppose that I have a residual hankering for a larger-than-life man, at the same time, and as much as I may want a go-getter, I can't help but think back on how difficult life with Connie was. Yet I hesitate. It doesn't seem like a good idea to hitch my fate to this warm and cozy little fellow with a cute body and a cleft chin. Where is it going to go anyway? As a result, I've put Benny off, keeping him at a certain emotional distance and telling myself that we we're just dating anyway.

The years with Connie keep circulating through my mind. After all that time, I had been nothing to him but an adjunct, the friend outside the family circle who didn't rate a mention in the will. I couldn't help but think how I stood outside the family circle watching alone as people lined up to give condolences to family members who had not shared a fraction of their lives with Connie. How was I to avoid being ephemeral at the end? Could this simple man really stay the course? How am I going to include him, compromise with him, settle differences and stay together and still keep my treasured independence? Is the life I want a life we could want together?

It is easy to avoid answers. Benny isn't the kind of person to push hard. We saw a lot of each other from the onset, but at some point, I knew that he had come to rely on the relationship. He would cock his head and look at me across the dinner table with those huge brown eyes that looked like they were trying their best to melt my heart, and mostly succeeding. You could see everything written in those large brown eyes. I knew, from the way he stared at me, that he had committed to me far beyond what I had done, so I've started to feel manipulated. Bit by bit there have crept into our conversations plans for the future. Little plans, usually, a trip next year or plans for Christmas. And then Benny said "I love you" one night and I said "I love you" back. And I began to wonder how far I would go and how much of that I really felt. That discrepancy became my secret from him and as time passed my doubts about us felt like a shameful thing between us, a wall waiting to be discovered, a pain waiting to be inflicted on a good and simple man.

You can put off the next step into eternity if events will allow. You can put one foot in front of the next, shuffle forward in a dead sort of motion, and put off forever any step that commits you to any real direction. I've begun to think that is how you end up on the tiniest branch of a tree, aflutter and dazed in that white, cold breeze. I'm catching my life's metaphor in action. What do I expect from shuffling and indecision? Even if I didn't know what I wanted, my philosophical internal debate could last forever. Events are going to play themselves out somehow with or without any direct action on my part, but now that there is a real question which has to do with the direction of my life, I am forced to face up to where I want to go. A failure to act will reveal my secret reluctance and hurt Benny. The time of equivocation is drawing to an end.

Before he left, Lace hired a punk girl with pink hair and a few pierced body parts to look after the store afternoons during the week. Her name was Karen and Karen did a wonderful job. She was happy and she engaged people in non-threatening conversation when they came into the store, chatting them up so that as often as not people left having bought something. We loved Karen. Benny and I would go out with her after hours for dinner. But then Karen met a guy who sold pharmaceuticals and her new boyfriend got transferred to Cleveland. Karen went along with him and out of our lives. At the same time, the restaurant Benny was working at went out of business and so now the question in the air is whether Benny should help with the store.

Our future spreads out before me. If Benny comes into the store, I'd be his boss, or his partner or what? Partner would be the only thing. Just how was that going to work? And what if we broke up or Benny didn't want to stay? But Benny has that same way with people that Karen had. He knows how to talk to them and bring them along without being intrusive. I think he always sold more salads and desserts than anyone else. People like him, which always showed in his tips. He's creative, too. It was his idea to hire out the store, with its homey feel, for dinners and special functions. That idea was a natural for him. He knows the catering business and we're all set for him to run at least that part of the business. He could even be the perfect choice to run the entire shop. If I don't choose to bring him in, I'll owe him an explanation.

I hear myself sharing these thoughts with Benny: I'm just not sure about this and I don't know about that and unsure about him and not very sure about me either. The world has begun to turn to dust under my feet. We go out to Fire Island and I leave him sitting on the beach reading a book to take long sunset walks by myself, or I sit alone watching the surf. I think a good deal about all these things but somehow nothing comes together and nothing gets resolved.

Karen gave a month's notice, but a month goes by faster than one would wish sometimes.

CHAPTER XXXI

Lace Whittaker rented a place on Calle Horatio Nelson, a street that runs in a diagonal line away from the more famous Avenida Costera Miguel Alemán in Acapulco. The apartment was in a district called Costa Azul that was cheap by American standards and, though not exactly close, his new home was within walking distance from the beach. The old streets were not in good repair. Old six- and seven-story apartment dwellings sat among auto repair shops, a car wash and vacant lots or half-built buildings that seemed to be forgotten in the slow, lazy meandering of time. Towards the end of Lace's block on Calle Horatio Nelson, old cement buildings hovered over the street like great stucco gravestones, quiet in the afternoon heat.

His apartment was small and crowded with heavy furniture in the Spanish style. Two chairs and a sofa had been upholstered in blue vinyl with large brass tacks around the edges. Cardboard reproductions of eighteenth-century French paintings hung around the dark rooms. He was four flights up and looked out to the back, which suited him fine. He felt weary to the bone and he didn't want to look out into the world so he settled in quietly and in time Lace began to wonder what it was that had made him run out of New York in such a rush.

At first, Lace did not go out except to dine at a small eatery on the neighborhood square or to buy food. One day, he bought a few flowers, too, and with that he began to recover from the heaviness that hung about him and weighted down his movements and his heart. At first, he would go to the zocalo and eat hurriedly, almost furtively, inside the restaurant, far to the back in the darkest corner. But his nature forced him, gradually, to reach towards the sunlight outside. He learned that the owner of the Restaurante Ontario spoke rather passable English and had lived in that Northern City for a time thirty years ago. Lace began to talk and then to move out onto the sidewalk and eat away from the street towards the back, but still outside and in the open air and under the awning. Finally, as the owner began to greet him as a friend and Lace could feel himself a regular, he ate towards the front of the outside area under those yellow umbrellas sporting the *Cinzano* logo or the names of beers. The umbrellas were slightly worn and somewhat dusty, but they carried him that final leg closer to the pedestrian traffic on the street.

One early evening, the owner, Sr. Gonzuiga, asked if he could sit down for a moment. The diffident man edged the legs of his white pants up a bit as he sat, leaning forward and brushing his hand across his moustache as he sported a sly smile, but in his eyes Lace noticed a question asked with sympathy.

"Ah, señor, I see you are coming here now for a few months, eh? Will you be staying in Acapulco for long?"

Lace didn't know how long. Maybe a year, perhaps? He mumbled a bit, but this made Sr. Gonzuiga lean in closer.

"Ah, señor, I see that you sit in the dark for many weeks, but now the weather, it draws one out a little, do you think? I live in

Ontario with my son, it is many years ago now, but he had his life there and a wife and I am Mexican, you see, and not a Canadian. Not an American, *non del norte*, if you know what I mean. It was not bad up there. They are good people, but I must come back here. There they lived in the dark, in the back of the rooms where they could be warm, but here it is the sun that I needed. I was sad to leave my son. He is my only family now, but life it takes you where it wants unless you stand your ground against it, no? I had to come back here and I could not stay where life took me. It was hard, because then I was alone and I think I need to be near my son, but the *restaurante*, it save me in the end. I buy it and return to my home and it save me. Save me, I think now, from sadness and being alone."

He began to stand up, but he continued as he swept his hand across the sky with a lazy, broad grinning motion.

"I am glad to see you come into the sun, señor. It is what we have to offer, here…that, maybe, and time, too. You see, I come back to take care of my sister and when she die, I buy the *restaurante* and stay. If not for my sister, perhaps I would have been still in Ontario and not so happy as I am now. It is the sun and also the business…" Again he swept his hand across the landscape of the tables and yellow umbrellas "and time after she die to make my peace."

He extended his hand and introduced himself and Lace, without standing, shook his hand and said, softly, "Lace Whittaker. They call me Lace. Señor Gonzuiga, thank you for introducing yourself."

Slowly, as in the small graceful steps of a minuet, Lace merged into the real life of the city and became a part of the ebb and flow of those who lived there, a regular at Restaurante Ontario. After several days, Sr. Gonzuiga would set him up with flatware and a water glass, as Lace sat down, after which he would bring a glass of red wine. The progress from eating alone inside the fourth-floor apartment to sitting beside the sidewalk and forming a part of the daily flux of people moving about their tasks was not achieved quickly. It took a full two months to move from eating alone in his living room, watching the old television and balancing a store-bought roasted hen or some beans and tortillas on his lap, to his first words with Sr. Gonzuiga at Restaurante Ontario. Then it took time to feel comfortable with the good Sr. Gonzuiga and the stories about his time in Canada. He was a drinker and a carouser up there and to hear him tell it, the women loved him, but as the story unfolded one could hear the fighting between a wayward father who drank too much and the good, Catholic son, and finally in disappointment his return to care for a dying sister, the trip back home and his ultimate salvation. Lace took another three weeks to move outside and then another two to move to the outer edge under an umbrella and in the full brightness of Acapulco's sun and the methodical movements of its citizens.

Another month passed and Lace took with him to the restaurant one noon a pad and pen and there he began to write some poetry. He had not written a word in how many years? It had been nearly two decades since he had begun to work for Mr. Myers and he had written nothing at all in those twenty years. He began to write verse that he knew to be excruciatingly bad, and still he wrote and the words poured out of him like a torrent of blood from a wound. At first, the poems had no shape or form; they seemed to be words placed one after the other without reason or sophisticated rhyme. But slowly he began to write about wanderers and dreamers and about failures of heart and soul. Then he wrote a series of small poems, almost Haikus, about climbing the stairs up and down and up and down again on MacDougal Street for half a century and the open question was whether he had anything to show for it but five published books of scatological verse and an antique store that was doing well under the supervision of a younger guy who worked for a fake flower wholesaler.

Then one morning there appeared a sensational article in the papers, which he read in his halting Spanish, about a boy who stalked and murdered a girl who wouldn't have anything to do with him. Finally, rage built up in him and he began to write about the uncertainty of life and the cruelties of people and little by little, when his bile ran out, he began to write about people he had known and how Patrick, who worked for the flower importer, also loved to dance well into the night. He wrote about lusty Patrick and his men and his hungry love of flesh and how uncertain and immature Patrick was still and Lace wondered how those things worked together, how adolescence could be drawn out over decades and he wondered if the nineteenth-century Romantics had been right to maintain that art was emotion, adolescence drawn out until it was taut and tight like a thread stretched to breaking? Perhaps they were more accurate, in the centuries before Romanticism, to admire the classics and to sense that art, including that art called living, took a mature and trained mind that included in its scope just a little wisdom. But how did one learn to live fully without drawing out the wild abandonment of adolescence into one's mature years?

Lace read the papers and wrote and threw away his poems and little essays with scraps of food left uneaten on his table at the Restaurante Ontario. His mind wandered and he wondered at how he had become experienced and maybe a little wise, but how was he to avoid becoming sad and ingrown. Could he somehow keep his abandon, too? How was that to be done?

Lace did not write about Agnes. She was too close to him. But he began to write about Anne Rose, finally, whose adolescence, her childhood as thought about it, had spanned her entire life and who had taken from her few experiences no maturity or lessons. She had lived like a little girl with no awareness of the concentric circles of her city and nation, little enough awareness even of her own extended family outside of the McGradys. What was her life but a succession of random acts over which she asserted a feeble pattern of forays out onto the same streets day after day in search of treasure? Out of the chaos of random acts, Anne Rose had struck her sturdy pose and wandered the streets out from where she lived with the regularity of a clock. And on Sundays she sat up with the women of Our Lady along Sixth Avenue and she stored and categorized her treasurers with the steadiness of a Dutch Burgermeister.

But Anne Rose crashed, one night, up against the random cruelties that make up so much of the world and none of her barricades against chaos had done her any good. In an instant, the pretty, simple girl of sixteen who had grown fat and silly and then silent in her wanderings, who had ultimately been loved by her neighbors, this little girl had been killed in an instant by a monster and there was nothing that could be done about it except that those things, too, must be acknowledged, faced and given their place in a messy firmament.

Then, Lace changed subject from those early poems that had been about things he did not understand very well: the mysteries of females and the ineluctable way they drew men to them and the way, it had seemed to him then, that they stole from men their semen and their proud erections and out of that thievery gave back life itself. "Yes," he thought now, "perhaps primitive peoples thought in that mystical, magical, sacred way." He did not really know about those things, living alone on the third floor of his apartment on MacDougal Street. They seemed far away and academic, like parsing the sentences of Chaucer. But he did know, now, about how messy random acts of kindness and random acts of cruelty are and how one must roam the streets in concentric circles and force down upon the chaos our own steady beat and rhythm so that we can live from one day to the next like simple human beings. But chaos is more powerful than we are, and sturdy as we try to be it will creep around us whatever we do and surprise us and take us away, however we may toil to keep it at bay.

After Lace had lived in Mexico for five months, he began to take Spanish lessons, starting as an intermediate because he had spent a good deal of time in Spain and had studied the language before. He became haltingly conversant quickly and it was perhaps because he could converse that he began to chat slowly with the woman who lived next door.

Where had Donna Elfiera Rosa Gonzago Natale been during those first five months? She had been living there next to Lace Whitaker, absorbed in her own errands. She was a widow five years now with a daughter who had married and emigrated to Chicago. They spoke each week on Sunday afternoon and on other days Donna Rosa came and went up and down the four flights of stairs and it is entirely possible that she passed Lace without noticing. But their meetings on the stairs became more frequent just as he was able to speak to her and so they began a conversation that within two months became an acquaintance and then they began to take tea together in the afternoons and Lace's Spanish became more fluid, if not fluent.

Donna Rosa was a conservative woman. She started each day with Mass and then bought each day's rations at the market. One day as Lace was departing for El Ontario, as he had dubbed the restaurante, Donna Rosa was in ascent with a package slightly wet with the blood of a newly dispatched hen. They met on the landing just outside Lace's apartment as he locked his door and she paused to look fixedly at the floor while she shifted her skirt with her free hand.

"Perhaps you would come for a small dinner tonight?" She said it in halting English encumbered by a heavy accent.

"No es possible," replied Lace who had suddenly become unaccountably nervous so that he replied, really, without thinking, and as a result he lied badly. Then in English, he continued, "I must go to El Ontario tonight" and then thinking better of it, he repeated in halting Spanish, "Tengo que cenar al restaurante Ontario esta noche." It was a poor excuse and he reddened as he told it, especially since he had planned to have a simple take-out dinner in and now he would have to eat twice in Mr. Gonzuiga's establishment.

Donna Rosa wrinkled her nose. "Is no good to go to restaurante always. You must have better food," and she glanced down at the package in her hand.

"Perhaps," Lace halted wondering if the word was possibly not in her vocabulary and started again with "Maybe…" He couldn't remember the words in Spanish, so he finally stuttered out a third attempt with "Tal vez…It is possible, maybe that I may come to dinner another time?"

"It is possible," said Donna Rosa Elfiera Gonzago Natale and she rose up stiff and erect, strong as a tiny frigate cutting through the waves as she continued her way into her apartment.

"What could have possessed you, old boy?" thought Lace audibly as he hopped as quickly as he could down the narrow staircase into the sun. "You're perfectly free and you say no in the most obvious way so that you've been insulting for no good reason and now what do you do because the fact is you'd like a meal and you're here all alone except for Sr. Gonzuiga and you don't know a damned soul."

Over some ceviche and a beer at lunch, Lace pondered his new dilemma. The puzzle worked on his brain. It furrowed his brow and twisted his mouth in a way that Sr. Gonzuiga found to be too tempting to let pass.

"Are you okay, Señor Lace?" He was suddenly beside the table at the very front of the café next to be sidewalk where Lace was seated. "I see you have a deep thought on your face."

"Ah, Señor Gonzuiga, señor, señor. I have a new little problem, you see. Just a little problem and I'm working it out in my head. Needs a solution, you know, and I just haven't quite got my mind to it yet."

"A problem and a solution. It is good, perhaps to have a problem to entertain one. No?" Perhaps the good señor had come to think that Lace was too preoccupied with nothing very serious, but his good nature was such that Lace didn't take umbrage.

"We'll know more about that when we have the solution, Sr. Gonzuiga."

"Ahh, a good solution for a problem. That will be just the thing. I will buy you another beer to help the solution come."

Lace nursed his second beer, looking out across the busy street and it came to him that he would have to approach the stern Donna now and somehow reestablish his invitation to dinner. But could he say, "I will come to your home, now, for dinner." He could rephrase it, perhaps. He could say, "May I come to your home, say tonight, for dinner?" but that was impossible to ask. One didn't say that to a stern frigate that had just sailed away from you up the stairs and into her apartment. "She might not have any hen that night and she might just say no and then where will we be, my boy?" Well, could he say, "Señora Rosa, I'm terribly sorry that I lied and said that I was going to the Restaurante Ontario the other night when actually I was so nervous and flustered that I didn't know what I was saying and what I really wanted to do was share your hen with you, which I know was absolutely delicious and really, Donna Rosa, wouldn't you give me another chance and may I come to your apartment for dinner, perhaps, even, this evening?" Lace stopped thinking altogether for a rather long moment, stunned, as he was, that he could even formulate such an outburst in his mind. Had he become a blathering schoolboy?

The second beer hadn't helped matters much when Lace stood up to retreat back into his little rented abode with the blue, plastic-covered sofa and the heavy black furniture. As luck would have it, the frigate disappeared for nearly ten days. Whether, for a time, she had sailed off over the horizon or not was impossible to say but somehow they did not meet on the stairs and the problem nudged at Lace without ever quite yielding to the firm resolution he was seeking. Then, suddenly, one day the frigate sailed across his bow, in a scene perfectly reminiscent of the earlier one, just as Lace was locking his door to go out.

"Donna Rosa, a pleasure to see you. You have been away…. gone?" Lace covered his bases by throwing multiple words in English, hoping one would match Rosa's vocabulary.

"Not gone, no. Here." She smiled with her lips a little upturned as if she was teasing him, enjoying his consternation. "Women," he thought. "She knows perfectly well I'm wound up like a top."

Then, straight out loud, "I am sorry that we couldn't have dinner when you invited me. Perhaps you would come to my apartment. Or we could go out." That was all wrong, it occurred to him suddenly. Eating out was what she didn't think he ought to do, but what alternative did he have at this point? He was in the middle of saying something and he had to make the best of it. "It would be a pleasure if you would have dinner with me sometime."

"Yes," she replied carefully, even thoughtfully, as if she wasn't entirely sure if Lace's time in purgatory was over, but she would be merciful even if the terms of reconciliation weren't entirely established. "Yes, we can eat at a restaurante if you wish."

"It is short notice…only a little time, but perhaps this evening."

"Yes, this evening is possible."

"I will come to your door at 9:00? Is this okay? And we will eat in a better restaurante than the Ontario. Maybe El Baraiso at LaCaleta? Es bueno?"

"Yes, 9:00."

So the problem had finally admitted to a solution. Not a solution entire in one gulp, but a solution laid out in stages because soon she began to fix wonderful dinners for Lace, sometimes sharing them over the same table face to face, but sometimes wrapping the food for him and giving it to him for his own enjoyment. But these things, too, took time. She did not hurry. Their first meals were simple, roasted chicken or a few vegetables and pulled meat with tortillas. Later the repasts were more elaborate as she took to mole sauces and clear broth soups with chilies and wonderful concoctions in rolled tortillas with piquant sauces that spiked across Lace's tongue.

And as time passed, Lace began to help clear the table and then to help wash the dishes as she dried them and put them away and so it was a natural event that one evening Lace's hand brushed against the back of Rosa's neck, quite accidentally it is true, but when it happened they both stopped what they were doing and Lace's hand stayed just so at Rosa's neck and then Rosa inclined her head just enough to the left so that it rested for a moment on his shoulder. They stayed that way for perhaps only three seconds, but although that is a very short span of time for most human endeavors, the three seconds during which Rosa's head rested on Lace's shoulder was a long time indeed. It was long enough that they actually had to begin moving again, like people learning to use an atrophied limb, so that Rosa began to wipe the dish that was left hanging in her hand and Lace began to swish the dish water and draw a wet rag across a plate, starting motions that were new to them both, somehow in tandem, somehow with a purpose. And at that instant Lace realized with a laziness that surprised him that the hurt in the bottom of his stomach was no longer there.

And so the second problem presented itself. But then it was only a problem if the moment when Rosa inclined her head just enough to lay it for three seconds on Lace's shoulder was to have any influence on the thousands, the millions or trillions of seconds that followed.

What did it mean? "But, dear boy, a woman can't lay her head on your shoulder with nothing at all following it. And Rosa is not coming onto you for sex, old man. Can't be that."

Then there was the odd fact that the hurt was gone. It was gone. There was no doubt of that, but was Donna Rosa the reason for it? Had time alone done the healing and now he was opening up for something new? Something he hadn't even been looking for?

Lace had lived in Acapulco for ten months when he wrote Agnes.

Dearest pussycat (alley cat?):

Is it possible to have such news? I have kept this from you before because I thought you would think me sillier than I am and perhaps even sillier because I am a man entering his dotage and whose emotions ought, therefore, not be trusted. But I am feeling fit again and take a long walk each day in the early evening. I have been writing some too, but ended up throwing it all away. You will understand that I have not been writing for posterity but to exorcize demons.

For a month or so, now, I have been joined on my nightly stroll with a lady of perhaps my own age, but who seems some years younger. That is a subject we have not discussed, as I am an honorable man. She lives next door to me, fixes me meals at times and at some unnoticed moment we began a steady habit of taking tea together in the afternoon.

She is a widow, not a woman of the world in that sense, but a woman who has raised a child successfully and lost a husband and who walks up and down four flights again and again to keep body and soul together and who has kept happy through it all. She goes to Mass each morning and she has taught me that I am lonely and that I am a person who can no longer climb flights of stairs to perform each day's errands for myself alone. I need someone at the top of those stairs or at the bottom of them to climb and descend to. I have asked her to marry me and she has consented.

I say this next thing only to you because I suspect you will assume certain things that are not true. My Willy has made no appearances at all in this sequence of events. To date, he is a stranger to the proceedings; hasn't even filed an amicus brief. I realize that I have not even mentioned the name of my beloved: Donna Elfiera Rosa Gonzago Natale, Rosa to you. Rosa is a good, Catholic woman and the carnal life is not for us before marriage. But as I say, I am a man nearing my dotage and it is difficult to say how important the—ahem—physical component of our life together will be. She is a wonderful cook and a comfortable presence and a good friend and I believe we will be happy.

We will be married when we arrive back in two months: January 24.

And I have begun to go to Mass with Rosa, too. At first, of course, it was just something to do together and a way of placing myself into her life. I've shared with you something of how I feel about these things. I don't think for a moment that Jesus came to wash away our sins or that the wafer becomes the body of Christ. What I do think—no, what I feel—is that the moment of the Eucharist reaches something ancient in me. Something in my cells, maybe. I doubt it's true, as some Freudian types would have it, that it harkens all the way back to some taboo against cannibalism, although I'm sure there must be a desire deep inside the human psyche to integrate ourselves, physically, with others. After all, the desire to meld with others, whether it is through their flesh or their semen or their penis, is elemental (my dear Watson!) and akin to that is also the desire to confess our deepest selves, to be understood and digested at the underlying levels of our souls. It seems that humans want to tell all to another soul, to be understood entirely by another—which is melding on an emotional and intellectual level—and perhaps confession addresses that. Primates eat each other and primitive humans have long eaten the dead, those they admire or fear or warriors fallen in battle so that their prowess can be absorbed and so that they, too, can merge with another human being. In some way, do we still yearn to do that?

And I admire, too, that Catholicism integrated the mother-god, the mother of god. It is a wise religion that transcends stern, rule-abiding male principles with the mysteries of creativity. I know, of course, that the idea of Mary in the Catholic Church has definite limitations, as you've strongly suggested to me, Agnes. Still, those dour Protestants make the universe entirely male, which it isn't and anyone can see that it isn't. To my mind, a religion that ignores the female persona entirely is a religion out of balance.

Then, too, for one thousand years, the Catholic Church with all its faults gave Western Man a common framework of belief. There is enough out there to cut people off from one another. In places like New Guinea, there are hundreds of tribes, indigenous peoples split into the smallest possible kinship groups that are engaged in endemic warfare and each speaking tongues unintelligible to one another. What it must have been like in Europe when one language, Latin, was spoken by educated classes wherever you went, and one frame of reference—The Church—tied everyone together. The Chinese have that sense of kinship, I suppose. They read a common language and they have thousands of years of Confucius and of seeing themselves as the center of civilization.

Maybe that's what I want. The widest sense of kinship instead of the smallest. After Luther, Christians have managed to split into thousands of tiny sects, each further splitting hairs, until now a simple congregation of worshippers can tear a store-front church apart over some small biblical interpretation. I look around myself and it seems that people barely listen to each other. They yell at one another. They look out from yawning chasms of self-absorption, from which there is no escape, until they have become strangers to one another.

But, to be sure, all this is history and academics, yet it isn't an intellectual exercise for me, Agnes. The heart of it is that I want to be united. Rosa is a Catholic and we can be Catholics together anywhere, here, the United States, anywhere, because the framework is, well, Catholic. We are, together, part of a system of thought that goes back two thousand years and unites the world.

So I've turned, with Rosa, to the Apostolic Holy Mother Church. You needn't tease this old reprobate. I'm tired, Agnes, and I want to be carried along with the currents of history and the tides of humanity. I don't need to buck any trends. I'm not a young buck. The more I'm exposed to Rosa's

Catholicism, the more it seems that it speaks to people's basic instincts, the basic instincts of human emotion and psychology. They take the Virgin Mary here very seriously, as you might imagine—just try to connect with the female force if you're a Protestant—which is to say that Rosa's sense of the church is that it treats us as fully human. Of course, they make a great deal of original sin, and I don't think I believe in that or find it a very helpful idea, but for her, these ideas offer a way for people to forgive one another for being who we are instead of forcing us to adhere to a set of impossible tenets that tell us that we are wretched creatures, inhuman beings just because we are human, and, therefore, expose us to even more unkindness than we would experience in the normal course of human events. And so with my dear Rosa, I am attending Mass and liking it, too.

I am happy to hear that you have been in touch with Patrick and that the store is doing well and that he seems to have met somebody new. He writes me and tells me about his progress. I think setting up living areas and bringing in furnishings such as place settings, silver, etc., was a wonderful idea. He tells me business is good and now you write to tell me the same things. I know you never liked him much, but he has improved with age, has he not?

There is still time to hear from you before I come back. I want to know how the book tour went and whether you are still speaking to Robert. Just how long will you stay constantly angry with him before something changes?

Your friend truly, my buttercup.

Lace

CHAPTER XXXII

It was only a small clipping in the *Friday Daily News* topped with a sensational headline announcing "Murderer Creep To Get His Due." What caught Agnes' eye was the tiny photo of a man staring out into space, eyes still, dark pools even in the grainy image on newspaper lying smooth over rough planks of the country house floor. She started for a second and thought back and then it came to her. The scene in the hotel room. Yes, that was it...the party?... no , it was an opening. The one at Lucille Lucifer's. He was older, but the photograph that accompanied the article was clearly a face she remembered. Ageless, in that vacant way, the look of it flooded her memory along with the feel of wet sheets and the burnt lampshade streaked with umber and black soot. She rocked back and forth, her feet slippered and soft in furry cat house-shoes, a gift from Robert. She hated the slippers as they caught her eye. "Throw the fuckers out as soon as I stand up," along with the little ceramic ducks Robert thought would make a cute collection. How had she put up with it? She was in the country to sell off or just plain get rid of their things. She had wanted silver brocade slippers. Robert misunderstood her again. Always listening but never hearing, obtuse Robert with his fucking soft baby shoe house slippers for her. But those thoughts, as the fuzzy fucking pink feet caught the corner of her eye, distracted her only a split second and as she steadied herself from shifting backwards from the momentary assault to her memory and the jolt from catching her silly feet, she was sure of one thing. The picture in the paper was of the man in the hotel who had stood her up, the man who fed into the nastiest instincts she could imagine, the ones she hadn't known she had, and she had gone along with it all. The memory flooded back: the wet toes and urine-flooded sheets, luxuriating in warmth and wetness. That man she had taken to the hotel she liked to use with lower East Side Miguel. Where would it have led if he hadn't gone out to Long Island to be with some john and then never returned? It caught her throat. She might have been killed. She had never been careful. One read of people in newspaper reports, murdered by people they took home. Those were always other people. People she could understand, certainly, even once a woman she knew, but other people nonetheless. And yet, she had slept with this man and the point drove home and made her think of Alan and weekdays and monogamy.

The news report had very little to say. It was only a brief, not a description of the trial. The single photograph showed a man being led into court for arraignment. The case would be going on now. Agnes called the Manhattan District Court for the date and times, the arraignment having been set for Monday, the following week. Then she finished boxing the garbage and the pottery and the stuff from Robert, the detritus of her country life, made arrangements for a house-sale and set off to the Metro-North station to take the 3:23 train back to New York City.

As the train jostled and clicked its way into the city, Agnes turned the *Daily News* photograph and its grainy felonious face over in her mind along with the emotions raised up out of those nights with the murderer. What was she up to, really? She hadn't meant to leave the country house so quickly when she went up there. There were still things to pack away; still work to do on the house-sale. Her mind wasn't quite made up when she started the trip down alongside the Hudson River, but by the time the train pulled into Grand Central, she knew that she would pay a visit to the courthouse. She had decided to find out from the Clerk of the Court when court dates were scheduled, but why come down earlier than expected? It seemed odd that she was so driven to pursue this inexplicable quest.

It turned out that something was scheduled for Tuesday afternoon, so that morning she awakened early and dressed, picking carefully through the closet off the entryway where her better clothing was stored, and found a Norell red suite, something bright in a nubbly fabric. She wanted to stand out. It surprised her, her vanity. Damn him, he went away and never came back. She hadn't thought it through before rummaging through the neatly hung and covered outfits, but as the suit came out and she reached up to pull down an appropriate pair of high heels, she began to laugh at herself quietly and then, as a foretelling of self-awareness began to dawn, she laughed a buttery laughter at the perfect silliness of it. Was she really going to seduce him out of the courtroom, as if he didn't have other things on his mind? She was still a pretty good-looking girl and she'd show that murderer bastard. Give him something to remember as they led him off to prison, the fuck face. He'd recognize her for sure and he'd have that everlasting memory of her sitting there in the audience staring at him, challenging him.

By the time she was dressed, hair and makeup in place, she wasn't so sure what she was doing, but she went on and took a cab down to the District Court in lower Manhattan. She imagined that earlier cases would be strung out and that this one would start late, maybe even an hour or two behind schedule. That made sense to her and she was prepared to wait; she had reading material with her. As usual, Agnes was prompt but to her surprise the court appeared to be running on time and some earlier proceeding was just being adjourned as she sat toward the front of the courtroom visitor's section. Odd how wrong her perceptions had been. She had expected a crowd, the constant mumbling of interested onlookers in a Perry Mason drama, but in fact she was the only person in the audience. Was that the word? Audience. She drifted off, wondering if there was another word.

The proceedings of the court continued in a hushed, business-as-usual tone followed by a period during which the judge left the room and then, after perhaps fifteen minutes—she checked her watch and indeed they were running twenty minutes behind schedule—the door opened and another judge walked out. She was not asked to stand. There was no announcement; the court, she imagined, was not formally in session for this hearing and she didn't quite understand what the participants were there for, but at last a door at the side opened.

Instantly, she recognized the man in plastic shackles. It was him, the very man. He was wearing a neat pair of jeans and a shirt tucked in, also neatly, as if his court-appointed lawyer had told him to be neat and clean for the judge. She had expected him in some sort of orange prison garb, but he was wearing normal street clothing like, maybe, someone's gardener or handyman or, it struck her, maybe like someone you'd pick up at a gallery opening like Lucille Lucifer's on a Sunday afternoon. What had they not done together, she and this murderer?

Her hand crept up the side of her neck and over her face and then she remembered that she wanted to be seen by this man who was supposed to see her and remember her and think to himself what a dame he'd lost. Wasn't it something like that? But instead, he looked up and through her and then, suddenly, she felt violated and then invisible. Did she feel raped or used or was it neediness and rejection that she felt at the bottom of it all? The court droned on and Agnes slipped into a reverie, remembering a hand, feeling caresses at school under the desk. She thought of a little boy in grade school, little Johnny, but no, that was memory playing a trick on her, tugging at her, making a joke. The name of the boy came back to her now, Jimmy Nagle. The name came back with his red hair and little freckles and the bulge in his neat gray school pants. She knew, finally, what it meant to be wanted by someone and when he touched her on the leg, her whole body tingled like it never had before until the inside of her glowed with a newly experienced hazy, yellow flame. She melted away to his touch, then, as she sat on the hard birch bench behind the classroom desk near the back of her fifth-grade room. Like a bank of clouds gathering into wispy, changing shapes, those years came back upon her in a storm. She was so lonely and thoughts came one after another in her dreamy reverie: "Mother and Father so involved with one another, they ate, slept and listened to the radio with each other, pushed me away…kept me busy with house chores and dressed me in awful clothes. Mother, a beautiful woman who made sure there was no competition in the house. She wanted nothing to do with childrearing or raising a daughter who might divert her husband's attentions, might get at him, take him away. Lovely, lonely little Agnes, kept ugly like a little ugly duckling and then little Jimmy wanted me and after that the other little boys, too. I learned to use them, I did learn to use them and turn to them when I needed them and get out of them what I needed out of them. Lovin', honey. Lovin', protection, favors. But the rumors, remember the rumors? I learned to fuck the rumors. I didn't care about the rumors after a while. Loose girl or not, I had a quick and wicked tongue and the boys were a little afraid of me and so they kept in line and then I got the fuck out of town. Came to New York where I could good goddamn act how I wanted."

Jonathan looked directly at her, but his eyes remained vacant. That vacant stare, she remembered it now in full force and how she'd tried to fill it up and make it matter to her. But that's all it ever was, just a vacant stare. Had he ever seen her? It suddenly occurred to her that he had never noticed her, just as he didn't see her now. Just like those awful cat slippers Robert gave her instead of silver brocade. Something expensive, beautiful. Would anyone who had ever seen her, truly noticed her, ever give her fuzzy cat slippers? As she sank into her reverie, men from her past stood in line towards the horizon of her memory, getting amber gray as they stood one after another back into time, and each one stared vacantly ahead as a sound beat against her ears like the sound of a butterfly beating its wings against a plastic container and then Agnes jerked abruptly to attention.

Unaccountably, without realizing what she did, almost like a nervous tic although Agnes had probably never done exactly this in her entire life, she opened the small handbag she'd plucked down from the closet shelf and pulled out a handkerchief and, absentmindedly, began to rub away her lipstick.

There he was, still looking at her, but looking past her. Was he crazy? A lot of the court conversation took place up at the bench and she wasn't privy to it. There was a prosecutor and a schlock attorney and the judge, and she gathered that the hearing was a formality of some sort. There was nothing to see here, almost nothing to satisfy her curiosity as to why he had killed Anne Rose. The man—had she ever known his name?—remained silent. He offered no explanations; there were no witnesses. Did she hear what they were saying correctly? Something about pleading guilty. Little catches of words in the air. No evidence of insanity by the state-appointed psychiatrists. Another date scheduled.

She thought to herself how silly she was. Poor Anne Rose. She hadn't known Anne Rose, but how upset Lace had been. What a violent murder, what little she knew of it. She thought of the aunt, the bereaved aunt who'd been drinking at the funeral. What was her name? What *was* her name? She'd forgotten that. What had pulled her down here anyway? Curiosity, vanity, horror at what might have befallen her? It made sense, as she sat there and the men droned on and the accused man who was pleading guilty sat stony-eyed. What a surprise that she would see the photo of that particular fuck from her past and learn that he was the murderer in a particularly gruesome crime and one that she knew about. That was a surprise, no doubt and then she thought back to his gaze, as he entered the room and the emptiness, she understood, was the gaze of a man unforgiving and unforgiven, standing before Pilate, she thought, and asking nothing of him but to walk straight into his fate.

It was the emptiness. The void he filled when they were together. He would do anything to fill the vacuum between them. He would do anything.

"I would have done anything, too."

Agnes folded the handkerchief back into her small purse and clutched it tightly to her side as she stood and left the courtroom. She wanted to call Alan and make sure they were still on for this evening. That was silly. Of course, they were on for this evening. But she had been sure of herself coming to downtown Manhattan this very morning, and now she wasn't so sure of anything. Alan was a dependable man and she knew he would pick her up at 6:00 tonight, but still, even so, she wanted to hear his voice and confirm something, anything, that would bedrock a foundation for her soul.

CHAPTER XXXIII

They called him Big Red for two reasons. That he was redheaded and big was the obvious one and he ran the white blocks of Greenhaven Prison with an iron and cruel hand. But if you did things his way, he could be all right enough. The second reason for Big Red's name, at least for those who knew him well enough or who had seen him in the showers, was the huge red knob that made up the head of his penis. That was the in-joke, an open secret. Plenty of young men had been broken in on that red knob. And some of the men, especially the ones who had grown up in Bible country and had a more than nodding acquaintance with Satan called it a devil's dick and seemed to know what they were talking about. So the guys laughed a little nervously at calling him Big Red, because he was devil enough to run the inside of Greenhaven where the worst criminals were sent to do their time.

Big Red was in for life on two murders committed during an armed robbery. Parole was an academic possibility, but he had been denied three times now and Big Red was getting along in years. The robbery was committed when he was 23. He had served 27 years and had a genius for manipulation. He would have made a good politician.

He knew how to punish and protect, serve your wildest needs, charm you until honey ran out of your mind onto the table he was dealing on while he planned to kill you without a thought.

That was how Big Red ran the white side of Greenhaven out of two cells side by side in one cellblock and another across the yard in a second block. The cells at Greenhaven were worn back to hard metal and cinderblock. Old dull green-gray paint from army surplus peeled away from the walls and dropped to floor limp with the steam that escaped from faulty pipes and radiators. Grime dripped from the ceilings and the air was close with sweat and violence and intrigue. In contrast, Big Red's cells were neat and painted white, and he had boys who kept them clean. That was the agreement. The guards and warden watched the walls; Big Red kept the white inmates in line and Lil' J Lowell ran the black side. Let the Puerto Ricans and the Latinos fall where they could, depending on how dark they were and how they acted. They tended to fall into splinter groups. Big Red and Lil' J divided them up, kept them at each other's throats and stuck a knife into the leader's ribs if one of the Latino groups got too strong. In prison, there were lines a man could not cross.

Detective Koklensky was at the precinct station the day Veronica called him breathless with a squirrelly, caged-up calm that he knew right away covered an emotional sickness of heart. She had found something leading to Anne Rose, something that had been taken out of her apartment. After that, the rest was easy. The murderer was a strange loner of a young man, but he fit a type. No one much knew him. He was the sort that came and went on the periphery of urban life, pretty much unnoticed. A floater, Koklensky thought. Some people use the city to make a neighborhood and weave their relationships out in concentric webs of friends and interests and activities. Others hide and flirt with light from just beyond the shadows. In that, the strange young man named Jonathan Perry wasn't so strange. Yes, he fit a type.

Nonetheless, Koklensky's perpetrator was strange because he didn't even try to cop a plea bargain. He seemed to pass the tests of sanity. He didn't confirm or deny anything. He said he didn't remember where he got the owl. He came to the station and they took his fingerprints. The perpetrator had not been careful. There had been fingerprints all over Anne Rose's apartment. Particularly good ones in the dirt and mud smudged against a table near her bed. Jonathan Perry's fingerprints matched. He had left them everywhere.

They booked him immediately. Koklensky wondered later whether Jonathan Perry actually was insane. The public defender assigned to his case was too busy to do an adequate job. The defendant made it easy. At first, he neither confirmed nor denied his guilt, but finally he pled guilty. He would not speak again before the court. He had done a horrendous thing, but before the bench it became a simple case. The public defender did not bother to work up an insanity plea. They let it go to a regular sentencing and Jonathan, still silent, heard the Judge: the rest of his life at Greenhaven Prison. And so there he went, for had not Christ kept silent before his judges? It was not these people who could judge Jonathan. Only creatures outside the boundaries of imagination knew the purpose of his deed. Not even Jonathan knew the inner and deeper purpose for his act, the ancient demand of gods that blood be spilt. Only God could judge him now and would judge humankind, too, on the basis of this great act of sacrifice, and self-sacrifice, too, that Jonathan had performed.

Jonathan kept silent and went to Greenhaven and became Big Red's bitch for three months until Big Red began to sell him off for favors.

At first, Big Red was fascinated by Jonathan and kept him close at hand, but after those initial months a new kid came along. The kid was younger; in prison because of a foolish moment. An acquaintance had been bugging him for some tabs of ecstasy and when the kid had gone and scored some and then tried to deliver them, the acquaintance turned out to be an undercover cop. This had happened during a season in which the public was aroused against drugs by simultaneous get-tough political campaigns. The district attorney, who was going to come up for reelection, made an example of the boy by getting him five years of hard time in a hard-ass penitentiary.

After the kid came along straight into Greenhaven prison and right into Big Red's embrace, Big Red didn't have any personal use for Jonathan. But Big Red ran the white side of Greenhaven because he had things that other people wanted. One of the side-by-side cells was filled with file cabinets that, in turn, were filled with cigarettes, booze, cocaine and heroin. Big Red had weapons in those cabinets and pornography and just about anything else anyone wanted or needed. The guards never looked inside those drawers, in fact never entered his cells, because Big Red kept order in the place and that's what they wanted. There were lots of ways to smuggle contraband: through kitchen deliveries and mail that passed under the nose of the guys who owed their easy-living office jobs to Big Red. Stuff came in with the laundry and sometimes with the guards themselves. They knew better than to look too closely.

After the kid came along, Big Red sold off Jonathan for a few cigarettes or some other item. Jonathan remained silent and pliable. A few guys who hadn't asked Big Red's permission raped him once, but after they ended up in the infirmary there was no more trouble. Anyone who wanted to use Jonathan would tell him that it was okay with Big Red and Jonathan would tell Big Red about it afterwards and that was all there was to it. Big Red got Jonathan a job in the janitorial service where he had access to a small supply room. That was the set-up. Jonathan led anyone who said, "Big Red says its okay" into the supply room and turned a trick for the boss and the piles of cigarettes and joints and the paraphernalia of power continued to pile up in the file cabinets on the white side of Greenhaven prison.

One day Big Red came up alongside Jonathan in the yard and whispered in his ear. "Hear there's a contract out on you, kid."

Jonathan said nothing.

"Word has it someone out there wants to get you. Know anything about it?"

"Don't know nothing. What do you know?"

"Just that someone's pretty mad at you for what you did. They want you dead." Big Red was a sadistic man. He played the father that Jonathan never knew at first when he had just come to Greenhaven, showing him the ropes, keeping him from the other guys, punishing the men who raped him, all the while reeling him in and making Jonathan his whore. But Big Red was a sadistic man. "I hear the order is to kill you in the worst way, so it hurts bad. Makes you twitch and scream." Big Red smiled his crocodile smile. "Don't know anything else. Don't worry, kid, I'll find out more and let you know. Big Red'll watch your back."

He patted Jonathan on the rear when he said that and smiled, showing a small row of white teeth and narrowing his eyes like a reptile that is about to take its prey. If anyone could protect Jonathan, Big Red could, but still sometimes things went on that no one, not the warden or the guards or the men who controlled the inside of the prison could foresee or control.

Jonathan heard nothing more for a couple of weeks until one Sunday morning a young Latino man he'd never seen before ran his hand over Jonathan's ass in the yard and whispered, "It's okay with Big Red." They went together to the storage room and the man closed the door behind them while Jonathan let the orange prison trousers drop around his ankles, spread his legs and lay with his arms outstretched over a worktable with his head face down against the hard wooden surface. He waited for the man to spit into his hand, open him up and enter him. As he relaxed his muscles in anticipation, he felt the slow edge of a smooth blade run against his throat. It didn't hurt, even as the blood spurted outward and covered his open arms. Jonathan didn't move nor was he surprised. He lay and let the blood pour out of his body, alone because the man left quickly, leaving him to die behind a locked door. He lay on the worktable with his arms outspread and his legs apart and he thought, "I am the lamb to slaughter, the warrior in God's army, the arbitrator before the throne of the Lord. I have been brought here by beings from beyond. Did Christ fight his executors? This is how it is for those chosen to bear the hardest task."

And as Jonathan had this thought, lying limp and dying against the workbench, he thought perhaps he saw a distant point of light before the end.

Big Red could not have protected Jonathan against the orders of people as powerful as those who sought Jonathan's death. He took the task on, knowing that he would profit and that if he fought it, Jonathan would die anyway and he would have gained nothing and beyond that, he would have lost a battle and with it honor and standing. His price was two bricks of pure heroin, a high price indeed. The knife was to have routed out Jonathan's innards as slowly as possible to keep him alive with the torture. This was an instruction from Vincent Morelli, sent inside Greenhaven through the battalions of powerful men with whom he was allied and the lesser men who served him. The order was to put duct tape over Jonathan's mouth and use the knife to gut him out while he was still alive. Big Red had elected to omit this detail in his instructions to the killer. Perhaps it would not have done for one of his boys to be killed in such a sadistic way under his watch. Still, in this, Big Red was true to his word. He had protected Jonathan after all.

CHAPTER XXXIV

Dearest Lace,

How I wish you were here. I know I don't write often enough and there's much you don't know, which is my fault. And how silly of me not to realize that Patrick is keeping you up to date. Yes, he seems to have met a perfectly suitable fellow who is watching the store on a temporary basis and turns out to be a very good salesman and lends a tasteful and suitable touch of his own. They are not living together, but it seems serious. I stop in the shop every now and then and we keep up that way. We're not bosom dinner companions yet, but perhaps in time.

Now my dearest, there must be some cosmic balance to be kept in these matters because just as you are attaching yourself at the hip to Rosa, I have severed the silver chord to angelic Robert Silbers and cast him into outer darkness. I had wanted to propel him to some place further away, but the astronomers tell me that I will have to settle for outer darkness.

I shouldn't rag on an old love and one with whom I lived for quite a while. And as you know he wasn't an evil or bad person, although that only made matters even worse because things between us weren't so bad that I absolutely had to break up, but they also weren't good enough to make me happy. I'm not sure I wrote you this, but after you left for Mexico I began to stay in town more and more. I'd drive out to the country sometimes and sometimes Robert would stay in town, but he has had more and more conventions and gatherings and political events to cover and those took him away for extended periods. The way out was the easy way out, actually. We just drifted apart, I started socializing with other people, met someone else and that was that.

And the someone else is to dear Robert what a Roadrunner is to a glacier, or something like that anyway. His name is Alan. He's in the rag trade, big and lusty and wears diamonds, but he knows his way around the opera, music, theater, that is to say around town. Savoir-faire, dearie, and all from owning a big off the rack ladies wear business on Seventh Avenue. He's a big tipper and orders "for the lady." Runs things like he's the one in charge, makes rough jokes and he has hair on his back and

I don't know what it is about him but he is fabulous in bed. He never asks me how it was for me, just fucks me until I'm limp and then he wines me and makes me feel like a trillion dollars and when I talk he listens and says something sensible back in return. He's married but sort of separated (wife in Hewlett, apartment on Lexington) and that suits me just fine because it leaves me time—by the clock and emotionally—for the book tour which went just fine, thank you very much for asking. And did I say he's wonderful in bed?

We can't wait to meet Rosa. The red carpets are at the cleaners as we speak. Your subtenant moves out January 15, which gives us time to check the place out, buy flowers and make sure the bed has fresh sheets. Maybe rose petals too? And oh yes, Alan bought me (yesss, she purrs, he buys me things!) a chic—much chicer, my dear than what he's made his millions on—dress for your wedding. He has a closet full of dark suits and you can bet he'll look stunning for the ceremony at Our Lady.

By the way, you know perfectly well I don't understand a thing you said about going to Mass. I'm a show-me girl, I guess, but I need a philosopher close by, honey, to explain things to me, so you can expound more about it later when we're sitting with each other face to face.

Now the strangest thing. You know they caught Anne Rose's murderer just after you left for Mexico, but the trial finally ended and he was shown on the news being led out from the sentencing. Do you remember Mr. Mysterioso from Lucille Lucifer's? Lace, I could swear it was him. I even went to the arraignment, or whatever it's called, to see him in person and I can't get it out of my mind. I really think it was the same person and I can't help but wonder why he didn't attack me. What was it about Anne Rose that made her the query and not me? I never told you much about that affair, but somehow I can see him doing something awful. For us, between us, the eeriness, of it was what fascinated me, but how it could have ended I can only imagine. And I don't think that they ever established a motive, or a reason, for the murder. What drew him to Anne Rose, I keep wondering. And how did I escape?

It is very peculiar out there. I'm glad you're coming back, Dearest. Only lunch with you keeps me sane.

As always,

Agnes.

CHAPTER XXXV

Dear Journal,

I've brought Benny into the shop on a sort of trial basis and he's started a catering part of the business more or less on his own. So far, it's turned out to be a wonderful idea. People give glorious dinners at the store, using the settings and the tables for gatherings distributed in groups of four or six among period vignettes. We bring in string quartets, a cabaret singer or a jazz ensemble. I must say that Benny does well, the partnership grows and catering is accounting for more and more of the business. But I haven't been too sure about where all this is supposed to lead…the personal stuff with Benny, anyhow.

Lace has returned, now, from Mexico with a new wife in tow. Benny and I dubbed her Rosie the Riveter because she is, to be kind, stout and looks like she ought to be doing construction work somewhere. But it's obvious they're happy. She went off to English classes first thing after they arrived. There she met up with some women and all of them cooked up an idea of selling regional tortilla and salsa and various other kinds of dishes that could be done at home and delivered daily to local restaurants. We've included some of her dishes in our meals to general acclaim. I would guess that there's about twenty years between her age and Lace's. It works out well that she is busy and eventually she could make a success out of her small business.

I suppose that one worker bee in a family was enough for Lace. He offered me a buy-out on the store, and at almost the same time the owners of Twenty-Eighth Street Flower have decided to retire, leaving me running the whole shebang for them. On top of salary, I can bill a commission for sales over an annual base. That will make a good income for me, so if things continue to work out with Benny, it makes sense to put him in charge of the store. So far, we've made a good fit, Benny and I, which has resulted in the fit between the Twenty-Eighth Street Flower Emporium and the store. This bodes well for the future. But even if Benny is working out well at the store I've still remained unsure, for reasons I don't fully understand, about how to go ahead with him. I sense that it might be best not to trust too much in how our personal relationship might work out.

There's a lot to attend to, and so just the other Sunday night I was upstairs visiting with Lace and talking a little business. I was supposed to be up there to iron out details on how I'm going to buy the shop, and I had taken to him a list of "what ifs?" and exacting details about how the store might operate. Lace's apartment, like mine, consists of a small living room with a galley kitchen along one wall and a tiny bedroom through a doorway to the left as you sit facing the kitchen. He and Rosa have a canvas curtain strung up to hide her work area from the living room. That night, you could hear her chopping and dicing and you could smell the aromas of garlic and onion and cumin sweep through into the entire apartment as if it were one large kitchen, which actually it is.

At any rate, I seemed to be going in circles. Somewhere deep inside I was scared to death of taking on the entire business. I knew I could run it. There's no problem with that. I've been running it for years now. It has taken time to realize what the tightness in my stomach is: a question that hangs over me about whether I'm capable of committing to anyone, really, but by now Benny's part of the business is significant. So long as Lace owns the shop, the business component between Benny and me and the intimate relationship between us can remain emotionally separate components. But to buy it from Lace means separating out what is Benny's and what is mine and by implication who Benny is to me and who I am to him.

I presented to Lace an endless number of considerations and worries that under any other set of circumstances would have been too small to discuss. I imagine Lace knew this, even if he didn't know why all of these simple stumbling blocks had suddenly appeared. Finally, Lace motioned to a book he was reading and said to me, "Patrick, let's take a break from business. I'm reading something that really interests me and I want to chat a little about something else. Do you mind?"

After my discussion with Lace about particle physics, his choice of reading material didn't surprise me. The book was on recent research into the human genome.

What was I to say? If his mini-lecture on physics and philosophy had gotten me to start thinking differently, perhaps I should be eager to hear what he had to say. Also, there was something particularly amusing about Lace that night. He didn't have his bridgework in so there was a gap where two teeth were missing right in the middle of his mouth and his words shot through the hole with a slight lisp, spewing out bits of spittle every once in a while. Lace has become very heavy and he reminded me for a second of a whale spouting philosophy through its blowhole. I imagined, for an instant, words in black type spewing into the air and settling over the tables and chairs of Lace's little living room, leaving a residue of ink and stray ideas. I'm glad we can't read each other's minds. Our secrets save us from one another sometimes.

"It turns out that mapping the genome is going to be simple compared to working out how the proteins unfold." He looked at me quizzically for a moment, unsure how much educating I needed before he proceeded. "You know, don't you, that the DNA sequences are really nothing more than instructions to make proteins? Then those proteins make not just our physical selves. They result ultimately, of course, in our physical selves, but what they really do is construct the parts of us, the individual enzymes and electrical impulses and all the other pieces of us that come together to make us living, human beings, or fruit flies or rhesus monkeys for that matter. But, you see, the proteins can also cause behavior. They create proteins that then chemically produce hormones and enzymes—chemicals that trigger actual, real-time responses. The little fruit fly uses a series of proteins, all made neatly one after the other in predetermined sequence, to create the exact sequence of steps in its mating ritual. Now you can say that humans are entirely more complex, but we also share about 65 per cent of our DNA with the fruit fly and a small increase in the complexity of the DNA results in an enormous leap in the complexity of what DNA is capable of doing. And, of course, humans have culture and self-consciousness which adds even more to the mix...adds a sentient mind if you want. The point is that fruit flies operate from a basic

template that has, at least in part, been inherited by us so it would seem that these proteins determine not only how we are constructed but they're partially responsible for our feelings and drives as well."

I supposed I had some idea of what he was talking about. It was a chummy evening, an evening made for discourse. It is winter and New York apartments of the kind we live in are hot and close, surrounding themselves around their inhabitants and against the harshness outside. Inside, Rosa's cooking enveloped us with an aroma that defined our space like a magic circle drawn to call night spirits.

I was increasingly interested in whatever theme Lace was developing. I was pretty sure he wanted to make a point and didn't quite know how. Perhaps he didn't know himself exactly what point he wanted to make. "Do go on," I said, and Lace continued.

"But the proteins are marvelous and devilishly difficult shapes, and they sort of just immediately unfold into these origami-like structures. The code on the DNA provides instruction for building the protein, but not for its exact shape so far as we know, so for research purposes we need to know how the genes unfold into specifically shaped proteins and the problem with doing that is that the possible ways in these molecules can unfold are hugely large. There are literally trillions of ways that a sequence of code can unfold into a protein, most of them into a sort of chemical rubbish. And not just for research, of course. If we want to actually cure a defect, or create something entirely new, knowing the DNA sequence for humans doesn't help much unless we can insert instructions to make not just the proteins that are necessary to that specific time and place, but the precise shape. It takes a modern computer an impossible time just to calculate the possibilities."

Lace got up and poured us both a brandy and the warmth of it mingled with an intellectual warmth, the realization that I could follow so far what Lace was talking about.

"If we're going to really know what the genome does, and even more to the point if companies are going to be able to make money by replicating what DNA sequences do, we need to be able to have a simple way to figure out how the fairly simple DNA makes these enormously complex structures. But, that's for the corporate types to figure out. What interests me is that nature figures it out almost immediately."

He looked at me and raised an eyebrow, as if he were reviewing a clue found by Sherlock Holmes. "Instantaneously," he added for emphasis, as if a game was afoot.

"People do have some ideas for how this could be. One is that the molecules are reacting to water. The theory is that some react negatively and some positively to the H2O molecule, so by avoidance or attraction they unfold automatically into incredibly complex structures. Not only incredibly complex, though, but also the one that the template needs at that precise moment! And they do it in a split nanosecond! Fascinating, huh? There are millions of possibilities, but underlying them is a deeper structure guiding them to emerge from chaos into orderly, beautiful and above all, workable creations!"

Rosie the Riveter looked out from behind the canvas curtain as if to check up on Lace. Lace had been talking quietly and it is doubtful she could hear him over the sound of her knife against the block and the low level of her voice as she hummed a droning tune to herself. Lace looked up at her and smiled and she flashed him a serious and curious look and popped back behind the curtain to resume her work.

"*So do you take anything from all this?*" I asked. *Was he making a point after all, or did he just want a break from my endless business niggling?*

"*Oh, my boy, the basic point to it all is that things are a crap-shoot, after all. I guess you know that's become my general philosophy ever since I discovered that the whole basis of existence is a fuzz-ball, which is my take on all that particle physics stuff. We just have to accept that there are a million possibilities to everything and everywhere there's a surprise. For instance, here's my dear Rosie. You meet someone and you size them up pretty well, but they still surprise you again and again. They react differently than you expected. They get mad when you thought they'd be happy with what you just did. They sleep through the alarm and don't wake you up and so they accidentally break an agreement that you never thought they'd break. I'm not just talking about Rosa here, my boy. She's perfect in every way, of course. Who would think that my sturdy Rosita would turn out to be such an entrepreneur! But you know how people are, they disappoint you and they have their own agendas and you continually wonder what in the world makes them tick. There's no telling how each day is going to unfold and yet it generally does unfold in ways that are more than adequate to the business of living.*"

We sat again in a short silence. It was time to go. I had promised to call Benny and there wasn't much more time to do it. The thought of that telephone call and the interlacing of our lives was a shadow across my mind and I withdrew into my thoughts to absorb the queasiness of it and ride it out as my insides tensed up. The silence became profound and, as good friends will do, Lace did not pry into it. He sat still, lost in his own world for a moment.

Still, I sat quietly and as I sat, an idea began to form, a dim globe of light moving into consciousness from the back of my mind. At the center of things lies an unknown quantity. This was Lace's teaching all along. I started in my reverie as I began to link this awakening idea to the uncertainties of my quandary. At the very heart of anyone lies a person unknown even to themselves. Just as Lace could not know that he reminded me of a whale spraying ink across the room, I am as much of a cipher to him as he is to me. I didn't know myself what I wanted or what my next thoughts would be as they raced through my mind. I remembered our talk at the restaurant just before Lace left for Mexico. I was reminded of neutrons scampering across space and time. Position or velocity, which could I measure? But still we make our lives with one another and even spend lifetimes with people who continue to surprise because they are unknowable. Even so people do know one another and sometimes with exacting certainty. How was this so? If the sweep of the stellar universe or even the center of a quantum particle dissolves just as we look at it, if velocity and position which give meaning to time, matter and energy, which, in turn, ought to give meaning to our very experience of reality, if these basic building blocks of reality can't be determined, then it should be impossible to be certain of anything at all. It should be impossible, if we lived in a logical place, to ever build anything at all. Even so, atoms come together to build creatures, even sentient creatures who are aware of themselves. Electrons somehow conspire to brighten the Northern sky. Holocausts of creation still twinkle overhead at night. Even if nothing can be certain, nonetheless simple structures unfold brilliantly to reveal shapes of stunning exactitude.

And it suddenly occurred to me that, just perhaps, a leaf trembling alone and cold at the end of denuded branch is at last a leaf about to be set free into the world.

Lace came away from his thoughts and began to talk almost to himself. He looked at me intermittently, but his eyes were really off to the right of my shoulder, looking upwards at an angle to the ceiling as if he were addressing random thoughts to a spirit that had answered the call into our magic circle. I let him go on.

"The difference between the time it would take to explore all the possibilities and the quick, elegant way nature finds its solution has a name actually."

Lace said this as a kind of afterthought. He was done, I thought, with his philosophies.

He sat, looking a bit confused, searching his mind, and then offered, "I think it's called the Leviathan, no Levitate…no no, it's called Levinthal's Paradox. That's it!" He sounded triumphant, a schoolboy remembering his lesson.

"And so people are undependable, it is true. Even those who love us withhold things from us. They tell us our poems are wonderful when they aren't. They grow away from us and time passes and they become completely different people from the ones we knew. And then people also have a secret inner self they don't share, and I'm convinced that those secret places verge on madness, too. It's hard to know what madness is, when you think about it, but I do think sanity is by its nature an experience of the world that people share together, the sense of reality that we share as a species."

As Lace talked, my irresolution came to mind. What is madness but not knowing what reality is? Yet that was, indeed, the human condition. Perhaps I could never know what would be real, what I could trust. What was Benny going to be to me? And as for me, what did I want to create with him? Did I want to make anything real at all? What was it about solid things, the things I confront and the things I make solid? I acted as if I didn't want anything to do with them. But now Lace had said something that finally struck me. Perhaps to provide motion and growth, a person has to make something solid out of uncertainty and the only way to do that is to proceed. Like Levinthal's Paradox, the correct solution would come not from endless, complex calculations but from the unfolding itself. This irresoluteness of mine lay between madness and sanity, knowing and unknowing. But it lay at the heart of what anyone can know about the world and each other. Was the inability to know what was real and my distrust of what I did know a kind of insanity?

"Yes," Lace repeated, looking directly at me out over his eyeglasses and making a point by half closing his eyelids, "I'm convinced that our inner voices verge on madness."

Had he heard my thoughts?

"Our inner voices tend to veer off until they no longer check with how other people see things. Just listen to people, particularly people who live alone or don't communicate with other people. Left to ourselves, individual perceptions begin to go a little screwy. We can't just be left inside our own heads because our senses can't really be trusted. We have to get feedback from other people and yet their perceptions are flawed, too, and what they tell is also colored by biases and

self-interest. We can never quite take the measure of a person; we never know quite what their trajectory through life will be or what's on their minds and yet it's still possible to understand our relationship to them with fair certainty."

Lace sat back and breathed for a moment, letting air in and out as if he had just come out of a meditation. We sat, basking for a glossy moment and Rosa peeked out again from around the dividing curtain to say, "Lacy, dinner ready soon" and gave him a look that seemed to mean, "Time for just the two of us, honey." I got up to leave and Lace stood up to show me to the door, which was hardly necessary since the door is barely three paces away from the chair on which I had been sitting, and I had visited upstairs possibly two thousand times over two decades. He walked with me and opened the door and stood for a moment leaning against the jamb as I stood in the hallway, not sure if he had something more to say.

"What amazes me isn't that people are so unknowable, it's that they are so dependable."

Lace paused, silently asking permission to go on. "I'm sorry if this is too pontifical. You know I can philosophize all night. It just makes Rosie laugh, you know."

But I felt a budding confidence and I looked back at him, attentive, smiling.

I heard Rosa call again and Lace leaned back and around the corner and called to her like a lovebird cooing at its mate, "Coming in a second, honey. I'll be right there."

Lace stood astride the doorway, his bulky frame almost filling it, and a silly grin came over his face. His hair was disheveled and he was wearing an old pair of workout pants and a stained tee shirt. The space between his teeth showed while he grinned and the air kept puffing out as he lowered his voice so that he couldn't be heard sharing a secret.

"You know," he started, "Rosie is very jealous of me. She thinks everyone has eyes for me and she's always on the lookout for someone who's going to come along and steal me away. God knows I don't know why. It's endearing, really and it's nice she thinks I'm gorgeous even if no one else does but…but…" he paused for a moment to consider what he was saying.

As he went on, an infectious grin spread across his face. "Well, Rosie knows you're gay and…and…"

With this, Lace broke into a goofy smile and looked heavenward, throwing his arms out akimbo and shrugging as if to say, "What can I do?" He looked for all the world like a big Howdy Doody doll and with a sputter that mixed up 's' and 'th' and 'p,' the words frothed merrily through his teeth.

"… Well, she knows you're gay and, well, she thinks you're after my ass, my boy. That's pretty much it. She thinks everybody, but including you, is after my pretty wide ass!"

So that explained Rosa's mood and why she kept looking out from behind the curtain. It was a silly thought. It was a completely unreasonable, outrageous and ridiculous thought totally divorced from any reality that anyone could possibly know. And yet it was a lovable impulse and I liked the fierceness of it. Rosa would stand by her man and protect him and fight with him and for him against foes real and imagined. The idea in its pure form was madness, but there was a solidity to it that could be trusted and it made me fond of her.

And, of course, in time I suspect she will see something closer to our version of truth and adopt our sense of what has made up our little world on MacDougal Street. All those things would change, but she would still be Lace's wife. That, I knew somehow, would not change.

Lace put a finger to his mouth, hushing me, and gave a conspiratorial wink that meant we'd keep this secret between ourselves. He began to giggle at the thought of it and the absurdity of Rosie's little mad jealousies. At the same time, my throat caught the giggle and I began to laugh quietly as Lace held his finger to his lips and "shushed" me again to keep our little conversation quiet. "Just thought you'd like to know why she keeps an eye on us."

Lace kept giggling as he stepped back into his apartment and closed the door quietly. I can still remember that goofy, toothless grin, the twinkle in his eye and the merry heaving of his paunchy stomach, and I admired the quirky fierceness of his wife. The silliness of it caught me again, like a wave that appears unexpectedly out of the surf and rolls across a wide expanse of beach. The laughter in my heart went from a giggle centered in the throat to a release that came out of the small of my chest and the pit of my soul so that I began to double over from a hunger for merriment and a laughter that carried me away on its shoulders. Tears welled in my eyes and I steadied myself against the banister. As I laughed, I turned to go downstairs and call Benny. And now I looked forward to doing that. He was a good man and we would make a good team.

It was then that I noticed for the first time in over twenty years a houndstooth pattern worn away in the old, dirty carpet. Small and elegant and precise but almost out of sight, it formed a pattern just beneath perception. As I stared at it, the pattern seemed to increase intensity. With its precise corners and jagged edges in my mind, I turned to grasp the railing and took the stairs down to my apartment.

Still I was laughing and the stairs held solid underneath my feet.